A Touch
of
Cashmére

All rights reserved. First published in 2011 by Xlibris Corporation.
Re-edited and Released in 2012.

ISBN: 0615654584
ISBN-13: 978-0615654584

Other Books by Regina Jeffers

Cast of Characters

Members of the Realm and Their Ladies

James Kerrington, Viscount Worthing–the leader of the Realm; the future Earl of Linworth; from Derbyshire; resides at Linton Park

Eleanor Fowler–Brantley Fowler's sister

Brantley Fowler, the Duke of Thornhill–from Kent; resides at Thorn Hill

Velvet Aldridge–the Fowlers' cousin; lives at Thorn Hall with Eleanor

Marcus Wellston, Earl of Berwick, Lord Yardley–from Northumberland; resides at Tweed Hall

Cashémere and Satiné Aldridge– Velvet's younger sisters; Cashémere resides with the Averettes; Satiné with Baron Ashton

Gabriel Crowden, Marquis of Godown – from Staffordshire; resides at Gossling Hall

Aidan Kimbolt, Viscount Lexford–lives in Cheshire; resides at Lexington Arms

John Swenton, Baron Shannon–lives in Yorkshire; resides at Marwood Manor

Sir Carter Lowery–second son of Baron Blakehell; a baronet from Kent; was given Huntingborne Abbey by George IV, the Prince Regent

Minor Characters of Importance to the Series

Shaheed Mir–leader of a band of Baloch warriors; seeks revenge on the Realm for stealing a fist-sized emerald

Murhad Jamot–Mir's agent in England

Viscount Averette (Samuel Aldridge)–the Aldridge girls' paternal uncle; raised Cashémere

Baron Ashton (Charles Morton)–the Aldridge girls' maternal uncle; raised Satiné

Ashmita–Brantley Fowler's first wife; attacked by Mir's band

Sonali–Fowler's daughter

Shepherd–the Realm's leader; so named because he gathers "lost souls"

Miss Grace Nelson–daughter of Baron and Lady Nelson from Lancashire; she is employed as a governess by the Averettes

Prologue

When we honestly ask ourselves which person in our lives means the most to us, we often find that it is those who, instead of giving advice, solutions, or cures, have chosen rather to share our pain and touch our words with a wrm and tender hand.
- Henri Nouwen

"Where have you been?" Marcus Wellston hissed.

"Attempting to find some place private–my stomach aches." His friend John Swenton pushed past. "Besides, what does it matter? We have been here for three days, and Mir has made one appearance," he grumbled.

Wellston nodded his head toward the other table. "Well, things are about to change."

Swenton shot a quick glance to where Wellston indicated. "Please tell me Fowler is not about to do what I think he is."

The third son of the Earl of Berwick groaned as he pretended to stretch, actually reaching for the pocket pistol he carried under his shirt. "It is Fowler; you know how he is. He has watched the girl's tent for over a day."

"Damn!" Swenton cursed under his breath. "Fowler will ruin everything. Some day he will place each of us in peril."

Marcus murmured, "Today is likely that day."

The words no more had escaped Marcus's mouth than Brantley Fowler stood and casually walked toward the tent's opening. The future Duke of Thornhill held a strong compulsion to save "damsels in distress." As best as Marcus could tell Fowler's father was renown for his debauchery, and Fowler blamed his father for his mother's death. On this particular day, Fowler predictably meant to save a young girl from the brutality Mir's men practiced on her. Just as true to form, one of Mir's men stepped into Fowler's path.

Wellston's heart lurched in anticipation. They would fight again. Within seconds, chaos would reign. Marcus watched in mocked chalance as Fowler raised his hands, pretending to accept the tribeman's silent warning. Thornhill's heir struck the warrior guard with an uppercut, sending the soldier reeling backwards, blood pouring from the man's nose.

Wellston shot the Baloch charging them in the knee, incapacitating the guard, and then he turned his attention to finishing off one of the two who assailed Swenton. Pulling a dagger from his boot, he attacked a dark-skinned warrior, quickly bringing the man down.

The next wave of Balochs streamed through the opening as Fowler elbowed his way towards the girl's tent. Even in the midst of the melee, Wellston wondered on the depth of Fowler's obsession to save the world. Fowler had always put himself in danger to save every abused woman he had encountered. The future duke, the would-be knight in shining armor, had never learned the lesson Marcus had learned long ago: Saving others did not make the pain go away.

"Now!" James Kerrington, Viscount Worthing, barked, and the Realm members responded in kind. Wellston delivered a lethal thrust to the throat of the man with whom he tussled, leaving the guard gasping for air.

Joining the others, he raced toward the waiting horses. From his eye's corner, Marcus saw Fowler ride off with the girl cradled before him. Wellston caught the reins of his horse, running along beside the animal before he could catch the saddle and physically pull himself onto the horse's back. Settling his feet into the stirrups, he kicked the horse's flanks and galloped away from the scene. Their band would meet again in three days at the Bombay safe house. As the pounding ride beat at his body, Marcus prayed that some day, he would find his own salvation.

Chapter One

Two Years Later

"I hate being soaked to the bone," he groused. The rain sheeted everything within sight, but Marcus rode on. The creek bed he followed into the Scottish backcountry had swelled from the downpour, but he had crossed it at its lowest point and was on safe ground. He had returned from Calcutta two months prior, having turned over the Sir Louis Levering affair to Viscount Lexford, and he had settled into the routine of running his estate and tending to Trevor, but Shepherd had sent word of Velvet Aldridge's possible abduction, and he had departed immediately. Evidently, His Grace, the Duke of Thornhill, had allowed the woman he loved to retreat to Edinburgh with her estranged family. Now, their old enemy Shaheed Mir had targeted Miss Aldridge in a dangerous game of "Who Has the Emerald?" Mir had marked each of his band of the Realm as co-conspirators in stealing a fist-sized emerald from the Baloch warlord. Mir's agents had staged a myriad of attacking, each proving fruitless.

Shepherd's message said the Realm's leader would send others to support Marcus's efforts, but Marcus knew he was pretty much on his own. That was why he had set a course across the back roads: He could save time, and he could avoid detection. He had stopped for a few hours overnight to allow his horse to rest, but Marcus felt he could thwart Murhad Jamot's plans just the same. Therefore, when he cut across the open field leading to Viscount Averette's land, Marcus had expected to explain his sudden appearance to the sometimes-difficult Samuel Aldridge, but nothing he discovered within had met his expectations.

❦

"Aunt," Cashémere Aldridge called as she entered the room. "Have we any news of Uncle Samuel?" The household staff rushed about in an attempt to respond to an unknown crisis, and with no one to assume responsibility, they crisscrossed the open foyer accomplishing very little.

Alice Aldridge rocked her daughter Gwendolyn, neither having had much sleep over night. They waited for news of the family patriarch, who had chased his eldest niece across southern Scotland.

Viscount Averette had been aware of the affection with which Velvet Aldridge had held Brantley Fowler, for Cashé's eldest sister had often professed she had loved the duke from the time they were children together. The household, having observed Velvet's despondency at having been separated from Fowler, had assumed Velvet had done the unthinkable: She had risked her life on the road to return to England. Therefore, Viscount Averette had given pursuit. Cashé was aware of how her Uncle Samuel had suspected the duke had arranged some sort of tryst with Velvet. Upon being made aware of his niece's disappearance, Averette had departed immediately to intercept the girl. He had been absent from the household since early yesterday afternoon, and, in truth, she thought Samuel Aldridge should permit Velvet her way. Cashé's elder sister held a schoolgirl fantasy in which the Duke of Thornhill played the role of noble knight. However, Cashé knew true love was a fallacy of the heart.

Lady Averette glanced up from her child to give Cashémere Aldridge a brief shake of her head, but she said for the child's benefit, "We should not expect to hear from my husband for several days. He must follow each lead on your sister. I am certain the rain has slowed his progress, and that is the reason we have heard nothing of yet."

A sharp knock at the door brought their immediate attention. "Possibly there is a message now," Cashé remarked as she stepped into the foyer. She could not condone her sister's actions, but Cashé recognized the depth of Velvet's misery. She had seen Velvet pine for Thornhill, and how her older sister had discouraged the many suitors their uncle had paraded before her. Yet, Cashé gave her uncle's actions merit: A woman's virtue was her crowning glory, and a lady must protect it. She was furious because the duke had led Velvet astray, and then he had deserted her. In the three months Velvet had resided with them, her sister had not heard one word from Thornhill. He had ignored Velvet's weekly letters, and now her sister might lose her reputation unless their uncle could prevent it.

Blane hustled to answer the door. Cashé looked on as the butler swung the door wide. Obviously, the butler had expected a messenger or even the viscount himself, but instead they all looked upon a stranger. "Yes, Sir?"

An autocratic voice announced, "The Earl of Berwick to speak to Viscount Averette."

Blane stammered, "His...His Lordship is unavailable, Sir."

The voice pressed, "It is a matter of great urgency."

Blane motioned the earl in from the rain. "I offer my apologies, Sir," the man began, but Cashé's sensibilities had returned, and she interrupted.

She had known the stranger as "Lord Yardley" and had not put his title with the familiar countenance she encountered once he removed his hat. "Your Lordship," she rushed forward, "please come in, Sir." She wondered what had brought the earl to her family's doorstep, very likely he had come at Thornhill's request. Perhaps the rain had slowed his attempt to reach Velvet before her sister's escape. Perhaps, it was he her sister had planned to meet, and the earl was to escort Velvet to where Thornhill waited. With so many unknowns, Cashé meant to practice caustion with the earl.

Berwick quickly dispensed with his hat and greatcoat before offering her a quick bow. "Miss Cashémere, might I speak to your uncle?"

"As Blane just explained, Your Lordship, my uncle is away at the moment. Please join my aunt and me in the drawing room, and perhaps we might be able to address the reason for this unexpected visit." Cashé turned immediately on her heels, expecting him to follow her. She had not allowed him time to protest. It pleased her he had trailed along behind her. She had not seen Berwick since the day after Prinny's party. Over a supper at Briar House, the Fowlers had celebrated Sir Louis Levering's downfall. Cashé had not understood the perfidy the Fowlers had practiced on the baronet, until her Uncle Samuel had inadvertently explained the situation when he demanded the removal of Velvet from the duke's household. In truth, Cashé had been sorry to leave so quickly; she had had no time to say her farewells to Viscount Lexford, who had shown her his attentions. It was quite heady for a young girl to have such a worthy gentleman's approval. It made her wonder if she had made a mistake by accepting an "understanding" with Mr. Charters.

"Aunt," Cashé called, obviously nervous, "the Earl of Berwick has come to pay his compliments." She rushed forward to take Gwendolyn from the woman. "Permit Edana to put our dear Gwen to bed. The child could use a nap." She lifted the child to her. "Excuse me, my Lord. My young cousin experienced a rough evening." She handed off the sleeping child to a waiting maid, before closing the door behind him.

Lady Averette belatedly stood to greet Wellston, who remained stolidly by the door. "Your Lordship," the woman gestured the earl forward. "Please join us. I apologize for my husband's absence."

Wellston glanced about the room, obviously displeased by the circumstances. He scowled before crossing to the chair Aunt Alice had indicated. "Might I ask, Ma'am, when His Lordship will return. I have urgent business."

The viscountess shot a quick glance at Cashé. Her aunt had depended on Uncle Samuel in social situations; she knew not how to respond. Therefore, Cashé answered. "It may be some time, Your Lordship."

"Then might I speak with Miss Aldridge? My business concerns your sister."

Cashé stood behind her aunt, resting her hands on the chair's back. "That too is impossible, Your Lordship." She smiled politely at the man.

"Miss Cashémere," the earl beseeched. "I have been sent to Scotland to offer your sister my..."

Cashé cut him off. "We are quite aware of why you have been sent to our home!"

Berwick looked aghast. "And why might that be?" he asked incredulously.

"You are an intimate friend of the Duke of Thornhill," she asserted.

"I am," he hissed. "Yet, even with that..."

Again, Cashé interrupted. "My uncle will foil Thornhill's plans and save my sister."

"Cashémere!" her aunt warned.

Her words had brought the earl to his feet. He advanced on Cashé. "You should explain," he demanded.

"You are in my home, Sir. Obeying you is not part of this house's rules." In defiance, her hands fisted at her waist. She attempted to meet his eyes with a resolve stronger than the one she found in his, but she felt like a tasty morsel in the path of a dangerous feline. Surprisingly, Cashé thought the earl strikingly handsome in all his fury.

⚬⚬⚬

He loomed over the girl. From behind him, Lady Averette gasped, but Marcus had no time to practice his manners. "You will do as I say if you wish to guard your sister's safety. I have come to protect Miss Aldridge." According to Shepherd's information, Murhad Jamot had planned his attack for this very day.

Regarding him with noteworthy self-assurance, the girl charge, "You are in Scotland at the duke's bequest, but you are too late!"

Marcus's temper flamed. "What do you mean 'too late'?"

6

A flicker of fear crossed her countenance before she tamped it down, and Marcus wondered what had brought on the emotion; but before he could explore the reason, the girl raised her chin in boldness. "As if you did not know, my Lord."

Marcus thought of turning her over his knee to teach the girl about respect, but he had no time to spare. He caught her by the arm and dragged her to a nearby chair, shoving her to a seated position. He saw Lady Averette take a step toward the bell cord, but he stayed her with a deathly stare. He seethed with anger. "Now, Miss Cashémere, you will answer my questions."

The girl rubbed her arm where he had grabbed her, and a moment of regret stabbed his heart. He was never one to treat females roughly, and he could not justify why he had done so. "I shall do no such thing!" she declared.

Marcus glanced at the cowering viscountess. The girl would protect Lady Averette. "I am certain your aunt will see things differently." He strode angrily toward the woman, but before he took three steps, Miss Cashémere jumped onto his back and began to kick and punch.

Marcus's hands protected his face as she swung indiscriminately, landing blows along his chin and ears. "Bloody hell!" he cursed, catching the girl's arms and whipping her before him and effectively clamping her arms to her side. Although she still attempted to kick him, she plastered his chest with her warmth, and a spark of tension flared between them. To free himself of the sensation, Marcus shoved her into a second chair. "Stay!" he growled, pointing his finger at her as if she were a dog.

His roughness brought tears to the girl's eyes, but she prepared for a second attack; however, her aunt stepped before the girl, effectively cutting off the exchange. "What is it you wish of us, my Lord?" Lady Averette spoke softly.

Marcus glared at Miss Cashé, before taking a stilling breath. "Could you please explain, Viscountess, where I might find your husband or Miss Aldridge?"

The woman turned first to Cashé, indicating the girl should sit. "Neither my husband's niece nor I know the answer to that question," Lady Averette said calmly.

Marcus thought this the most bizarre mission Shepherd had ever assigned him. He ran his fingers through his hair. Taking another calming breath, he said, "What might you tell me, Ma'am? I give you my word as a gentleman..." He heard the girl snort, and Marcus leveled a warning glare on her before he continued. "As a gentleman...that it is not my intention to bring shame upon your household."

The viscountess again motioned Marcus to a chair. She sat beside Cashé, taking the girl's hand. "Are you telling us the Duke of Thornhill did not send you to Edinburgh?"

Marcus wondered how much he might honestly share with Averette's family, but these women were also Fowler's family so he attempted a version of the truth. "Although His Grace now knows of my mission to your home, I did not come at his bidding."

"Then who sent you?" the girl demanded before her aunt placed a calming hand on Miss Cashé's sleeve.

"That I am not at liberty to say, Miss Cashémere, but I will tell you I received word of a former enemy of the men you met at Briar House after the Prince's party. This man had planned to exact revenge on Thornhill by hurting your older sister. As I live in Northumberland, I was dispatched to intercept the attack."

The viscountess's hands trembled. "Velvet did not leave to meet His Grace?"

Her words slammed into his chest. "Miss Aldridge has left this house?"

"Yes."

"When?" The word exploded in the room.

"Yesterday morning."

"Oh, my God!" Marcus was on his feet and pacing. "Tell me the rest."

The viscountess reluctantly obliged. "A servant observed my husband's niece in the orchard. The man went on about his duties, but within a quarter hour, he observed a carriage racing from the area. When Gillis reported what he had seen to my Samuel, we conducted a search. Unfortunately, we were not successful in locating our eldest niece. My husband, Sir, believes his family has departed our home to meet the Duke of Thornhill. He gives chase."

Marcus had heard from Carter Lowery how distraught Thornhill had been at Miss Aldridge's departure, but he knew Bran would never lure Velvet from her uncle's home. To claim the woman he loved, Thornhill might "storm the castle," so to speak, but he would never devise a secret betrayal. It was not Thornhill's style. "Lord Averette will not find your niece with His Grace."

"How can you be so certain, Your Lordship?" Miss Cashé charged.

8

"Because Shaheed Mir has other plans for your sister."

"Such as?" she demanded, but a slight shake of his head said she would not want to know. Before he could say more, she stood before him. "You must assist her," she asserted.

Marcus wanted to remind the silly chit assisting Miss Aldridge had been his plan. Wished to remind her he had ridden all night through a rainstorm to do his best to foil Mir's plans. She had stated the obvious. "We must determine whether Mir's agents have your sister. Have either of you noticed strangers in the area?"

"We ran a foreigner from the stable," Lady Averette shared.

"When was that?"

"A week or so ago. He claimed to be seeking work. Lord Averette did not like his looks so he sent the man away."

The girl caught Marcus's arm. "A dark man followed Velvet and me when we shopped two days ago. We noticed because he asked Edana if he might buy her a butter tart. When she refused, he continued to ask about the household."

"Damn!" Marcus grumbled.

"Your Lordship, I must insist that you not curse in my uncle's house," Miss Cashé reprimanded.

Marcus blinked in confusion, unaware he had uttered an expletive before a lady. He had spent too much time of late with his duties to the Realm and in a bachelor's household in Northumberland. "I apologize, Miss Cashémere." Ashamed, he purposely walked away toward the window, taking up a position to look out upon the gardens. "Did you observe this stranger?"

"No, Sir, but we might bring in Edana to describe him."

Marcus considered it, but he suspected it would be a waste of time. "I am assuming Miss Aldridge had at least a two-hour lead on Lord Averette," he said to the expanse before the house.

"Closer to three," Lady Averette shared.

"So, we are not certain whether His Lordship actually followed Miss Aldridge."

Miss Cashé asked, "What do you mean, Sir?"

Marcus turned to look at her. "My informant says Mir's man plans to travel to Liverpool and wait for a ship. I doubt Lord Averette could have known of the stranger's plans? And I am certain the rain will eliminate any opportunity of his actually following the coach in which the man holds Miss Aldridge."

"Your assumption holds merit." The girl appeared very nervous. "I hold my doubts also."

"Explain." Marcus waited for more information.

Miss Cashé looked about sheepishly. "I heard Uncle Samuel order his driver to set a course for Derbyshire. My uncle assumed the duke would lure Velvet to Eleanor's home at Linton Park. It would not be so long of a journey. Not as if Thornhill planned to lure Velvet to Kent, and Uncle realized Viscount Worthing and Eleanor would be happy to give both Velvet and Thornhill refuge."

"So, your uncle chases his prejudice while your sister is in real danger?" Marcus could not resist this bit of censure.

"Lord Averette protects my sister!" the girl defended her foolish uncle.

"Actually, Miss Cashémere, I suspect His Grace, as well as several others of our acquaintance protect Miss Aldridge."

"I thought you said His Grace had nothing to do with your being here!" Again, the girl was on the offensive.

"I said," he emphasized the words, "when I began my journey, His Grace knew nothing of this situation, but I am certain he has since received notification; and knowing Thornhill's affection for Miss Aldridge, he must be on his way to Liverpool."

Miss Cashé looked to her aunt for confirmation. "Then we must locate my uncle and see him to Liverpool as well."

"Surely, you jest, Miss Cashémere?"

Again, her fists came to her waist. "I do not jest, Your Lordship! We must find my sister before His Grace has the opportunity to ruin her."

"Miss Cashémere," Marcus mocked, "your sister's reputation is already ruined: She travels alone with a foreigner. However, it is her life of which you should be concerned."

Lady Averette finally reacted. "But if Samuel can aid in Velvet's release, we might still hush up her absence. Other than our servants, no one knows, and they are a loyal lot." Marcus doubted the Averettes could control the gossip, but he kept his opinions to himself. "We will spread the rumor Samuel and his niece have traveled to Derby because Lady Worthing has taken ill. If my husband can return with Velvet, no one will be the wiser. Lord Averette is most concerned for propriety."

"I could go," Cashé declared. "I could go after Uncle Samuel."

10

Lady Averette reached for the girl. "It is a great responsibility."

"We will tell everyone the earl came to escort me to Linton Park. Lady Eleanor, obviously, is my family also."

Marcus suddenly realized what they planned. "I beg your pardon. I must follow Miss Aldridge's trail."

"Then I will go alone," Cashé declared.

"Miss Cashémere, that idea is folly. The roads are too dangerous for a woman alone."

"We can trust no one else, Your Lordship." Lady Averette turned her eyes on him in supplication. "If we are to save Velvet's reputation, my husband must be involved."

Marcus realized their determination. "Then I will follow Lord Averette."

Miss Cashé stood before him, her damnable chin lifting again. "Uncle Samuel will never believe you. He is aware of your relationship with His Grace. You must take me if you expect him to accept your words."

Wellston wished he could curse again. The exclamations seemed to clear his thinking when he felt the frustrations. He attempted to analyze what he might achieve if he went toward Liverpool first. Miss Aldridge and Murhad Jamot had, at least, a four and twenty hour advantage. "Might Lord Averette have access to his bank if we must ransom Miss Aldridge?" he asked.

"I shall give my niece a blank draft to take to her uncle," Lady Averette assured him.

"Might your maid accompany us?" he needed to clarify what he should expect.

"I shall take Edana with me," Cashé declared.

"I would go," Lady Averette excused herself, "but Gwendolyn would be devastated. Plus, we must keep up appearances."

Marcus did not understand the viscountess's attitude. He would give away every thread of propriety to have Maggie back. He would stare down Society for the pleasure of Maggie's laugh. Marcus quickly planned their departure. "We must be on the road immediately. We have much time to recover. Is there a coach the ladies might use or should I see to renting one?"

"You may take my husband's small coach," Lady Averette declared. "We have another the servants might use if we require supplies or if we experience an emergency."

"And a driver?" Marcus pressed.

"I shall see to it, Your Lordship." Lady Averette caught her niece's hand. "You must hurry, my Dear. I shall send up the maids to assist you in packing."

The girl started for the door. "Miss Cashémere," the earl called, "do you recall what your sister wore yesterday?"

"A light blue gown."

"Are you certain."

"Absolutely, my Lord."

Marcus nodded. "Might you bring an item belonging to Miss Aldridge among your things? If we must use the hounds, it would be helpful to track your sister." Thankfully, the girl acknowledged the sensibility of what he had said before excusing herself. "I will see to my horse and assure myself of the coach's soundness. I hope to use some of the back roads to save time."

"I understand, Your Lordship." Lady Averette led him to the door. "We will be ready within the hour."

The rain had stopped, but the earlier downpour had washed away some of the trails he might have chosen, but Marcus figured they could reach the border by nightfall. He had hoped by using the lesser-traveled roads they could recover a half-day or more on Lord Averette's pursuit. Although he was admittedly often inebriated and traveling with a pack of rabble-rousers, Marcus had traveled this part of Scotland many times in his youth. In those days, he had attempted to kill the pain of losing Maggie, but Shepherd had pulled him from that useless life and slammed him smack into the middle of political intrigue. First, he had spent nine months with the military, and then he had known real training. Thank God for Shepherd's insights. Otherwise, Marcus would be dead, and there would be no one to see to Trevor.

"Your Lordship," Miss Cashé's head appeared at the coach's window, "when might we be stopping?"

Marcus maneuvered his horse closer to the carriage. "At dark, Miss Cashé."

"Could we not stop earlier?" She snarled her nose as she glanced at her maid. "Edana is not feeling well."

Marcus ducked his head to peer inside the coach. The maid appeared embarrassed by the attention, but he noted no discomfort on the woman's countenance. "There will be no place to stay before then." He directed his statement to Miss Cashémere, who, obviously, placed her own discomfort on the maid. "Hopefully, your maid will be able to withstand the rough road a bit longer."

"Your Lordship, I insist," she began, but a glare from Marcus stopped her short.

"When it is safe, Miss Cashé, we will stop and not before then." Marcus nudged the horse ahead, ignoring her orders. He was not often rude to anyone, but something about this girl set against his nature. His friend Aidan Kimbolt, Lord Lexford, affected Cashémere Aldridge. The viscount had been absolutely intolerable after Miss Cashé's withdrawal from London. On the Calcutta trip, Lexford had snapped at everyone and was often angry for no reason, but Marcus could not see the attraction. The girl was pretty enough–coal black, silky hair and mesmerizing emerald eyes, but she ruined every kind thought with her shrewish tongue. He certainly was not about to take orders from some immature female.

Cashé watched him ride away; she found the Earl of Berwick to be the most infuriating of men–his rudeness irritated her beyond belief. However, she could not forget his body's heat when he caught her before him or his strength when he clasped her arms to her side. His strong, muscular arms had held her tightly in place, and Cashé still flushed with the remembrance of her back pressed against his chest.

She had reluctantly taken pleasure in his dark, deep-set eyes and his aristocratic nose, as well as his powerful chin line. He resembled a Roman orator; she could easily picture the earl in a toga and addressing the Roman Senate, but those thoughts brought on images of an improperly clad Marcus Wellston, and that figure bothered her more than she understood.

Never once had Cashé possessed such a thought. In fact, her Uncle Samuel would have had her doing some sort of penitence if he knew. So, Cashé forced her musings away, but each time she turned her head to glance out the window at the countryside, she would see Yardley and be reminded of her errant thoughts, or she would not see him and be reminded.

Cashé had only accepted the attentions of two men in her life: Lachlan Charters and Aidan Kimbolt. Charters, her uncle's preference as a suitor, had called often at The Ridge to sit with her. Everyone assumed Charters would make his intentions known when she turned nineteen in four months. If Uncle Samuel and the church approved, they would marry before she reached her twentieth birthday. Having lost his first wife some four years prior, Charters was nearly twice her age. She would have a ready-made family as Charters had two children. The Scot certainly did not possess either the earl's or Lord Lexford's physique, but Charters was a pleasant-enough looking man, and, more importantly, he was a leader in the parish. Cashé had thought it best to choose someone with the same religious beliefs.

When she had traveled to London in the late spring, she had met the earl's friend Viscount Lexford. The viscount, like the earl, held a previous acquaintance with both her cousin Brantley Fowler and with Eleanor's husband, Lord Worthing. Uncle Samuel did not totally approve of Cashé keeping company with the viscount, but her aunt had convinced her husband Cashé would be more willing to choose Charters if she had had an opportunity to enjoy other men's attentions. Reluctantly, her Uncle Samuel agreed, but he had insisted on chaperoning Cashé's every encounter with Lord Lexford. Only once, at the infamous Vauxhall Gardens, had she come close to being alone with the man, if one can consider herself alone in a crowd.

And although Cashé had found Lord Lexford exceedingly handsome, she had never once pictured the viscount as anything more than what she had Charters. She had missed the viscount's company when her family suddenly departed London, but, in reality, Cashé realized she had missed the excitement of the London Season more than she had the man, a fact she could not share with anyone. She was sorry to admit the viscount's coffee brown eyes did not hold the smoldering passion she had observed in the earl's slate gray ones.

In the late evening, the small carriage rolled into the hard-earthen drive before The Square Bow Inn on the British side of the border. Because the storm had moved from north to south, the yard was well on its way to being full. The earl had dismounted and had opened the carriage door to assist her and her maid to the ground. "It might be best," the earl whispered close to her ear, "if we register as brother and sister. Even with your maid in tow, it would be unseemly of us to travel together."

Cashé's eyes grew in size. "I am not of the habit of offering an untruth, Your Lordship," she hissed through tight lips.

He casually adjusted the angle of her bonnet, and Cashé felt the air rush from her lungs. She wondered if his careless shrug meant he had ignored her objection or whether it was part of his ploy. He murmured, "I

Regina Jeffers

understand, Miss Cashémere; yet, I only make the suggestion to protect you."

Cashé searched his countenance for the truth of what he said. Finally, she reached to straighten his cravat. Although she told herself it was all for show, it was an intimate moment, one she never thought to share with any man, but one which felt so natural. "I shall agree to being your cousin, Your Lordship."

The earl smiled deviously. "Yardley."

"I beg your pardon?" Cashé glanced to where Edana waited.

Assuring their privacy, he leaned closer. "My cousin would know my name. I am Marcus Wellston, Lord Yardley."

Cashé ducked her head in embarrassment. "Of course. I recall from the Prince's party." She bit her bottom lip. "Thank you, Lord Yardley."

He placed her hand on his arm and led her into the inn. Recognizing quality, the innkeeper rushed forward. "Yes, Sir."

"My cousin and I require rooms for the evening." She observed how Lord Yardley's eyes surveyed the common room. She supposed he searched for acquaintances.

"I have only two small rooms available, Your Lordship. I will be happy to serve you, but I must warn you one is off the kitchen and is a bit noisy." The innkeeper smiled a toothless grin.

"Yardley, this is unacceptable," Cashé said aristocratically. "I cannot sleep off the kitchen, and I certainly cannot condone the Earl of Berwick doing so."

The innkeeper dropped his smile. "The Earl of Berwick? My Lord, I will personally see to your accommodations. We will make the necessary adjustments. Might you and your cousin step into the private room? I will send in some of my wife's best while I have my man bring in your trunks. There are two other gentlemen in the parlor, but I am certain they would welcome your company."

"Thank you. My cousin and I appreciate your solicitous service."

He returned her hand to his sleeve, and her heart skipped several beats. "I thought you refused to twist the truth," he mocked.

"I did not offer a prevarication," she declared. "I said I could not condone my sleeping in such a room nor would I see you do so. If the innkeeper read something into my words, then that particular fact is not my fault."

The earl laughed. "I suppose it is not." He held the door for her, and they stepped into the shadows. Before either could adjust to the darkened room, someone called out, "Wellston!"

Chapter Two

Marcus's head snapped around, searching for the source of the sound when his eyes fell on Lucas Sampson, a former colleague. Leaving Miss Cashé by the door, he strode toward the man. "Sampson!" he slapped his friend on the back and shook his hand rather than to offer a proper bow. "My God, Man, it must have been nearly eight years!"

Sampson gave Marcus a sly grin. "More than that. One day we were riding Northumberland's back roads, wreaking havoc, and the next you were gone, with no word to anyone."

Marcus ignored the probe into his past. "It was time to do something besides carouse with the likes of you," he mocked as a diversion.

Sampson took on a serious mien. "I was grieved to hear of your father's passing."

Marcus glanced away as if seeing something others did not. "His Lordship anticipated his end: The earl planned for all contingencies."

"And you have assumed the title?" Marcus slowly turned to where Miss Cashémere waited a bit impatiently. She was tapping her foot in the most delightful manner, and he found the scene amusing.

Distractedly, he said, "I serve as Trevor's regent." Again, Marcus declined making additional comments.

Sampson trailed along beside Marcus as, like a fly to sugar, Marcus returned to her side. "Would you care to introduce me, Wellston?" He watched with annoyance as Sampson's eyes scanned the lady's appearance. Sampson's close assessment of Miss Cashé's ample bust line brought Marcus's ire. His fists tightened in response.

Noting his former friend's interest and easily interpreting Sampson's assumption that Marcus planned an assignation, he pointedly said, "Lucas Sampson, may I present my cousin, Miss Aldridge." He possessively returned Cashé to his arm, conveying his protection of the girl.

Sampson smiled cheekily. "I never knew you possessed such attractive relatives, Wellston." The bounder bowed properly to Miss Cashé before giving Marcus a knowing look.

He quickly read Sampson's conjecture: Miss Cashé was likely Marcus's mistress or a local girl upon whom he practiced an affair. To allay Sampson saying something inappropriate, Marcus shared, "My cousin's family has been summoned to Linton Park. Unfortunately, her uncle with whom she resides was unable to accompany her; therefore, I have taken on the task." Marcus liked the way he had worded the remark; except for the cousin part, he had spoken the truth. He had mimicked Miss Cashémere's earlier remark.

Sampson's countenance relayed his surprise. He stammered, "Linton... Linton Park? You are related to Linworth, Miss Aldridge?" His lecherous gaze switched to respectability.

Marcus recognized how the girl had carefully observed the spoken and the unspoken interplay between Sampson and him. She had taken note of his disapproval of Mr. Sampson's tone, and her ire pinked her cheeks added her own reproach, "Yes, Mr. Sampson. Lady Worthing's mother and mine were first cousins. My older sister resided with Thornhill after our parents' untimely deaths." She raised her chin defiantly, daring the man to question her further.

It was one of the few times during this long exhaustive day that Marcus had admired the girl. She had effectively placed Sampson in his social strata by mentioning both the earldom and the dukedom in her explanation. Cashé Aldridge had announced quite clearly that she held powerful connections. Marcus took pleasure in watching Sampson take a step backwards, literally, increasing his distance between himself and the girl.

"Then I did hear correctly," Sampson spoke again to Marcus. "Lord Worthing took the Thornhill daughter for his wife?"

"You did."

"Did you not serve with both men?" Sampson kept probing. "I had heard you served together in the East."

The continual questioning began to wear on Marcus. "It appears, Sampson, you have an excellent source of information. If only the British government had had such connections during the war, we could have shortened the struggle by several years." Before the man could respond,

Marcus brought the conversation to an end. "You will excuse us. My cousin and I are quite famished, and the innkeeper has brought our meal."

"Of course, Wellston." Former friends were no longer equals. A plain "Mister" could not detain a peer, no matter their previous connection.

The lady accepted the seat to which Marcus guided her. "I apologize, Lord Yardley, if my presence keeps you from your acquaintances," she whispered as he bent to adjust her chair.

"Believe me, Miss Cashémere, it is of no significance." He glanced to where Sampson rejoined his companion. "I chose to leave behind what Mr. Sampson regards as important. I hold no regrets."

She nodded her agreement. "I would say it quite fortuitous we did not tell the innkeeper we were siblings. I assume Mr. Sampson knows your family. I heard him mention your father. I was unaware of your loss."

Marcus stiffened. A very private man, he swallowed his comment. "My father was ill for a prolonged time."

"But it was only a few months since his passing. Surely you must still be grieving," she declared.

Marcus bit back his instant anger. The girl held no idea of what his life consisted before the earl died. "How I honor the earl's passing is my own accord."

She helped herself to some of the shepherd's pie. "Yet, you do not wear a black armband."

"The earl is aware of my breaking with propriety." Marcus started with a piece of bread and some cheese.

Characteristically, the girl pointedly put down her spoon with a huff. "You are the earl, Lord Yardley," she insisted.

"I am a minor son, Miss Cashémere, and I am a fake."

♪♪♪

She thought to protest, but one of his deadly stares stopped her cold. Cashé did not understand, but it really made little difference. After they reached Linton Park, she would never see him again, so attempting to solve this irascible man's mystery appeared an effort in futility. Yet, privately she would admit the possibility was intriguing. Instead, she concentrated on the meal and on making plans to find her Uncle Samuel. She refused to end the evening the way the day had started: in an argument with Lord Yardley.

Within an hour, Edana assisted her in the larger of the two rooms assigned to them for the evening. Earlier, she had looked on as Lord

19

Yardley had hired a man to ride to his estate and to return with a small trunk. His Lordship had brought little with him and would require a change of clothes if they were to travel far. She noted he had paid the man very well to ride through the night. From what she could surmise from eavesdropping on the hostlers, if she and the earl had hugged the eastern coastline, they would have come across his estate shortly after entering into England. She wondered about his estate. Would it resemble those she had seen in Derbyshire or would it have more of a rugged appearance, like some of those, which peppered the western Scottish border. Under the earl's direction, they had traveled east across the central border counties toward Harwick.

Watching him had become a bit of a game while she was confined to the coach. It had amazed Cashé how efficient Yardley appeared when he had organized things, but how impersonal he became in his social interactions. The man did not even openly grieve for his father. Cashé could not comprehend such a thing. She would give anything to have had her parents until she had reached Lord Yardley's age. An additional five and twenty years with her family. She would grieve for them, not as she did at age three when all she had known was to cleave to her grandmother's skirt tail and to cry. At such a tender age, not only had she lost her parents, but Cashé had also lost her sisters in one fell swoop. Satiné had been sent to live with Uncle Charles in Cheshire and Velvet to the Fowlers. They had both thrived in their respective households. Everyone had left her all alone to survive in a home where love had taken a permanent holiday. The thought shook her composure.

Although Cashé had always assumed the previous Lady Averette had loved her, if for no other reason than the fact she was Edward Aldridge's daughter, her paternal grandmother had not believed in showing affection. Cashé's grandmother had loved her eldest son to distraction. Kentigerna Aldridge lived up to her name. Kentigerna means "ruler" or "great lord," and Cashé had experienced how the woman had ruled her household with an iron hand. Even Uncle Samuel had suffered under Kentigerna's reign; in fact, he had not married Aunt Alice until after his mother's passing. Cashé always assumed her uncle had not wished to subject another to Lady Averette's bitterness. Yet, however hard the woman had been, Cashé had spent a year wearing black in remembrance. She had grieved for a woman who never once showed her love, while Yardley had offered no such honor for a man he obviously respected. She could not conceive of such stubbornness!

◯◯◯

Marcus could not shake the feeling of unrest which had followed him to his chambers for the evening. Being reminded by both Sampson and the girl of how he had stumbled into the earldom had not set well with him. Each day, Tweed Hall reminded him of how he had come into the position. How he had not deserved one "Your Lordship" or one point of deference. Like Sampson, he should simply be a "Mister," not "Master of the Estate," the highest-ranking aristocrat in the area. He smiled with irony at how God had dealt him a hand he had never expected. A hand where the youngest of four children became an earl."

◯◯◯

"It appears, Miss Cashémere, your uncle has taken the main roads across Northumberland, meaning Lord Averette will cross Nottingham and mayhap even part of Lincolnshire." Marcus escorted her to the coach. They had not broken their fast together; he had pointedly sent a tray to her room, assuring she did not lie abed half the day. He wished an early start to their journey.

"And how may one be so assured, Lord Yardley?" Miss Cashé asked sarcastically.

Marcus taunted, "It is my business to know such details, Miss Cashémere."

"I thought your business was the earldom, Sir," she hissed, stressing her words.

"Berwick is my title, but I have other interests." He glanced over his shoulder to where the driver assisted the maid to the coach. "Do you suppose I might make a comment," he whispered, "without your correcting or censuring it?"

"I do not..." she began, but quickly clamped her mouth shut. Through gritted teeth, she whispered, "Explain, Lord Yardley."

Marcus's hold on her arm tightened. "I will protect you and see you safely to Linton Park, but I will do so without an argument centering upon every interaction between us." He paused and waited for the girl's response, but when none came, he continued, "I questioned your uncle's staff before we departed, and I have done the same at each stop we have made. No one has seen Viscount Averette or the livery, which means His Lordship travels by a different route."

21

She nodded before grudgingly saying, "Thank you, Your Lordship." Marcus assumed her brief words were the closest he would receive in apology. "Do we have the means to overtake my uncle?"

"I doubt it," he leaned closer where he might speak only to her. "Although a bit slower, by taking a more direct route, we should arrive in Derbyshire within a few hours of your family."

"Shall we reach Linton Park today?"

"Tomorrow." He braced her entrance into the coach.

She stared deeply into what Marcus hoped were noncommittal eyes. Without wishing to do so, he noticed her heat when he was so close to the woman. "Then we remain cousins a bit longer, Lord Yardley."

"A bit, Miss Cashémere." He closed the carriage door and walked purposely away.

Cashé watched him move, entranced by his maleness. She had been in his presence only three times prior to this journey. He had come to Linton Park to celebrate Viscount Worthing's marriage to Lady Eleanor Fowler, and then he had attended the Prince Regent's party, along with the follow up celebration at Briar House. But at each, she had entertained Viscount Lexford's attentions and had had very little discourse with the earl. Obviously, Lord Yardley did not have Lexford's affability, but she had to admit he held a hidden intensity, which she found quite intriguing.

Marcus rode casually beside the carriage. Occasionally, he had caught a glimpse of the girl, sitting very prim and proper on the forward facing seat. Her alabaster skin made the silky black of her hair more apparent, and he had never seen such beautiful eyes, but her attitude and her caustic tongue ruined every kind thought he possessed of her. Perhaps, if he could find a woman with Miss Cashémere's looks, but possessing a milder temper, Marcus might become as besotted as his friend Aidan Kimbolt. With his accession to the earldom, he had accepted his duty to the title. He had understood he must marry and set up his nursery, but, in reality, Marcus would prefer that particular responsibility to fall to Trevor or even to Myles. It was never his destiny to hold the earldom. Only by a fluke of nature and an unexplained tragedy had Marcus received the title, and even after four months of holding the position and the prior six months preparing for it, the title still felt foreign. Felt as if he had robbed his older brother of his destiny.

Thankfully, true to her resolve, Cashémere Aldridge had done as he asked. She had offered him no censure throughout the day. At least, not directly. She had criticized the rough terrain, the many holes in Northumberland roads, the lack of proper springs in her uncle's carriage; the weak tea served at the afternoon's inn, and the lack of conversation to pass the time. Very little had pleased her. Marcus had considered riding in the coach, rather than on horseback, but he did not trust his patience with the girl. It was safer if he remained in the saddle.

"This is not much of an inn," Miss Cashé snarled as Marcus assisted her to the ground before the Salt Journey's Inn.

"It is nearly twenty miles to the next one if you care to continue on, Miss Cashémere." He fought hard to keep the smirk from both his mouth and his tone.

She reluctantly accepted his arm. "No, Cousin, I think not."

"Then let us make the best of it," he cautioned. "Despite the roads' poor conditions, we have made excellent time. We should reach Linton Park late tomorrow morning."

"Do you instruct everyone in how he should act and what he should know, Your Lordship, or am I a special project?" the girl hissed.

Marcus looked askance. "I assure you, Miss Cashémere, I offer no purposeful offense."

∞

"Somehow, I doubt your words, Your Lordship." Cashé turned her head so he could not observe her need for his approval. It was foolish: this desire to please a man she did not like or respect. The innkeeper rushed forward to greet them. Not as crowded as last evening's stop, the proprietor quickly showed them to his best rooms. As Yardley held the door for her, Cashé hid how his finding fault in her had affected her. Admittedly, she did not totally understand her dependency on this man's opinion; no one else's recognition of her worth had ever mattered. She had never permitted her vulnerability to show. "I believe I shall take my meal in my room, Lord Yardley. I would prefer to turn in early."

Cashé stared at her reflection in the mirror. Lord Yardley's censure had hurt. She had met people before who had not approved of her usual frankness, but it had never bothered her until now. She normally would assume such people lacked her natural astuteness, but Cashé could not say the same of Marcus Wellston for the earl was as intelligent as he was handsome.

"Well, you are nothing to me, Lord Yardley," she declared as she straightened her shoulders and turned from the foggy reflection. "Lachlan Charters does not think me a misbehaving child. Mr. Charters finds me quite charming." She crawled in the bed and blew out the candle. "After tomorrow, I shall never see His Lordship again." That particular thought bothered her more than Cashé would care to admit. She would prefer to learn more of the Earl of Berwick. What made him act as he did to her?

For some unexplained reason, Marcus had hoped she would change her mind; yet, the lady gave no sway. "As you wish, Miss Cashémere." He bowed over her hand. "I will see you in the morning then." He released her hand reluctantly. With this particular woman, he was often akilter, and Marcus did not care for the feeling.

"Good evening, Lord Yardley." She turned quickly into the room and closed the door. He stood watching it for several elongated seconds before shrugging his disbelief.

Later, Marcus had sat in the chair before his room's empty hearth. A nip in the air had told him they must soon light the fireplace at Tweed Hall on a nightly basis. However, tonight, his thoughts remained not on the hearth but on the hurt he had observed in Cashé Aldridge's countenance. He had not realized he had used his "professor" voice with her. Unfortunately, he had done so out of habit. He regularly instructed Trevor in what Society would expect, and Trevor required constant reminders. Marcus had hoped he had not transferred that particular tone to others, but he, obviously, had done so with Lord Averette's niece.

Mayhap he should find a woman, or, at least, a group of friends with whom to spend some "normal" time. Attempting to prove himself worthy of the title thrust upon him, Marcus had devoured his father's papers and ledgers. Perhaps if he socialized more, Miss Cashé's immaturity would not bother him so deeply. As he retired for the evening, Marcus resolved to treat the girl with more civility in the future.

They had barely spoken since departing the inn shortly after daybreak. Every time he looked upon her, Miss Cashé purposely turned her head rather than to meet his eyes. Finally, he had brought his horse along side the coach and had leaned down to speak to her through the open window. "Linton Park's gatehouse is just ahead." He nodded toward the road.

Regina Jeffers

"Thank you, Lord Yardley." She busied herself with her reticule and looked away.

Marcus wondered if something beyond their disagreement had upset her; he could not conceive how anything he had said would bring such rancor. Uncertain of her temperament, he simply touched his hat with his riding crop and nudged the horse forward to lead the coach onto the Linworth property. Three-quarters of a mile later, they had arrived on Worthing's doorstep.

As he led Miss Cashémere toward the entrance, her anxiousness showed. "I certainly hope my uncle is present, and we have not missed him."

Marcus could not resist adding, "As do I, Miss Cashé." He saw her flinch and knew instant regret at having caused her additional pain, but before the girl could respond, the estate door swung wide, and Worthing's butler greeted them.

"Lord Yardley. Miss Cashémere." Automatically, Mr. Lucas shot a glance over their shoulders to see if others were in the party. "Please come in."

"Thank you, Mr. Lucas." Marcus handed his hat and crop to the man. "Might Lord Worthing be available?"

The butler stepped back, evidently uncertain how to respond. Lucas's response told Marcus something was amiss. "His Lordship is out at the moment. However, I will inform Lady Worthing of your arrival. Please escort Miss Cashémere to the blue drawing room, my Lord. I will see to the refreshments."

"Certainly, Mr. Lucas." Although he would prefer to question Worthing's man further, Marcus caught Miss Cashé's elbow to steady her on the stairs.

"Why did you not ask after my uncle?" she demanded through tight lips.

He taunted, "Do you not believe it proper to speak to the master of the house before asking after his guests?"

"I do not care for proper, Your Lordship. I simply want this journey to end," she growled.

Marcus pulled her to an abrupt halt. "I did not take on being your escort for your sake, Miss Cashémere. I executed my duty for His Grace and for your sister. And, by the way, you might have considered extending your gratitude just once in the past three days!" He stalked away, angry with her once again and angry she had stirred emotions in him he thought long dead. Marcus wondered how many times he had lost his temper with the girl. It was not like him. Normally, it took something devastating for him to react emotionally.

The girl caught her skirt tail and strode after him. "Why should I offer gratitude, Lord Yardley?" she barked to his retreating form.

Marcus turned on her. "Have you no sense of propriety? How do you call yourself a Christian and treat others so poorly?"

She breezed past him, entering the room in a huff. Then she came to an unexpected standstill, causing Marcus to curtail his chase. "How dare you question my Christian charity? At least, I worship regularly!"

Intentionally, he crossed to a cluster of chairs and sat. "And what do you learn in God's house, Miss Cashémere?" he demanded.

However, before she could respond, Lady Eleanor Kerrington appeared at the drawing room door. "Cashémere. Lord Yardley."

Marcus scrambled to his feet and offered Lady Worthing a bow. "Lady Worthing, thank you for receiving us." Marcus noted the girl came to her senses and executed a belated curtsy.

Lady Worthing gestured to the chairs. "Please be seated." Once they were situated, she continued, "How might I serve you?"

Wishing to stifle Miss Cashé's tendency to speak out of turn, Marcus took the lead. "The fact you did not ask immediately why Miss Cashémere and I traveled together tells me you are aware of our situation, Lady Worthing."

Their hostess inclined her head. "I am, Lord Yardley." She accepted the tea tray the maid delivered.

Unable to remain quiet, the girl interrupted. "Then my uncle is at Linton Park? Or my sister? I insist you make them aware of my arrival; I shall see either immediately." Tinges of their previous conversation, evidently, still lingered for she demanded and coerced. The girl had not learned sugar captures flies quicker than does vinegar. Irritated once again, Marcus clenched his fists at his side.

Lady Worthing leisurely poured tea, ignoring Miss Cashé's attitude. "I am afraid," she said as she graciously served the cakes, "I have seen neither Lord Averette or my cousin since His Lordship and I took our leave of your family in London." She directed the last remark to her stunned relative.

Miss Cashé placed her cup down hard to emphasize her point. "That is impossible! We trailed my uncle to Derbyshire!"

Marcus gritted his teeth in anger; yet, Lady Worthing smiled indulgently at her cousin. He admired the woman for maintaining her composure. He wished he could imitate her good manners where Miss Cashé was concerned. "I did not say Lord Averette had not come to the neighborhood," Lady Worthing responded sweetly. "I simply said your uncle did not call at Linton Park."

"Go on, Lady Worthing." With a warning glare, Marcus overrode any objections Miss Cashé planned to make. He would not permit the girl to insult the Captain's wife.

"Our day yester morn appeared quite routine, but things altered quickly. Viscount Lexford made an unexpected call." Marcus glanced at Miss Cashé to gauge her reaction to the knowledge her former admirer was close, but the girl showed no interest whatsoever. He assumed Lexford might know another heartbreak if he continued to pursue the girl. "Then my brother arrived seeking Lord Worthing's assistance in rescuing Velvet. Bran possessed the information you had sent him, as well as some additional facts from Mr. Shepherd. Before we could organize a liberation, Lord Hellsman arrived."

Marcus raised an eyebrow, but neither he nor Lady Worthing vocalized the irony of Carter Lowery's older brother Lawrence becoming involved. Lady Worthing continued, "Lord Averette had asked Lord Hellsman to intervene upon his behalf. As you are both aware, the viscount assumed His Grace had arranged to meet our cousin at Linton Park. As we attempted to convince Lord Hellsman of the error of Lord Averette's assertions, Sir Carter arrived to add to the chaos. The baronet had tracked Brantley to Derbyshire. It appears Mir's men have staged a double kidnapping. The one known as Talpur has taken Sonali toward Cornwall; the other has taken Velvet toward Liverpool. Poor Brantley knew not what to do so my husband took control. Lord Worthing and Sir Carter have assumed Sonali's rescue. They will set up at our brother Amsteadt's estate in Devon. James has sent Lexford, who has connections in Cheshire, with Bran to Liverpool."

"And my uncle?" Cashé asked sarcastically.

Marcus noted Lady Worthing's controlled expression. "It is my understanding Lord Averette continues his search. Lord Hellsman has accompanied Viscount Averette to London." Marcus quickly realized how Sir Carter had recruited his brother to mislead Averette.

"So, did no one tell Uncle Samuel that Velvet has likely been kidnapped by the duke's former enemy?" the girl's sharp tone of insinuation remained.

Marcus took pleasure in Lady Worthing's devious smile. "As Viscount Averette never presented himself at Linton Park, it was impossible to dissuade him from his misconceptions."

Marcus had not known much of Lady Eleanor Fowler prior to Worthing's announcing he would make the woman his wife. All he had known was the woman's shame. Of the degradation under which she had lived with the former duke. And of the elaborate plan executed by the Realm against her tormentor Sir Louis Levering, but he had liked Thornhill's sister immediately. She possessed an innate intelligence and a willingness to take on a difficult situation. Worthing, obviously, based his choice on more than the lady's elegance and beauty, and Marcus quickly judged Lady Eleanor the perfect match for his former leader. "Shall you continue to seek your uncle, Miss Cashémere? It appears Lord Averette will discover nothing of import in London or Kent to satisfy his anger." Marcus had turned his attention to his very spoiled traveling companion.

Miss Cashé paused, apparently considering what he said. "It appears more prudent to chase after His Grace and Viscount Lexford." Again, Marcus searched for an emotional response to her mentioning of Lexford's name; yet, nothing appeared. He wondered if he should warn Lexford of his pursuit's futility. "Besides, Satiné is in Manchester."

He asked curiously, "Satiné?"

"My twin...the Fowlers accepted Velvet when our parents passed. I remained with Uncle Samuel, but Satiné resided with my mother's brother, Baron Ashton of Chesterfield Manor."

Marcus heard her words, but none of them registered beyond the words my twin. He had known on some level that another Aldridge sister existed, but he was not aware the third was Miss Cashémere's twin. Just the word twin brought a groan to his throat, which he worked hard to swallow.

"I forgot about Satiné being in Manchester," Lady Worthing was saying. "I am certain Bran will not recall. When was the last time you saw Satiné?"

The girl stiffened. "Nearly three years ago."

Uncomfortable with the talk of twins, Marcus placed his cup down. He wanted to be doing more than sitting around sipping tea. "How long has His Grace been in Cheshire?"

"Since yesterday evening."

He thought aloud. "I am certain he and Lexford are in Liverpool by now. I doubt if Jamot arrived before today. We pressed to reach Linton Park as quickly as we could. Jamot had rougher terrain than did we. Plus, I know time-saving secondary roads."

From nowhere logical, Cashé announced. "We shall leave for Cheshire this afternoon, my Lord."

Cashémere Aldridge might be beautiful, but she possessed the ability to set the hairs on the back of his neck on edge. And not in a good manner. She was singular in her ideas, thinking very little of anyone but herself. She did not consider what would become of his estate while he escorted her across the countryside nor the danger in which she had placed them by her shortsightedness. Now, she expected him to continue this escapade by escorting her to Cheshire. He would definitely express his disdain with Shepherd regarding this assignment. "You wish me to continue to serve as your escort?"

♦♦♦

Cashé wished he might be a bit pleased by her offer, but Lord Yardley, evidently, found her contemptuous. Hurt by his resentment, she retorted, "Obviously, Uncle Samuel would not approve; yet, we have traveled this far together, and as long as I have Edana with me, we shall persevere. In addition, Lord Averette does not approve of how Lady Worthing has conducted her life prior to coming to Linton Park." The viscountess blustered, but Cashé persisted in repeating what she had heard her uncle say on more than one occasion. She did not consider her insinuations as anything more than the truth. "Even Eleanor's aiding Lady Amsteadt in the delivery of the woman's child is not acceptable for a woman of refined Society, no matter how admirable the act might be. My uncle would not agree with my staying at Linton Park without him or Aunt Alice, so it is best if I continue to seek my sister."

"You are quite misleared, Miss Cashé," the earl accused.

"Rude, my Lord? Or honest? It is a matter of perspective." She raised her chin defiantly. She saw the anger seethe beneath his composure, but Cashé no longer cared about his holier than thou opinions.

"From my perspective, rudeness is a long way from truthfulness. You accepted the hospitality of Lady Worthing at Linton Park and of her brother at Briar House, and then you repeat malicious, hurtful words spoken about their family. You are incorrigible."

29

She flushed when she observed the earl's displeasure and her cousin's discomfort. Belatedly, Cashé added, "I apologize, Eleanor; you are my cousin, and my family is thankful to yours for my sister's care; yet, things were quite different within our households." She mimicked her uncle by snarling her nose in distaste.

Marcus watched closely as Lady Worthing busied herself with the tea service, using it as a distraction while she took several deep breaths to steady her hand. Finally, she said flatly, "As I would not judge you, I would wish you to offer me the same. Do not forget what the Good Book says, 'He who is without sin among you, let him throw the first stone.'"

Marcus thought Eleanor Kerrington chose her response well, but Miss Cashé looked offended. "Such misapplication of the scripture will not silence me or my opposition to depravity. Besides, what might be said of censure for Uncle Samuel's family?"

Lady Worthing stood suddenly. She surprised Marcus with her composure, however. How did one address the girl's naiveté? The viscountess's voice held a deadly warning. "As Peter warned when referring to Paul's letters, some things are hard to understand by those who are untaught or are unstable and who twist to their destruction the scriptures. Cashé, you make everything black or white, but the world knows not such extremes; it is covered in variations of gray." Lady Worthing paused to calm her breathing. "You wish to know of what I might criticize Viscount Averette. Let us consider the fact your uncle would see a woman and a child die simply to keep the lines of propriety? Or that you have not known your twin in nearly three years, and until recently, not Velvet for over four? How about the fact that not once did your righteous Uncle Samuel send one quid of support for Velvet's upbringing? I imagine it is so for Satiné, as well. I know this to be a fact for the past six years because as father became more incoherent, the estate ledgers became my duty to oversee and to update. How about the fact that when Velvet came of age, no one in your family acknowledged it with an appropriate dowry? Again, it was that depraved man known as William Fowler, my father, who bequeathed your eldest sister a dowry of thirteen thousand pounds. But even more importantly, it was my family who saw to Velvet's education, who tended her when she was ill, who nourished her hopes and her dreams. You may be Velvet's sister by blood, but I am her sister in life. Despite our depravity and our ill breeding, my family gave Velvet a home when your righteous grandmother and Uncle Samuel would not." Lady Worthing presented Marcus a quick curtsy. "Your Lordship, I shall see to your and Miss Cashé's carriage. I assume you will play the gentleman and will accompany her west."

Marcus certainly wanted nothing more to do with Miss Cashémere, but he would not leave the girl to plague Linton Park with her misconstructions. He refused to subject Worthing's wife to such a fate. He would remove Cashémere Aldridge from the viscountess's household if he had to physically carry the spoiled brat all the way to Cheshire. "Unfortunately, Lady Worthing, my parents raised a gentleman."

"And the world is a better place for it, my Lord." Lady Worthing rolled her eyes in disbelief. She plastered a cordial smile on her lips when she turned one last time to meet Marcus's gaze. "Tell my brother I pray for the speedy and safe return him and his associates."

"Yes...certainly, Lady Worthing," Marcus stammered. Then she left them alone in the drawing room. Marcus waited until Lady Eleanor's receding steps had told him she had departed before he vehemently attacked Miss Cashé. "I have traveled through much of the Continent, as well as the East. I have known schemers and liars, but not in all the years of my life have I known anyone who spoke with such hatred and such ignorance! What is it about you that makes you so despise the world? To see nothing but evil and iniquity? To place yourself as judge and jury? I can conceive of your immaturity, Miss Cashémere, but I cannot comprehend your desire to lash out at everyone."

Tears misted the girl's eyes. "I am not immature, Your Lordship. I have learned my lessons well. You have no idea..."

"Then tell me, Miss Cashé. I will understand. Explain it to me, and I will make whatever troubles you, right. I swear by my honor."

"I require not your honor nor your understanding, my Lord!" She stood quickly. "I also do not require your protection. I release you from your promise to escort me to Cheshire. It is still daylight, and Edana and I can be at Chesterfield Manor in a matter of hours." Cashé reached for her reticule and bonnet. "I thank you, Lord Yardley, for your concern for my well being." She made a curtsy to leave.

Marcus caught her arm. "If you think I will permit a mere girl to travel alone even for a few hours, Miss Cashémere, you are sadly mistaken."

She hissed, "I am not a girl, Lord Yardley."

"You are not yet a woman for you act as a child," he growled.

She flushed with color. "I am nearly nineteen. My uncle intends for my betrothal after my next birthday. If I am woman enough to marry, I am no longer a girl."

Marcus studied her countenance. Cashé Aldridge was an enigma to which he held no answer. "I will see you safely to Baron Ashton's estate and then will join my friends in your oldest sister's rescue."

Her bottom lip trembled. "As you wish, Your Lordship." She jerked her arm from his hold and raced from the room.

Marcus simply shook his head. "No, as you wish, Miss Cashémere."

Chapter Three

"Miss Cashémere, we must speak immediately." Marcus assisted the lady into the waiting coach. "I could ride with you, and Edana could join the driver for a few minutes." He breathed the words into her hair. He had spent the last twenty minutes in a private conversation with Lady Worthing. Eleanor Kerrington had pleaded with him to assist Miss Cashé in breaking the hold Viscount Averette held over the girl. In tears, Fowler's sister described a jovial Samuel Aldridge and the carefree child she remembered. "Find a way to reach her, Lord Yardley," she had begged. "I fear it is too late for her uncle, but Cashé always possessed the most generous heart. Assist her in finding her humanity again before she becomes a bitter old woman."

Marcus did not understand why Lady Worthing entrusted her remembrances to him. She should have directed her discourse to Viscount Lexford. The man held the girl in affection. He supposed Eleanor Kerrington simply needed to give voice to her concerns, and he was the only one available; and, although he had promised his captain's wife that he would see it through, now Marcus wondered about the sanity of his vow.

Red rimmed the girl's eyes, but she refused to look away from him. "Our only business, my Lord, is to find my Uncle Charles. He shall see to Velvet's safety and to mine. Escort me to Chesterfield Manor, and then your services shall no longer be required." She stepped into the carriage and motioned for Edana to join her. With a shrug, Marcus folded the stairs into the coach and secured the door. With a nod to the driver, he swung up into the saddle to cover one more British shire. He glanced at the girl as he rode forward to take the lead. Cashé Aldridge dabbed at her eyes before looking away. The sadness reminded Marcus of someone else he knew: him.

&

"Yes, Sir."

Marcus stood before the Chesterfield Manor butler. "The Earl of Berwick and Miss Cashémere Aldridge for Baron Ashton." He noticed how the butler stared intently at Cashé.

The man stammered, "Certainly...Sir. Please...please come in, Sir." The butler accepted Marcus's hat and gloves.

Marcus assisted Cashé with her cloak, but she turned to the butler and demanded, "Please ask my sister, Miss Satiné, to join us."

With the security of an upper servant, the man replied evenly, "I will inquire if Miss Satiné is available." He returned his attention to Marcus. "This way, Your Lordship." The butler led them to a nearby drawing room. "Baron Ashton will be with you shortly, Sir." He bowed from the room.

Marcus desperately wanted to leave the girl to her own selfish devices and to join his friends. His few private moments with Eleanor Kerrington had convinced him Lexford and Thornhill required his expertise in capturing Murhad Jamot. The faster he could dispense with Cashémere Aldridge, the better. He would share Lady Worthing's concerns with Lexford and permit the viscount to address Miss Cashé's shortcomings.

"Your Lordship," Baron Ashton stepped through the open door, "how good of you to call upon us, Sir, and to bring our Cashémere with you." He bowed to Marcus and opened his arms to his niece.

"Uncle Charles," she cooed prettily. "It is so good to be at Chesterfield Manor." The girl, evidently, ran hot and cold, and it discomposed Marcus to know she had thought so little of him to show only her disdain.

"I am always amazed, my Dear, how much you and your sister resemble each other." The baron sat the girl away from him and took a closer look at her countenance. "Absolutely uncanny," he murmured.

"Where is Satiné?" Marcus watched with some angst as the affable Cashémere reappeared. She acted as if this was simply a social call.

The baron shot a quick glance at Marcus. "Your sister will be down momentarily; she has been riding and must wash away the trail dust." He motioned Cashé to a chair. "Meanwhile, perhaps the Earl of Berwick might enlighten me as to why you two travel from Edinburgh together."

"I can explain," she began, but a raised hand from her uncle smothered her words. Thankfully, she acquiesced to the baron's wishes.

"I would prefer to hear it from His Lordship, my Dear."

Although he perfectly understood, Marcus did not appreciate the implication behind the baron's words. "I am Marcus Wellston, and my estate is in Berwick. For many years, I have been a close associate of the Duke of Thornhill."

The baron's eyebrow rose in curiosity. "William Fowler?"

"No, Sir. Brantley Fowler. His Grace assumed the title several months prior."

"I was unaware. My niece and I recently returned from a journey to Wales. I must have been from the country when the transition occurred." The baron took a seat and motioned Marcus to one.

Marcus did not wish to discuss confidences. "As the late duke was ill for several years and not in Society, I assume Fowler's accession was not as well known as one might suspect."

The baron inclined his head in affirmation. Marcus then continued, "Thornhill and I served together on the Continent and have continued our association after returning to Britain." He swallowed hard. "Perhaps, Sir, I might make a very complicated story shorter. Viscount Averette recently spent time in London with the Fowlers. When he returned to Scotland, he thought it appropriate that Miss Aldridge change her residence to his. The lady has dwelled with the viscount for some three months. Recently, the British governmental agency for which His Grace and I both served intercepted word of a possible kidnapping of your eldest niece. Because I was closer to Scotland than Thornhill, I was dispatched to Edinburgh to thwart the attempt. Unfortunately, I was too late.

"Not understanding the situation's true nature, Lord Averette assumed Miss Aldridge was a runaway and was on her way to meet Thornhill, as they have expressed an affection for each other. The viscount chases his niece toward London. Miss Cashémere thought we might overtake her uncle and set him to right, but when we reached Linton Park, Lady Worthing informed us that His Grace and Viscount Lexford rushed to Liverpool to seek word of Miss Aldridge."

"Why did you travel to Linton Park, Cashémere?" Charles Morton asked, the unusual turn of events still not clear.

"Lady Eleanor married Viscount Worthing four months prior. When Uncle Samuel learned of the duke's passing, he set an immediate course to Kent. He feared Fowler's Cousin Leighton might assume the title as no one knew of Brantley's whereabouts, and my uncle would not permit such a man to claim Velvet as his own." The girl wrinkled her nose in disgust. "At the time, we, too, were unaware of His Grace's return to the title. As Fate would have it, our coach broke an axel outside of Linton Park, where we discovered Lady Eleanor in residence and awaiting her nuptials. As His Grace, Velvet, and the Dowager Duchess of Norfield made their way to Derby, we tarried with the Worthing household until the wedding ceremony. When Velvet went missing, Uncle Samuel, naturally, came to the conclusion my sister returned to Thornhill."

"And Samuel in his righteous mind believed Linworth would look the other way while Thornhill staged some sort of tryst with my niece. It amazes me the narrowness of the man's opinions!" The baron leaned forward to press his point. "And never once did it cross Aldridge's mind to keep me informed of these changes regarding Velvet! The gall of the man! He broke the dictates of his brother's last testament."

Marcus cleared his throat to refocus the conversation. "James Kerrington, Lord Worthing, Sir, served as our commander. He and Thornhill are intimates."

Baron Ashton smiled knowingly. "And now brothers. I am pleased to hear Eleanor found contentment. She has a family, at last. The Kerringtons are of the first ilk." He now rested his attention on Marcus. "Were you and Thornhill and Kerrington all Realm?"

Marcus stammered, "You...you are...familiar with the Realm, Baron?"

"Intimately." A secretive smile graced Ashton's lips. "When I was younger...I served as such also."

Before Marcus could stop his chin from dropping in surprise, Miss Cashé squealed, and Marcus turned to see a woman the spiting image of Cashémere Aldridge. The same height. The same coal black wavy hair. The same dark brows and pale skin. The same delicate features and heart-shaped face. The same green eyes. Although he had spent the better part of the last week with Miss Cashé, this time his breath caught in his throat.

"My niece, Your Lordship." Ashton took the newcomer's hand in a loving gesture. "May I present Miss Satiné Aldridge? My Dear, this is Marcus Wellston, the Earl of Berwick."

The woman presented a proper curtsy. "We are most pleased you have brought Cashémere home to us, Sir, but how might I address you, Your Lordship? Berwick?"

"Yardley. I am Lord Yardley." Marcus's eyes traced her face, memorizing each line.

"Let us order tea, Your Lordship." Ashton hustled everyone to nearby chairs. "We must inform Satiné of Velvet's situation, and I have many questions to which I require answers. Afterwards, Lord Yardley and I will confer. Develop a plan in case Thornhill and Lord Lexford fail."

Only a few moments ago, Marcus had desired a speedy exit. Now, he had nothing better to do than sip tea with a beautiful woman.

ⓛ

If Marcus had bothered to look upon Miss Cashé's countenance, he would have easily noted the girl's discomfort. His attention to her sister had not escaped Cashé's notice, and she seethed from the knowledge it was her personality to which he objected and not just her lack of experience. "Come sit with me, Satiné," she requested. "When her sister joined her on the settee, Cashé said innocently, "I have missed you, Satiné."

"And I you," her sister responded with polish. Satiné's every gesture spoke of refinement, and Cashé felt awkward and unworthy.

"It has been several years, I understand," interjected Lord Yardley.

Satiné supplied, "Nigh onto three years, Sir."

Cashé rolled her eyes in disbelief. Yardley already possessed knowledge of her family's situation. "Edinburgh is a long way from Manchester," Cashé murmured.

"No more so than a journey to Kent and London," Yardley said cockily, and Cashé again despised his righteous censure. Nothing she attempted pleased the man, and she hated herself also for even attempting to do so.

ⓛ

Over the next two hours, Baron Ashton and Marcus formulated a plan to follow Thornhill and Lexford to Liverpool. Marcus had wanted to leave the ladies in Cheshire where they might remain safe, but, much to his chagrin, Miss Cashémere had insisted on being in a position to protect her elder sister's reputation by traveling to the seaport with her uncle. "My Uncle Samuel would expect me to protect Velvet from the gossipmongers," she had declared, and Marcus's disdain grew more acute.

Miss Satiné thought to go only because her sister might require the emotional support. "Velvet must be terrified," she said quietly.

And so Marcus rode beside Baron Ashton's carriage. It was late when they departed Cheshire, but the journey to Liverpool would take only a few hours. Although Marcus assumed Lexford and Thornhill had already taken up residence in Liverpool, before they departed the baron's estate, he had sent a message to Lord Lexford at Lexington Arms.

The Aldridge twins sat together in the baron's carriage. Marcus shot several glances at the girls. Uncanny is what Ashton called it, and

Marcus saw the truth behind the baron's words. However, he suspected the differences in the women's personalities would make it quite easy to delineate between the twins. Miss Cashémere certainly did not have Miss Satiné's sweet disposition. Cashé Aldridge was obstinate and demanding and shrewish. Even the reasons the women had chosen to accompany the men to Liverpool highlighted their differences: Miss Cashé wished to make a religious statement about a woman's virtue, while Miss Satiné offered comfort before propriety.

Ashton brought his horse along side of Marcus's. "Liverpool is only another mile or two. We will put in at The Golden Apple. If your friends followed protocol, they will be lodged there. It is a familiar stop for those associated with the Realm.

Marcus liked the baron–respected the way the man's mind worked– recognized how Charles Morton might have once played his part in keeping Britain safe. "I pray we are in time."

Reaching the inn before nightfall, Marcus immediately recognized Lexford's horse in the stable. He and Ashton dismounted, handing off their reins to a waiting groom. "They are here," he told the baron in a hushed tone. "Allow me to locate my friends while you tend your nieces." He motioned to where the baron's carriage rolled into the inn yard's entrance.

The baron nodded his agreement while Marcus turned toward the main door. Stepping into the dimly lit open room, he paused to permit his eyes to adjust to the darkness, and then he saw him: The viscount made his way toward the stairs. Marcus pushed past some of the locals to reach the man. "Lexford!" he called.

Aidan Kimbolt turned quickly upon hearing his name. Recognizing his friend, Viscount Lexford turned in greeting. "Yardley! Why are you here?"

"Miss Cashé and I followed Lord Averette, but we changed our course when the lady recalled the maternal uncle and her twin were in Cheshire. Therefore, we traveled to Chesterfield Arms. Baron Ashton, unbelievably, is former Realm," he whispered in hushed tones. "With the baron's backing, we followed you in hopes we might be of some service."

"Miss Cashé is here?" His friend's voice rose in anticipation as he peered over Marcus's shoulder, expecting to see the girl.

Marcus had the strange feeling handing Miss Cashé off to the viscount would be a mistake. But for whom? The girl? His friend? Or him? Giving his head a good shake, Marcus purposely shoved such thoughts away. The girl held no sway over him, and Lexford could freely have her. "The baron assists his nieces from the carriage."

Lexford pushed Marcus toward an open door. "Thornhill is in the private dining room. Go on in. I will meet the baron."

Marcus looked up in amusement. "And Miss Cashé's twin?"

Lexford stopped short. "Do they truly favor each other?"

"Let us just say you should be aware to whom you address your attentions." Finally enjoying himself, Marcus found it satisfying to laugh at his friend. Marcus realized he had been out of sorts since he had received Shepherd's note for him to seek the Aldridges. It would be liberating to be rid of Miss Cashémere. Chuckling lightly, Marcus strolled toward the private dining room.

He was barely in the doorway when Thornhill greeted him. "Yardley! I thought you sought Lord Averette."

"Miss Cashémere believed it best if we journey to Liverpool instead. She wished to protect her elder sister from ruination." Marcus purposely swallowed the words, which sprang to his lips: protect her elder sister from you! "I brought Baron Ashton and Miss Satiné with us; they reside quite close to Lexford."

Thornhill shook Marcus's hand and ushered him into the room. "I had forgotten about Satiné and the baron being so close at hand." The duke gestured to the food spread out upon the table. "Yet, how could Miss Cashé be of use?" Marcus half agreed with Thornhill's sentiments. The girl knew nothing of danger.

Marcus reached for the sliced dark bread and cheese. "Speak to the baron, Thornhill. The man is former Realm, and Ashton has an idea of how he and the girls might foil Jamot's plan."

Before they could discuss it further, Lexford ushered the baron and the Aldridge twins into the room. "Look who Yardley brought us, Your Grace." Marcus could not keep his eyes from looking upon Miss Cashémere. She docilely accompanied Lexford, acting very ladylike, not like the hellion Marcus had suspected she really was. Her eyes met his, daring Marcus to defy the image she presented.

The duke's voice brought Marcus from his thoughts. "You will see to rooms for the baron and the young ladies."

Marcus silently thanked his friend for the escape. "Of course, Thornhill."

When he returned to the private dining parlor, the men had planned their attack while the ladies retired to freshen their clothing. Lexford's man, Henry "Lucifer" Hill, had brought word he had located the Baloch warrior for whom they searched at a portside warehouse. Lucifer had actually followed the man to a boarded up storage building.

Always impulsive, Thornhill would have stormed the warehouse, but all the men preached caution. Jamot could possess additional men inside the locked building, or he could have rigged an assault on Velvet Aldridge to squash an attack. "I could go through an upper level," Marcus suggested. Each Realm member possessed special talents. Marcus's was his ability to easily scale heights. However, Thornhill had demanded to be the one to stage the rescue. The duke needed personally to secure his ladylove's safety. "With your permission, Your Grace, I will examine the building and advise you how best to proceed."

"I would appreciate it, Wellston."

Although only the viscount had voiced his discontent, neither he nor Lexford liked the idea of involving the young ladies. When he had asked Miss Cashé about the color of her older sister's gown, Marcus had thought that it might assist him in locating her. Plus, he had realized the Baloch's belief in the power of color. The blue meant the sky. Jamot would lift up Velvet Aldridge to a great height. Whenever he had discussed such mysticism with Englishmen, they scoffed at the uncivilized percepts, but Marcus had placed a great deal of store in the things beyond the explainable.

After he had the opportunity to examine the site, Marcus provided Thornhill with specific instructions on how to tie off the ropes to avoid a fall. The precarious part would be making a "bridge" between the buildings. Thornhill had had little experience with heights so Marcus had instructed him on the basics. With the daylight, they had taken positions outside the warehouse and had waited for Jamot to make his appearance. Their plan involved a bit of luck and a certain amount of "sleight of hand."

Some time later, Marcus and Miss Satiné stood outside a pawnshop. They stared into the window, pretending to be admiring the items when, in reality, Marcus had used the window's reflection to watch the street before the warehouse and to watch for Lexford's signal. The viscount hid behind a wagon piled high with barrels.

Marcus held Miss Satiné's elbow as if they were a couple. He watched her shallow breathing, the lady's nerves controlling her thoughts. "If it is too much, you should wait in the church," he whispered close to her ear.

Satiné glanced up at him. "You must think me the biggest ninny, Your Lordship."

"You misjudge, Miss Satiné. I am not of the persuasion that women should take unnecessary chances. It probably sounds as if I am quite antiquated, but I believe a woman should seek a man's protection emotionally and physically." He smiled at her. "I know women who charge into battle, but it is not for every woman."

"Why do you not simply enter the warehouse in force and remove my sister?" she asked quietly.

Marcus glanced over his shoulder to make certain nothing had changed. "We have dealt with Murhad Jamot previously, and we know the man is unpredictable. Jamot may have an accomplice in the warehouse, waiting for our attack before killing Miss Aldridge. He might even hold your sister at another location, some place we may not discover until it is too late. We must capture Miss Aldridge's abductor rather than to kill him."

"You speak of killing as if it is commonplace." Miss Satiné's eyes grew in concern.

Marcus took time to word his response carefully. "Those who have seen battle...who have experienced war...speak of death more often than do others, but we do not take that commonality as acceptance. We respect death for its power. For its all-encompassing strength. For good and for evil. Sometimes bringing about a death makes a difference in many lives. In that case, it is necessary." He paused, uncomfortable with his own thoughts. "Do my thoughts make any sense?"

Tears misted her eyes, and Marcus wished to protect the woman. "They make perfect sense, Lord Yardley. I had never thought of death in that particular manner." She touched his arm, and Marcus felt her empathy.

From behind him, in the glass, Marcus observed the door to the warehouse opening and noted when Jamot appeared on the street. As if stretching his neck and shoulders, the Baloch rolled his head before turning to fasten the door. Jamot glanced quickly about the street before strolling casually toward a nearby inn to break his fast. "It is time," he said flatly. Miss Satiné's apprehension showed. "Stand by the alley's opening. You know what to do, but take no risks."

"I shall be well," she said with little confidence.

Marcus squeezed her hand. "I will be close. I will permit nothing amiss to happen to you."

Cashé waited with her uncle, outside a nearby blacksmith shop. "You seem very composed," Ashton said as he leaned away from the side of the building to peek at the open street leading to the warehouse.

"I am not the type to have a case of the vapors," she assured him, but Cashé quickly added, "Yet, if I appear calm it is purely a nice façade."

Her uncle took her hand in his and brought it to rest over his heart. "I have longed to see you again. It grieves me we have had so little time together. Your mother–my sister–never wanted you girls separated. My heart beats a bit easier today knowing you are before me. Even with Velvet's crisis, it is important for you to know that."

Cashé stared deeply into his eyes, noting how the lines creased his temples. She had always wondered how Uncle Samuel and his mother had chosen which sister had gone to which relative. She wanted to ask the baron how Satiné had come to him, but she did not want to know Uncle Charles had left her behind because she was the least loved or even the least lovable. "We should make an effort to be together more often." She cupped his face with her free hand. "I would like to know my mother's family...to be reacquainted with cousins and aunts. It is difficult with the distance between us to be more to each other, but I will try, Uncle Charles. Truly, I shall."

"As will I," he whispered quietly. "Now that you are before me, I will have a difficult time allowing you to return to Scotland."

"I will write Uncle Samuel and ask his permission to extend my visit with you."

Cashé noted his slight frown, but before she could respond, the baron took a tighter grip on her hand. "It is time to move into position."

With trepidation, they followed the dark skinned man. He made his way to the inn, and she and the baron crossed to the pawnshop and entered. Cashé noted how her sister waited by the opening leading to the alley, but she did not turn her head. Although any passerby could identify the similarities between them, it was important not to appear to be together. She also allowed her eyes to follow Lord Yardley's retreat between the buildings surrounding the warehouse. Without conscious thought, she said a prayer for his safety.

At a run, Marcus darted between the buildings and climbed a high fence to guarantee Thornhill had made it into the building's upper level. If the duke had failed, it would fall to Marcus to complete the assignment. He waited in the alleyway as Thornhill managed to lower himself over the building's edge and to secure a finger-hold on the window frame.

"Anything?" he hissed through gritted teeth.

Thornhill peered through the window and shook his head in the negative. Then the duke began to frantically kick at the window, sending shards of glass tumbling to the ground. Marcus took cover, but he watched carefully for Thornhill's success.

"Stop Jamot's return!" Thornhill ordered before crawling through the window.

To Marcus, Thornhill's entreaty meant his friend had found Miss Aldridge. Leaving the duke to his job, Marcus scrambled over a low wall and dropped onto the street level just as Jamot exited the inn. As if he had no cares, the Baloch carried a loaf of bread under his arm. He strolled leisurely toward the warehouse. The man actually whistled a tune. The docks and their ever-changing population were a good place for the Baloch to blend into English society. In London, among those who tended shops and went about their business, Jamot would stand out.

Marcus motioned to Satiné to cross the busy street. On cue, she darted from beside the warehouse and crossed behind a merchant's cart, before racing into a dead end alleyway.

As predicted, Jamot took notice of the blue dress and coal black hair. The man threw down the loaf of bread and walked quickly to the alley's opening. Marcus raced to the pawnshop, bursting through the main door and pushing his way toward the rear entrance. The plan was for Satiné to enter the building through the back, but when he reached the door, boxes blocked the entrance. Had Baron Ashton not made arrangements with the shop owner? "Damn!" He began throwing boxes to the side to reach the door. If Jamot caught Miss Satiné, the man would kill her!

"What is it?" The baron realized the problem and began to shove boxes left and right. "Hurry!" he ordered, but Marcus already had broken furniture and glass items with his frantic pace. The baron turned to Cashé, who waited for her turn to appear. "Tell Lexford!" Morton yelled as he lifted a huge carton.

Cashé ran for the front, but when she reached it, neither Lexford nor his man of all means was in sight. It was upon her shoulders to save Satiné.

Taking a deep breath, she edged toward the opening. She could hear the dark-skinned man curse as he turned over stacked boxes. Cashé had no idea where Satiné hid, but it was only a matter of time before the man found her. So, brazenly, Cashé stepped into the opening and purposely cleared her throat. She paused but a second to assure their enemy had seen her, and then she hurried across the busy street into the blacksmith's shop. They had planned for the foreigner to follow her to the church, but she did not have time to reach the building's safety before the Baloch would overtake her, so Cashé chose the smithy instead. Luckily, the young apprentice had not seen her enter. Neither had he seen her hurry pass the tack room and exit the stables, where she caught at the fence rail to steady her knees. "I made it," she said with some triumph in her voice. Taking a few quick gulps of air, she raced for the church.

☙❧

Marcus caught the door's handle at last. He could hear Satiné trembling against the wood as he jerked the door wide and pulled her roughly into his embrace. Her heart raced as did his, and he refused to release her. Not since Maggie had he felt the frustration of not being able to control his fear.

"Excuse me while I see to Cashémere," the baron said, but Marcus only nodded his agreement. He had told Miss Satiné he would protect her, and he had come very close to failing again.

"Look at this mess!" The shopkeeper complained from behind him.

Marcus glared at the man. "I should slit your throat from ear to ear," he growled. "When I finish my business, I will be back to settle with you." He did not say whether he would take revenge on the man or pay him for his damages. At the moment, even Marcus did not know which was the truth of his words. He opened the back door again and led Satiné to the rear of the church. She would wait there while they lured Jamot to the building.

Meanwhile, the baron had followed Murhad Jamot to the blacksmith's, where he found the Baloch strong-arming the smith's apprentice. Not observing Cashé anywhere, Ashton assumed the guise of a blundering aristocrat. "What goes on here?" he charged.

His interference had irritated Jamot, but it had stopped the Baloch from inflicting pain the young man. Having broken up the tussle, Ashton stepped aside as Jamot shouldered his way past the baron. "Out of my way!" Jamot had shoved the baron hard against the doorframe.

44

As he turned, Ashton saw her. Cashé paused on the church's threshold and then entered the building. The baron admired her bravado; she had played her part magnificently. Immediately, Jamot followed, so Ashton apologized to the youth and exited through the back of the stables to join the others at the church.

.൦൨൦,

Marcus had given the signal before entering the church. He led Satiné to an alcove and told her to wait, and then he realized Lexford was alone. "Where is the baron and Miss Cashé?" he demanded.

"Cashé leads Jamot on a merry chase." Lexford peered through the shutters at the street.

Marcus stormed forward, heading toward the church's main door. "She does what?"

"Relax." Lexford stepped before Marcus to block his exit. "She is coming this way."

Marcus removed his gun from an inside holster before assuming a position behind a shuttered window where he might observe the street. Seeing Cashé hurrying toward them from the stable, he allowed himself to breathe again. He did not like to involve innocents, especially women, in Realm business.

Cashé breezed into the church, quickly closing the door behind her. Exhilarated by the intrigue, her eyes glowed with excitement. "Did he see me?" she asked as she saddled up beside Marcus to peer around his shoulder.

Her presence. His fear. Her excitement. His dread. All compounded, and forgetting himself, he caught Cashé by the arm and dragged her toward the alcove where her sister hid. "Are you crazy?" he demanded, without giving her time to respond. "Are you attempting to get yourself killed? Stay in there, and allow Lexford and me to handle this!"

"Jamot is headed this way!" Lexford called, redirecting Marcus's anger.

Marcus gave Cashé a warning glare before taking an offensive position on the other side of the door. He and Lexford waited. Guns cocked and ready, but nothing happened.

When Jamot had not follow Cashé into the church, it had taken Marcus and Lexford only a moment to realize their plan had turned. "Stay here!" Lexford ordered as he ran for the door.

"What if?" Cashé began, but Marcus cut her off.

45

"What if, nothing, Woman!" he barked. "We have not time for your silly games!" Then he darted through the door, making his way to the warehouse. Seeing Ashton exit the stable, Marcus motioned the man toward the church.

Lexford joined him as they squatted beside an overloaded wagon, preparing for what might come next. "What was all that about?" Lexford hissed, as they checked their guns.

"Nothing!" Marcus growled and stepped from behind the wagon to access the warehouse door.

A shot rang out, and both men hit the door in concert. Shoulders exploded against the wood. Breaking away as they hit it a second time, crushing it to pieces; the door ripped free of the frame. Marcus went low, and Lexford high as they dove into the darkened building. A second shot blazed past them before they had time to even adjust their visions to the dim light. Lucifer, who had appeared from the back of the warehouse, cried out, but he did not stop to acknowledge the wound. The man blocked Jamot's retreat.

Murhad Jamot whirled in place and then scrambled up the stairs to a narrow room. Marcus gave pursuit, but Thornhill's raspy voice froze all three of his cohorts in place. "Forget Jamot!"

Above them from the warehouse rafters the Duke of Thornhill swung from a rope. Jamot had rigged an elaborate gallows for Velvet Aldridge. Her arms clung to a rope above her head. Marcus immediately recalled his own prediction: Jamot had truly lifted Velvet Aldridge toward the heavens. If her grasp slipped, the rope's other end would serve effectively as a noose. To prevent her demise, Thornhill now supported her weight and his from the makeshift gallows. Miss Aldridge wrapped her legs about Thornhill's waist and held onto him for dear life.

"Would you like a moment, Your Grace?" Lexford taunted; all three men avoided looking at the lady's fully exposed legs as she dangled above them.

"Just get us the bloody hell down!" Thornhill growled.

Chapter Four

"What did I do wrong?" Cashé whined as her uncle offered a comforting embrace.

Charles Morton held both women close to him. "Absolutely nothing, my Dear. I was quite proud of your resourcefulness." He chucked Cashé's chin and brought her eyes to meet his. "The earl spoke without thinking. His actions were improper. Understandably so, but, nevertheless, inappropriate. Lord Yardley likely experienced the anxiety of our putting Satiné in danger. The shopkeeper's not removing the boxes as instructed nearly destroyed our intricate plans. We actually have your quick thinking to thank for the success we experienced in luring Jamot away from Satiné."

"Then I saved the day?" she asked hopefully.

"Mayhap not the whole day, but part of it," he assured her. "Now, allow me to check on the status of the duke's assault. You girls wait here. I will return for you in a few minutes."

Marcus and Lexford restacked the wooden crates scattered about the area, while Lucifer sat on the bottom step grasping at his chest.

"One more." Marcus used his shoulders and back to shove the large wooden box above his head.

Lexford called out to Thornhill. "Drop down. You can stand on the box."

Thornhill touched the highest level with the toe of his boot. "I can, but Velvet cannot. And I will not leave her!"

Marcus obediently lifted another of the heavy crates. "Will this do, Your Grace?" He wedged the two-foot deep box under Thornhill's foot. Realizing they had given the duke an escape, he and Lexford backed away from the wooden tower and turned their heads to provide Thornhill and his Miss Aldridge some privacy. They had avoided looking directly at Miss Aldridge's exposed legs and under garments. Impatiently, Marcus and the viscount waited for Thornhill to free himself and his ladylove.

They heard the duke and Miss Aldridge whispered endearments, and then Thornhill called for assistance in freeing the woman. "Tell the smithy I require an instrument to cut the chains." The stacked structure wobbled, but Thornhill straightened slowly, maintaining his balance.

Marcus grinned mischievously at Lexford. "I have it." He darted through the open door into the busy street and came face-to-face with Ashton's frowning countenance.

"Thornhill and my niece?" The baron asked without prelude.

Marcus whispered, "Safe for the moment, but not totally free. Miss Aldridge is chained to the rafters. I am to the blacksmith's."

The baron nodded his understanding. "I will wait a few moments before I bring Velvet's sisters over."

"I should go." Marcus took a step away, but the baron caught his arm.

"Cashémere can be quite frustrating, Your Lordship. She is a product of Samuel Aldridge's sickness. However, she does not require your censure for doing the correct thing. You owe my niece an apology, Lord Yardley."

Marcus paused, listening closely to what the baron did not say. In four and twenty hours, two of the girl's relatives had cautioned him on how to handle her. He did not understand why his actions and his words had taken on such importance in regards to the girl, but he recognized the folly of his earlier lack of composure. "I will do so, Ashton." Marcus could not explain why Cashé Aldridge so enflamed his thinking. He did not need such chaos in his life: He required peace and quiet and contentment. Marcus had attempted to forgive himself for his inadequacies, so why could he not forgive a beautiful woman for hers?

He hurried to the smith and borrowed a metal cutter Thornhill could use to free Miss Aldridge. Returning to the warehouse, he gingerly climbed the lower levels of the pyramid, handing the tool to a half bent Thornhill. When the duke straightened, the boxes rocked, and Marcus grabbed them to steady his friend's maneuvers. His expertise in heights proved beneficial, and the quickly constructed tower righted itself.

While Thornhill cut the chain's links, Marcus lowered his weight to the warehouse floor before rushing to Lucifer Hill's aid. "Allow me to have a look," he told the former cavalryman. "You have a nice hole gaping at me, old Man," he taunted in a male bonding sort of way.

"Been hit worse than this," Lucifer mustered.

Marcus looked up when the metal lock crashed to the floor. He folded his handkerchief to stop the blood flow and replaced Hill's hand over the wound. When he looked again, the duke was handing Miss Aldridge to Lexford's waiting arms; therefore, Marcus announced, "I will find a physician. Lucifer requires tending."

"So do I," Thornhill added flatly.

Marcus nodded and disappeared again into the street. From a distance, he observed Ashton approaching from his left with the twins; defensively Marcus turned to his right and darted between the bustling wagon trades: Watching both girls grapple with the demon Jamot had frightened Marcus beyond reason, but he was not proud of his actions and required alone time to decide what to do next. Instinctively, he looked for the signage of an apothecary, catching a passerby by the arm, "Where is the nearest physician?"

"Two streets over, Sir."

Marcus was on the move, weaving his way through the busy streets. Finally, he spotted the marked office. Bursting through the door, he called out, "Anyone here? I have two injured men in a warehouse by the water!"

⨏⨎⨏

Cashé spotted the earl walking briskly away. Coward, she thought. No civilities! she amended. "May we leave for Cheshire soon, Uncle Charles? I tire of these games." She had thought to prove something to Lord Yardley. Prove to him she was not the spoiled girl he had thought her to be. She was brave and mature: A woman worth choosing. She did not understand why she desired to prove anything to the cantankerous lord, but deep inside she had recognized her weakness. It is not as if I need Lord Yardley in my life! she had declared to her confused mind. I have other options!

When they entered the warehouse, Cashé's mouth had gaped in surprise. Despite others milling about them, her sister and the duke embraced intimately. Just as Uncle Samuel suspected, she thought. Only when the baron cleared his throat did the couple cease the kiss, and even then, Thornhill had refused to release her sister from his embrace.

When she followed the duke's gaze, their presence became evident to Velvet, but only a slight blush betrayed her sister's "cozy" display. Yet, Velvet's pure delight at discovering them brought Cashé a jolt of loneliness. She had for so long been the odd one out. It hurt to know she did not fit into this happy family.

"Uncle!" Velvet squealed before rushing into Ashton's welcoming arms. "How did you come to be here?" However, before the baron could answer, Velvet grabbed both Satiné and Cashé in an encompassing hold.

49

Their oldest sister alternated kissing both their cheeks. "I am so pleased to see you. You have no idea what your presence means to me," she whispered lovingly to them.

The baron took possession of Velvet's hand. "Lord Yardley escorted Cashémere to Chesterfield Manor," he explained to her, "and, of course, we had to assist the duke in your rescue."

Velvet appeared stunned by his statement. "To think you came to support His Grace's efforts."

"Your sisters did more than come to Liverpool to support you, Velvet. Look at how they are dressed." Baron Ashton gestured to the twins. "They distracted your kidnapper long enough for Thornhill to stage your rescue. They were quite bold."

"My Goodness!" Her sister gasped in wide-eyed acknowledgment. "You are each quite remarkable. And look at us. We could be triplets!"

Cashé wrinkled her nose in disgust. Before she thought about her words, she whispered, "Except that you are so unkempt."

Satiné warned in a hiss. "Cashé!"

While Thornhill reclaimed Velvet, Cashé considered her twin's reprimand. She had again overstepped the boundaries of propriety; yet, her revulsion had been as much for the situation as it was for Velvet's unseemliness. Cashé found it all quite odd; Uncle Samuel and Aunt Alice had taught her intimacy of any kind was purely for the procreation of children, never for pleasure. Yet, Velvet showed no regret for her actions, and Uncle Charles offered no censure. She did not understand how no one other than her found Velvet's ruination repugnant. Had they all left their morals behind?

The earl reappeared with a physician in tow, and everyone moved quickly to tend to Velvet, Thornhill, and Hill. When the physician decided to transport his patients to his office, a clean up of the incident became the next phase. The viscount saw to the wounded, and Yardley reported the incident to the local authorities, as well as settling the damages with the shopkeeper.

Ashton announced, "I will escort the girls to Chesterfield Manor. I assume, Your Grace, you will see my niece safely to Cheshire."

The duke bowed in respect. "Velvet is under my protection, Your Lordship."

Regina Jeffers

Cashé pulled at her uncle's sleeve. "Do you think it best, Uncle, to permit Velvet to travel with Thornhill? Uncle Samuel would object; we should consider Velvet's reputation," she whispered.

"By his actions, His Grace has shown his affection for your sister," he assured her. "Thornhill will protect Velvet with his title. The man is part of our family; can you not see he loves your sister and will bring no shame on our name?"

⠶

From the rooftops of the neighboring building Murhad Jamot watched as a middle-aged English gentleman, the one he had encountered in the blacksmith's stables, departed the warehouse with a young lady on each arm. The women were obviously twins; from the distance, Jamot could discern very little difference between them. Now, he fully understood how the Realm had tricked him. The women bore an uncanny resemblance to Velvet Aldridge, and they both wore dresses of a similar shade. They had made him see things that did not exist. A nice illusion. And he had fallen for it, but Jamot would not permit such deception again.

He would change his operation. Mir would not be happy with Jamot's lack of success. He had begun this campaign with the Realm's leader James Kerrington and had persued Brantley Fowler when Viscount Worthing had proved too honorable for thievery. In all honesty, Jamot had never suspected either man of possessing the emerald. Both boasted high principles. However, Mir had ordered Jamot to seek those two Realm members first; his leader thought Worthing's and Thornhill's honors a façade. Mir did not understand how these Englishmen thought, but Jamot did. He had lived among them for the past year. He had felt the chill of their winters and the warmth of their springs. He had seen the hatred for foreigners in English eyes, and he had recognized the English attitude of superiority. The Realm had fooled him this time; yet, he would not permit it to happen again. He would regroup and find the weaknesses among the others. Murhad Jamot would find the missing emerald, and then he would return to his homeland.

⠶

"To think, Uncle, my sister is to be a duchess," Satiné said for the third time in an hour.

Cashé rolled her eyes in exasperation. "Why is that particular fact so important?"

51

The baron good-naturedly explained, "A duke is the closest to royalty this country offers in the social strata. When Velvet becomes a duchess, your sister will hold great sway in society, which plays well for your own places."

"I am so pleased we postponed my Come Out," Satiné gushed. "To be known as the sister of the Duchess of Thornhill shall open doors left closed otherwise."

Cashé sat back into the coach's soft squabs. She crossed her arms before her chest, symbolically closing herself off from reason. "You make the assumption, Satiné, that Uncle Samuel will permit Thornhill to marry Velvet, and I can assure you Uncle shan't agree."

"How might Averette prevent the joining?" the baron demanded.

"As Uncle Samuel has assumed Velvet's guardianship, he may speak to her choice of husbands until she is of age. That is reason Velvet came to stay with us in Edinburgh. Uncle objected to the duke's attentions to our sister. He actually caught them in an intimate moment," Cashé shared. Her uncle had attempted to hide the reason for their hasty removal from London, but Cashé had overheard Thornhill's servants gossiping about what Samuel Aldridge had said to His Grace.

Ashton sat forward, as if to hear better. "What do you mean? Averette assumed guardianship of Velvet?"

"Just as I said," Cashé smirked. "Uncle Samuel found Velvet and Thornhill kissing in the duke's London library. He demanded Velvet return with us to Scotland. Thornhill quickly relinquished Velvet when Uncle Samuel threatened to expose Eleanor for the truth."

"I require a fuller explanation," Ashton insisted.

With a sense of importance, Cashé told him of the scene at the Prince Regent's party. Of Sir Louis Levering's charges. Of the baronet's attacking the Prince. And of how the Fowlers had led Prince George to believe the Averette's governess was Lady Eleanor's traveling companion. "Uncle Samuel confronted Thornhill regarding the former duke's debauchery. My uncle spoke to Thornhill of his benevolence in looking the other way because Lady Eleanor deserved a better life with an honorable man, but Uncle Samuel could not permit Velvet to return to Kent with His Grace without a chaperone."

"And Thornhill refused to make an honest woman of your sister?"

"No, His Grace made an offer," Cashé continued, "but Uncle refused."

The baron leaned back. "And why would Aldridge refuse to accept a duke's offer? That is the real question. What is in it for him?" A touch of bitterness laced his words.

"Uncle just wished to protect Velvet's name," Cashé asserted.

Ashton laced his fingers across his waistcoat. "I wish Samuel held altruistic motives, but I doubt Aldridge would make a move, which did not benefit him."

Cashé puffed up with indignation. "Uncle Samuel had Velvet's best interest in mind."

"My Dear, I realize your allegiance to Samuel Aldridge, but your eyes cannot be so closed to the truth."

"What truth?" Cashé demanded. "All I know is Uncle Samuel has given me a home and affection."

Satiné responded, "And you think the Fowlers and Uncle Charles did less for Velvet and me?"

Cashé blushed, but she continued. Such accusations against the only family she had known did not set well with her, but she could not deny the baron and the Fowlers had done honorably by her sisters. "Uncle Samuel welcomed me into his family because he loves me!" she asserted.

The baron reached across the coach and patted her hand. "Cashé, I have never believed otherwise, but you must also recognize Aldridge's weaknesses."

"Such as?" Cashé demanded.

"Such as requiring Uncle Charles and the Fowlers to pay him before he doled out children to their care."

Cashé bucked at the idea. "You speak an untruth!"

"No, Satiné does not," the baron said evenly. "Both William Fowler and I gave Samuel Aldridge five thousand pounds for Velvet and for Satiné. If you care to check my ledger for proof of the transaction, I will gladly share it with you. The implied threat was if the Fowlers and I did not respond, you girls would be sent elsewhere."

"Then he must have loved me best!" Cashé's eyes misted with tears. "He could not part with me!"

Neither Ashton nor Satiné spoke their thoughts, which made Cashé squirm inside. "The point is," said the baron evenly, "Aldridge likely believed he could make a better settlement with someone other than Thornhill. Has Aldridge presented suitors to Velvet while your sister resided in Scotland?"

"Of course." Cashé raised her chin defiantly. "Uncle Samuel has chosen husbands for both Velvet and me."

Ashton smiled grimly. "As I suspected. Cashé, Samuel has overstepped the boundaries set for your sisters. He cannot question my guardianship of Satiné or that of the Fowlers for Velvet. He had no legal right to remove Velvet from Thornhill's home. As Thornhill has assumed his father's title, he has also assumed Velvet's guardianship. In fact, there will be more stigma to young Fowler marrying his ward than any public show of intimacy. Thornhill must marry Velvet in a speedy manner for everyone to save face, even Samuel Aldridge. Once they marry, every indiscretion will be forgiven."

"Then you believe Uncle Samuel will agree?" Cashé challenged.

"I believe Samuel Aldridge will attempt to stop Velvet's joining for he sees a means to line his own pockets, but I will take up Thornhill's cause. Velvet, obviously, loves young Fowler, and a marriage based in love holds great sway with me."

"Did you say Uncle Samuel has chosen a husband for you?" Satiné questioned.

"Yes, Lachlan Charters and I have an understanding."

The baron sat forward again. "Has not Viscount Lexford also expressed interest? The earl led me to believe it is so."

Cashé flushed. "Viscount Lexford spent much of his time in London in company with my family, but I counted his attentions to be only part of his friendship with His Grace."

"Yardley appeared to think there was more to Lexford's regard," the baron shared.

"Uncle Samuel would never accept the viscount," Cashé claimed.

The baron spoke seriously. "Cashé, do you not see a pattern? Samuel would give Velvet to a man without a title rather than permit her to marry a duke, and he would give you to plain Mister Charters rather than see you as a viscountess. What gentleman would refuse a title and a place in British society for his nieces? Samuel's manipulations make little sense." He paused briefly. "Tell me. Does Mister Charters hold a place of distinction in Aldridge's church?"

"Mister Charters is a church deacon."

The baron continued his questioning, "And he is several years older than you?"

"Mister Charters is a widower; he has two small children," Cashé confided.

The baron nodded his head as if processing the information. "Again, as I suspected."

Cashé could not understand her Uncle Charles's obvious dislike for Samuel Aldridge. Somehow Charles Morton described a man Cashé did not know. She believed in her Uncle Samuel, but Satiné felt as strongly about the baron. They both could not be correct. Had Uncle Samuel truly "sold" her sisters to the baron and the Fowlers? And, if so, why had he chosen to keep her over her sisters? There were too many questions and too few answers.

⁂

"Would you care to explain what happened today?" Marcus and Lexford returned to Chesterfield Manor. They had seen to the incarceration of Jamot's hired driver and had provided the local magistrate and dockside officers with an "edited" version of what had occurred.

Marcus anticipated his friend's censure. "It was nothing."

"It was something," Lexford corrected.

Marcus silently prayed for patience. How could he explain the turmoil he had experience from his first view of Cashémere Aldridge? "I became upset when we could not reach Miss Satiné. I had promised the lady to protect her." He ran his fingers through his hair. "And then Miss Cashémere acted on her own, placing herself in real danger." As he said the words, Marcus wondered at whom he was really angry: himself for losing control or Cashé for acting impulsively. Did the girl not realize it was a man's province to protect the woman? A tight knot formed in his chest. Every time he thought of Maggie and how he had failed her, Marcus cringed in agony.

"Miss Cashémere acted sensibly under the circumstances," Lexford defended the lady.

Marcus simply nodded his head. He would not argue against his friend's intended reprimand. "I have assured the baron I will offer my apologies to Miss Cashé."

"Then, I thank you also for your magnanimity."

⁂

"Miss Cashémere, might you walk about the room with me?" Marcus bowed to her. By silent assent, they had avoided each other through most

55

of the evening; even over the rather boisterous supper conversation, Cashé and he had exchanged no discourse.

Marcus could tell she considered refusing, but the girl said, "Thank you, Lord Yardley."

Marcus placed her hand on his arm and began a slow promenade about the music room. Her twin entertained everyone on the pianoforte. They strolled for several elongated minutes without conversation. Marcus directed her steps to a recess in the back wall. "Miss Cashé, I wish to extend my apologies for my uncouth behavior earlier today. I spoke out of turn, and I pray you will offer your forgiveness."

The girl raised her chin defiantly. "Is this your idea, Lord Yardley, or is it an edict from my uncle?"

Marcus flinched. "Baron Ashton expressed his discontent with my actions, but I was aware of my abhorrent behavior prior to your uncle's comments."

"So, you would have asked for my forgiveness without Uncle Charles's prompting?" Her voice held cynical strands.

He regretted making his apologies if it was to cause a scene. Marcus simply wished to terminate his connection with Cashé Aldridge. She brought out the worst in him. "I am not a heathen, Miss Cashémere. I understand what is acceptable in polite society. I was upset when we were unable to secure your sister's safety. I feared for her life, and then you improvised, placing yourself in danger also. I reacted to the peril."

"I am surprised, Your Lordship, that you were successful as a government agent if you so quickly lose your control."

Marcus bit back the hateful words that sprang to mind. He considered telling her she caused his bad behavior with her infuriating actions. Instead, he said, "I assure you, Miss Cashémere, my standards were never in question."

"Then it is only with me you act so rudely?" she demanded.

Marcus's ire rose quickly. Anger mixed with the churning in his stomach. "Will you accept my apology or not?" He forced the words through clenched teeth.

Cashé's hands fisted at her waist. "When your apology comes from your heart and not from your conscience, then speak to me again, Lord Yardley!" Her cheeks burned red. She shoved past him, returning to the chair she had vacated earlier.

Marcus watched her go. He wished they were alone so he might teach Miss Cashémere a lesson in civility. But what would he do? Images of turning the girl over his knee turned to one where his fingertips stroked the softness of her cheek. "Bloody hell," he groaned. "From where did that come?"

Marcus would have preferred to depart for Northumberland the following morning, but as the next day was Sunday, he postponed his leaving. Then Thornhill had announced his intention to marry Miss Aldridge as quickly as possible. Ashton had championed the duke's cause, and Thornhill had sent to Linton Park for permission to marry his cousin in the estate chapel. Lady Eleanor had responded in the affirmative. All they required was the return of James Kerrington and Carter Lowery with Thornhill's daughter Sonali. So, Marcus tarried in Cheshire.

As a group, they had attended services with Baron Ashton. Marcus placed Miss Satiné on his arm as they entered the chapel. Church members sat agape as the three Aldridge sisters assumed their places on the baron's pew. The twins caused more than one double take, but Velvet Aldridge's similarity created quite a stir. Add to that novelty the presence of a duke, an earl, and a viscount, and the gossips buzzed throughout the sermon.

Marcus could not remember the last time he had attended Sunday services. It was not as if he did not consider himself a religious man; he believed in an avenging God, but he had ceased praying when his prayers for Maggie had fallen on deaf ears. He had asked God to take him instead, but the Avenger had refused. He did not know of the benevolent being of which these villagers believed. Yet, he sat quietly, his own thoughts not adverse to those of the sermon, but also not in alignment with the vicar's words.

Seated directly behind the ladies, he searched the profile of each twin: the long sleek neckline, the soft white shoulders, and the heart-shaped jaw line. If he had not known which was which, Marcus would have thought it impossible to tell Miss Satiné from Miss Cashé. That flaw would only last until the women opened their mouths. Cashémere Aldridge spoke with such negativity it riled even the good-humored baron. The only one who did not seem to notice was Lexford. His friend had accepted everything the girl professed in stride, almost as if the viscount acknowledged Miss Cashé's opinions as commonplace. Perhaps, love was not only blind but deaf, as well.

"What did you think of the sermon, my Dear?" Ashton inquired of Cashé when they returned to the estate.

"It was a noble effort," she began, "but your Mr. Whistman is short sighted in his congregational responsibilities."

The baron smiled kindly. "How so?

Cashé repeated what she had heard in her Scottish home. "Your Mr. Whistman still believes he can service the poor, but the gentleman does not understand that throwing money at the poor will not solve the problem. The poor always outnumber the needed funds. Plus, simply handing impoverished people money does not resolve their condition."

"And how might a congregation go about aiding those who most need it?" The baron appeared interested in what she had to say.

Cashé puffed up with pride at being consulted on such a weighty topic. "At home, we have divided the parish into 'proportions.' The church elders and deacons visit every home to determine what each family can provide for itself and then dispense aid to close the deficit."

"So, Samuel Aldridge follows the tenets of Thomas Chalmers?"

"He does, Uncle."

The baron laced his fingers before him. "An admirable application."

"Lachlan Charters and Uncle Samuel serve the parish."

Ashton nodded his head in understanding. "I am afraid, my Dear, that particular disclosure is not a revelation! Aldridge and this Charters fellow control parish funds meant for the poor."

"Uncle Samuel and Mr. Charters take their responsibilities very seriously," Cashé assured her uncle.

"I imagine they would. Your tale rings of what I know of Averette."

Her Uncle Charles's words betrayed nothing, but his tone spoke volumes. She debated on whether she should defend her Scottish uncle, but with most of those in residence set against Uncle Samuel, Cashé bit back her retort.

"What occupies your time?" Marcus walked with Satiné in Chesterfield Manor's upper gardens.

Satiné rested her hand on the earl's arm. "Oh, the usual for a lady: painting, embroidery, overseeing the house. Probably my most scandalous interest is horses. I love to ride, and I take satisfaction in recognizing quality in an animal."

"You should speak to the viscount. Lord Lexford prides himself on his stables," Marcus observed. "Have you traveled much, Miss Satiné?"

"Nothing of which to speak." She took a seat in the arbor, and Marcus followed her lead. "I suppose you have seen much of the world, Lord Yardley."

"I have experienced more than I would have wished. Much of my time abroad was spent in the East. In India and Persia."

Satiné's interest increased. "Is the lifestyle there as decadent as people say?"

Marcus chose his words carefully. The lady was an innocent; she knew not what she asked. "It is quite different from what we know in England. Some would call India, for example, uncivilized, but I never thought so. People wear clothing appropriate for the weather. They eat foods available in their region. They worship their gods. Humans are very resilient. They learn to live and love wherever they call home."

"I am not certain I could tolerate such drastic changes."

Marcus smiled at her. "A woman should not be forced to experience a lifestyle so foreign to her. Leave the spices and the extreme heat behind and, instead, enjoy the best England has to offer."

Satiné stood. "May we return to the house, Lord Yardley?"

Marcus followed her to his feet. He considered what the lady had to offer a man: She possessed the face of an angel and the disposition of one, as well. Satiné Aldridge was what he required in his life: Stability. Something he had not known for a dozen years.

◦◡◦

Carter Lowery rode into the circular drive early Monday morning with the news for which they had all waited: Sonali Fowler was safe. Thornhill's composure relaxed, and he rejoiced in the news.

"And Worthing is safe also?" Marcus implored.

"As I explained to His Grace," Sir Carter related, "the captain suffered two broken ribs, but he eliminated Talpur. That fact means Jamot is alone at this moment. Shepherd came to Devon to meet with Viscount Worthing. They decided to send Swenton and Crowden to follow Jamot's trail. There is confirmation the Baloch has a connection to a shipment of opium from the Orient. They seek the drug's origin."

"The opium trade is a bad business," Lexford added. "I do not envy John and Gabriel's mission."

Sir Carter nodded his agreement. "Neither do I."

59

Marcus reached for his gloves. "Lexford and I are to Lexington Arms today. I assume you have no desire to climb in the saddle and to join us." He jokingly slapped Sir Carter on the back.

Sir Carter's obstinate look said it all. "Lord, no. I chased Thornhill from Kent to Derbyshire. Rode from Linton Park to Devon and then to Cornwall and from Thomas Whittington's estate to here in a little over a week. I will pass on the pleasure of riding for a day or two."

"Then, His Lordship and I will see you at week's end. Thornhill plans a speedy union," Marcus good-naturedly teased. "Lexford has some pressing business with his tenants, and I have promised the viscount my opinion on his latest Tattersall's purchase."

Sir Carter mimicked Marcus's tone. "Should I keep Miss Aldridge's sisters company in your absence?"

Marcus's smile widened. "You will notice Lexford's disposition has improved with Miss Cashé's presence."

"I never!" Lexford objected.

Sir Carter countered, "Oh, yes, you did!"

Lexford self-mockingly laughed aloud. "Well, maybe just a little." The viscount stood to follow Marcus from the room. "Actually, you might keep an eye on Miss Satiné for the earl, Lowery. Our friend appears to affect the lady."

Sir Carter smiled knowingly. "So Thornhill says. In your absences, I will enjoy both ladies' companies."

Early Friday of that same week saw Marcus and Lexford riding beside the baron's coach as it made its way to Linton Park. Thornhill had arranged everything. By special license, he and Miss Aldridge would marry at the Linworth chapel. They had anticipated Kerrington's return, and he would bring Thornhill's daughter Sonali to her father. The only sour grape in the bunch was Lord Averette's notice of the joining. The baron expected an ugly scene in dealing with Samuel Aldridge's objections.

Although he knew very little of the family history other than what he had heard since beginning this assignment, Ashton, in Marcus's estimation, appeared calm about the upcoming confrontation, which seemed a bit unusual to him. With one point of interest, Marcus readily saw the baron's stance: Marcis had agreed with Morton's opinion of Miss Cashé's upbringing. The girl required a more genteel attitude.

The three Aldridge daughters, all products of the households in which they were raised, differed greatly. Miss Aldridge was a woman thought to be as delicate as fine china, but she had survived a week of hell and of fear, with what appeared to be no major ramifications. Although she was not to his liking–requiring constant compliments regarding her beauty, Velvet Aldridge had proved feistier than people had given her credit for being. Miss Satiné, on the other hand, reflected Ashton's country values. She excelled at running a household and was an accomplished artist. She enjoyed a mental challenge and a robust ride across her uncle's estate. And then there was Miss Cashémere. She spit out vinegar and brine as she repeated Lord Averette's percepts. Marcus did not understand the girl. One moment she expressed the most prejudicial responses he recalled hearing, and the next she showed the deepest compassion. Of course, her compassion was never directed at him. He regularly received a full dose of narrow-mindedness. It bothered him he recognized the sadness the girl attempted to bury. "Count your blessings, not your uncertainties," he warned his foolish heart.

The three days he had spent at Lexford's estate, Marcus had attempted repeatedly to engage his friend on the topic of Miss Cashé's appeal, but, for the life of him, he could not find the words. Marcus had reasoned it was none of his business to whom Lexford paid his attentions. He would not welcome such interference into his own life, so Marcus had swallowed his objections to Lexford's choosing the lady. As long as he did not have to feather his bed with Cashé Aldridge, his friend's taste in women would not be Marcus's concern.

Thornhill had met them upon their arrival at Linton Park, as had Lady Worthing and Viscount Averette. Marcus looked on with amusement as Ashton caught Averette by the arm before the viscount had publicly berated his oldest niece. "Samuel, how pleasant to see you." Ashton effectively blocked the viscount's approach.

Aldridge grudgingly had presented Ashton a courtesy bow. "Good afternoon, Charles."

Marcus dismounted, handing off the reins to a waiting groomsman. The shadows, which flitted across Averette's countenance, drew his interest.

With his larger than life presence, Ashton graciously greeted Eleanor Kerrington and then steered everyone into the house.

"Uncle," Cashé gave Aldridge a curtsy. "Are you well?" Marcus heard the tremble in her voice, and worry for the girl caused his heart to lurch.

The man harshly grasped Miss Cashé's elbow to lead her into the house. "As well as a man might be whose wishes and rights have been undermined by his family."

"I could not reach Velvet in time, Uncle." Marcus, who walked behind them, observed fear crossing the girl's face, and that particular fact did not set well with him. He wanted to know the source of that fear.

Aldridge glanced at his niece. "You did your best, Girl. I could expect nothing more from a woman. At least, you thought to take a maid with you to protect your reputation." Again, Marcus observed the girl's disappointment. She, obviously, sought her uncle's praise for her efforts to save her oldest sister. A thought struck him deep in his chest. Miss Cashé had wanted his praise of her daring in Liverpool, and, instead, Marcus had berated her. He swallowed his embarrassment at being no better than Averette, a man of whom he thoroughly disapproved.

The party retired to a drawing room where Lady Worthing and Miss Aldridge served tea. "My husband's parents will join us for supper," Eleanor Kerrington announced. "The earl has long suffered from poor health, but he has shown improvement of late."

While Marcus found a chair where he could simply observe, the baron assumed the bulk of the conversation. "I am certain Linworth must thrive under your care, my Dear. I remember when you insisted you would be a physician so you could save your mother."

Lady Worthing laughed easily at her youthful aspirations. "No one informed me only men could train in the medical arts."

Ashton smiled indulgently. "And why should we, my Dear? Who knows? Mayhap some day that restriction will change. The world continues to spin."

Aldridge blustered, "Why do you speak such rubbish, Morton? Women are meant to serve their husbands."

Marcus flinched, as did Thornhill and Lexford. The vehemence in Averette's tone ricocheted through each man's body. Marcus thought the man's words went a long way in explaining Cashé Aldridge's attitude.

The baron took a sip of his tea. "I am sorry you feel that way, Aldridge. Thankfully, your brother Edward held more respect for his wife–my sister." He took a second sip. "However, we will discuss such matters in private. Now is not the time. We will speak of family in congenial terms."

Marcus heard some of Aldridge's mumbled objections, but the viscount permitted Ashton his way.

The remainder of the afternoon and evening found the Linton Park inhabitants and guests avoiding the invisible taboo in the conversation. Viscount Averette's contempt colored everything and everyone. Conversations existed only to fill the emptiness. Finally, after supper, Ashton requested Lady Worthing's permission to use Kerrington's study for his "inevitable" discussion with Samuel Aldridge. Everyone breathed a bit easier with Averette's removal. Although no one voiced his relief, Cashé Aldridge felt it; therefore, she sat very prim and proper, overseeing the group in her uncle's absence.

It was the first time Marcus had felt pity for the girl. The last few hours had opened his eyes to Miss Cashé's daily life, and Marcus had quickly discovered he did not approve of Aldridge's parenting skills. Although he still condemned the lady's actions, Marcus now understood why the girl acted as she did. She had been taught censure as the standard for her interactions with others. It was a sobering realization of what the lady had suffered, and he began to understand Lady Worthing's earlier caution.

Thankfully, Averette did not return to the drawing room after his conversation with the baron. Marcus wanted to question Morton as to what he had said to the man, but good manners required Marcus to swallow his curiosity. So, he directed his attention to Miss Satiné. He had joined her for loo, and Marcus believed it one of the most enjoyable evenings he had experienced in quite some time. As the lady confided the baron's plans for her Presentation, he began to consider the merits of the upcoming Season.

"Then you are anxious for the rigors of balls and soirees and musicales?" Marcus teased.

Miss Satiné played her cards before answering. "Oh, yes, Lord Yardley. Most young ladies my age have already experienced their first Season."

Lady Worthing assured, "When Velvet and I made our Come Outs, the gentlemen appreciated the fact we were not green girls straight from the school room. You will do well, Satiné. You should consult Velvet regarding protocol. I am ashamed to admit your sister far outshone my efforts."

"Who will serve as your chaperone, Miss Satiné? I mean with Ashton being a widower." Marcus played off the cards Lady Worthing had discarded.

"My uncle has not decided, Lord Yardley. He has another sister, but my aunt has her children and grandchildren."

Eleanor suggested Velvet. "Although your sister is quite young, she shall be a duchess, and, as Bran often says, the duchy is a powerful force in British society."

Miss Satiné smiled broadly. "Yours is an excellent idea; I shall speak to Uncle Charles about the possibility."

Marcus considered the likelihood of being a regular caller in Miss Satiné's drawing room in London. It was the first time he had found the rigidity of the Marriage Mart worth his time.

☙❧

"Good morning, Your Grace." Ashton strolled into the room. He bowed to the women, filled his plate, and then joined Lady Linworth to continue a conversation they had begun the previous evening. Still curious regarding the baron's confrontation with Averette, Marcus had hoped to speak privately to Charles Morton, but his hopes were quickly extinguished. The unease he had experienced regarding Miss Cashé had lingered, and he felt compelled to act on it.

The room soon streamed with life and conversation. Misses Aldridge and Satiné spoke of new clothing and fashion. Sir Carter provided Lady Eleanor minute details of the attack the Realm had staged to rescue Thornhill's daughter while Lexford and Thornhill planned a fall hunting trip. Thus engaged, no one, but Marcus, noticed Cashémere Aldridge's appearance in the morning room doorway until Miss Velvet looked up and gasped.

Marcus immediately wanted to comfort the girl: Tears smudged her face, and her hair streamed undressed down her back. His fists balled at his side. Someone had hurt her, and Marcus wished to dole out justice. She trembled, and her shoulders rose and fell with silent sobs. Not since Maggie's passing had he seen someone so distraught. That someone was he.

When the room fell silent, Miss Cashé demanded, "Which of you did this?" She held a letter aloft. "Which of you drove him away?"

Miss Aldridge rushed to her sister's side. "Come," she attempted to coax the girl toward a nearby chair, but Miss Cashé physically resisted. "Cashé," Miss Aldridge whispered close to her ear, "Allow me to assist you. Tell us what has happened. Of what do you speak?"

The girl pulled away from her sister's grasp. "This!" She thrust the letter at the entire group in accusation.

64

With the others, Marcus looked on: a terrible tableau coming to life before his eyes. No one moved; everyone remained suspended waiting for what would happen next.

Miss Aldridge slid her arm around her sister. "Come; sit down. We cannot make things right if we know not of what you speak."

Again, instead of obeying, Miss Cashé shrugged off her sister's embrace. In the morning light streaming through the tall window, her coal black hair was haloed with a rim of light, and her eyes were shimmering emeralds. Marcus stared at the girl, allowing his heart to slow from its unexpected leap to life. "Do not touch me," she hissed. "It is your fault—yours and the Fowlers. You drove Uncle Samuel away! He left for Scotland this morning!" Just saying the words took all the girl's energy; her posture slumped in defeat. Tears consumed her. Her words of injustice revealed the fierce pride Marcus had come to associate with the girl, but then her vulnerability announced its presence. "He left me," she whispered softly, and Marcus heard the feeling of abandonment rattle in his own heart. Miss Cashé wiped her tears with the back of her hand. "What will I do now?" Marcus wanted desperately to wrap her into his embrace and to comfort her with understanding. It was not fair for one so young to know such desolation. He had learned that particular fact first hand when he was just a youth.

Ashton, however, did the deed; he gathered Cashé to him and with a shift of his wrist, the baron slipped his handkerchief into the girl's hand. "After Velvet's wedding, you will return to Cheshire with Satiné and me." The girl sobbed openly. "Your Uncle Samuel did not desert you, my Dear. He and I spoke of a Season for you and Satiné in the spring." Ashton released his hold and instead cupped Cashé's jaw in his hands, bringing her chin up where he might speak to the girl's countenance. "It was a practical move; plus, Samuel missed his wife and daughter. Everything will be well, Child. Permit Velvet to escort you to your room and assist you in dressing for the day." He kissed Cashé's forehead and turned her into Miss Aldridge's waiting arms. "I will explain more when you rejoin us."

Once the sisters escaped the room, the baron apologized to the remaining houseguests and his hosts. "It seems my discussion with the viscount spurred the man to action. Unfortunately, it was not executed as I had hoped, but the results will prove true. The girls are in my care now, and I most hardily agree to His Grace's proposal for Velvet."

Marcus turned to slap Thornhill on the back and to offer his friend his genuine well wishes. However, he could not shake the feeling something was amiss. Averette had given up too easily. It did not make sense that a man would chase a girl from Edinburgh to London in order to prevent a marriage and then just walk away when he met with opposition. Marcus barely knew Lord Averette, but from what he did know, the viscount's response was not typical for Samuel Aldridge. This realization made him wonder what Baron Ashton had said to bring about so great a change of sentiments. Plus, why would Aldridge leave behind the girl he had raised as his own? It seemed more logical for the viscount to take his niece with him. The way the baron had manipulated the situation identified Ashton as a worthy adversary, and Marcus would do well to remember as such.

◌◌◌

In the late afternoon, Cashé followed her elder sister outside to greet Lord Worthing's coach. Still stinging from her uncle's abandonment, the picture of happiness displayed by the coach's inhabitants rubbed her raw. James Kerrington greeted his wife with a passionate kiss, while Thornhill scooped his daughter from the carriage's open door and swung her around in total disregard to the child's deportment. The image was one of which she would have once gloried. She was like all girls, dreaming of finding a loving husband and having a brood of children, but now she knew not what she should feel. Her traitorous imagination made her yearn for the comfort of a man who would revere her as a partner in her life. Her nerves tightening with uncertainty as she looked on.

With her Uncle Samuel's speedy departure, Cashé had found herself in a world she really did not understand. She had experienced Society briefly when the Aldridges had spent time with Thornhill after Eleanor's marriage. However, she was very much out of place during this brief respite. Cashé eyed the goings on with great reluctance. Instability and befuddled feelings warred within her. While her family had tarried with the Duke, she had attended several of the Season's programs, but Uncle Samuel had been very selective and often spoke of the depravity on display. And although she had seen nothing wrong with the entertainment, Cashé had verbally agreed with her uncle's evaluations.

Now, that same uncle had abandoned her to the people he had often criticized. Did she mean so little to him? What had she done to make Uncle Samuel punish her as such? How could she earn his love again? And did she want to return to Scotland? Satiné appeared very content with Uncle

66

Charles, but could she also know happiness in Cheshire? Cashé simply did not know which way to turn. For a brief moment, she allowed herself to daydream of being accepted in her Uncle Charles's life, but the baron had committed himself to Satiné's happiness. Was there room for her in the baron's life?

Although she noted Velvet's anxiousness, Cashé could not completely stifle her standard speech. As if she wished to punish her sister for finding happiness, Cashé sniped, "Such displays demonstrate a lack of good breeding. Are you certain you wish to align yourself with such a family?"

As if she recognized the shielded pain in Cashé's words, Velvet whispered, "Such displays demonstrate love. Do I want love in my life? Absolutely!"

Cashé watched her elder sister walk into the duke's open arms. Then Velvet had taken Sonali up with her. The child clung to Velvet's neck, and they spoke of becoming a family. As the little party reentered the house, they left Cashé standing alone and displaced. She suppressed the rage swelling into her chest. "No more," she murmured. "No more shall I be the person everyone overlooks."

Without knowing what to do with this new resolve, reluctantly, Cashé had followed the group, but instead of finding her way to the drawing room for tea, she had sought privacy in a deserted alcove in the Kerrington library. Here, she could sit without being seen by someone just passing by the open door, and she could plan how best to proceed.

In the silence of the room, Cashé tallied what she knew and what she had yet to discover. She did not understand how she had ended up with nothing. She had practiced her religion and had done the correct thing all her life, but for some reason God had punished her. All around her, families formed. Her cousin Eleanor had married Lord Worthing and had been accepted by the man's parents and his son as their own, and Eleanor exuded happiness. Her cousin even carried Viscount Worthing's child. Eleanor had been raised in depravity, but now Ella had a family and a title and contentment.

Her twin sister had been given an exemplary education in Uncle Charles's household. Her uncle had treated Satiné as a valuable person, not as a subject under a man's jurisdiction. And the baron planned a Season for Satiné. He had offered Cashé a Season also, but it was not the same. He had given Cashé one from obligation; the baron presented one to Satiné from love.

Then there was Velvet. Her elder sister had replaced her natural family with the Fowlers. Velvet and Eleanor both had said it: They were sisters of the heart. So, Velvet, who believed in princess tales and conquering heroes, actually found that type of love in Thornhill. Velvet would be a duchess, and Cashé recognized her own aspiration to be a wife: Miss Charters, had been set too low.

They would all know happiness except for her. No one really wanted her–well, no one except mayhap Viscount Lexford. Cashé liked the man, but could he make her happy? She did not think so. Lord Lexford accepted all her weaknesses; he did not make her want to be a better person. She would hate to have no other options than His Lordship.

A noise signaled the presence of another of Worthing's guests, and Cashé looked up to see the man she most wished to avoid standing in the open doorway. If he knew of her misery, the earl would gloat with satisfaction, but he had not seen her in the shadowed corner. Curious, Cashé watched Lord Yardley make his way to a shelf holding poetry. She had never considered him the type who would enjoy poetry.

As she looked on, a dark smile crossed his countenance, and he selected a thin volume before taking a seat near the single lighted lantern in the room. He was lean and muscular, a warrior god. He moved with a confidence of a lion surveying his kingdom. Belatedly, she realized she should have revealed her presence before he had taken up the book, but she had held too long. Now, she would remain in hiding.

The earl thumbed through the volume until he had found the piece for which he had searched. He leaned back into the chair and raised the book where the light might fall upon the page. Cashé watched in awe as the man, who she half feared and half admired, read aloud a favorite poem.

Farewell! if ever fondest prayer
For other's weal availed on high,
Mine will not all be lost in air,
But waft thy name beyond the sky.
'Twere vain to speak, to weep, to sigh:
Oh! more than tears of blood can tell,
When wrung from guilt's expiring eye,
Are in that word–
Farewell!–Farewell!

Surprisingly, the earl's voice cracked with emotion as he pronounced the words aloud, and Cashé wondered of whom he thought as he read. A former lover, perhaps. She had not considered how a woman would find him attractive, but, obviously, Satiné had done so. What did the others see that she had missed?

These lips are mute,
these eyes are dry;
But in my breast and in my brain,
Awake the pangs that pass not by,
The thought that ne'er shall sleep again.
My soul nor deigns nor dares complain,
Though grief and passion there rebel;
I only know we loved in vain–
I only feel–
Farewell!–Farewell!

Cashé's first thoughts were of her own loss–of her own loneliness, but that was not the source of the tears bubbling in her eyes. Her tears were for the man who read from Lord Bryon. Her tears were for the man who challenged her at every move. An image of an arriving coach had her waiting for someone as had Eleanor earlier, but the man who had caught her up in his embrace was the earl. Cashé jammed her fist into her mouth to stifle the gasp of surprise. She suddenly recognized her fascination with Lord Yardley. Recognized why she required his approval. Yet, he was a man who essentially despised her. A man who preferred her twin. "Oh, my…" Her lips formed the words, but no sound escaped.

"Ah, Maggie…" his voice brought Cashé's attention. "You left me too soon."

Cashé swallow the hurt swelling her throat closed. Lord Yardley grieved for another. The poem was for an unknown woman. He had loved someone so deeply, and now he bemoaned his loss. Cashé wondered what it would be like to have a man such as Marcus Wellston to love as her own and to have him return that love. She concluded Lord Yardley would love as passionately as he hated.

With a deep sigh, he set the book on a nearby table and stood to take his leave. Without looking back, Yardley strode from the room.

Cashé edged from her hiding place. She looked toward the door through which he had exited–actually considered following him, but instead she reached for the book he had left behind. Clasping it to her chest, Cashé rushed to her chambers. She would read the poem and cherish the moment.

The next morning, the duke rode to Matlock to procure a special license. By the same time next week, the marriage would occur. Thornhill's friends and Velvet's family would celebrate together. They would remain at Linton Park until the ceremony. Out of loyalty to her Uncle Samuel, Cashé had sent a letter reporting the transactions. She had informed her family of the upcoming nuptials, and she had broken her vow to be strong by begging Aldridge to allow her to return home. She had promised to do whatever he wished of her, but Cashé realized her uncle rarely relented when he had made a decision.

"Miss Cashé." Sonali Fowler passed Cashé in the upper hallway. The child belatedly made a proper bow. "Will Gwendolyn come to Linton Park?"

Cashé bent to speak to the child. "No, Darling. Gwendolyn remains in Scotland." Sonali and Uncle's daughter Gwen had become fast friends when the families had dwelt together.

Sonali frowned. "I had hoped..." The child glanced quickly toward the maid assigned to tend to her until the girl's governess Mrs. Carruthers arrived. "There is not much to do in the nursery. They have not had a girl in the children's room since Lady Georgina was a child."

Cashé smiled at Sonali's manipulations. "Would you care to take a walk a bit later, Darling?"

"Would you, Miss Cashé?" The child's smile grew.

"I have a few errands, but I will come to the nursery soon."

The girl giggled, dropped a curtsy, said her "thank yous" and skipped away.

Marcus did not look forward to spending another week away from his own properties. Neither could he sit through more discussions on the wedding. The women were all atwitter with dress fittings and flowers. Kerrington, still recovering from his broken ribs, judiciously agreed to escort the women wherever required. Sir Carter and Lexford had decided to deliver a personal invitation to the wedding to Carter's brother, Lawrence

Lowery. Lord Hellsman had distracted Averette while the Realm had staged Velvet's rescue. The Lowery estate was a two-hours' ride north of Linton Park; however, Marcus had declined to join them. Instead, he had agreed to take Worthing's son fishing for the day. Therefore, he and Daniel Kerrington walked toward the largest tarn on the Linworth estate.

"Do you enjoy fishing?" Marcus asked the boy as they approached the lake.

Daniel's face glistened with a patina of sweat. "Oh, yes, Sir, but I am not often permitted to do so."

The boy reminded Marcus of his brother Trevor: all rambunctious enthusiasm. The eleven-year-old favored his father, his quick mind indicating the boy's intelligence far exceeded his years. Marcus had always enjoyed being around Daniel. He had observed bits of himself in the boy: Daniel had spent most of his time with adults, and so the child's mature vocabulary sometimes shocked an onlooker. Yet, he was still a boy-exuberant and boisterous, and the contrast made people uncertain of how to react to him.

"Well, it is a fine day for fishing." Marcus ruffled the boy's hair. "Not too warm nor too cold."

"Will you show me how to cast, Lord Yardley?" Daniel double stepped to keep astride of Marcus.

Marcus stopped suddenly and peered curiously at the boy. "Surely, you jest! You know how to bait cast!"

Daniel had paused along with Yardley. "No, Sir. I have seen my father do so, but overhead branches are all I seem to catch."

Marcus smiled, genuinely feeling the pleasure of being young and green again. "Then we must correct the situation immediately. You must learn to cast over hand." Daniel returned the smile. "We may find no fish today, but we will master your casting skills. It will likely take an hour or so to correct your technique. Are you up to it, Boy?"

"Yes, Your Lordship." Daniel straightened his shoulders to stand taller.

Marcus pointed to the nearby lake. "Then let us begin." They found a semi-shady spot along the bank, but with few low hanging branches, which might cause the boy trouble. Marcus set the bait. "Now, you must not become frustrated if you are not successful immediately. I was serious about an hour or two of practice. However, when you master the technique, you will place the bait exactly where you want it. Put it right in the fish's mouth if you wish." He winked conspiratorially at Daniel. "If you are prepared, permit me to observe your grip. Take the rod."

Daniel caught up the pole and assumed his normal grip on the rod. Marcus chuckled. He had recently attempted to teach Trevor the different grips, but his brother preferred to splash the water and create ripples. "I detect part of your problem. You permit the pole to control you rather than your mastering the hold." He started maneuvering Daniel's fingers to adjust the boy's grasp. "Have you ever held a tennis paddle, Daniel?"

"Yes, Sir."

"Then we are going to use that hold on this handle." Again, he adjusted Daniel's fingers. "We will place your thumb and index finger in this V," he said as he demonstrated with his own pole. "That V should be dead center. See." He held out his hand so Daniel could observe the proper clasp.

"Yes, Sir."

"Remember: The grip must be relaxed, or the rod will end up on the ground." Marcus easily cast his line some twenty feet away.

Daniel mimicked Marcus's movements, but his line barely traveled five feet. The boy frowned and then looked to Marcus for assistance.

Marcus retrieved the line and set the boy's hand in the proper position. "You locked your wrist when you brought the pole back," he explained. "That lack of movement forced you to use more power than was required. Try again and relax your hold."

Daniel took a deep breath and tossed the line again. The action was smoother, but still not accurate.

"You are going to learn to hate this word, Boy, but do it again."

"Yes, Sir."

"Could we drop the Sir, Daniel? Sonali calls me Uncle Marcus. Would you mind addressing me as such? Or you may just say Marcus if the uncle part makes you uncomfortable."

Daniel thought about it but for a split second. "I would be honored, Uncle Marcus."

Marcus sat down on the bank. "Again."

The boy chuckled, "I already do not like the word." Daniel brought the line back in and reset it before casting once more.

ꙮ

Cashé and Sonali had taken a picnic basket from the kitchen. "Where shall we go?" Cashé asked as she lifted the box.

"The lake," Sonali responded without hesitation.

"And why the lake?" Cashé inquired as she followed the child skipping along before her.

Sonali turned in place, letting her skirt tail spin about her legs. "There are flowers, and we can play princess."

Cashé rolled her eyes. Sonali resembled Velvet in her appearance and in her belief in fairy tales. Maybe her sister's family would blend after all. "There are no knights or dragons," Cashé stressed her practicality.

"We do not require knights," the girl declared. "My new mama and I beat the bad men too. My papa assisted mama, and Uncle James saved me; but Mama and I were both brave, just like Scheherazade."

The child was so certaom of what she said that despite being skeptical, Cashé had to agree. "Then we shall be princesses," she conceded. "We shall make flower wreaths for our hair and our wrists." Happy to have her way, Sonali ran ahead, humming a tune Cashé had sung as a child. "Did my sister teach you that song?" she asked as she caught up to the child.

"My new mama and I danced for papa, and Mama sang this song." She hummed again. "Mama gave me some blue silk, and we wrapped it around us, just as Scheherazade did."

Cashé's eyebrow rose in surprise. "My sister danced in blue silk for His Grace?"

"Yes," Sonali declared. "Then Papa read us a story of Sinibad."

Cashé said no more. At first, the thought of Velvet dancing as a harem girl for Thornhill scandalized her, but then as she thought about it, she envied her eldest sister's freedom. Cashé had never experienced scandal. Even when Viscount Lexford had escorted her through the crowd at Vauxhall Gardens, she had maintained her principles and her propriety. She had enjoyed seeing the waterfall and the fashionable couples, but scandalous behavior had never crossed her mind. Now, as they walked along the smooth pathway, the image of dancing–swaying her hips provocatively before a man–sprang vividly before her inner eye. Then she and Sonali came around a bend in the road, and the man from her musings stood before her. Without thinking, Cashé blushed and then blustered, "Your...Your Lordship."

༺

Marcus looked up at the sound of her voice. She was the last person he had hoped to encounter today, but his breeding took control of his actions, and he offered the woman a curt bow. "Miss Cashémere. Miss Fowler."

Sonali giggled. "Uncle Marcus, you know my name."

"Actually, Pumpkin, Miss Fowler is your proper name." He caught the girl in his arms and lifted her to him. "Your Papa has told you that particular fact previously. I have heard His Grace do so."

"Must I be Miss Fowler, Uncle Marcus?" Her forehead crunched in a frown.

"As your Aunt Ella is now Lady Worthing, you are the next female in the family to carry the title. It is how Queen Charlotte will address you if she should make your acquaintance." He chucked the girl's chin with his knuckle. "Good manners never go out of style. It will be appropriate for your family and friends to speak of you as Sonali, but it is important for you to also practice the proper form so you will not forget to respond when someone speaks to you. Do you understand, Sweetling?"

"Yes, Uncle Marcus," she said with a bit of petulance.

"And what would you call me if others, not our friends, were present?" he prompted.

Sonali smiled largely. "Your Lordship."

Marcus held her gaze. "Or?"

"Lord Yardley."

"Perfect." He kissed Sonali's cheek and placed her on her feet. Marcus turned to Miss Cashé. "What brings you ladies out today?"

Cashé pushed the last visages of her dance away. "Miss Fowler and I are taking a picnic in that field of clover." She pointed to a nearby slope.

The earl's eyes followed her gaze. "And what will you do in a clover field?"

Cashé had actually anticipated his tease. "What every fine lady does?" she mocked. "We shall make floral wreaths for our heads." She caught Sonali's hand. "We may even abandon propriety and dance among the forget-me-nots."

Marcus had expected a caustic remark, but Miss Cashé's response had caught him totally off guard. "Dance with...wild abandon," he stammered, and a picture of a happy Cashémere Aldridge materialized before his eyes.

"Yes, Uncle Marcus," Sonali answered as if he had lost his reason. He glanced toward the lady, and she offered him a perfectly executed curtsy. Despite his best efforts, Marcus smiled. Miss Cashémere was playfully teasing with him, and he found great comfort in that particular fact. The sun suddenly warmed the back of his neck, and he felt the familiar tug of desire in his groin. He was out of step with this new development.

Miss Cashé said coyly, "Would you and Master Daniel care to join us, Your Lordship? I am certain there is more than enough for everyone in the basket." She lifted the box to verify her words.

Lord Yardley looked to Daniel for agreement. When the boy nodded his head, Marcus reached for the box. "May I carry this for you, Miss Cashé?"

"Thank you, Lord Yardley." She smiled brightly at him, and Marcus's heart jumped to attention.

Silently, they walked to the slope. Behind them, Daniel and Sonali laughed and teased each other about what cook might have packed in the box. He stole several quick glances at the woman beside him. She was the exact copy of her sister Miss Satiné, but somehow very different, and he did not know what to make of the girl.

When she pointed to a flattened area upon the slope, Marcus spread the blanket Sonali handed him and then placed the basket in the center.

"Sonali," Cashé ordered, "why do you not pick some clover while I lay out the food?"

The girl immediately rushed away toward the white-topped flowers leading to the lake. Marcus addressed the boy, "Daniel, make certain Miss Sonali does not slip and fall in the tarn."

"Yes, Sir."

Marcus took the cheese and knife Cashé handed him and began slicing the wedge. "Thank you for sharing your feast," he said without looking up.

She murmured, "You are welcome, Lord Yardley." He wished he had had the nerve to make eye contact with her. He would like to look closely into those emerald orbs and to determine what lay behind them.

"The boy and I planned to fish, but I am spending my time teaching him how to cast overhand," he said lamely in explanation.

"You sound disappointed," she remarked, finally looking at him.

"No. No. Not at all." He was struck with how long her lashes were. Why had he not noticed previously? "I...I enjoy the boy. I have my brother Trevor at home. The innocence of childhood is refreshing, especially after all the war and devastation I have experienced over the past few years." Marcus looked off as if seeing something she could not. "Trevor keeps me humble."

Cashé did not know how to respond; his words genuinely had surprised her. At first, she had thought the earl as a gruff, obstinate aristocrat. A man who was relentless in his disdain for his fellow man. Of late, her opinions had softened as she found herself requiring his approval. Now, he presented a totally different countenance. The earl grieved for a woman whom he had lost, and he spoke kindly of his younger brother. She had been surprised to find him teaching Lord Worthing's son how to cast a fishing line, but not surprised in a negative manner. Would he make a good father? The thought both scared and delighted her.

"Is that enough?" Sonali asked as she laid several handfuls of clover in Cashé's lap. Daniel brought another stack of white-headed stems in his hat.

Cashé gratefully accepted the boy's offering. "I believe we shall persevere," she teased. "Let us have something to eat first." She motioned for the children to find a seat on the blanket. Cashé prepared Daniel and Sonali a plate containing fruit, cheese, dark bread, and cold pork.

*

Marcus had watched her closely. When Miss Cashé had given each child a generous portion, he had approved. He believed growing children should eat heartily at each meal. Miss Cashé had handed him an empty plate so he might serve himself. Marcus chose bread and cheese, leaving her the last of the cold meat, along with a small portion of each of the other items. "Are you certain, Your Lordship?" she asked when he shoved the plates in her direction.

"Miss Cashé, you must understand I am not the type of man who would take food from women and children." Marcus actually blushed with his admittance.

The girl's eyebrow rose. She stammered, "I...I...could never conceive you would be, Your Lordship." She paused, brushing the hair from her face, tucking one loose strand behind her ear. "Might we split what he have equally?" she murmured.

Marcus watched her movements, thinking he might like to be the one who assisted her with that errant curl. The thought shocked him. Cashémere Aldridge was definitely not a choice he would make. He supposed his newfound interest had come from his attraction to her twin. Realizing he had not responded, he purposely smiled before saying, "That is most tactful, Miss Cashé."

"I have my moments of diplomacy, Lord Yardley," she mocked.

"I am happy to see you more carefree, Miss Cashé. You have been under a terrible strain of late. I would not have you suffer in any way." Marcus could not explain why he had expressed such sentiments; yet, it seemed important to say them aloud. He truly would not have the girl know any more anguish in her life.

.ᴼℓℓᴼ,

His avows had taken her unawares. She had thought to chastise him for making assumptions about her life, but now, she could not consider such an reaction. The earl always appeared to dislike her, but he had spoken of sincere concern, and Cashé had felt a warmth peak the nipples of her breasts. It was not a sensation with which she was familiar, and, in a moment of panic, she glanced down to view the phenomenon before flushing thoroughly.

.ᴼℓℓᴼ,

Marcus noticed her skin's pinking and her downward glance, and his eyes naturally followed hers. However, he had never expected what he beheld. The girl's apparent embarrassment colored her skin; yet, something more had occurred. Her corset raised her rounded breasts to tempting swells above her dress line, but, more importantly, the corset lifted her breasts where the nipple might be seen behind the thin muslin. The buds hardened, indicating her sexual desire, and Marcus's groin reacted to that knowledge. Blood rushed to his erection, and he could not resist licking his lips as he considered the pleasure of tasting her.

.ᴼℓℓᴼ,

Shocked by their mutual response, Miss Cashé noticed his interest and purposely turned her back on him to speak to Sonali. As she told the child to hand over some of the clover, she fought the thoughts bombarding her sensibility. Against propriety, she had enjoyed the sensations coursing through her veins, and now she wondered what it might be like to know this man intimately. Behind her, she could hear the earl gathering the used plates and silver. Meanwhile, Sonali handed her flowers to create a floral chain. Cashé tied the flexible stems of the first bud into a knot and threaded the second flower through. Without any discussion, she laced the flowers together, creating a necklace and sash and crown for the girl. "Miss Cashé," Sonali whispered loudly, "will you be my aunt when Papa marries my new mama?"

Cashé glanced at the child. "I had not thought about it, but I assume it is possible. I am your papa's cousin, so we would be cousins, at the least. Why do you ask?"

"Daniel said you would be my aunt, but Uncle Marcus is really not my uncle. None of Papa's friends are my real uncles." Sonali shot Daniel a mutinous stare. Cashé pulled Sonali closer to her before looking to Lord Yardley for an appropriate explanation. Thankfully, he took the hint.

Marcus placed the last of the dirty plates into the picnic basket, something he had been doing to fill the gap left by Miss Cashé's purposeful withdrawal. Then he reached for Brantley Fowler's child; Marcus lifted Sonali to his lap. "Come here, Pumpkin." He stroked the child's head. "Daniel is correct in some ways, but not others." He kissed the top of Sonali's head. "Miss Cashé is Miss Aldridge's sister, and as a wedding is planned between your father and the lady, Miss Cashé will become part of your family. However, because Miss Aldridge is not your natural mother, Miss Cashé is what is known as a step-aunt, meaning you are related through a second marriage on your father's part."

"Step-aunt?" Sonali wrinkled her nose in disapproval. "I do not like the word."

Marcus chuckled. "I did not think you would, Little One."

"Why can I not call my new mama's sister Aunt Cashé?" Sonali insisted.

Marcus looked quickly to the lady to observe her feelings on the subject. When she smiled and nodded, he gave relief's sigh. To the girl, he said, "I imagine that might be possible–the same as it is possible for you to call me and Daniel's father and all the rest of your papa's friends uncle. It is true we are not your uncles through blood, but we are through our hearts. When your papa rescued your mother from those bad men, Uncle Carter, Uncle Gabriel, Uncle Aidan, and all of the rest of us fought beside your father to free Ashmita. We all shared in protecting your mama and later protecting you. We are part of your family whether we share the same blood or not. Do you understand, Sonali?"

The girl threw her arms about his neck. "Yes, Uncle Marcus. I did not want to lose all my uncles."

Daniel maturely added, "I apologize, Sonali. I did not mean to cause you pain. I wished only to explain the differences."

Marcus ruffled the boy's hair. He liked how Kerrington's son had taken responsibility. It spoke well of Lord and Lady Linworth's guidance.

"Both of you have many people who care for you. I am Daniel's uncle also because his father and I share a brotherhood even though we are not truly related."

Daniel wisely said, "Yes, Uncle Marcus."

Marcus sat Sonali from him as he stood. "Come, Boy, it is time we returned to the fish."

"May I come too, Uncle Marcus?" Sonali caught his hand.

Marcus's eyebrow rose as he watched for Miss Cashé's approval. When she laid back on the blanket in complete relaxation, he accepted her action as agreement. "I believe we can arrange a bit a time with the fish," he told the girl. "We will permit your Aunt Cashé to have a few minutes to herself." Marcus purposely did not look at Cashé Aldridge. The idea of her resting on the blanket brought other thoughts he refused to permit at this point. Instead, he tightened his grip upon Sonali's hand and returned to the tarn's bank.

Chapter Six

"Sonali, we should return to the house," Cashé called to the child.

Predictably, the girl lodged her objection. "Must we?" Sonali kept her attention on the pole she held with Lord Yardley's assistance. The trio had removed their shoes and stockings and had waded into the water. His Lordship had loosely secured the girl's skirt tail to her waistline.

"We have been away longer than anticipated. People will worry," Cashé countered.

Sonali whined, "Plea...se, just a few minutes more."

Cashé sighed deeply in exasperation. The child's attitude caused Cashé to regret she had brought the girl out for the afternoon. Obviously, Thornhill gave his daughter too much freedom. Too much attention. Cashé did not wish to play the "overly strict aunt" in this scenario. For nearly a half hour, through slitted eyes, she had watched the earl and the two children playing in the water. Observing their interplay had created a longing she was sore to identify. She never had much of a childhood. Her grandmother had believed children should never soil their clothes–never make too much noise–never interrupt adults in conversation. Now, as she stood along the tarn's bank, she imagined herself as part of the group.

Wellston handed Sonali over to the boy, instructing Daniel not to permit Sonali to go any farther into the water, and then he slugged his way to the shore. "Come join us, Miss Cashé." Lord Yardley extended his hand to offer his support.

Cashé automatically took a step backward, shying away from the contact. "I could not, Your Lordship," she protested.

Marcus did not withdraw his hand. "Miss Cashé, the children and I would enjoy your company. Have you ever fished?" He did not understand why he did not just permit her to return to the house alone. He could handle the children if she chose to leave Sonali in his care, but somehow it seemed important to extend his time with this particular woman.

He smiled again and heard her breathing quickened. "No...No, I have never held a fishing pole," she stammered.

Marcus motioned to the children. "Even a child can do it, Miss Cashé. I promise I will not permit you to fall in the water."

"Remove your shoes," Sonali encouraged. "The water tickles your toes."

Marcus pointedly extended his open palm to the woman. "I promise."

She bit her bottom lip in hesitation. "Are you certain, Your Lordship?"

"Absolutely," he assured.

She found a rock upon which to sit to remove her shoes, and then turned her back on them to remove her every day stockings. When she stood, after hiding her footwear behind the rock, she finally accepted Marcus's hand.

"You may wish to tuck in your skirt tail," he warned.

Miss Cashé bristled, "I think not, Lord Yardley."

Marcus chuckled. "As you wish, Miss Cashé." He picked up the extra pole and handed it to her. Then he led Cashé some fifteen feet into the water. "Do you wish my assistance?" he asked. Her wet skirt floated about her legs, and Marcus found he enjoyed peeks of her bare feet and ankles.

"I will be fine, Lord Yardley." Although she had no idea what to do, she attempted confidence, and he found her determination amusingly engaging.

Reluctantly, Marcus stepped from her and sloshed his way to where Sonali attempted to cast her line directly before her and failed. "You have your pole too up and down," he told the girl as he adjusted her hand on the handle. "Try again."

ઠઠ

Cashé wondered how she had gotten herself into this situation. The water had looked so inviting, and, in truth, it was quite cool on her feet and legs. However, the pebbled bank had been rougher than she had expected. She had told the earl she could handle the pole and line, but as she caught the handle in her dominant hand, she realized how foolish she had been not to accept Lord Yardley's assistance. "Nothing ventured," she mumbled as she raised her arm above her head and whipped the line behind her with the intention of bringing it forward, but it was not to be.

Cashé's arm jerked hard, but the pole flew from her grip as the hook caught on a low tree line behind her, leaving the wooden pole swinging from the tree like the pendulum of a longcase clock. She screeched as the tree wrenched the pole from her grasp. Spinning to see what happened, the water splashed the front of her day dress, taking her breath with the surge.

♦♦♦

Marcus lurched at the sound, but was too late to catch the pole before the line wrapped itself about a river birch. When the water splashed into her face and chest, he could not stifle the laugh that burst forth. "It appears our Miss Cashé has caught herself a big one," he teased. He motioned Daniel to remain beside Sonali's side before returning to where Miss Cashémere waited.

"Miss Cashé caught a big tree," Sonali corrected.

"I never guaranteed anyone would catch a fish," Marcus good-naturedly sloshed through the water toward the shoreline. "I believe Miss Cashé has won the day," he said as he reached for the tangled line.

The woman, at first, had opened resented his taunt, but she quickly forgave the jest at her detriment, and the corners up her lips tugged upward. "I did not see you do as well, Your Lordship," she charged in a sweetly mocking tone.

Dutifully, he broke the tree limb and unwrapped the line. "I am not in your class, Miss Cashé," he said in a pretense of calm detachment.

♦♦♦

The children continued to laugh at their banter, and Cashé involuntarily joined in, having never experienced this type of personal embarrassment before. From the time she was a small child; she had strived for perfection. Today, she relished her mistakes. It was quite freeing to own up to one's flaws. Her laughter escaped, sweet and intimate and filled with promises of girlish fantasies.

♦♦♦

Marcus looked up as the sound of her laughter drifted to where he stood. Observing the girl enjoying herself standing in mid-calf water, he had the strangest feeling he was seeing her for the first time, and Cashé Aldridge was beautiful: She, literally, took his breath away. For a moment, he froze–no longer unwrapping the string. Her lips appeared soft as silk. Her eyes twinkling emeralds buried in a cloud of purest white. Marcus wished to possessher–to break away the walls of her reserve–to storm her defenses and to know the girl's complete surrender.

82

Regina Jeffers

"Is something amiss, Uncle Marcus?" Sonali called, noting his strange behavior.

Marcus dropped his gaze quickly. "Nothing, Poppet," he assured as he loosened the line from the last twig holding it. He motioned to Daniel to assist Miss Cashé in pulling in the line and to reset her hold on the pole. Marcus did not trust himself too close to her at the moment.

"I am prepared, Lord Yardley," she teased from the water line as she held the pole aloft as if it were a cane. "You may wish to move, Your Lordship. I believe I will attempt to catch myself a larger branch this time."

Without thinking, Marcus stepped to the side. Cashé's teasing and laughter cast a spell on his sensibility: His breathing had become shallow, and his heart raced. An image of a nude Cashémere Aldridge danced in his head. He glanced up to see her bring the pole back to cast it once again. "No!" he called, impulsively striding forward to stop her. However, before he realized what he did, he caught Cashé from behind–his left hand coming about her narrow waist and splaying his open palm upon her lower abdomen to hold her in place and his right hand cupping hers with his on the pole. Effectively, he spooned her body with his–the same as he had done with both Daniel and Sonali, but Cashé Aldridge was not a child. She was a woman, and her slim figure blanketed his chest and upper thighs. Marcus's breath caught in his chest for the second time in less than a minute. The smell of sunshine and sweat and female filled his nostrils with the scent of her, and, instinctively, he turned his head to bury his nose in her hair–to catch the scent of jasmine. It was a moment he would remember later as exquisite hell.

"Lord Yardley, what do you think you are doing?" she hissed through tight lips, bringing him from his musings.

Marcus felt embarrassment heat her skin. "Noth...nothing," he stammered. "I did not think before I moved." He spoke softly to her ear, and Marcus made no move to free her. Her lithe body belonged in his embrace.

"Then release me," she ordered under her breath. "Remove your hand from my person."

Minutely, Marcus tightened his hold. "If we jump apart as if we have completed an indiscretion, the children will tell everyone of our error in judgment." He paused briefly to allow his words to register. "Allow me to assist you with the pole, and then I will casually step away." Marcus repositioned her hand, but no other muscles responded to his need to move.

It was as if his body took satisfaction in the feel of her without his mind agreeing to the embrace. "Otherwise, we are embroiled in scandal." He breathed the words. Finally, she nodded her agreement. "That is correct, Miss Cashé," he said for the children's benefits. "If you lock your wrist, the pole's tip falls away to the ground." Marcus physically moved Cashé's arm, locking her grip with his and placing the bait some twenty feet before them. "Did you feel the difference?" He released the pressure and stepped away from her, but her heat still clung to his body, and he knew he absolutely could feel the difference.

oOo

Miss Cashé still flushed, but she forced herself to turn and face him. "Thank you, Lord Yardley. I did feel it." Her words echoed in her head. She most certainly felt his hardness up and down her back, but to her surprise, she wanted to feel it again.

oOo

Marcus observed the color rising to her cheeks, and desire sparked in her eyes. He rasped, "I believe it is time to pack up, Daniel." He took a deep breath to control the racing of his heart. "Your father will have my head if you miss your afternoon lesson with Mr. Weston."

"Yes, Sir." Not surprisingly, the boy did the chivalrous thing. He caught Sonali's hand to lead the girl to the shoreline.

Marcus swallowed hard. He was grateful to the tarn's cold water on his legs. It kept him from displaying his unanswered desire to the world. "May I assist you, Miss Cashé?" He extended his hand, but silently prayed she would not take it. He did not want to touch her again so soon.

oOo

Aghast, Cashé looked at his hand, but the girl recognized the necessity of not creating a scene, so she reluctantly placed her fingers in the earl's palm. His long fingers closed about hers, and she took her first unsteady step along the pebbly up slope. The weight of her wet skirt tail slowed her progress as she paid more attention to the man bracing her than to her actual footing.

And then it happened. An unpredictable combination: Some sort of fish bumped her left ankle. With a shriek of surprise, she abruptly shifted her weight just as her right foot slipped on the smooth surface of one of the larger rocks lining the gentle slope. As if in slow motion, both of Cashé's feet flew in the air as her skirt tails wrapped about her legs. Her arms windmilled as she fell backwards. Then he was there, scooping her up in his strong arms, lifting her from the impending soaking. For a split second she fought him, but then Cashé's instincts told her this was where she belonged. She wrapped her arms about Marcus Wellston's neck.

He had moved by design when her footing slipped. Marcus had not thought about the ramifications of touching her again so soon. He caught her as her feet became tangled within her soaked day dress, and she stumbled backwards. One arm had encircled her small waist, and the other had come under her knees to cradle the lady.

"Lord Yardley!" she gasped, but she did not fight him. Instead, she had clung to his neck, their faces only inches apart. Marcus could see the incredibly long length of her lashes, thick and black with golden tips.

He pushed the renewed desire away. "I have you, Miss Cashé," he assured her as he waded through the shallow water, making his way to the grassy slope. So close, he again filled his lungs with the scent of her and his eyes with her image. For the longest time, Marcus just held her close, then he realized the impropriety and placed her on dry ground; but a beauty mark caught his eye, and he artlessly remarked, "I have never noticed the mark on the back of your neck. It resembles a star."

"Both Satiné and I have one. However, hers is on her shoulder where she can hide it from prying eyes," she sniped.

Noting the uncomfortable flush of her cheeks and the censure in her tone, he, finally, sat her before him. "Are you...are you injured?" he asked softly.

"No, Sir," she mumbled and looked quickly away, adjusting her clothing with the turn of her back to him.

Marcus swallowed hard. The sun kissed delicate skin, soft and white as the finest china. The memory of how her lips formed a perfect bow made his lips tic with the desire. "Why do you not take the children to the house? Daniel can carry the basket. I will secure the fishing equipment and follow you." It seemed important to separate himself from her: He required time to think. Without looking back, he sloshed into the water to retrieve the abandoned pole, making a show of capturing the line and giving himself time enough for Miss Cashé and the children to don their shoes and make their ways to the manor house.

She followed the children at a leisurely pace. Sonali danced and twirled, her floral crown and necklace swaying with her. Daniel chased her in circles as he swung the basket freely, both of them giggling and playful as children tend to be when left to their own devices. And, today, Cashé had no intention of interfering with their amusements. Her mind rested on the irascible earl and the lingering excitement she had felt when he had lifted her so easily into his arms.

She reluctantly acknowledged she did not want to think of Marcus Wellston; she had fought the good fight in that matter, but it was to no avail. She had thought of him often of late–too often for her own sanity. Of course, such ruminations served no purpose. The earl affected her sister Satiné, and his friend Lord Lexford had offered his attentions to her. Yet, Cashé held no affection for the viscount–no more than she had done for Lachlan Charters.

"Neither Mr. Charters nor the viscount stirs my interest," she murmured. The earl's heat remained, along with the image of his charming grin. Up close, his dark penetrating eyes–eyes as stormy as the blackest clouds over a Scottish moor–had hit her like a blow to her chest. "Could I undermine my own sister?" she asked silently as the house came into view.

♁

Marcus paused as he gathered the fishing lines for the three poles. The day had taken an unexpected turn. From the beginning of their acquaintance, he had detested everything about the lady. He had considered Cashé Aldridge a spoiled, self-centered woman, but today he observed the softer side of her.

He actually felt an erection when he had embraced her, which definitely vexed him because he had convinced himself he had wanted nothing to do with her. "It is because she is identical to her sister. It happened only because I had Miss Satiné on my mind." However, Marcus knew better. There was a sense of heartbreak, mixed with an air of opposition about her, and the combination made Marcus wish to comfort her and to wash away the lady's vulnerability. Miss Cashé's presence had shaken his world.

"Damn!" he cursed aloud. "I cannot be attracted to Cashé Aldridge," he growled. "And if I am, what of Lexford?" Marcus had suffered through the viscount's depression when Shepherd had separated Lexford from Miss Cashé by sending them on a mission to Calcutta. Lexford had made them all miserable because he had pined for the girl. Obviously, he could not come between Lexford and Miss Cashémere. He the viscount had known

86

similar tragedies, and Marcus credited his friendship an important link to his current peace of mind, something for which he had struggled for many years after Maggie's death. "This is all a fluke," he said the words aloud, trying to make them so. "It is Miss Satiné who stirs my blood." Yet, despite the confidence he had infused into his tone, a nagging doubt clung to his mind.

ﾉﾉﾉ

During the evening, Marcus made a concerted effort to ignore Miss Cashé by doubling his attentions to Miss Satiné, but try as he may, he could not withdraw his eyes from the lady. Miss Satiné was everything he had thought he had needed in his life, and, at first glance, a person could not tell the sisters apart, but there were distinct differences. Charles Morton had guided Miss Satiné in the niceties of Society. Bred as a genteel lady, the woman possessed nothing but admirable qualities: good manners, ladylike accomplishments, and acceptable opinions. Yet, was his admiration of Miss Satiné's perfection settling for the boring, something Marcus had never done in his life?

Then there was the entity known as Miss Cashémere. Equally as beautiful as her two sisters, Miss Cashé posed no concerns in that manner. All three sisters were more than a bit handsome. Difficulties occurred in other areas, however. She often spewed prejudice and offending remarks, but she possessed an appealing vulnerability, which had made him want to protect her, even from herself. She was admittedly one of the most vexing females he had ever encountered. She was impetuous and unpredictable and strong-willed, and the woman knew exactly how to bait him into saying and doing things he would not normally do.

ﾉﾉﾉ

"Would you care to walk in the garden, Miss Cashé?" Lord Lexford extended his hand.

Cashé had considered refusing, but a quick glance at Lord Yardley told her the earl danced attendance on Satiné. "That would be pleasant." Cashé had kept the earl in her view, and she had known each time he had looked upon her. She could not help but wonder what would happen if she had met Lord Yardley first. Uncertain, she placed her hand in Lord Lexford's and permitted the viscount to lead her through the open patio doors.

"Lord Yardley speaks of providing fishing tips for you today." Lexford turned his head in her direction.

The fact Yardley had spoken of her sent a shiver down her spine, but the fact he had found it necessary to share their encounter with Lord Lexford said the earl had not experienced what she did today. She could speak to no one of it, not even her own reflection in the mirror. Cashé glanced away, again remembering the brief intimacy she had shared with Lord Yardley. "It was a spontaneous thing. His Lordship had taken Daniel to the tarn, while I entertained Sonali. We came across each other quite by accident."

"Should I be jealous?" Lexford teased.

Cashé thought, if only, but she said, "I must protest, Lord Lexford. We do not possess that type of relationship."

The viscount stopped under a shadowy rose arbor. "Miss Cashémere, you must be aware of my interest. It would please me greatly if you would permit me to call upon you while you are with the baron."

Cashé kept her eyes downcast. "You must understand, Lord Lexford, this is all very new. In Edinburgh, Uncle Samuel had come to an informal agreement with Mr. Charters. Now, I am to live with Uncle Charles, and everything has changed. The baron has indicated he will bring both Satiné and me Out into Society. That particular fact permits me a mere six months to learn a whole new way of thinking."

Lord Lexford caught her hand in his. It was an intimate gesture, and Cashé fought the urge to snatch her fingers from his grip. "I understand your reticence, and I am sympathetic to your dilemma. You are being ripped from the only life you have ever known, but the baron only has your best interests at heart...as do I. If it suits you, I will temper my needs with the understanding I will make my suit known when the Season begins."

Cashé hushed an overwhelming urge to run from him and to find solace in the strong arms, which had held her earlier. "Your suggestion appears prudent, Your Lordship." She forced herself to smile at him. "I appreciate your understanding." It was not that the viscount was a poor choice. She knew women who would think her a complete idiot to refuse the viscount's attentions. He was very handsome; yet, Lord Lexford's affections were not reciprocated on her part.

The viscount either could not or would not recognize her indecision as a stalling technique. He lifted her chin with his fingertips and lowered his head to lightly brush her lips with his. "So sweet," he murmured as he withdrew.

Cashé flushed in embarrassment. His was her first kiss, and she hated it had come from Lord Lexford. It had lasted but a few seconds. He had placed no pressure upon her nor had he taken her into his arms. It was nothing more than a sweep of his lips across hers. No passion. Simply a common regard.

Like most young girls, Cashé had always thought if she married, it would be for love. She realized she had not loved Mr. Charters, but she had held him in highest respect, and she always assumed love would follow once they had had time to know each other more fully. She had often prayed for someone who would love only her. When she permitted herself feminine dreams, she had imagined a man who would cherish her even if she were sometimes outspoken or had broken with propriety; he would love her because he had chosen her. She had never known anyone who preferred her above all others. Even Uncle Samuel's love had come with its limitations: She had been thrust upon him after her parents' unusual accident. Because of duty, her uncle "had to" love her. She may not have been raised as Velvet was, but Cashé shared one thing with her sister: She wanted her own "happily ever after."

"As I suspected...pure perfection," the viscount whispered.

Cashé opened her eyes, a bit shocked she had not resisted the intimacy, although she certainly could not count it as an immodest act. However, she must find a means to dissuade the viscount from escalating the relationship. "Lord Lexford, you must accept the fact I cannot allow you such liberties. It would not be proper," she chided.

Lexford smiled widely. "I will remain a prefect gentleman in your presence, Miss Cashé. I simply wanted you to realize the depth of my regard."

"Then we shall forget this unseemly behavior," she asserted. "I am honored by your interest, Your Lordship, but I will hold you to your promise of gentlemanly manners."

The viscount nodded his agreement. "We should return to the house." He presented his arm, and Cashé reluctantly took it. His Lordship cupped her hand with his free one. "Thank you, my Dear, for tolerating my indiscretion," he said softly.

"As long as you do not repeat the act any time soon, we shall speak no more of it."

Marcus had attempted to ignore his friend's escorting Miss Cashé from the room. However, his mind said one thing, while his body said another. So, when Worthing had inquired as to the whereabouts of Lord

Lexford, Marcus had volunteered to seek the viscount about the grounds. He exited through the same patio doors, as had the couple earlier. Crossing the graveled path to the lower garden, Marcus had come up short. Standing in the rose harbor, Lexford bowed his head to kiss the upturned face of Cashémere Aldridge. Marcus made himself look away. Made himself turn on his heels and execute a ready retreat. However, the pressure building in his chest cut off his ability to breathe normally. Only a few hours earlier, he had held the lady in his arms; her body plastered to his chest wall, and the scent of her hair and the warmth of her skin had tempted him beyond control. Now, she had offered those lips he had craved to one of his best friends.

Rather than permit the others to know of his discontent, Marcus had crossed behind the house to follow the circular drive toward the stables. He required a few moments to sort out his newfound feelings for Cashé Aldridge. "I cannot seriously be interested in the girl," he said aloud for his own benefit. "I simply require a woman to sate my desires. I have been busy with the estate, and today was the first time I have held any woman for a very long time. That is why I reacted to the lady. I simply need to call on Rose when I return to Northumberland." The widow would take care of his male desires. "A night in Rose's bed." He did not finish his thoughts because in his mind's eye, the lithe figure of Cashé Aldridge replaced the image of Rose Hardesty's full bosomed body. "Bloody hell!" he growled as he ran a hand across his face to push his crazed thoughts away.

For the next few days leading to Thornhill's wedding, Marcus spent much of his time alone or in the company of his friends. Beyond what was expected in polite Society, he had even avoided Miss Satiné, the lady's appearance reminding him of her twin. "Does something bother you, Yardley?" Worthing had asked as they shot a round of billiards.

Marcus paused for a moment, tallying his words carefully before he spoke. "Nothing in particular. I just have many responsibilities in Northumberland, which require my attention. Instead, I am whiling away my hours in Derby. Trevor requires my presence to know stability. I do not like to be long away from him."

"If that is truly what disturbs you, then I will keep my piece." Worthing broke the ball set before he lined up his first shot. "Yet, if there is something more, I am still here to listen."

Marcus tilted his head as if considering Worthing's words. Finally, he surrendered to the temptation to put words to his thoughts. "Have you," he began, "wanted something...something you knew was wrong for you?"

Worthing straightened, the cue stick chalked for the next shot. "I suppose it would depend upon what a person wanted." Frowning, Worthing leaned over the table before he said, "We make our plans, and then God laughs and sends up something quite unexpected. Does this have something to do with Miss Satiné?"

Marcus shook his head in the negative, shoving down a pang of guilt. "It is not Miss Satiné. The lady is all that is pleasant."

"Then something else?" Worthing walked around the table's edge.

Marcus continued to mull over his response. "You remember Maggie."

"I recall what you have shared." Worthing no longer pretended to be interested in the game. It had been an often-used ploy with the men who had served under him.

In some twisted sense of reality, the normalcy of his former captain's gambit had provided Marcus the safety of sharing his thoughts. "Maggie used to irritate me beyond belief. Sometimes I wished to throttle her. She was opinionated and determined and downright stubborn. Yet, she was easily persuadable and required my protection." Marcus stopped suddenly; the pain of how he had failed Maggie remained hauntingly clear. "And she..." But Marcus did not finish. He could tell no one Miss Cashé was just like Maggie.

When Marcus stopped, Worthing thought he had understood, and he said, "You blame yourself for something you could not prevent." His friend still spoke of Maggie while Marcus had thought only of Miss Cashémere.

An image of the woman materialized: her heart-shaped face and mesmerizing eyes. Knowing his former captain expected a response, Marcus said enigmatically, "Some ghosts are hard to lay to rest."

⁕⁕⁕

Starting with the evening the viscount had kissed her, Cashé had begun a close observation of Satiné and the earl. Lord Yardley had paid his attentions to her twin. Designed seating charts provided them time together, and they had sat side by side during meals and the various evening entertainments, but Cashé could detect no genuine interest on either's part. They had laughed and had played cards together: yet, Cashé observed nothing, which had convinced her to believe the earl and Satiné were anything more than fond acquaintances.

"Satiné prefers to ride out across the estate with Lord Lexford," she told herself as she watched the pair from her bedroom window. "My sister has more in common with the viscount than do I."

"Did you say something, Miss Cashé?" the maid asked as she laid out a morning gown across the bed.

"No, Lily," Cashé turned quickly away. Her Uncle Samuel had taken Edana with him to Scotland. Cashé and Satiné shared the same maid while they resided at Linton Park. Uncle Charles had told her she could choose someone as her regular maid at Chesterfield Manor. "I was just watching my sister leave for her morning ride."

The maid carefully straightened the dress's seams. "Miss Satiné loves being about the horses."

"I do not know why," Cashé remarked as she turned to the room. "They are smelly animals."

"You do not like to ride, Miss Cashé?" The maid brought the brush to dress Cashé's hair.

Cashé shook her head in the negative. "If I must, I can sit a horse, but I certainly prefer another form of travel." As the maid continued to tend to Cashé's hairstyle, she returned to her earlier musings. She had decided both she and her twin suffered from poor matchmaking, and Cashé wanted none of it. Despite knowing little of the maneuverings of courtship, she had decided she would have the man she desired. Yet, before she could earn the earl's approval she would have to convince her sister to do the unbelievable: to perform a switch of a sham.

,ºℓℓ,

Worthing had asked Marcus and Lexford to join him and Thornhill in the Linworth study. "What is amiss?" Lexford asked as they entered the room. Marcus had said little to anyone over the past few days beyond common civilities, and he had wondered for a moment if Worthing would take up the conversation they had had in the billiard room two days prior.

"Have a seat," Worthing gestured toward the two empty chairs before the hearth. "Do either of you wish a drink?"

Both declined. It was rare for Worthing to be so grim, and Marcus instinctively felt the importance of what they had shared.

"The captain and I wished to make you aware of something about which we both felt strongly," Thornhill began. "You two witnessed Miss Cashé's tear-stained rant on the morning of Samuel Aldridge's departure."

Lexford played with his watch bob. "It was quite a spectacle. My heart wanted to find a way to make the pain go away for Miss Cashé."

Marcus felt his chest tighten; he, too, had wanted to soothe the lady's anguish. "We were all relieved for His Grace's sake, the last barrier to his marriage removed. Yet, like Lexford, I felt quite sympathetic for the lady. Her uncle's abandonment was devastating for Miss Cashé. What she perceived as Averette's goodness was often a conversation topic as we chased Thornhill to Liverpool."

"That is just the point," the duke continued. "Viscount Averette vehemently opposed leaving Velvet with me. At Briar House, after our evening at Vauxhall, Averette found Miss Aldridge and me in an embrace. When I assured the viscount my intentions were honorable and I would make Velvet my wife, Averette fervently refused."

Lexford asked, "How could he deny his niece a duchy?"

"The viscount disparaged my reputation as William Fowler's son, but more importantly, he threatened to expose the farce we had practiced on Sir Louis by publicly announcing Miss Nelson traveled with him and not with Eleanor to Derby." Marcus noted how Worthing's fists opened and closed with the threat to his wife. Marcus understood completely. He would have responded likewise for any member of his family. Family had always been his first priority. "In order to protect Eleanor, I permitted Velvet to walk out of my life–to leave with Averette for Scotland."

Lexford grumbled a curse while Marcus swallowed his. Marcus had seen firsthand the subordinate position Viscountess Averette assumed in her own home. Not for the first time, he began to wonder what Aldridge had done to Miss Cashé.

Thornhill continued his tale. "When I arrived at Linton Park, Averette was already in residence. Eleanor and I met with the man in this very room. Averette unreasonably brought his conspiracy conjectures over Velvet's disappearance to the table. He believed I had staged Velvet's abduction in order to earn the viscount's gratitude. And despite both Eleanor's and my reasonings, Lord Averette still objected to my union."

Lexford whistled under his breath. "Even with Miss Aldridge's ruination? The man would see to his niece's loss of reputation?"

Thornhill added, "Neither Ella nor I could make Averette see the error in his judgment. The viscount countered our every point with his hatred."

"Then how was Morton able to convince Averette so quickly?" Marcus observed.

Worthing leaned forward to emphasize his words. "That is the very gist of this conversation. Baron Ashton, a former Realm member mind you, spoke to Aldridge for less than an hour, and then Averette up and leaves, without even saying his farewells to Miss Cashé, who has lived exclusively with the man since the age of three. It does not make sense."

"What could Ashton know about Aldridge that would change the viscount's mind?" Marcus's senses lurched into action.

"That is the question." Worthing grimaced.

Thornhill's countenance held a troubled expression. "Lord Worthing has sent a letter to Shepherd. We are guessing Ashton blackmailed Averette into complying, but what he has on the man is still an unknown."

"Would Averette's letter to Miss Cashé provide us any clues?" Marcus asked as he began to analyze the situation.

"That is another key issue," Thornhill confided. "Do either of you know what happened to the letter?"

Lexford glanced quickly at Marcus. "I suppose Miss Cashé still has it."

"No," Thornhill rasped out. "She does not. Without making an issue of it, the baron eased the letter from Cashé's hand and slipped it into his pocket while he held the girl in his embrace. I watched him do so."

"What could the letter hold that might make the baron want it?" Marcus became thoroughly engrossed in the possibilities.

"Maybe nothing," Worthing's voice was softly lethal. "Maybe everything. Thornhill and I believe Averette's personality would cause the man to include some of Ashton's charges as part of his tirade. However, when we examined the baron's room, we found no trace of the letter. Either the man destroyed it, or he has hidden it very well."

Marcus swallowed hard. "If no letter is readily available, the only source of information is Miss Cashé. Would she have knowledge of Ashton plans? Could it put her in danger?" He felt the sudden desire to find the lady so he might protect her. It was a betrayal of trust to even consider such an action, but Marcus could not control his chest's constriction.

"At the moment, we have no way of knowing for certain," Worthing summarized. "Averette may have written nothing of importance in the letter. Then again, the viscount may have railed against Ashton, and Miss Cashé either did not read the whole letter or she did not understand the implications. However, Thornhill and I wish to discover what Ashton knows of Averette."

94

"I will question Velvet about what went on in the viscount's household, but I do not wish to set up an alarm. However, my instincts tell me something is quite rotten." Thornhill's gaze intensified.

"I can add my insights having been in the household recently," Marcus thought aloud.

Worthing nodded his head in affirmation. "Why do you not make yourself some notes, and I will send them off to Shepherd?"

"Should I question Miss Cashé?" Lexford asked.

Marcus interrupted Worthing's response. "It does not seem prudent to grill Miss Cashé regarding her uncle." To his shock, he felt an intensity, which caused another tightening of his gut. "The lady is suffering from Averette's withdrawal and being thrust into a household foreign to her experiences. I believe questioning Miss Cashé would only increase her resistance to assist us. She would do better if she is permitted to share naturally with someone she trusts."

"And how do you have such first hand knowledge of how to handle Miss Cashé?" Lexford's gaze scoured Marcus.

Marcus willed away the panic he felt at exposing himself to his friend. "I do not know Miss Cashé other than our interactions during this mission, but she reminds me of Maggie."

They all knew of Maggie. As Thornhill had spoken often of Miss Aldridge and Worthing of his first wife Elizabeth, Marcus had spoken of Maggie. He noted Worthing's raised eyebrow, but he knew his former leader would say nothing of what Marcus had just relayed. "Then let us act cautiously," Worthing suggested. "First, we must convince Miss Cashé to trust one of us."

Thornhill teased, "That should be your domain, Lexford."

Marcus dropped his eyes before saying, "Then we will each gather what information we can and send it to Shepherd."

Worthing stood to end the conversation. "Wellston's summary speaks of our current operation until we know more about Ashton and about Averette."

Thornhill rose to his feet also. "I plan to examine my father's correspondence with the Averettes whenever Velvet and I return to Thorn Hall. Mayhap there is something among his papers to assist us."

Worthing added, "Do not forget Murhad Jamot is still at large."

Marcus lazily followed them toward the door. "I had hoped when we returned to England all of which we would deal would be estate affairs."

95

Worthing drew a deep breath. "We will know such peace soon. We have dispensed with Talpur; Jamot cannot succeed alone."

Chapter Seven

In the evening before the wedding, the Kerrington household teemed with activity. In addition to his Realm friends, Bran's aunt and his cousin had made the trek from nearby Nottingham, and Lowery's older brother Lawrence and his parents, the Baron and Baroness Blakehell, who lived but two hours north, also attended.

"Miss Cashé, would you honor me with a dance?" Marcus asked. The Duchess of Norfield, Bran's cousin, who was with child, had assumed the duties of the pianoforte.

The lady glanced up in surprise, and he thought for a moment she might refuse. Finally, she said, "Thank you, Lord Yardley." She tentatively placed her hand in his.

Marcus was uncertain what had come over him. He was not particularly fond of dancing, nor did he consider it the wisest idea to bring attention to his ever-growing need to be near Cashé Aldridge. He watched as the men had taken turns in approaching the women, providing the ladies few opportunities to rest. Marcus had previously danced with Lady Worthing and Miss Aldridge, but when he had spied the Duchess choosing a waltz, his feet directed him to where Miss Cashé sat. He wanted to compare this evening with their time at the tarn. He would also claim Miss Satiné's hand and consider the differences between his reactions to the twins.

Marcus placed his left hand on her waist when the music began, and all the couples realized theirs would be a waltz. With his right he caught her ungloved hand in his. Stepping into the first turn, he saw Cashé bite her bottom lip, and Marcus whispered, "Is something amiss, my Dear."

She blushed prettily, and Marcus enjoyed the flush of color in her cheeks. He wondered what it might be to look upon her in the throes of passion. "Although I recently learned the steps, I have never danced the waltz, Sir," she confided.

Marcus noted her nervousness and smiled indulgently. "Never fear, Miss Cashé; I will not permit you to falter. And even if you do step on my foot, I will consider the experience delightful. I will be forever known as your first waltz partner."

"You may laugh, Your Lordship," she warned, "but when you must hobble to the chapel tomorrow, you shall regret this."

Marcus thought he could, at least, claim one first in her life. "I will endure your worst, Miss Cashé." Deviously, he directed her through an elaborate double twirl about the corner just to hear her squeal from the experience.

"That was magnificent," she gasped, her eyes twinkling with excitement.

Marcus felt his heart leap into his throat. "Would you care to do it again?" he breathed in her ear.

"Oh, yes, please," she giggled.

Marcus tilted his head back and laughed heartily. "As you wish, Sweetling." Then he steered her between two other couples, and in the open, he half lifted her into the complicated step. Marcus found he thoroughly enjoyed dancing with Cashé Aldridge.

She sighed audibly. "Thank you, Your Lordship. I have never had so much fun."

"Neither have I, Miss Cashé." He smiled largely at her.

Silence held the next few minutes as a desire brewed between them. Marcus felt it in his groin and on her skin's heat. Quietly, he said, "After tomorrow, I must address you as Miss Aldridge...when your sister relinquishes that name."

"I thought of the same earlier. I am certain I will not respond when I am thus addressed." She glanced about the room. A comfortable pause rested between them. "May I ask you a confidential question, Your Lordship?"

"Always, Miss Cashé. I would never deny you anything," he whispered close to her ear.

The lady dropped her gaze before she spoke. "Do you believe in love? I mean...do you believe His Grace loves my sister?"

When she modified her question, Marcus felt more comfortable with his response. He did not wish to discuss the concept of love with her. With an innocent. Personally, he no longer believed in love: He had refused to love anyone because everyone he had loved had left him–his parents and Myles and Maggie, and likely Trevor, too, very soon. "I can honestly tell you Thornhill spoke only of your sister in all the years we served together. I believe the duke truly loves Miss Aldridge."

"Then why did he marry someone else?" she demanded. "If His Grace truly loves Velvet, as you say, how could he take someone else as his wife?"

"It is not my secret to share," he said cautiously.

Miss Cashé frowned. "I should have known you would not trust me," she accused.

Marcus regarded her unsmilingly. "I will tell you this. In her looks, Ashmita favored your sister, which I believe was His Grace's initial reaction to his wife. As a member of Thornhill's family, you must know the duke had never planned to claim his title. Therefore, he could not propose to your sister. And Ashmita was in desperate circumstances before His Grace rescued her. It is my opinion Thornhill felt responsible for Ashmita's life."

Miss Cashé studied his countenance, as if to assess whether he spoke the truth. "Then answer me this: Why did Thornhill not write to Velvet while she was in Scotland?"

"You will not enjoy my answer," he warned.

"But I would hear it just the same. No one believes I can tolerate the truth." She set her mouth in a defiant line.

Marcus nodded his head in agreement. "Your uncle threatened to make the former duke's lifestyle public knowledge, and Thornhill chose to protect his sister and his daughter, as well as the Kerringtons."

"Uncle Samuel did that?" she whispered as he spun her to a stop.

"Yes, Miss Cashé," he murmured as he led her from the floor. "Viscount Averette made those threats and many more."

He felt her fingers tense on his arm. When they reached her chair, Cashé turned to him. "Thank you, Lord Yardley, for the dance and for the conversation."

"My toes survived," he breathed the words close to her ear.

Cashé smiled sweetly at him. "I had not considered my successful first waltz. You gave me much upon which to think, Your Lordship."

Marcus brought her hand to his lips as he bowed one last time. With an uncontrollable need to taste her, he actually kissed her knuckles. The feel of her skin under his lips sent a shockwave through him. "It was my pleasure, Miss Cashé." He walked away slowly with the image of a breathless, happy female implanted on his mind.

"It was good of you to waltz with Cashémere," Miss Satiné told him as Marcus passed her in a country dance several minutes later.

Marcus circled the other couple before returning to face Miss Satiné. "I did not know it would be a waltz," he lied.

The lady placed her hand in his as they passed down the line. "My sister has had a difficult time adjusting to Uncle Samuel's speedy retreat. Cashémere hides it well, but she is lost."

As they parted, Marcus considered what Miss Satiné shared. Although both held vulnerability beneath the surface, the girl he had observed in Scotland and the lady with whom he had waltzed earlier differed in many ways. When he came face-to-face with Miss Satiné again, he said, "Then it is to Miss Cashémere's advantage that she join you and the baron at Chesterfield Manor." Unfortunately, for him, that would be the worst place for Miss Cashé. She would be in Lexford's backdoor, and he would be five shires away in Berwick.

The day of the wedding dawned, but Marcus felt a twinge of regret. Tomorrow, he would leave for his estate, and he would not see the girl who had suddenly become very important to him again. In some ways, he did not know why he still thought of her as a girl, rather than a woman. Maybe it was his means to protect himself from the obvious hold she possessed over him. Maybe it was the undercurrent of susceptibility he had observed in her.

While the others admired Miss Aldridge's entrance, Marcus found his eyes drifted to the long line of Miss Cashémere's neck. He could see the star mark at the base, and he wondered what it might be like to run his tongue over it–to kiss his way up her nape–to feel her shiver with his ministrations. A ghost of a smile played across his lips. He imagined kissing her slowly, her slender arms clinging to his neck. He felt his groin harden, and he adjusted his position to cover the evidence of his thoughts. He took a quick note of his friend, Viscount Lexford, but Lexford exchanged a quick comment with Worthing, rather than to enjoy Miss Cashémere's profile.

Tomorrow, he thought again. Tomorrow, I must leave her. What will Miss Cashémere do in those months leading to her Season? Will Lexford claim her before then? Marcus frowned with the thought. His friends supposed he had favored Miss Satiné. Little do they know! Last evening's dance had been the defining element. Miss Satiné had looked the part, but she never challenged him–never made his body feel alive–to feel anything after feeling nothing for so long. It was important he find a means to remain in contact with the baron's household. Yet, he must move slowly–to not sever his friendship with Lexford.

"It was a beautiful ceremony," Lady Worthing asserted. "I have never seen Velvet look lovelier." They were seated at a long table, along with others enjoying the wedding breakfast.

Worthing countered, "You were equally as lovely, my Dear." He slipped his arm about his wife's waist.

Marcus had learned from Fowler that Lady Worthing was already expecting her first child. "Less than six months ago, it was you, Captain. Now Fowler. Who among us do you suspect shall be next?" Marcus took a sip of his wine as his eyes searched for Miss Cashé.

Lord Worthing glanced about the room. "We suspected you might follow, Yardley. Miss Satiné is quite attractive. Or, perhaps Lexford and Miss Cashé."

Marcus schooled his countenance to hide his dislike of Worthing's assumptions. "It would seem Lexford holds a better opportunity. Lexington Arms is much closer to Chesterfield Manor than is my estate. I am not likely to see either lady again unless I choose to partake of the next Season's offerings, and that possibility is months away. What of Crowden?" Marcus wished to deflect the attention being given to him.

"The marquis is not ready. He still has too much anger–too much to resolve before he can start anew." Worthing looked lovingly at his wife. "I can only attest that marriage to the right woman is the only light to leave burning."

"Oh, James," Lady Worthing blushed and turned her face into his sleeve.

Worthing laughed. "Now, I have gone and embarrassed my wife. A man cannot tell the truth and not have his words misconstrued."

"I believe any of our unit would be happy to know what you have obviously found with Lady Worthing. You have set the standard high, Captain." Marcus raised his glass in a salute.

ഛ

With so many guests coming and going, the Kerringtons had opted for a leisurely supper after such a momentous morning. The servants had set up everything in the morning room. The hosts encouraged their guests to avail themselves of the offerings on their own schedules. Unable to control his need for her, Marcus had purposely waited for Miss Cashé's entrance into the room. "Ah, the new Miss Aldridge," he stood upon her arrival.

Miss Cashé smiled largely. "I believe you are the only one aware of the change, Lord Yardley."

101

Marcus motioned to his place setting. "I was just about to prepare a plate. Might I fill one for you also, Miss Aldridge?"

Miss Cashé mockingly curtsied. "That would be pleasant, Your Lordship."

Marcus held the chair next to his setting for her. "Please join me, Miss Aldridge." He winked at her.

"You are prepared to use my new moniker until I accept it. Is that correct, Lord Yardley?" She placed the serviette upon her lap before returning his wink.

"It is a tedious undertaking," he teased. "But I am up for the task...Miss Aldridge." The delay brought a genuine smile to Miss Cashé's countenance. "You are quite exquisite when you smile," he whispered close to her ear.

Miss Cashé blushed, but she did not look away. He enjoyed her vulnerability and her boldness. "Thank you, Your Lordship." She glanced about the empty room. "It appears the household has taken to its bed after such a busy morning."

"It is my understanding Lady Worthing has escorted Sonali into the village. Lord Worthing, Lexford, Sir Carter, your sister, the baron, and Daniel have chosen to ride part of the way with the Lowerys. I believe they required the exercise after the last few days of joyful confinement."

Miss Cashé looked closely at him, as he placed the plate before her. "And you chose not to join them, Your Lordship?"

He clutched at his heart as if he were wounded. "Please do not tell me you cannot tolerate my company, Miss Aldridge." His mood was quite carefree.

Sounding rather pleased, she said, "I only meant you must have wanted to ride with your friends."

Marcus could not keep the huskiness from his voice. "I prefer present company. Besides, I spend enough hours in the saddle."

"I fear I am a poor rider. I have little experience," she admitted.

Marcus seated himself on her left. "Then someday I must teach you," he declared. "I was successful with both casting a line and with the waltz."

The lady provocatively held his gaze. "Some might say you are conceited, my Lord," she taunted.

Marcus saw her tongue caress her dry lips, and he privately thanked the Kerringtons for providing the serviette for his lap–to cover the sudden rush of blood to his manhood. "While others would attest I am talented, Miss Aldridge."

Something hot flashed between them; it was an understanding and a desire. "Tell me of your estate," she breathed the words. "I am very interested in where you call home."

For the next twenty minutes Marcus describe his property and the area surrounding it. "Berwick is really not part of Northumberland," he explained. "We have had an illustrious history, being literally on the Scottish border. Berwick has belonged to the Scottish and to the English. Richard, Duke of Gloucester, captured the village in the late 1400s, and we have been English ever since. Although we were never formally annexed into England, with the Wales and Berwick Act, we officially became British property. Yet, we are a shire in our own right and have our own MPs in Parliament."

"I believe I would enjoy Berwick," Miss Cashé said wistfully. "I have spent my whole life in Scotland, and I consider the task of meeting English standards quite daunting."

Marcus smiled broadly. "And this comes from the girl who propelled herself onto my back to attack me. Most soundly, I might add."

Miss Cashé dropped her eyes in embarrassment. On closer inspection, Marcus could see how different her looks from her twin. Her lashes were thicker. Her eyes a deeper green. Her nose with a bit more of a bump in the middle, as if she had once taken a blow to the soft bone. "I suppose I should apologize for my actions."

Marcus cleared his throat to force the desire from his speech. "You fought for what you believed. I cannot fault you for that fact, but I suggest we simply call a truce. Neither of us were at our best during that time."

"Thank you, my Lord," she murmured. After an awkward pause, she added, "Berwick keeps the flavor of both countries. It would be heavenly in that way. I do not imagine Uncle Charles will relish my ideas or my habits. I will appear a hoyden compared to Satiné's refinement."

"You will do well, Miss Cashémere. I sense in you a bit of resilience. I have no doubts of your success." He returned to his plate in earnest to hide his susceptibility to the woman.

Miss Cashé tilted her head in an acknowledgement of what he said and then inquired, "And you have sheep on the estate?"

He smiled indulgently at her. The lady's inquisitive mind must keep her awake at night. "My father, who passed but months prior, began breeding our region's Teeswater sheep with Bakewell Dishleys. The result has been quite productive because they can be fattened quickly. We also have some

Shorthorn cattle. Since my taking over the title, I have invested heavily in a railroad system to replace the canals, as well as both a shipbuilding business and the production of brine from the Walker pit."

Cashé sat mesmerized. "You are a man with a vision."

Marcus laughed good-naturedly. "I do not know about a vision, but I am a man who does not believe the aristocracy will survive if it does not make changes. The wealthy middle class will no longer accept being treated as an insignificant entity." He motioned to a footman to refill Cashé's wine glass. "Those of us from northern England see things differently from those in London. Maybe it is the land's wildness and the harsh weather. We breed a different type of Englishman in Berwick."

"I now understand how you traversed the Scottish back roads so easily, Your Lordship."

"I am ashamed to admit that in my youth I spent too much time carousing about the bordering villages."

Cashé smiled sweetly. "You learned from your mistakes. Not many men do."

Marcus thought the conversation had taken a serious tone, and he wanted desperately to see her smile again; therefore, he returned to his teasing, "And you have known many men who suffer from repetition, Miss Cashé."

"Do not bam me, Lord Yardley. You are aware of my upbringing. From all the guests at the wedding, only you and Velvet have seen my home."

Marcus kept the tone light, despite feeling a twinge of guilt for flirting with Miss Cashé behind Lexford's back. "I believe I prefer it that way. I was the first to teach you to fish, to waltz with you, and the first Englishman to spend time in your Scottish home. I propose I start a list of firsts to accomplish with Miss Cashé." Marcus did not want to consider her first kiss.

"And when might I reciprocate and have you offer me a first," Miss Cashé countered innocently. She held no idea what images her words brought forth. Most profoundly, an image of being the first man to make love to her.

As much as he enjoyed their bantering, he felt he must issue a warning. Marcus lowered his voice and leaned close. "Permit me to provide you a bit of advice, Miss Aldridge. Never throw down the gauntlet with a man who has seen the world as I have. I have very few firsts remaining in my life to share with anyone."

Before she could respond, the riders returned. Their voices could be heard in the opening hallway, and although they had done nothing untoward, she and Marcus set further apart.

"Look who did not wait supper for us," Lexford announced as he entered the room.

Marcus forced himself to meet his friend's gaze. "We had no idea of your plans."

Worthing suggested, "Permit us to freshen our clothing and we will join you." He gestured to the main stairway. "Has Lady Worthing returned?"

Miss Cashé responded, "I overheard Mr. Lucas say Eleanor was in the nursery with Sonali."

Worthing nodded his understanding. "I will check on my father and find my wife. I will see you in a few minutes."

"I may attempt to convince Miss Cashé to join me in the garden," Marcus explained. He noted Worthing's raised eyebrow–the second time his former leader registered a visual objection.

When they were gone, Cashé whispered, "Were you aware of Eleanor's future confinement?"

Marcus thought it unusual the girl spoke so openly to him. "I have recently been informed of the happy event."

"What do you think of it? It seems a bit odd that Lady Worthing is with child so soon. Of course, with William Fowler as her father..."

Marcus scowled. "Miss Aldridge, I am honored you feel comfortable in asking me about subjects not often shared between a man and a woman, but permit me to offer you another warning. First, a woman's confinement is not a subject for an innocent, and, secondly, as we have discussed previously, Lady Worthing is your cousin. Protect her reputation because indirectly it affects yours. That is the way of the ton."

Cashé flushed. "But is it not unseemly?"

He deliberately paused, drawing her full attention to his words–making certain Cashé understood the importance of what he shared. "James Kerrington lost his first wife in childbirth. I would hate for the delivery of this child to be marred by silly gossip. Whenever the child was conceived, it was formed in love, and that particular fact is more important than the date. To think in our society how many children are abandoned to their nurses, I celebrate a child who will know the love of both his parents."

Miss Cashé blinked back her tears, and he knew instant regret for bringing her any qualms. A stilled moment held their thoughts, and then she said, "I have never considered the end result, my Lord. I have been taught only how the life begins in reference to children."

"I truly do not offer you censure, Miss Aldridge," he buffered his tone. "I have seen countless children during the war who were orphaned by the battles. I suspect most of them would have traded legitimacy for the embrace of a loving parent."

Cashé swallowed her dismay. "Why is it, Your Lordship...that you speak to me differently from the others?"

"I do not understand, Miss Aldridge." Her unshed tears clung to her lashes, and he wanted badly to take her into his embrace and to tell her he would make everything better for her.

"Sometimes...sometimes I suspect you do not like me." He started to protest, but Miss Cashé touched his lips with her fingers. "That you actually detest me. Then other times, you treat me with tenderness. But whether it is with disdain or with compassion, you have always spoken to me with frankness. I have not consistently appreciated your opinions, but I am aware your brute honesty is like a dam breaking over me, washing away the woman I have always been."

"I do not wish to injure you," Marcus whispered. "I could not live with myself if I brought you pain."

The lady smiled shyly. "It is not exactly painful, but your opinions are important to me, Your Lordship."

Again, the entrance of one of Marcus's companions interrupted their conversation. Miss Cashé dropped her eyes immediately, while Marcus cut his ham into smaller bites, he wondered what else might have been said if time had permitted.

"I am starving," Sir Carter announced as he lifted the lid of a warming dish.

Marcus chewed the cheese he had speared with his fork. "Worthing's staff has prepared an excellent array of hot and cold dishes."

Without notice, Miss Cashé suddenly stood, and Marcus obediently followed her to his feet. "If you will forgive me, Lord Yardley, I believe I shall return to my chambers. The day has been quite tiring." He realized the awkwardness of being in the room with him and Lexford. Too many excuses to make.

Marcus hid his disappointment; he had hoped for a few more minutes alone with her. "Of course, Miss Aldridge. Thank you for your company." He brought her hand to his lips for a brief caress. Miss Cashé held his gaze but a flicker of a second, but Marcus saw what looked like disappointment in her eyes also. He bowed briefly before she exited.

Sir Carter joined Marcus at the table. "You should beware, Wellston. Lexford will not appreciate your keeping company with Miss Cashé," he taunted.

Marcus's hands fisted on his lap. "It is not as if I could avoid the woman," he snarled.

Sir Carter's raised his hands in submission. "Hey, I was just making a poor jest!"

Although to him both still seemed strained, Marcus managed to control his breathing and the tone of his voice. "Miss Satiné asked that I show Miss Aldridge a kindness. Miss Satiné feels her twin is having difficulty adjusting to all the changes of the past fortnight."

Sir Carter appeared to accept Marcus's explanation. "It had slipped my mind Miss Cashémere is now Miss Aldridge. Does the young lady answer to her new title?"

"Whose new title?" Lexford asked as he entered the room with the baron. Marcus observed the viscount closely to see whether his friend would take notice of Miss Cashé's departure, but Lexford left any objections unspoken.

Sir Carter said, "Miss Cashémere is now Miss Aldridge."

Baron Ashton accepted the soup a footman served him. "I suppose we all must adjust to the change. As it is rightly hers by birth order, Cashémere will assume Velvet's title of address."

Marcus realized he should keep his opinions to himself, but he could not permit Miss Cashé to leave with the baron without having his say. "It seems to me Miss Aldridge will have many adjustments to make. I have seen the home in which Averette raised the girl. It is much more structured than what I observed in yours, Ashton. Miss Aldridge will require a healthy dose of understanding."

Ashton eyed Marcus carefully. "It appears you have taken an interest in my niece, Lord Yardley."

Marcus could feel Lexford's questioning gaze, but he did not turn his head: He looked only upon the baron. "You may be unaware, Ashton, that I have an older brother. However, Trevor suffers from mental problems, and I serve as his regent. I must often correct Trevor's actions because he knows nothing else. I observe the same susceptibility in Miss Aldridge as I do Trevor. Both respond based on limited experiences; both require a compassionate hand. You were correct to chastise me for snapping at the lady in Liverpool, but I would encourage you to not forget your own cautions."

Ashton's eyebrow arched in surprise. Marcus suspected the man was rarely called to task. "I can see how you would consider these equivalent situations. I thank you for your insights."

Lexford added earnestly, "Wellston was always the planner amongst us. Give the man a roomful of files, and he can reduce all the information into the minimalist of facts."

Although he offered little to the continuing discourse, Marcus lingered at the table. His mind remained on the one room in Worthing's great house where Cashé Aldridge could be found. It was crazy, but he thought he could feel her through the brick and mortar. How had things changed so dramatically in a fortnight?

Very soon, Miss Satiné and Lady Worthing joined the men. Miss Satiné assumed the empty setting vacated by her twin. That placed her between him and Lexford. Surreptitiously, Marcus took in the woman's countenance, identical to Miss Cashémere's but somehow lacking in the brightness he had discovered in her sister's eyes. "You were missed today, Lord Yardley," Miss Satiné said sweetly.

"I will have a two-days' journey as it is, Miss Satiné. I take no pleasure in spending hours in the saddle." Marcus motioned for more wine.

Sir Carter complained again about his recent trek across the southern half of England as he first raced to warn Thornhill of Sonali's kidnapping and later in the girl's rescue.

Lexford taunted, "Yet, today, you wished to see your family home."

Sir Carter laughed lightly. "That is because I have had several days out of the saddle. And two hours is much less than what I experienced in Sonali's rescue."

Lady Worthing rightly added, "My family appreciates your devotion."

"What time do you depart, Your Lordship?" Miss Satiné inquired.

"Some time after I break my fast." Marcus finished off his drink. "If you hold no objection, Captain, I will spend some time with Daniel before I leave. I taught him some casting techniques a few days ago." Marcus stood, all the while thinking he had wasted precious time arguing with Cashémere Aldridge, and now he must leave her.

Worthing nodded his agreement. "I have heard nothing else. You made quite an impression on my son. Daniel is in the nursery with Sonali."

Marcus bowed to the room. "I will see everyone a bit later." As he left, he noted how Lexford and Miss Satiné discussed equine bloodlines. He momentarily wondered if he could convince Lexford that his friend had chosen the wrong twin.

Marcus took the main staircase two at a time and made a sharp left toward the nursery. It was no sham, he truly wanted to speak to the boy; he liked children. His late father had laid the groundwork years ago for Marcus to assume Trevor's care. Even if Myles had survived, the former earl had set aside an allowance for his oldest brother's care. Recently, when he learned of Lady Worthing's upcoming confinement, jealousy had sprung to the forefront. Worthing had a wife, a son, and another child on the way, and Marcus wondered if he would ever know such contentment. Of course, his unstated reason for seeking out the boy lay in a need for a few stolen moments with Miss Cashé. She had quickly become an obsession, and this wing also housed her chambers.

He spent twenty minutes with the boy, jokingly teasing Daniel about his early attempts with the fishing pole and also giving Sonali some extra attention. Although she seemed quite hardy, Marcus worried the child might have suffered from her recent abduction. Obviously, Thornhill had similar thoughts. The duke had made arrangements with Sir Carter to escort Sonali and her governess, Mrs. Carruthers, to Kent. All the Realm members had taken turns attending to the girl since her birth. When Shepherd had sent Thornhill on a mission, one of the other unit members remained with Sonali. That was how they all had become her "uncles."

He hugged Sonali in farewell and ruffled Daniel's hair before stepping into the connecting passageway. Marcus paused, wondering whether he dared to approach Miss Cashé's chamber when suddenly a door three rooms away opened, and his imagination had come to life.

"Lord...Lord Yardley," she stammered when she saw him.

Purposely pushing away from the doorframe, Marcus approached her slowly. He spoke softly so others could not hear. "I...I said my farewells to... to the children." He gestured toward the nursery stairway.

Miss Cashé's eyes grew in anticipation. "You are all kindness...to think of the children. Most adults would not." She gulped in a deep breath as he drew nearer.

Marcus stood before her, and he was satisfied just to be close to her. Neither spoke, each letting his eyes fill with the other's presence, as if memorizing every detail. "Miss Cashé..." he rasped.

Instinctively, she raised her chin as he inched closer. "Shall you bid me farewell also, my Lord?" Her breathing became shallow. "Shall you offer me a similar gesture?"

A smile turned up his mouth's corners. "I do not believe you would appreciate my disarranging your hair as I did with Daniel." As he said the words, images of a disheveled Cashé lying across his bed shot heat to his loins.

The lady blushed, but, as before, she held his gaze. "And you bestowed a like form of affection on Sonali?"

Marcus's voice came out husky. "No, she I embraced."

Cashé did not respond, but a dark eyebrow rose in a question.

A deep sigh escaped as Marcus accepted the unspoken invitation. With a swift movement, he backed her through the still opened door, closing it with his boot's heel before taking Cashé into his arms. A feeling of completeness filled his lungs as he held her, breathing in the jasmine he had craved of late. "Cashé," he whispered, lifting her to him.

She buried her face in his chest. Her breasts swelled in a prelude to something she did not understand, and her sigh hardened him instantly.

Marcus placed his fingers under her chin and raised her eyes to his gaze. "This is madness," he growled. "Everything about this is wrong. Lexford is my friend, and I know he has kissed you. I observed his doing so in Worthing's garden." He felt the heat of her blush. "Yet, I find I can think of nothing else." As he professed his desire, Marcus brought her inexorably nearer, where she might feel his erection against her stomach.

A frown appeared between her eyes. "A woman does not consider it a true kiss unless she willingly seeks it," she said faintly.

Marcus chuckled lightly; she wielded a power over him of which she had no knowledge. "Might I assume you seek my attentions, Ma Chère?" He spoke in hushed tones. When she nodded her agreement, excitement flooded his veins.

As Marcus lowered his head, he murmured one word, "Madness," before his mouth took Cashé's hungrily. He forced himself not to devour her, as he so wanted to do. With her finally in his arms, his heartbeat skittered frantically. He loved the taste of her mouth, and he slid his tongue along the line of her lips. Thankfully, Cashé opened ever so slightly, and Marcus swallowed her gasp as he deepened the kiss.

In some far off place in her mind, Cashé could hear her uncle and the church leaders describing this moment as one of lasciviousness, but she could not believe anything, which felt this exquisite, could be wicked. All she wanted to do was cling to Marcus Wellston and never let go. His mouth had to be one of the seven deadly sins–the sin of over indulgence, for she would die if she could not have this forever.

His mouth's warmth sent shivers of delight through her heated veins. He held her tightly to his muscular frame, and Cashé wished to rub her breasts against his chest to relieve the ache, which had swelled them. He tilted his head to better take her mouth, and she realized she had not resisted in the least. This was perfection, and she wanted more of the hot swirling emotion seizing her body. His kiss destroyed every notion of denying him. The earl was the one man with whom she belonged: Cashé held no doubt to that particular fact.

Reluctantly, he eased his grip and lessened the pressure of his mouth on hers. They clung to each other, seeking the heat, which held them in desire's grasp. Marcus's breath came in short bursts as he forced himself not to escalate the situation, but releasing her mouth did little to decrease the passion coursing through his body. This woman was more than he anticipated.

"Oh, my Goodness," she breathed the words without opening her eyes or releasing her fisted hold on his lapels.

Marcus smiled confidently. Lexford may have kissed Cashé first, but the lingering desire he recognized in her body said she belonged to him. He kissed her temple before brushing his lips over her ear. He murmured, "I sincerely hope that is approval I hear in your voice." He sucked on her ear lobe before peppering her neck with a series of light kisses, taking a moment to circle his tongue around the beauty mark.

Cashé sucked in a deep breath. "It was…it was like nothing of which I ever dreamed." She shivered, and he pulled her closer still.

"Then you have dreamed of me?" He breathed the words into her hair. The resulting flood of heat told Marcus all he needed to know. "You do not need to say the words, Ma Chère. I feel it also."

Cashé's palms leisurely stroked his chest muscles. "I have dreamed, my Lord," she confessed.

Although he continued to feather kisses across her face and neck and shoulder blade, he insisted, "I must leave. We cannot be found together."

Cashé slid her arms about his neck. "I do not wish you to leave." She kissed along his chin line.

"Ah, Ma Chère, you must know it will take a Herculean effort." Marcus lifted her chin again where he might brush her lips with his. "Yet, we have no choice. I must return to Berwick and tend my estate and my brother, and you must recapture your family."

The lady loosened her hold, but she still rested against his body. "Will you call in Manchester, my Lord?" There was pain in the reality of their situation, and it rested plainly in her tone.

Marcus intentionally stepped away from her. Her kiss-swollen lips trembled, and so he caressed her cheek for comfort. "My calling at Chesterfield Manor might be a bit awkward with Lexford's regular appearances." He hated the sound of jealousy ringing through his words. "The viscount remains one of my most loyal friends, and I will not see him know pain again. I will remove myself from the picture before I permit that to happen."

Cashé wanted to argue with him, but beyond anything else in her life, she knew this man meant what he said: Marcus Wellston would never betray his friend. "Come to London," she said, a plan hatching as she watched self censure arrive. "Lord Lexford will look elsewhere," she asserted.

"I mean what I say, Cashé. I will not have Lexford hurt; the viscount suffered greatly when he returned to England."

"Promise me you will come to London." She caught his hand and kissed his palm. "I will find a means to divert Lord Lexford's attentions without his feeling the loss."

Marcus cupped her cheek. "If it were so..."

"You will come?" she demanded.

"Yes, Ma Chère, I will come." He bent to kiss her lightly. "For the short Season–before the weather changes."

Regina Jeffers

"Thank you, my Lord."

"Marcus," he corrected. "After what has occurred between us, it seems only appropriate."

The lady smiled largely, and he thought her the most handsome woman of his acquaintance. "Marcus."

The sound of his Christian name on her lips renewed his desire, and he recaptured her lips. Marcus realized this could be the last time he kissed her so he went slowly, savoring every moment–implanting the feel, the smell, and the taste of her in his memory. "Cashé," he breathed her name against her ear. "I can stay no longer." He kissed her temple. "Freshen your looks, Ma Chère. You appear thoroughly delightful, but thoroughly kissed." He reached for the door handle. "I will see you downstairs with the others for the evening entertainment."

Although it had no taste, Marcus had eaten the last of his breakfast. He simply had gone through the process. He was the only person in the morning room. Still very early, Marcus assumed Lord Worthing had seen to his having several choices of meals, so he dutifully partook of the dishes and offered appropriate praise. He had left a note of thanks with Mr. Lucas to give to Worthing, along with the information on Lord Averette for Shepherd.

Last evening, the ladies had entertained the household guests with music, and then they had set up card tables, but Marcus had had little patience for either. His mind constantly drifted to those few stolen moments he had shared with Miss Cashé. He wanted nothing more than to grab the lady's hand and return to his room to finish what they had started–to sate his growing desire for her. She sat at a table with Lexford, her twin, and Sir Carter. Observing their group, Marcus sadly discovered he would enjoy pounding his friend into the ground–an irrational response–but nothing about the green-eyed monster was rational. Unable to watch without a violent response, he excused himself early, claiming this morning's journey as a pretext. His last image of her was when he bowed over Cashé's and Satiné's hands. He felt cheated by the formality.

Unable to dwell any longer, Marcus made his way through the still shadowy hallways and out across the open expanse of the manicured lawns to the stables. He had ordered his horse saddled by six, wanting to cover more than half the distance to home today. A sleepy groomsman motioned Marcus into the stable before stumbling toward the estate kitchen. Driven to know where she was in the manor, Marcus turned one last time to search the many windows, illogically hoping Cashé stood at one of them–her requiring him as much as he required her. Seeing nothing but drawn drapes, blocking out the sunrise, he had dejectedly entered the dark building, only one lantern indicating the stall, which held his waiting mount. For the hundredth time today, he wondered if he had been wise to kiss the lady last evening. It created a gaping hole he could not fill with anyone else.

Making his way along the line of stalls, his hand caught the latch where Khan pawed the hardened earth in restlessness. Yet, when he opened the gate, a force propelled itself from the shadows, hitting his chest with an impact that sent Marcus staggering backward against a wooden support with a "Thunk!"

Chapter Eight

Marcus caught his attacker by the shoulders, ready to snap the interloper's neck, when his senses said "Female" and then "Cashé," and he released his grip before basketing her in his arms and sitting on a nearby bench. With shaking hands, he soothed her trembling form. "Sweetling, never surprise me as such again." He kissed the top of her head. He had wanted her with him, but his heart lurched with the knowledge of how close he had come to harming her. "Tell me you are not injured," he pleaded in hushed tones.

"I...I am well," she whispered.

Marcus moved her away where he might look upon her countenance, to confirm she had not suffered from his rough handling. Realizing Cashé had worn her hair down, he ran his fingers through the soft coal draped across her shoulders. He had imagined her as such when he had watched her last evening. "Darling, I am thrilled to see you, but why the secret assault?" Marcus drawled as he kissed her cheek.

"It was never meant to be an attack," she asserted with her usual defiance, a trait he had thought to despise, but now found quite adorable. Cashé gestured toward the stall. "I wanted to hide–to surprise you." Her bottom lip trembled. "But that...that animal..." She pointed her finger at Khan. "Does not like me."

Enjoying the spontaneity of her actions, Marcus watched her face's animation. She had come to him of her own free will, and his body reacted instinctively. "Khan will not harm you," he assured as he pulled her close again.

Cashé rested her head against his shoulder, mindlessly stroking his chin line with her fingertips. "He is so large," she weakly protested.

"A man requires a horse upon which he can depend." With his knuckles, Marcus lifted her chin. "Tell me what happened."

"I heard you speak to the groom, and I slipped into the stall to surprise you. But your horse also heard you and pushed me against the enclosure's side."

Marcus doubted Khan actually nudged her. More than likely, Khan shifted his weight, and Cashé panicked. "As long as you are uninjured..." He leaned forward to take her lips. His efforts brought her arms about his neck, and Marcus deepened the kiss, taking up where he had left off yesterday. Surprisingly, Cashé had learned her lesson well; her tongue danced with his, and she sucked lightly on his bottom lip. When they parted, Marcus huskily said, "Thank you for seeing to my departure."

"I...I should not...it is not proper," she whispered.

Marcus smiled tenderly. "But I will cherish this memory during the time we are apart." He brushed his lips against hers. "It is a special gift."

She pulled herself closer. "Would you give me a gift?" Cashé kissed his neck and ear.

Marcus thought if she would continue to kiss him as such, he would give her anything. "If I have the means," he breathed the words as he closed his eyes to the sensation.

Cashé ran her tongue about his ear, and Marcus groaned his pleasure. "I require a token...something by which to remember you."

Marcus growled, "Am I that forgettable?" He did not think he could become more aroused.

Cashé innocently rubbed her body against his. "I want something that is just mine...something I must never share with anyone else."

Marcus took her mouth again, bringing his hand from her waist to brush against the underside bust line. He ran his knuckles back and forth, caressing the lower swell of her ample endowments. He drank deeply of her lips and enjoyed how she clawed at his shoulders. Finally, he palmed her left breast and massaged it gently, lifting it to the edge of her gown's neckline. Cashé moaned, and Marcus sent his finger across her nipple, budding the hard tip with his touch. "You are so beautiful," he rasped, his lips returning immediately to hers. He thought he might explode with desire.

"Marcus." Cashé pushed further into his palm. "I cannot bear it."

He smiled at her smoke-filled eyes. "There is so much more, Sweetheart." He slid his fingers along the lace opening, touching her nipple. He knew from holding her she wore no corset, evidently dressing quickly to meet him. Nothing would keep her from his gaze if he dared to lower the dress. "Darling...permit me to look upon you," he begged. "I will not hurt you...you must trust me, Ma Chère." Marcus lightly squeezed the nipple between his fingertips.

She did not answer, but Cashé lay out across his arm, inviting his attention. Marcus shifted her weight and then maneuvered the material off her shoulder; he lowered the dress's front to expose her breast as he untied the ribbon of her chemise. He heard his own gulp for air, but he reached for the glorious globe. He had never seen someone lovelier. Marcus squeezed the nipple again, noting how Cashé's hips undulated to a primitive rhythm. "Breathtaking," he murmured as he leaned across her to run his tongue around the nub. Then he sucked lightly.

ꝏ

Cashé understood what he had asked of her, but she had wanted this. She had wanted a man who would love only her, and although she realized on some level the earl was worldly, she did not believe he would steal her innocence and then walk away: She had always recognized him to be an honorable man. His breath caressed her exposed breast, and she held a twinge of guilt, but then he said she was breathtaking, and Cashé knew she had made the correct choice. She relaxed into his manipulations, allowing her body to feel something she had never expected. To be able to give herself to this man would prove the most intelligent thing she had ever done.

ꝏ

He continued to circle the dark tip with his tongue feeling the smoothness of her skin with the rough textures of his mouth. Such an arousing contradiction! He realized he was close to taking her like some doxy in a stable, and it took everything in him to withdraw. When he raised his head, Marcus gently restored her clothing as he kissed her neck. "Cashé," he groaned, "if we stay... "

She opened her eyes and flushed in embarrassment. She looked terrified. "What...what must you think of me, my Lord." She turned her head from his gaze.

Yet, Marcus would have none of it. "Look at me, Cashé." He waited until she obliged. "What I think of you, Ma Chère, is nothing as you imagine. You are obstinate and head strong, but you are also thoughtful and tender and passionate." Her eyes grew in amazement. "I have never met a woman who angered me more or one I have wanted more. You are a conundrum, and I will spend my life learning your many secrets."

Cashé's eyes misted with tears. "You hold feelings for me!"

Marcus chuckled. "Believe me, Sweetheart, if I did not care for you, I would not have stopped. You deserve better than a smelly stable for your first time."

Cashé innocently asked, "Where?"

Marcus kissed her cheek. "Darling, please do not set me thinking of where I might wish to make love to you." She was the most puzzling woman he had ever met. One moment she spouted strict Biblical interpretations and the next she pondered where they might take pleasure in each other's bodies. Needless to say, Cashé Aldridge had much to learn about life before this could go further.

He stood and set her on the ground before him. Marcus cupped her chin. "You need to return to the house before someone realizes you are missing. The servants are up, and others will soon follow."

Cashé went on her tiptoes and kissed his cheek. "My gift, Your Lordship?" she teased.

Marcus ran his fingers through his hair. "I do not know what would please you." He thought on the items in his bag that he might offer her.

"Something you would never give another," she insisted.

Then Marcus knew what it should be. He released her hand and strode to where Khan still stood. Fishing in his saddlebag, he found exactly for what he searched. Cupping it in his palm, he dropped a yellowed piece of lace in her open hand.

Cashé looked on in dismay. "It is lace, my Lord." Her eyebrow rose in question. "I never thought you as the type who kept lace in his bag." She suspected it belonged to his mother or his grandmother.

"I carried it with me through all the years I was away from Berwick. It has survived battles and the worst of conditions."

Cashé smiled brightly. "Then I shall cherish it until we meet again. Was it your mother's?" She delicately folded the scrap of material.

"No, it was Maggie's"

He could not disguise the pain that flickered in his eyes. "Tell me," she whispered. "Who is Maggie?"

His Adam's apple worked hard, but Marcus managed to say, "Maggie... Margaret Wellston...my twin."

He said no more as Cashé walked into his arms; there she remained in a silent embrace until they heard voices in the stable yard. She touched his cheek with her fingertips and then turned quickly toward the rear door. "Farewell, Lord Yardley."

Marcus automatically caught Khan's bridle, but he watched the sway of her hips before she had disappeared from sight. Then he walked the animal outside to mount. He would draw attention away from her return to the house.

The head groomsman spotted him. "Is something ill, Your Lordship?"

"No," he said jovially. "I just seem to be a bit distracted this morning." Marcus accepted the man's boost into the saddle. "When you speak to Lord Worthing, tell him I appreciated his hospitality."

"I will see to it, Lord Yardley."

Spotting the pale blue of her dress crossing in the direction of the lower gardens, Marcus turned Khan twice in a circle to maintain the men's attentions. Then he rode away–his heart folded neatly in the palm of her hand–all his love wrapped in a small fragment of lace.

Cashé had little time to think about what had happened with Wellston in the Kerrington stables. She had rushed from his embrace to the privacy of her room, clutching the lace he had placed in her hand–a piece from his twin sister Maggie. She had known he had had a brother for whom he cared, and she had known His Lordship's parents no longer lived, but he had never mentioned a twin. Even when she had disclosed Satiné's existence, Lord Yardley had said nothing. She now understood why the man had understood her better than anyone she had ever met. Understood why she had required his approval. What was it that had so devastated the earl that he had clung to a scrap of lace? And why had he shared it with her? Yes, they had shared an intimacy she had never expected from any man. Yet, when he had handed her the lace, Lord Yardley had touched her soul, not just her body.

Returning to her room, Cashé had stripped away her gown and had returned to bed. Pulling the blanket around her, she had buried her head into the pillow and looked upon the lace as it lay beside her on the bed linens. She placed her hand over it and closed her eyes to imagine the earl rested beside her–holding tightly to her hand. Cashé never felt so much love. She kept telling herself Lord Yardley truly cared for her, or he would not have shared his token.

Later, she would analyze how he had touched her–how her breasts swelled just thinking of him–how a heated dampness appeared in her most private place. When His Lordship's mouth suckled her, fireworks, like those she had witnessed at Vauxhall Gardens, exploded before her eyes. She had wanted him to do more–to touch her in other places. Uncle Samuel would think her a pure wanton; he would denounce her actions–would call her the most vile names–would force her to confess to the entire congregation and do a very public penitence. Yet, Cashé readily accepted the fact if Lord Yardley walked through her chamber door, she would welcome him to her bed. "What has happened to you?" she asked herself, but the only answer was a piece of lace–her connection to the Earl of Berwick.

"I need to discover more of Maggie," she announced as she attempted to calm her nerves and return to sleep. "Lord Yardley's relationship to his twin will tell me how I fit into the man's life. If he has agreed to share his demons, then I must be prepared to assist him."

Marcus's body still strummed with life an hour after he had ridden from Kerrington's stable. He would never be able to look at that building again without seeing Cashé's form stretched across his lap. Just the thought of it brought another rush of blood to his groin. How he managed to withdraw, he still could not explain. Marcus wanted her more than he had ever wanted any woman. Yet, instinctively, he knew once would never be enough. He would never sate his desire for her–even if he had her every night for the rest of his life.

"You gave her Maggie's lace," he chastised his actions aloud, but despite the words, Marcus felt no regret at having done so. He had never expected his actions would feel so right. He had cut the lace from the hem of the dress in which his parents had buried Maggie. At the time, Myles had criticized the impulsive act, but Marcus's mother had told her second son to allow Marcus his grief. And that lace had been with him every day since Maggie's funeral–every day, until today. Today, he had entrusted it to Cashé Aldridge. Would the girl understand how the delicate yellow threads were his connection to his sister? Would Cashé treasure it as he did?

"What do ye mean? She be gone?" Lachlan Charters demanded. The Scot had shoved Samuel Aldridge against the drawing room's wall.

Aldridge attempted to smile and to loosen the man's grip from his neck. "Not...not gone," he croaked, lodging his fingers around his attacker's and sucking in air. The viscount pulled at his cravat and straightened his waistcoat as Charters took a backward step. "Cashémere is visiting her sister and her maternal uncle. That is all."

"I be hearin' ye allowed the older one to marry her English duke. I thought ye be against their joining." Charters fisted and unfisted his hands in a constant threat.

Aldridge smiled purposely as he edged away from the wall. "My niece had her heart set on being a duchess. Plus, the connection is a good one for my family." Averette spoke with a false bravado. "I escorted Velvet to Derby, where she and Thornhill chose to speak their vows before family and friends. Thornhill's sister is with child, and the future earl would not permit his wife to travel." He turned the truth to his own devices.

"And ye be leavin' Miss Cashémere behind?" The big man circled the desk to threaten Averette again. "The girl belongs to me. I paid ye, Averette. Paid ye a tidy sum to be making the girl me wife. What if Miss Cashémere be choosin' that fancy viscount she be keepin' company while in England? That would be makin' me most unhappy."

"I assure you, Charters, my niece will have nothing to do with Viscount Lexford. She is a good girl and knows the punishment for going against my moral lessons. In fact, I expect Cashé to convert others to our ways." Averette actually believed much of this speech. He had no doubt about his influence on his ward. "It is best to give Cashémere some freedom before she weds. She will make you a better subject then." Averette poured himself a glass of claret and took a sip.

"Then we be lettin' the girl taste her freedom with the baron and her younger sister, but I warn ye, Averette, I will give the girl but three months. After that, I be not responsible for what happens. I mean to have Miss Cashémere or me money–you must decide." Charters stormed from the room, leaving the door rattling in his wake.

Aldridge sank into his chair before taking a deep drink of his wine. He had made it a habit to drink only in the privacy of his home. "There must be a way without Morton's interference," he murmured. "I must find an ally to bring Cashé home."

*

"What do you think of Viscount Lexford?" Cashé asked as she shared tea with her twin in one of Linton Park's smaller drawing rooms. Lord Yardley had departed eight hours prior. Cashé knew how long he had been gone because her eyes involuntarily traveled to the ormolu clock on the mantel. Despite her best efforts, they had done so repeatedly since her early morning farewell. Predictably, the baron had announced they would retire to Chesterfield Manor tomorrow, and Cashé anxiously had put her plan to rid herself of Aidan Kimbolt's attentions in place.

Satiné looked up suspiciously. "Does it matter what I think of the gentleman? He seems to find you irresistible. The question might be more appropriate directed to you. What is your opinion of Viscount Lexford?"

Cashé did not respond immediately. She had concocted a plan of which she had hoped her sister might partake. Since becoming aware of her growing need for Lord Yardley's approval, Cashé had carefully observed Satiné's interactions with both Yardley and Lexford, and she had thought Satiné held a preference for one and not the other. Cashé elongated the pause as part of her scheme. "I suppose the viscount will call often at Chesterfield Manor."

"It is in close proximity to Lexington Arms," her sister noted.

Cashé nodded her understanding. Her nerves added a small squeak to her words. "The viscount is very handsome."

She watched closely for her sister's reaction and found it satisfying to hear Satiné stifle the sigh that slipped from her lips. "Indubitably–he is extremely attractive."

Again, Cashé waited, increasing her sister's interest. "As is the earl."

Satiné smiled obligingly. "Yes, the earl is a striking man."

Cashé's voice automatically softened to a breathy whisper. "Dark penetrating eyes–strong aristocratic nose–ruggedly handsome face–wide shoulders."

Thankfully, Satiné had taken the bait. Both her sister's tone and her stare betrayed Satine's puzzlement. "I had not noticed His Lordship's eyes." She stammered, "I mean…I have looked at his eyes, but never found depth there."

"Lord Yardley's eyes speak of his soul," Cashé protested. "When he is angry or when he is pleased or when he is frustrated." Images of the earl's eyes dazed with desire sprang to her mind, and Cashé felt her breasts swell in response.

Satiné leaned forward, pressing her own opinions. "But they cannot compete with the viscount's coffee brown ones–nor does his appearance– the way Lexford's sandy blonde hair falls over his forehead, teasingly blocking his vision, as if he is looking at a person through a screen."

Cashé stared contentedly at Satiné, totally enjoying how her sister had disclosed what Cashé had secretly observed. Cashé spoke the truth when she admitted, "I find the viscount's constant battle with his hair a bit distracting."

Satiné smiled privately. "Really? I find it quite endearing."

They sat in quiet companionship for a few brief moments, each considering the man she affected. Cashé broke the silence, "May we speak honestly?"

"Absolutely."

"Although we are sisters of the same blood, we have not known each other. Uncle Samuel demanded a different type of obedience from Uncle Charles. We are the same, but we are different." She recognized the moment Satiné understood and acknowledged the truth of Cashé's thoughts with a tilt of her head. Encouraged, Cashé continued, "I have had a longer acquaintance with Viscount Lexford, and I find him quite agreeable company, but he does not stir my soul."

"And the earl does?" Satiné's countenance held a bit of mischief.

Cashé's turmoil–the feelings exploding every time she thought of Marcus Wellston–rolled on. What the Averettes had taught her was in stark contrast to what she had felt when the earl came near her. "I often despise the man, and I am likewise certain he cannot tolerate me, but I admit I cannot remove my eyes from him." She turned to her sister. "I acknowledge requiring Lord Yardley's approval, and I believe you feel the same about the viscount."

Satiné bit back a laugh. "I might."

"Then what shall we do about it? How do we convince Lexford and Yardley they affect the wrong twin?" Cashé enjoyed the secret of how Yardley would require less persuasion than the viscount. She moved to sit beside Satiné.

"Can they tell us apart?" Satiné began, hatching her own plan. "Mama and Papa never could. When anyone first meets us, he searches our countenances for the differences, but finds none." They both paused in contemplation of the possibilities. "The differences, at the moment, lie in our experiences. I suppose I could become a bit more outspoken and you a bit more conservative."

Cashé caught her sister's hand. "We could teach each other about our respective lives."

"That endeavor would require total honesty between us," Satiné cautioned. "Are you prepared to do so, Cashémere?"

Cashé answered quickly. "I suspect the differences are quite striking. Although I am curious about the lessons you have already mastered in preparation for your Come Out, likely, you shall be more astonished than I." Satiné nodded her head in agreement, but Cashé noticed her sister's raised brow, indicating Satiné might change her mind. "We shall see neither man," Cashé continued quickly, trying to squash any qualms Satiné held, "for some time once we return to Uncle Charles's estate. We could teach each other–become different women, sharing a common experience. If Lord Yardley wishes more of your ladylike softness, Cashé will adopt those qualities."

"And if Viscount Lexford prefers Cashé's obstinacy, I can learn to be more like Cashé," Satiné insisted. They sat in quiet contemplation for several minutes.

Finally, Cashé giggled uncertainly. "I have been considering how we might begin. I thought we could start with discussion sessions and then look at our clothing choices, before, finally, executing the occasional switch on Uncle Charles or the servants. Eventually, we shall fool Lord Lexford."

"If we can fool Uncle Charles, that proof shall be the true test." Caught up in her sister's excitement, Satiné giggled also.

"Then we are in accord?"

Satiné spontaneously hugged her, and Cashé breathed an early sigh of relief. "We have more than concurrence; we have a compact for love."

"With a touch of Cashémere."

"And one of Satiné."

◦◦◦

"When did the Viscount Averette return?" Murhad Jamot sat in a small inn situated on Edinburgh's outskirts. The Baloch hated the country's dampness, but the area's rough terrain along the English border had provided him with several places where he could hide and re-evaluate his efforts after the failure of his last encounter with the Realm.

"The county be back near on a month now," said the groomsman with whom Jamot had made a connection over a shared drink and some cut powder to which Jamot had access. The Baloch had followed Mir's orders, but he had seen no reason he could not profit from a side venture in opium while he spent time searching the British countryside for Mir's emerald. "A man must eat," he had told himself on more than one occasion.

Jamot took a sip of his drink. The ale did not sit well with his constitution, but he feigned contentment. "And neither girl returned with

124

the man? That appears odd." Jamot had taken time to reflect interest but not an obsession with the man's story.

"It all be most suspicious. For months old Averette be crowin' 'bout marryin' off them sisters to Charters and 'nother man he chooses. Then neither returns." The man swayed in place. The weakened drug and weaker ale having an effect on him. "Charters put the hurt on the county on Tuesday last. Jemmy be sayin' Charters told Averette he had paid good money for the younger girl, and he wanted her back."

Jamot had heard all he required for the time being. He no longer suspected either Kerrington or Fowler had Mir's emerald, but he did believe they knew of its whereabouts. Now, he had the names of those he could approach to assist him with the next suspects on his list. "Think I will find my bed," he slapped the groomsman on the back and turned toward the exit. "I will find you again soon, Friend." However, Jamot thought the groomsman had served his purpose.

♦

"Uncle, it is terrible what the Averettes have done to Cashémere in the name of love," Satiné sobbed. She and the baron had ridden out together on the pretense of visiting several of the tenants, but they had shared a secluded outcropping less than a mile from the main house. Satiné had asked the only parent she had ever known to accompany her for she had required someone with whom to share her sister's confidences. They had returned to Chesterfield Manor a week prior, and as she and her sister had agreed, she and Cashé had set about teaching each other about their respective lives. Satiné did not explain to their uncle what had precipitated these sharing sessions, but of what her sister had spoken she had felt compelled to tell the baron.

Ashton's body stiffened, and she recognized the anger coursing through him. "Tell me what your sister has confided. Before I can protect Cashémere, I must know it all."

"I am ashamed to say I would have crumbled long ago," Satiné declared. "The Averettes have an unusual lifestyle. In some ways, they practice what we think of as Society-arranged marriages, men's supremacy, and rules of propriety. Yet, there are extremes also." Satiné hiccupped as she swallowed her sobs. "The worst part is Cashé believes much of what the viscount does is acceptable. My sister does not question Lord Averette's authority."

"I understand." The baron placed his arm around her shoulders. "It must be difficult on a young woman of your station, but it is important,

125

Satiné, that you tell me everything just as Cashé has explained it to you." For a moment, she questioned whether she should share Cashé's confidences with her guardian, but Satiné held no experience to determine what should and should not be made public from her sister's story. She had never heard of anyone being abused by a loved one, but most certainly Lord Averette had done so to Cashé.

"Our grandmother," she began with a deep inhalation, "required Cashé to spend hours on her knees in meditation whenever my sister misbehaved as a child. Once, Cashé had torn and muddied her dress, and our grandmother locked Cashé in a broom closet for a whole day without food and with only a chamber pot in the space. Another time, Cashé forgot to do her chores, and Uncle Samuel placed her on her knees before a room full of guests and forced her to read the book of Exodus aloud. She was not permitted to stand until she had read the entire Biblical passage. Cashé was eight at the time."

Her uncle bit back his reaction, which Satiné took as encouragement. Uncle Charles's anger mirrored Satine's. "What else?"

"None of the women are permitted opinions, nor are they given privileges within the church. Such contradictions are difficult to accept. Although parties are condemned as evil, Uncle Samuel permitted His Grace to escort the Aldridges about London recently."

The baron spoke through gritted teeth. "I suspect Aldridge uses his religion as an excuse for avoiding what he does not wish to do. It is his mantle–something he brings out when convenient."

"Cashémere brags of the good deeds the church accomplishes. My sister speaks of the schools established for the poorer children, and you are aware of what she says regarding the church's protection of the needy families; yet, when she speaks of the power of both the parochial elder and of the deacon, I fear something is amiss."

"Your fear is well placed," Ashton warned. "Satiné, you must continue to persuade Cashémere to entrust you with her memories, and then you must make me aware of each experience your sister shares–no matter how insignificant that particular memory may seem."

"Yes, Uncle." Satiné breathed freely. Some day Cashé would thank her for the trouble she had encountered in setting things right.

"Now, my Sweet, share with me the rest of what you know, and then we should return to the estate. You must promise me you will not tell

Regina Jeffers

Cashémere of our discussion. Your sister must not know you turned to me for comfort."

Determined to do well by Cashé, Satiné said, "I understand, Uncle, but you will protect Cashé, will you not? My sister cannot return to Lord Averette's household."

Ashton kissed her forehead. "I promise Cashémere will never return to Scotland."

It had taken Marcus two days to reach his estate. He had spent his first night on the road dreaming of making love to Cashémere, waking hard with desire. He had ridden steadily through the day, taking only a few breaks to rest his horse. Subconsciously, Marcus realized he should put the miles between him and the woman he had kissed so passionately or else return to Linworth and claim her. His conscience had bothered him as he had ridden away: He had betrayed one of his closest friends. Yet, images of Cashé's trusting countenance clung to his mind's recesses, and Marcus knew he would kiss her again if provided the opportunity.

"You are home," Trevor said when Marcus entered the drawing room.

Marcus sat close to where his brother and his companion played cards. "I apologize for being away so long. Have you and Jeremy completed your lessons today?" Marcus nodded to the young man he had hired to stay with his older brother.

Trevor placed a card on the table with a flourish. "Jeremy made me clean my room today," Trevor declared.

Marcus smiled indulgently. "Jeremy was correct. A gentleman does not leave extra work for his servants."

Trevor protested, "Jeremy is not a gentleman."

Jeremy Ingram had been a Godsend. The young man, a by-blow of one of his father's dearest friends, had agreed to become Trevor's companion for ten years. In return, Marcus's father had educated Ingram in the finest schools and had set aside a sizeable trust for the man when he finished his time with the family. Marcus had already identified a youth in a similar situation, who would replace Jeremy when the man left the Wellston household. It was an unusual business arrangement to which Marcus gave his father the credit for developing the position. With Trevor's condition, the family held no idea of his brother's lifespan. The doctors had not given them much hope. In fact, the physician had encouraged the former earl to place Trevor in an asylum, but Lionel Wellston had adamantly refused. Because Trevor had a man's body, but a childlike mind, Jeremy's employment provided Trevor stability, and it relieved his father, and now Marcus, to tend to estate business. Marcus likened the situation to hiring a destitute female as a governess or a lady's companion.

Thankfully, his brother's companion had kept his opinions to himself, but Marcus corrected, "Jeremy is a gentleman, Trevor–the same as I. Jeremy is a minor son also."

"I am a number one son," Trevor asserted.

"That is correct," Marcus motioned for the tea tray to be place where his brother could reach the cakes and finger sandwiches. "You were father's first child."

Abandoning the card game, Trevor had taken the plate the maid handed him. "We had different mothers."

Marcus frowned when Trevor spoke before swallowing. He motioned for his brother to use his serviette. "Yes, our father remarried."

"My mother died after I was born." The maid judiciously handed Trevor a half-filled cup of tea. Over the years, the household staff had adapted to Trevor's poor coordination skills. They had cleaned more than one of his brother's accidents. "My mama died and your mama died and Papa died and Myles died and Maggie died..." Trevor recited in a singsong rhythm.

Marcus swallowed the predictable desperation creeping into his chest. The litany of his family history set poorly with him. "We have suffered too many losses," he said softly.

Suddenly, Trevor looked very agitated. "When you die, Marcus, who will see to my care?"

It was the type of question young children asked of parents when a beloved grandparent passed, and Marcus answered as he would in that situation. "First, it will be a long time before God calls me to Heaven, but you should not be afraid. Father and I have made plans for your care. You have nothing of which to worry."

As if he did not recall the conversation, Trevor changed the subject. "Did the duke marry?"

Marcus smiled, "Yes, His Grace took a wife. Do you remember Brantley Fowler?" He knew Jeremy would have read Marcus's letter to Trevor.

"I remember names," Trevor revealed triumphantly. "Jeremy says I remember names better than anything else. There is Brantley Fowler and James Kerrington and Carter Lowery and Gabriel Crowden and..."

128

Marcus interrupted, not wishing to hear Kimbolt's name and be reminded of his irrational desire for the viscount's love interest. "I must change my clothes and rid myself of the trail dirt." Marcus stood to emphasize his point. "Then I will be in my study, addressing all the correspondence Mr. Dylan has waiting for me." Marcus presented Trevor an abbreviated bow, reminding his brother of his manners. "I will see you at supper, if not before."

ﾟｏﾟ

"Surely you practice an untruth," Cashé accused.

Satiné strolled about the room, playacting at being at a Society party. "I am quite serious. A woman may use her fan to speak secretly to an established suitor or a potential one. Now, watch this." Satiné took the open fan in her left hand and delicately fluttered it before her face. "This means, 'I wish to speak to you.'" Satiné demonstrated again. "It is your turn."

Cashé reluctantly mimicked her twin's actions. "What else?"

"Oh, there is a whole language." Satiné took up the lesson. "If a woman fans slowly, she is telling a man she is married, and if quickly, she is engaged."

Cashé looked puzzled. "Then what does a woman do if she is too warm and simply requires a bit of air? The lady could be saying something, which is not true. I am neither married nor engaged, but fanning myself after a robust dance might be saying otherwise."

"Oh, silly, it just is not the same," Satiné assured with a bit of petulance. "As new debutants, we shall wear white, and the men will know we are not involved in a serious relationship." Cashé rolled her eyes in vexation, but Satiné ignored her sister's stubbornness. "These are the important ones." Satiné took the fan again to demonstrate each maneuver. "Drawing the fan across the man's cheek means, 'I love you.' Pulling the fan through the hand tells the man you care nothing for him. Touching your right cheek means, 'Yes,' and, of course, 'No' is the left cheek. A fan placed near the heart tells the man he has won yours, and a half opened fan pressed to the lips means you will accept his kiss."

Cashé thought about the passion she had shared with Lord Yardley. She held no fan then, but the earl knew she had desired his kiss. Still desired his kisses. Feeling flustered by her unexpected wantonness, Cashé blushed.

"Did I say something that brought on your color?" Satiné laughed lightly. "Oh, do not tell me, Sister, that you have never been kissed."

Cashé thought instantly of Wellston, but she quickly hid her fluttering heart. "I have been kissed," she asserted.

"By your intended? By Mr. Charters?" Satiné teasingly questioned.

Cashé's countenance answered the tease. "No, not Mr. Charters."

"Then who?" Satiné demanded. "A kiss when you were ten does not count."

Cashé walked away, partially turning her back on Satiné. "No, not when I was ten. This past week, in fact."

Satiné flinched. "Lord Yardley?"

Cashé hid her amusement. She liked seeing her sister at a disadvantage. "Actually, Lord Lexford."

Satiné puffed up in denial. "You said we are to convince Lord Yardley and Viscount Lexford each had chosen the wrong twin!"

Cashé trailed her finger nonchalantly along a bookshelf. "We did, but the viscount kissed me before we came to our agreement."

Satiné crossed her arms across her chest in disbelief. "Lord Lexford would not have done so. He is a gentleman."

"His Lordship most certainly kissed me!" Cashé declared in triumph.

Satiné admitted, "I am not certain I like the idea. If we are to switch affections, I would prefer the viscount knew you less rather than more."

Cashé quickly realized her sister's insecurity. In some ways it provided comfort to know the polished Satiné held her own self-doubts. "You must remember Lord Lexford and I hold a longer acquaintance." She paused, recognizing Satiné required more comfort. "His Lordship wished to ease my feelings after Uncle Samuel's departure. It was not as if I encouraged the viscount," she protested. "Trust me! I hold no desire for a repeat of Lord Lexford's affections."

"Was the kiss deplorable?" Satiné appeared suddenly concerned over Lexford's abilities.

Cashé chuckled. "No, nothing as such. His Lordship's kiss was very tender–not demanding."

"What do you mean, not demanding?"

A light turned on in Cashé's understanding. "You have never been kissed!" she blurted out.

Satiné's hands fisted at her waist. "I will have you know Lord Yardley kissed me before he departed!"

"You speak an untruth!" Cashé declared.

Satiné grimaced. "I am not of a habit of being dishonest," she snapped. "Lord Yardley offered me a farewell kiss, just as Lord Lexford bade you adieu."

The possibility of Yardley rewarding Satiné with his attentions enflamed Cashé. "I extend my deepest sympathies, Satiné. You are deceived, Sister!"

Satiné's voice rose in desperation. "It is true! Lord Yardley kissed me!"

Cashé strode to the door. "I pity you for your weakness," she declared.

"What weakness?" Satiné challenged.

Cashé turned on her twin. "Your true vulnerability. It provides me recompense to know you do not possess all the answers."

"Why do you not believe me?" Satiné shouted.

Cashé smiled deviously. "Because Lord Yardley kissed me repeatedly before he left for Northumberland, and I can assure you, Sister Dear, tenderness had nothing to do with the earl's show of affection!"

Chapter Nine

"Did you dance at the duke's wedding?" Trevor asked as they had dined together. Marcus had returned to his estate a week earlier, and he had repeatedly answered his brother's questions about the wedding.

Marcus looked up and smiled. Images of his waltzing with Cashé readily materialized. He had dreamed of her each evening, and in the privacy of his chambers, he had brought Cashé to pleasure. At least, in his mind, he had done so. "It was a small gathering, and we celebrated during the evenings leading up to the exchange of vows."

"But did you dance?" Trevor insisted.

Marcus indulgently answered, "Yes, I acted the gentleman and escorted several ladies onto the floor."

"Then there were pretty girls at the party," Trevor asserted.

Marcus barked out a laugh. "And why would you think there were pretty girls in attendance?"

Trevor presented him the silly, lopsided smile Marcus treasured. "You do not enjoy dancing, so if you danced, it must have been with a pretty girl."

Marcus choked on his wine. "I...I suppose...your assumption makes sense."

"Were they very pretty?" Marcus accepted a mental reminder that although Trevor had a child's mind, his brother possessed a man's body, holding a young boy's interest in girls. As the oldest, at the age of four and thirty, If not for his limitations, Trevor should have been the Earl of Berwick: His brother would have inherited. Trevor's mother had never delivered a child, and his brother's birth had brought disappointment. The physician had said the countess had passed her prime years for delivery–her being in her early forties when she had given birth to Trevor. The first Lady Yardley had passed when Trevor was not quite one, and twenty months later, the earl had married Marcus's mother. Lady Margaret Sterling Wellston quickly delivered forth an heir, Marcus's brother Myles;

and two years later, he and his twin graced Tweed Hall. Little did anyone in the family realize only the oldest and the youngest would survive.

"Yes, very pretty." Marcus joined in the banter.

Trevor put down his utensils and focused his attention on Marcus. "Tell me."

Marcus purposely paused in a teasing manner. "There were four women residing at Viscount Worthing's estate." Another pause. "First, Viscountess Worthing is quite tall and statuesque with golden blonde hair and green eyes."

"Lady Worthing is tall like His Lordship," Trevor observed.

"Yes, very much so."

"Then they will have a tall baby." Jeremy, who sat beside Trevor, attempted to caution his charge about appropriate mealtime conversations, but Marcus gave a small shake of his head to allow Trevor to continue. He was always interested in his brother's musings.

"Lord and Lady Worthing will soon welcome their first child, and I will most certainly convey your observation to Kerrington. I am certain the viscount will be amazed by your logic." Trevor seemed pleased with Marcus's evaluation. He paused again before asking, "Should I continue with my descriptions of the ladies?" A quick nod from Trevor sent his agreement. "Miss Aldridge is His Grace's new bride and his distant cousin. The lady is very petite, and she possesses dark hair and blue-violet eyes."

"His Grace is tall, and she is short." The combination appeared to bother Trevor.

Marcus chuckled. "Yes, Fowler's children could be short or tall." Trevor asked Marcus to continue his description, and Marcus became more guarded with his words. "Miss Aldridge has two sisters, and all three ladies favor each other in hair coloring and height. Unlike the new duchess's blue eyes, Miss Satiné and Miss Cashémere have green ones."

"Which of the two sisters is prettier?"

Marcus knew which he preferred. "The ladies are twins. There is little difference between them."

"You and Maggie were twins," Trevor announced before returning to his meal.

Marcus hesitated. He rarely spoke of Maggie to anyone, at least, not since his years with the Realm. "Miss Satiné and Miss Cashé are both females and look alike, where Maggie could not look exactly like me. She would have been an unsightly lady if that were true, and we both know Margaret was quite beautiful."

"You would have been an unsightly man if you and Maggie were alike," Trevor declared.

Marcus threw back his head and laughed heartily. "I certainly would have."

"Which lady was the best dancer?" Trevor continued.

"Miss Satiné was raised by Baron Ashton as a refined lady, but I enjoyed Miss Cashé's innocence tremendously."

Trevor appeared confused. "Why did the baron not raise Miss Cashé as a lady?"

"I should have explained. The three Aldridge sisters lost their parents when they were very young. Miss Aldridge resided with the Fowlers, Miss Satiné with Baron Ashton, and Miss Cashé with an uncle in Scotland."

Trevor frowned. "I am glad we live together."

"So am I." Marcus frowned also. "The circumstances placed Miss Cashé in the worst situation." Marcus thought of Fowler's father, but the late duke had never come near Velvet Aldridge. Even with the shadow William Fowler's depravity hanging over the late duke's household, Miss Cashé had known a different, more lasting violation. Cashémere's mind had been flooded with messages of hatred and censure. "The lady suffered greatly with Lord Averette."

⁂

"Uncle Charles," Cashé sat with the baron and Satiné for afternoon tea. She and her twin had called a truce; neither had acknowledged the argument of two days prior. Cashé had accepted Satiné's silence as an apology. "Would you object if I wrote to Uncle Samuel and Aunt Alice?"

"If you feel a necessity, then I would hold no objections," the baron said warily.

Cashé read the question in his tone. "I will not ask Uncle Samuel to come for me if that fact speaks to your concern. I have spent much time reasoning the why's of this situation, and although it has been thrust upon me without regard to my own feelings, I have come to peace. Yet, I cannot pretend to be comfortable with not offering my farewells to Aunt Alice and to Gwendolyn. Besides, I would wish to have some of my personal belongings and clothing sent to me. You have been generous, and Satiné has shown true compassion in sharing her items, but I wish for my memories not to be stolen from me." Cashé noted the baron's frown at her use of the word stolen, and she had taken a certain pleasure in seeing her uncle's ruffled composure. She still stung from how easily everyone had dispensed with her objections.

"I imagine Samuel would welcome the request more so if it came from you." The baron sat his teacup on a side table. "However, do not fret about the expense of a few extra dresses. I would stand it gladly to have my dear Chenille's children in my home." He stood to take his leave. "Have Mr. James frank your letter for you when you are ready. By the way," he turned to the sisters, "I have asked some of the family to join us for a few days next week...before the weather changes. Your Aunt Charlotte and your cousins are thrilled to reacquaint themselves with you, Cashémere. Satiné, if you will see to the menus and arrangements, I would appreciate it."

"Yes, Uncle."

When the baron exited, Cashé turned to her sister. "What do you say to our attempting a small switch or two when Aunt Charlotte and our cousins visit? Nothing elaborate–just having tea or sharing a few minutes to see if they notice the difference."

Satiné's composure faltered. "I am no longer certain this is a good idea."

Cashé expected as much. What she had learned of her twin spoke of Satiné's refinement, but also of her sister's weak resolve. "Then you will accept Lord Yardley when your heart tells you otherwise?"

"Why could we not simply tell the gentlemen the truth? There is no need for deception."

Cashé fought the desire to roll her eyes in exasperation. "Gentlemen never realize what serves them best, and you must recall Lord Lexford and Lord Yardley have a long-standing friendship. Neither would interfere in the other's relationship. We might lose them both if they thought we refused their regards. Men possess such weak egos."

Satiné argued, "It appears the earl has already interfered in the viscount's life."

Cashé immediately came to Marcus's defense. "Lord Yardley is not at blame. I encouraged him. I wished to compare the gentlemen, especially as I held no desire to mislead Viscount Lexford if my affections were engaged elsewhere."

"Of course," her twin observed reluctantly, "it would be indecorous to treat His Lordship falsely." Satiné lowered her voice. "I am unsure whether I might attract Lord Lexford. It appears both gentlemen prefer you."

Perversely, Cashé rejoiced in Satiné's lack of confidence. To her, Satiné was everything she could never hope to be, and to observe her twin's doubts had given Cashé the nerve to see this plan through. She moved quickly to sit beside her sister. "Dear Satiné, please do not turn this a into competition. Lord Lexford sees only my face, but yours is equal in every way. I have watched the two of you together. You and the viscount complement each other. For example, I despise riding, but you are an accomplished equestrian; and Lord Lexford plans to develop a line of thoroughbreds. He and I are mismatched. If you permit His Lordship to woo you as me, it shall prove it is you for whom he truly cares. Entice the viscount in my name, but secure his affections in yours."

"His Lordship and I do seem to share many of the same interests," Satiné agreed wistfully. After a short pause, she added, "Do you truly believe such a plan will succeed?"

Cashé wanted to shout how she would accept nothing less than success, but she had recognized her sister's tentative personality, so she said, "Fear of failure is why we shall attempt our deception in small doses on Aunt Charlotte and our cousins–walking through a room, answering a question as each other, enjoying afternoon tea–everyday actions. If we are caught, we can laugh and claim it a twin trick. Everyone expects twins to act as such as children."

"Yet, we are no longer children," Satiné protested.

Cashé countered, "However, for no fault of our doing, we have known a life-long separation. It is natural for us to regress."

"I would not wish to disappoint Uncle Charles." Satiné wavered.

Cashé bit back her retort. "You will not disenchant the baron. He desires for us to discover a sisterly relationship. This joint venture will prove him correct."

"I suppose we could practice carefully orchestrated switches," Satiné reluctantly concurred.

Before her twin could retreat from the scheme, Cashé said, "Then you must tell me more of Aunt Charlotte, as well as John and Rose. I have not seen our cousins since we were children."

Cashé and Satiné spent an hour making plans, and then Cashé excused herself to write her letter. A bit later, with trepidation, she approached her uncle's secretary. "Mr. James, Uncle Charles said you would frank these letters for me." She feigned nonchalance, when, in reality, her heart pounded double time.

"Of course, Miss Aldridge." The man accepted the two letters she held in her hand. He marked the first one with the baron's authority. However, when he looked at the second, he shot Cashé a questioning glance. "You have not written the direction on this one, Miss Aldridge." He meant to return the letter to her.

However, Cashé, intentionally, refused. She purposely giggled in the way of schoolgirls. "How silly of me! They are both going to my uncle's home. The one you hold is for his daughter Gwendolyn. The child must be highly disappointed with my not returning with Uncle Samuel. In the letter, I explained my extended absence. If you will post it, I will mark it to her attention."

"Certainly, Miss Aldridge." The man poured the hot wax to seal the pages and placed the baron's signet symbol in the quickly drying liquid. "Should I post these for you?" he asked with a great deal of self-importance.

"That shan't be necessary, but I appreciate your offer. I plan to walk into the village," she assured him.

"It is nearly three miles, Miss Aldridge," Mr. James protested.

Cashé smiled sweetly. "Nothing of significance. I do not mind a long walk. I welcome the exercise."

"As you wish, Miss Aldridge. However, if you should change your mind, I will order the carriage for your needs."

Cashé squeezed the back of the man's bony hand. "Your kindness is so noted, Mr. James." Squelching the giddiness that had sprung to sher step, she left him.

ℭℓℓℭ

"Do you understand what I require of you?" Jamot asked the man he had hired to learn of Ashton's daily habits. With cautious questioning, Jamot had discovered Morton's identity. He had only seen the baron once–at the blacksmith's shop. His inquiries had revealed the man was the maternal uncle for the Aldridge sisters, and the baron had accepted Satiné Aldridge as his "daughter," while Viscount Averette, the paternal uncle had taken in the middle girl Cashémere. Originally, Jamot had thought finding the Realm culprit would have been easy, but he had already spent a year in England, and he was no closer than he had been on the day he had arrived on English shores.

"I understand," the out-of-work shopkeeper said.

"You hold a previous acquaintance with Morton?" Jamot confirmed.

The shopkeeper ran a finger under his tight collar. "I conducted business with the baron on a regular basis."

"I wish to know everything you might discover. You will meet me here, one week from today with the information." They sat on the steps of a deserted hunting lodge, which Jamot had used of late for his hideaway. "You are to tell no one of our connection."

The Englishman nervously swallowed. "And I will be paid at that time?"

Jamot understood the man's reluctance to do business with anyone of Jamot's skin color. The English had a natural dislike of anyone not like them. Their prejudices fueled his desire to prove Mir correct. "Ah," Jamot pretended to comprehend. This man he hired as his eyes desperately required money because of an ailing wife and four small children. "You wish some assurance of your trouble being compensated. Am I correct?"

"I...I did not mean," the man stammered.

He had learned in his dealings with the English to assume their speech and their mannerisms. It assisted him in hiding the fact he despised the English race. The Englishmen who had stolen Mir's emerald were the reason he had been banished from his homeland. Mir would not welcome Jamot home until the Baloch knew success. Biting back his anger at the injustice, he pretended real concern for the man's misfortunes. "It is of no consequence. We know each other not." He reached into his pocket and withdrew ten pounds. He thrust the money into the man's hand and closed the shopkeeper's fingers about the paper. "Take this as a sign of our agreement."

The man looked relieved. "Thank you," he gushed. "I will not fail you."

"I knew you a man of trust when I first laid eyes upon your countenance." Jamot lied. "You are a man of honor."

*

He had returned to Berwick a little over three weeks prior, and each day Marcus had talked himself out of saddling Khan and riding to Manchester to claim her. Marcus's heart ached for something he might never have. He would not interfere if Lexford had chosen Cashé: Somehow Marcus would find the strength to walk away. Yet, the thought ripped his heart of shreds. If that scenario became a reality, he would find a means to divorce himself from Kimbolt's acquaintance. Marcus could not tolerate seeing Cashémere as Kimbolt's viscountess. Either way, destiny might cost him Lexford's friendship.

"A post, Sir." Marcus looked up to find his butler.

"Thank you," he said as he reached for the letter. Marcus turned it over to see the baron's insignia embedded in the wax, and his breath caught in his chest. "That will be all, Mr. Spear," he mumbled, deep in thought. Last week, he had received an update from Worthing on what "Shepherd" had learned of Averette. The irascible government contact had suspected Averette of siphoning off funds donated to the parish poor. However, the Realm required more specific information on Ashton's knowledge of Averette's perfidy, but their suspicions appeared true: The baron had, obviously, blackmailed Aldridge into leaving both Her Grace and Miss Cashémere behind.

With a deep breath and noticeably shaking hands, Marcus broke the seal on the letter and unfolded the pages. Then his heart lurched in surprise; the letter had come from her–from Cashé. Unconsciously, he brought it to his nose and inhaled deeply of the scent of jasmine–whether real or imagined, the fragrance would forever be implanted in his memory and associated with her. How she had wheedled her way into his very bruised soul, he did not know, but the lady's beautiful countenance lingered with him.

Marcus sipped the claret he had set aside only moments before. Leaning into the chair, he wondered whether he should be wary of Cashémere's words. His first response when he had seen the letter had been one of delight, but now his eyes searched the paper for words of endearment. If Cashé was to tell him she never wished to see him again, he did not want to read the page. Other than Trevor, he had lost everyone in his life for whom he cared deeply. Marcus was not certain he could tolerate losing her. The thought shocked him because he had never thought of her in that respect. Was she truly his to lose? His eyes fell to the first line to read,

My dearest Marcus,

I am certain receipt of this letter shall surprise you. I must admit to being quite devious in executing this sham. I have secured the baron's permission to write to Uncle Samuel, which I did, but for this second letter to my cousin Gwendolyn, I asked Mr. James to frank it before I wrote the directions. So, mayhap I should retract my salutation and instead say, "My dearest Gwendolyn."

Marcus laughed softly. She was a most ingenious creature. He would need to keep that particular fact in mind if he was to claim Cashé as his own.

Now that you understand how I have broken with propriety, my Heart, will you continue to read these words–words from someone who pines for your attendance, or will my inappropriate bravado spur you to throw these pages into the fireplace?

Throw the pages into the fire? Never! They would remain with him forever. He would place Cashé's words in a safe place–a place of honor–he would carry the letter near his heart, as he had once carried Maggie's strand of lace.

I suspect I should inform you of my manipulations with Lord Lexford. My commitment to directing His Lordship's attentions elsewhere are progressing. As I suspected, Satiné holds a tendance for Lord Lexford, and I have recruited my sister's aid in securing the viscount's interest.

Only Cashé, he thought. She was the one woman who would move a mountain if it foolishly stood in her way. Maybe that unconquerable determination fact was what he had recognized in her from the beginning–a certain boldness, which both infuriated and enticed him.

Satiné and I have agreed to a switch of sorts. Except for our upbringing, few people can tell us apart. So, we have begun to teach each other. Satiné is offering me lessons on deportment, and I have shared my experiences in Scotland.

Marcus thought of Ashton's closeness to Satiné. He would inform Worthing how the baron likely had first hand information on Averette's daily life. Marcus doubted Cashé realize what she knew of her uncle's Scottish home could play out in the bigger plans of the Realm. He would tell Worthing some story of how he had received a "thank you" letter from the baron's household as part of Marcus's saving of Velvet Aldridge from Murhad Jamot.

Regina Jeffers

In the next few days, the baron's sister, Lady Charlotte Resnick, and her children will pay a visit; and Satiné and I have agreed to an experiment in identity recognition–nothing elaborate–a walk through a room or a conversation over tea. As for His Lordship, Lord Lexford has not called at Chesterfield Manor since our return...

Marcus let out relief's sigh. He had spent several sleepless nights visualizing Kimbolt kissing Cashé as Marcus had kissed her. She had quite effectively allayed his fears without directly addressing his ego. He wondered if this knowledge of other people came naturally to her, or did Cashé only open herself to him?

As for His Lordship, Lord Lexford has not called at Chesterfield Manor since our return, but the baron has invited the viscount and others to an evening when Aunt Charlotte is in residence. If Satiné and I are successful with our relatives, then we shall mask our true identities with the viscount. I believe Lord Lexford bases his interest purely upon a faulty first impression. The viscount has never once asked my opinion or any topic or asked of my childhood. He knows nothing of my true person, and while he and I are reduced to such mundane topics as the weather, His Lordship regularly discusses politics and horses and other interests with my sister. Lord Lexford holds much in common with Satiné, but he has placed his affection with me. All we must do is to allow the viscount to woo "Cashémere" in Satiné's form. Then he will discover the truth: His Lordship affects Satiné, not Cashémere.

Marcus, too, had taken note of the ease with which his friend addressed Miss Satiné. He had based his hopes on the possibility. If he had admitted it, Marcus wanted a "happily ever after" for each of them.

Cashé's manipulations had impressed him. It was a courageous move, and he almost pitied Kimbolt. She had maneuvered everyone into doing her biding. Marcus recognized how even if Lord Lexford saw through the switch, Cashé would make his friend aware of his misplaced ardor simply by exposing the plan to mislead him. He wished he could be there to observe Cashé in action. He thought of the birthmark and wondered if Lexford had ever taken note of it.

I am not certain, my dearest one, if I shall have the means to inform you of the success or failure of this convoluted plan, but be aware, my Lord, of my sincerity in bringing Lord Lexford to know his heart and in allowing me to know mine. You once remarked on my comfortably asking you questions not suited to a lady of fashion, but surely you recognize that "comfortable" feeling, as something quite spectacular. I know little of the world, but in our separation, I have discovered a void of which I held no previous knowledge–a void which could only be filled by your presence.

Marcus, too, understood the void. He had experienced a powerful yearning since returning to Northumberland.

I realize what I write reeks of incommodious behavior, but I believe you will forgive me when I speak of our brief time together as the most important event of my short life.

It had been a turning point for him also. Since discovering Cashé, he had quit lamenting his losses, especially that of Maggie, and had begun planning a future.

I was changed by our encounter, and I question whether Fate finally brought into my life someone who saw me–saw Cashémere–and liked me even with my faults. I pray this letter has not lessened your regard for me.

Marcus recognized Cashé's unspoken need to find someone to love her. He had seen it written upon her countenance when she rushed into the Linworth morning room clutching her uncle's letter. Marcus had wanted to protect her from the evident loneliness; he had recognized a bit of himself in her anguish. Who did he have who loved only him? And he had missed her also: He had missed the sound of her laughter, the tilt of her defiant chin, the sparkle in those emerald green eyes, and the feel of her lips under his.

I must bid adieu, my Lord. Until we meet again in London, I remain your faithful friend with a heart devoted to your well being. My daily prayers begin and end with a plea for your safety and happiness.
In affection,
Cashémere

Although Marcus had understood Cashé's carefully worded closing, the fact she had not proclaimed her love bothered him. She had expressed her continued loyalty to him. He assured his heart it was too early for declarations of love; yet, he had wanted Cashé to love him. Marcus had required a balm as much as she.

Rather than to return to his ledgers, he reshuffled the letter's pages and began to reread it. He doubted he would be able to put it down–at least, not until he had memorized each word. "Ah, Cashé," he moaned aloud. "Thank you, Sweetling, for realizing I required something upon which to place my hopes."

ꞁꞁꞁ

"Aunt Charlotte," Satiné called as she led Cashé into the room. "We are so pleased to have you at your former home again." Satiné kissed Morton's sister. Cashé wondered on her own mother. How would Chenille Morton Aldridge have looked if she had not died in a freak accident? Except for her eyes, Cashé had never thought she had resembled the Aldridge clan. She and Satiné possessed a brighter version of their father's features; but now as she searched the countenance of the woman who was her mother's elder sister, she saw Velvet's eyes and the rich black hair they each possessed. Mayhap she belonged with the Mortons, after all.

Cashé's dropped a curtsy and murmured, "Lady Resnick."

"Oh, give me none of that, Girl," the woman enveloped Cashé in a tight embrace. "I am forever your Aunt Charlotte." She set Cashé from her to study Cashé's countenance. "My–my. You do so look like our Satiné and your mother, our Chenille."

Cashé could not resist a snide remark slipping out, "I suppose that resemblance would make me your Cashémere."

Her aunt barked out a laugh. "I suppose you are, Child." She snaked her arm about Cashé's waist before turning to the baron. "She has Chenille's spunk."

The baron smiled indulgently. "That she does, my Dear. Our Cashémere possesses Chenille's nature."

Cashé basked in their praise. She always wanted to belong somewhere. Although she had given them her absolute loyalty, she had never felt a part of Samuel Aldridge's family. Now, her aunt and uncle's references to her mother made Cashé wonder if that particular fact was the secret to her grandmother Kentigerna's constant reprimands over Cashé's too defiant

143

personality. Was she too much like Chenille Morton, a woman Kentigerna had never thought good enough for Edward Aldridge?

"What am I?" Satiné demanded, not happy–a bit jealous of the attention Cashé garnered.

"Oh, Darling," Aunt Charlotte caressed Satiné's cheek. "You are our mother reincarnated. Is she not, Charles?"

The baron looked lovingly at Satiné. "She very much is, Charlotte. Satiné embodies our mother's elegance."

Charlotte turned Cashé toward the twenty-something year old man and woman waiting politely for their part of the reunion. "You must remember your cousins," Lady Resnick continued.

Cashé flushed. She had seen neither for more than decade. "I assure you I would not have known either."

The young man stepped forward to accept Cashé's extended hand. "We are pleased to have you among us, Cashémere." He brought her hand to his lips.

"Thank you, John." She smiled largely. "When last I saw you, you were off to school and thought yourself quite above the rest of us."

"I do not recall it that way," he blustered.

But his very enceinte sister interrupted. "Miss Cashé recalls it exactly. You were quite the prig for the first two years."

Despite being a bit envious of her cousins' relaxed interplay, Cashé laughed. "I am pleased to see you, Rose." She had missed so much of her life while locked away in Scotland.

"All of me." Rose Croft, Viscountess Simonson, lovingly patted her stomach.

John assisted his sister to a chair. "Yes, all of you, Rose," he teased.

"Let us have tea and catch up on family," the baron declared as he motioned to a maid to bring in the waiting tray. "Satiné, if you will serve, I would appreciate it. You are the most accomplished of hostesses."

Cashé noted how Satiné preened with their uncle's words, while recognizing the man knew his ward's weakness for praise. Learning how each member of her family responded to the other was turning into a heady experience for Cashémere.

"Look who I found in the village," the baron announced to the room as he led Aidan Kimbolt through the drawing room door. Cashé saw Satiné cringe with the viscount's entrance. After a successful walk through during the morning hours, Cashé had convinced Satiné to attempt a longer switch over tea with their Aunt Charlotte. Their cousins had called on their paternal half brother, and the twins had thought, which really meant Cashé had thought, with only their aunt present, they might practice their deception. Cashé had assured her sister even if they misspoke, Aunt Charlotte would be unaware of the error.

Now, with Uncle Charles and Viscount Lexford as members of their party, they must tend to detail. Catching her sister's hand, Cashé led Satiné in a curtsy. She could feel Satiné's racing pulse and trembling fingers. "Your Lordship," Cashé murmured and made herself look the viscount in the eye. Satiné barely whispered his name.

Lexford came forward and took Cashé's right hand and brought it to his lips. "Miss Satiné," he said, "it feels an eternity since we last saw each other."

The fact he had called her by the wrong name gave Cashé confidence, and she smiled largely at him. "Lord Lexford, we did not expect you until the end of the week." She gave her sister's hand a squeeze to bring Satiné to attention.

"'Tis true." He laughed softly. "But I called upon my man of business in Manchester and stopped to take a small meal at The Orange Frog, but your uncle spotted my horse and insisted upon my accompanying him to Chesterfield to greet his sister."

Cashé stepped slightly to the side and gestured to Satiné. "Of course, you will say your greetings to my sister first. I assure you Lady Resnick will demand your undivided attention." She giggled from the excitement and the absurdity of the situation. "Is that not correct, Aunt Charlotte?"

Her aunt rose slowly to her feet. "As the baron has spoken so highly of the gentlemen who aided in our dear Velvet's rescue, I am most anxious to form an acquaintance with the viscount."

"Remember, I warned you, Your Lordship." Cashé giggled again.

Lexford smiled indulgently. "Then I will claim Miss Aldridge's hand before I devote myself to Lady Resnick's inquiry." He took Satiné's extended hand, much as he had Cashé's, but the viscount lingered a few extra second over Satiné's knuckles. Cashé watched carefully as Satiné blushed and a spark lit in Lexford's eyes. She had been correct about their natural connection. "You are looking well, Miss Aldridge."

"Thank you, Your Lordship." Satiné's color rose higher.

The baron touched Lexford's shoulder. "Permit me, Lexford, to introduce my sister, Lady Charlotte Resnick." Charlotte offered him her hand while Lexford bowed again. "Charlotte, may I present His Lordship, Aidan Kimbolt, Viscount Lexford, of Lexington Arms in Cheshire."

"I have heard good things of you, Sir. You must know you hold a tender place in my heart for what you and Yardley and Thornhill did for our family."

Lexford nodded his head in acknowledgment. "It is what is expected of a gentleman," the viscount insisted as he supported Lady Resnick to her seat. "Besides, Thornhill and Yardley and I have established a kinship many years ago. They would serve me in a like manner."

Charlotte Resnick smiled at her brother. "Charles once knew a similar relationship with five other gentlemen, but time and distance has weakened their bond."

The baron corrected, "Not weakened so much as delayed...my friends and I have all taken on families and titles and responsibilities, but our devotion to one another remains."

"We were seven strong," Lexford confided. "Thornhill and Yardley and I share our memories with James Kerrington, Viscount Worthing; Sir Carter Lowery; Gabriel Crowden, the Marquis of Godown; and Baron John Swenton. We have been quite inseparable for nearly a decade, but both Worthing and Thornhill have married. Soon, I am certain we will mimic Ashton's experience." Neither the baron nor Lexford mentioned the Realm, but all understood the implications.

The baron glanced at the girls. "Satiné, why do you not serve the tea?"

Without thinking, Satiné began to pour before she realized they all looked at her askance. They saw her as Cashé. She blushed, but managed to say, "I apologize, Satiné, I did not mean to usurp your position in Uncle Charles's household. In Scotland, serving tea was part of my domain, and I reached for the set before I thought."

Cashé expelled a deep sigh. "I hold no qualms, dear Sister, in occasionally abdicating my responsibilities to you. Uncle Charles does not mind, do you, Sir?"

"Of...of course...I possess no objections," he stammered. "I have depended upon Satiné to serve as my hostess for years, but I should have thought you should also assume those duties. You are my family...our family. Forgive me, Cashémere, if I have inadvertently slighted you in any way."

146

Cashé bit back the tears as her twin answered in her stead. "I was never offended, Uncle Charles," she whispered hoarsely. "You have given me a home," Satiné confessed what Cashé had said only last week, "when no one else would."

Cashé bit her lip harder to stifle the emotions. "Let us not become maudlin," she declared on a rasp. "This is a time for celebration. We are together."

"Here, here," the baron agreed. "We will always be family."

Chapter Ten

"We did it!" Cashé declared with gusto when she and Satiné slipped into her twin's room. "It was exhilarating!"

"I was petrified." Satiné sank into a nearby chair.

"I thought we were surely discovered when Uncle Charles brought Lord Lexford to tea." The excitement bubbled over. "And you, dear Sister, were so clever. When you starting serving, I expected Uncle Charles to expose our scheme, but you acted quickly and distracted him."

"Look at my hand," Satiné extended her open palm. "I am still shaking."

Cashé caught her sister's hand and knelt before Satiné's chair. "Yet, it proves what we surmised all along. The viscount does not affect me as a person. He could not tell us apart, and I know you felt his regard when he kissed your hand."

"It was quite singular," Satiné gushed.

"I suspect we should not attempt a switch at Uncle Charles's dinner party," Cashé advised. "But during the evening, I will suggest His Lordship should call upon the household soon. When he does, you must make him lose his heart to you, not to a face, which happens to resemble mine."

A frown crossed Satiné's countenance. "What if His Lordship turns against me because of our deceit?"

"It shan't happen. Even if Lord Lexford discovers our perfidy, the man will never turn his back on love. Lord Yardley confided how the viscount had suffered a loss when he first returned to England. The viscount seeks a love match."

Satiné sighed heavily. "As do I."

"When did ye last hear from Miss Cashémere?" Charters calmly asked Samuel Aldridge. He had made himself call on the viscount before he chose his recourse.

"We received a letter just yesterday." Averette did not hide his disdain.

Charters, likewise, did not hide his disgust. "Ye would not be tellin' me if'n I did not ast. Ye be less than willin' to keep me informed of late."

Aldridge walked around the desk. "What do you want, Charters?"

"I wish to know when my intended plans to return to her childhood home." Charters sat forward to press his point.

Aldridge snarled, "Do you wish to read the letter yourself?" The viscount reached behind him to lift a stack of correspondence from his desk.

Charters did not give an inch. "Ye may summarize."

"Cashémere is with her maternal uncle, Charles Morton, in Manchester, and she and her sister Satiné are preparing for a London Season."

"And why would Miss Cashémere be requiring a London Season if'n the girl be promised to me?" Charters grumbled.

"I am no longer making the decisions for my niece," Aldridge confessed.

"Then who be doin' so? This other uncle?" Charters cracked his knuckles.

Aldridge resumed his seat. "Charles Morton has assumed control of his nieces."

"Kin ye not do somethin'?"

Aldridge's anger showed. "It is not within my power at this time. The Duke of Thornhill, Viscount Worthing, and my brother by marriage hold the power in an English court, especially over an Englishman living his entire life in Scotland. I am in a no man's land when it comes to my legal rights."

"I thought ye be sayin' the girl simply be requirin' some freedom. Now, it be soundin' as if Cashémere not be returnin' ever," Charters accused.

Aldridge swallowed hard. "I am afraid your assumption is the gist of the situation. Ashton has assumed Cashémere's care. I have no recourse."

"Then ye be findin' a way to repay Charters," the man spoke of himself in the third person. He rose to his feet, his business finished.

149

"I will be expectin' payment within a fortnight," he warned. Then he strode from the room, not looking back.

Outside, Charters' servant scrambled to bring the man's horse around. "Ye be gonnae home, Sir?" he asked, giving the man a leg up.

"For the moment," Charters disclosed. "But I be havin' other plans t'morrow."

Marcus sat on the nearest hillside looking down upon his estate: gazing upon his grounds men as they attended the landscaping and at the busy stable yard; yet his mind was full of thoughts of her, as it was, at least, fifty times per day. Of late, he had envisioned Cashé on his stairway, by the open window in his drawing room, and waiting by the door for his return home. "God, it is a long time until the new Season," he grumbled, as the image of her faded. "Can I exist without seeing her for another four months?"

Over the past few days he had considered riding to Manchester on some business pretense just to be close to her–just to call at the baron's estate and have tea in the same room as she. He would ride however many days it would take just to be her companion for a few hours. He suspected himself quite addicted to the woman, even though, he had actually only held her in his arms four times–at the tarn, on the dance floor, in her chambers, and in the Linworth stables. His heart knew each moment well. "Dare I chance it?" he questioned.

Before he could decide, the stable yard's increased activity caught his notice. The head groomsman ran toward the servant quarters, and Marcus looked in the direction to which one of his tenants pointed. A plume of smoke rose in the early morning, graying the sky with a curtain of ash. "The mill," he said in recognition, and immediately he slapped Khan's flanks with his heels.

"My Lord," Cashé dipped a curtsy as she joined Lexford on the balcony before the baron's other guests gathered for the evening's supper.

"Ah, Miss Aldridge," he said as he turned to her. "You look lovely this evening." Lexford captured her hand to kiss her knuckles.

Cashé swallowed the urge to jerk her hand away. Although this evening played into her overall plans, she felt disloyal to Marcus. "Thank you, Lord Lexford." She stood beside the brick balustrade leading to the upper gardens. "It is good to have you in my uncle's home again, Sir."

"I would have called sooner, Miss Aldridge, but I thought it appropriate to allow you time to recover your family." He sat on the ledge, making them closer in height. "Yet, you must know, Miss Cashémere, my heart decried the action."

Cashé forced a smile to her lips. "I fear our acquaintance shall suffer this evening. Uncle Charles plans for me to meet many of his dearest friends. That scenario is why I sought you before I am called away to my duties." She touched his arm lightly to press her point. "I had hoped I might prevail upon you to call at the end of next week, once Aunt Charlotte and my cousins retire to Shropshire."

A full smile lit Lexford's countenance. "I would be honored, Miss Aldridge."

Cashé bit back relief's sigh. "I must warn you, Lord Lexford, I have been taking lessons from my sister. You may experience moments when you think yourself speaking to Satiné."

Lexford frowned. "I hope not too much so. I find I am quite fond of Cashémere Aldridge."

"Yet, my Lord," she said coyly, "I have taken note of how my sister holds your interest equally as well as I." Cashé feared Satiné might forget her role, and she meant to counter her twin's mistakes in advance.

"Be still, my heart," Lexford taunted. "Perhaps the lady finds herself jealous of her own sister."

Cashé thought, if His Lordship only knew. "You cannot claim, my Lord, that my countenance outshines Satiné's, as we have the same look," she reasoned.

Lexford scowled. "Obviously, there is a marked resemblance, but you wound me, if you think I might not recognize the difference."

Cashé swallowed hard to hide her amusement, but a smile broke her mouth's line. "I would hope you recognize the differences, my Lord," she said merrily, realizing he had not known Satiné had been she when they last met. "You must agree, my Lord, you and my sister find a commonality, and I plan to make myself more aware of what interests you, Lord Lexford."

"I am touched by your willingness to acclimate yourself to my world."

Cashé realized her over zealousness; she did not want Lord Lexford's regard to deepen. She quickly decided on a different tactic. "You must admit, Sir, Satiné would make any man the perfect companion."

"Absolutely," he acknowledged. "I am certain Lord Yardley would agree."

Cashé schooled her expression, but the idea of Yardley preferring Satiné did not sit well with her. "I love my sister, but I cannot conceive of her with the earl," she countered. "If for no other reason than Northumberland being a much harsher climate; Satiné might find survival in the shire's remoteness foreign to her."

Lexford looked away, a recognized grief dulling his eyes. "I would not wish the earl to know another loss."

Cashé heard Marcus's voice saying something similar of Lexford. "I agree. Each of us deserves happiness wherever he finds it. I would sincerely wish you such contentment, my Lord, whether that happiness involves me or someone like my sister or even some other woman."

Lexford's gaze narrowed. "That is very magnanimous of you, my Dear, but I have no intention of looking elsewhere."

Cashé realized she had pushed her own agenda too hard. "I meant speak no disrespect. My words only acknowledged the fact you and the earl have sacrificed much for your ideals. It would be an aberration if your sacrifice did not lead to a fulfilling life upon your return home. As Viscount Worthing did with Eleanor and His Grace with Velvet, you must permit nothing to stand in your way. Choose what brings you happiness."

"That is a very mature statement, Miss Aldridge," he observed warily.

Cashé thought it time to pull in her lines. She was using Marcus's casting lessons, after all. "I, too, Lord Lexford, have had a less than stellar way, and I am determined to know contentment, and you must promise me you shall seek the same, no matter which path you must follow."

"Of course, Miss Aldridge. I would deny you nothing."

Cashé looked over her shoulder to the open doorway. "We must join the others, my Lord. I am certain Uncle Charles wonders of my whereabouts. Might I have the pleasure of your arm, Sir?"

Lexford stood and offered his support. "You never cease to amaze me, my Dear."

Marcus collapsed into a chair in his chambers. He had fought beside his men and his tenants and the local villagers for hours, but they had managed to save the mill from complete structural ruin; however, he had lost two men in the blaze–two families who would know Death intimately. Sometimes, he felt his efforts brought nothing but evil to Tweed Hall. Exhausted, too weary to argue even with himself, Marcus rubbed his dirty palm over his face. "I require a bath," he grumbled as he struggled to his feet. "And I must call upon the families of the deceased to assure them I will not turn them out."

Tomorrow, he would lead his men in repairing the mill. He held no choice. The harvest rested in the surrounding barns. Winter would call within the next month. His tenants and the estate required the mill so they might prepare the different crops. Marcus would work night and day to make things right.

"This chaos is what happens when I covet what is not mine. It is God's warning," he chastised himself, but Marcus knew he would never turn his mind and his heart from Cashé. Even partnered with a touch of wariness, he accepted his fate whole-heartedly.

Marcus had no idea what had awakened him. The house creaked and moaned, but every house did. Yet, he remained on alert. Over the years with Wellington's army and as part of the Realm, he had learned to listen to his instincts, and those instincts told him something was amiss. He edged the coverlet away from his body and swung his legs over the bed's edge. Reaching for his breeches, he drew them on before slipping a shirt over his head.

Another board popped loudly in the hallway, and Marcus retrieved his gun from the nightstand. Someone moved through the empty passageway. A brush of a soft shoe on the carpet told him his suspicions proved accurate. He crossed the cold floor of his master chambers–quickly and quietly and eased the latch. Then his heart stopped: A shadow had entered Trevor's room.

Taking a deep breath to steady his nerves, Marcus slid out into the darkness–clinging to the wall–surveying each dark corner and recess for other intruders. Yet, before he could surprise the interloper, a blood-curdling scream set him into action.

Marcus burst through the door to Trevor's room, immediately diving forward and rolling to a squatted position. Gunfire and a guttural scream welcomed his entrance. Marcus, pointing his gun at a man he recognized despite the darkened room, came to stand in the room's middle. Murhad Jamot held Trevor by the neck, squeezing his brother's Adam's apple. His sibling attempted desperately to free himself, but the Baloch was too strong for Trevor's pudgy body.

"Release him," Marcus demanded. "Your fight is with me, Jamot."

The Baloch grinned sinisterly. "Ah, Yardley, it is nice to know you expected my arrival." Trevor attempted to break away, but Jamot tightened his hold.

Marcus shot a glance at his brother. "Trevor!" he barked. "Stop fighting him."

The anger in Marcus's voice quailed Trevor's struggle, and Jamot minutely loosened his hold so Marcus's brother might breath easier. Marcus silently gave thanks. He knew Mir's henchman was capable of snapping Trevor's neck.

"What do you want?" Marcus growled as he edged closer, looking for a clear shot. The moon streaked the room's occupants on the left, and the dying fire added a glow on the right, but Marcus could not delineate Jamot's and Trevor's forms completely.

"The emerald," Jamot flatly replied.

Marcus snarled, "There is no emerald."

"There is, my friend, and I will find it." Jamot tugged Trevor backward, dragging him toward the open doorway.

Marcus and the Baloch were in a slow dance of death, each circling to remain facing the other. "If there is an emerald, you will not discover it at Tweed Hall. I brought nothing with me from Persia besides a hatred for Shaheed Mir's justice."

"It was Fowler who removed Ashmita from our camp. You and your friends have stolen our women and our jewels," Jamot accused.

"Is that the reason you are in England, Jamot? You were not enough man to defend the woman you wanted, so you pay your penitence in this blind search?"

Jamot back stepped to reach the door. "It is you who are blind, Yardley. One of your group knows of the emerald's existence, and he puts the others in danger. Mir will never rest until the emerald is returned."

154

As he spoke the last word, he shoved Trevor into Marcus, sending both to the floor.

Marcus wrestled Trevor from him, ordering his brother to stay in his room, as he rushed into the hallway to follow Jamot. Marcus listened closely to the man's retreat before giving chase. The Baloch made his way toward the second level. Footmen from the lowest level of the house could also be heard racing toward his location, but Marcus concentrated on Jamot's breathing. He could hear the fear as another vase crashed to the floor.

"My Lord?" Jeremy appeared in a doorway, a raised fireplace poker in his hand.

"Stay with Trevor!" Marcus ordered and began his descent to the lower level–his gun leading the way. He jumped over the banister and landed nimbly on the carpet runner just in time to see Jamot crawling through a draft window. A small salute heralded the Baloch's escape before the man descended a rose lattice.

Marcus turned instinctively toward the footmen rushing up the main staircase. "Outside!" he ordered, shoving past his men. "He went out the window!" Despite being barefooted, Marcus bolted to the latched doorway, jerking it open, and set off at a run. Rounding the house's corner, he saw Jamot mount a waiting horse. Although he knew the distance too much for the handgun he carried throughout the chase, Marcus took his best shot.

"Shall we follow him, my Lord?" one of the footmen asked as he skidded to a halt behind Marcus.

"Have several men secure the area, but our interloper will not return tonight." Marcus turned toward the house.

The footman still stared in the direction of the retreating form. "Did you recognize him, my Lord? Should we contact the magistrate?"

"I will speak to the authorities, but Lord Summers will never find our trespasser. The man will resurface only when he is ready." He motioned to his men. "Let us see what damage has been done. Send someone to the kitchen and have him bring tea to my brother's room. Trevor will be quite frightened."

"Yes, my Lord."

Marcus returned to Trevor's room to find Jeremy with his arms about Trevor's shoulders, actually rocking Trevor in place. If the situation had not been so dire, Marcus would have found the scene comical.

Jeremy was nearly a head shorter and likely three stone lighter, but he encompassed Trevor in his embrace and gave Marcus's older brother the necessary comfort.

"Did you catch him?" Trevor demanded as Marcus entered.

"No." Marcus surveyed the room. His brother's clothing lay scattered about the floor. "He had an open window and a waiting horse."

Trevor's lips trembled. "I was afraid the bad man would kill you, and I would be left all alone."

"Murhad Jamot cannot kill me," Marcus said with a false bravado, as a means to allay Trevor's fears. "He has attempted to do so before, but Jamot is simply a hired henchman. He has no real interest in me." He reached for his brother's hand to pull him to his feet. "Jeremy will stay with you and help you straighten your room. Someone will bring you tea. I must secure the other rooms of the house. I have men outside guarding the grounds. No one will bother us again." Marcus gave Trevor a brief hug and led him to nearby chairs. "I want you to assist Jeremy with your room."

"Yes, Marcus." Trevor smiled shyly. "You were very brave."

"Just as were you, I was very frightened, but I was trained to fight the 'bad men' and to protect others. I will protect you, Trevor. I promised our father you would always have me."

"I know." Trevor looked at Marcus with renewed admiration. "I loved Myles, but I am glad you are the brother with whom I am to live."

"So am I." Marcus ruffled Trevor's hair. "Now, I must see to the estate. I will check on you in a bit."

Marcus reorganized as much of his study as he could. It would require a thorough cleaning, as would many of the rooms. Jamot had rummaged through closets and drawers, searching behind furniture and mirrors and paintings, but other than the disorder the man had created, the Baloch had caused no real harm.

Nearing three in the morning, he sat completely exhausted, unable even to muster enough energy to climb the steps to his chambers. Trevor had finally returned to his bed with the condition Jeremy would make up a pallet on the floor before the fireplace. Marcus had written Shepherd, Kerrington, and Fowler to tell them of the attack. He ought to notify the others, but he had convinced himself Shepherd would see to it, but, in case he judged poorly, he added an additional page to Kerrington's note, asking his former captain to inform Kimbolt, Crowden, and Swenton. Lowery would know when Shepherd was informed. In retrospect, none of his former associates mattered: The only one who mattered to Marcus was Cashé. He felt a compulsion to warn her, but he would be taking a great chance in doing so. If someone discovered his caution, he would be expected to declare himself. That possibility did not scare him as it once had done, but the discovery would destroy his friendship with Kimbolt, and, in reality, he wanted to protect the viscount's heart.

"What should I do, Sweetling?" he whispered to the empty room. Marcus took a sip of brandy and listened to his heart. Six weeks ago, Jamot had kidnapped Velvet Aldridge, and Marcus's life had altered. With a deep sigh, he took up his pen. He would warn Cashé directly; he could not tolerate the idea she might become Jamot's target. Whether he or Kimbolt acknowledged her, Cashé could become an objective for the Baloch. Jamot had proved previously he would use women and children in his fight against the Realm. Marcus would make the effort to warn her.

Ma Chère,

I must risk sending you this message. I will do everything possible to assure no other becomes aware of our communication. Yet, something extraordinary has happened, and I fear you may be in danger because of it.

Yesterday, my staff and I were called to a fire at the mill. It was minor as the damage is reparable, but we lost two good men in the effort. Although I held no inclination of this being more than an accident, this evening's events have led me to other conclusions.

Murhad Jamot, the man who kidnapped your sister, invaded my home after midnight, briefly taking my brother Trevor prisoner. Unfortunately, the man escaped before I could stop him. Do not stress yourself, my Dear. My family and staff are safe. However, Jamot's entrance so close to the mill accident appears more than suspicious.

Therefore, I am throwing propriety to the wind and am sending you this warning. You are my concern. I cannot bear the possibility of your being in danger. Please, my Darling, act prudently. Permit the baron, and even Viscount Lexford, to offer you protection in my absence. I realize you are a strong, independent woman, but promise me you will accept the good intentions of others in your behalf.

I will send this to you by my former batman. Mr. Breeson is an excellent man: He will be very discreet. I must ask you not to tell the others. I am certain Lord Lexford will receive the details of Jamot's invasion of my home from Kerrington, as will your uncle; yet I assumed they would act the gentlemen and would hide the facts from the women in their lives. I thought it best to speak to you directly, without interpretation. I also wished to allay any fears you might have of my safety if you heard it secondhand.

Please, my Dearest, practice caution in your actions. You must know my heart rests in your hands. There is not a day to go by without my reflecting on our short time together. I count the days until we are reacquainted in London. Your happiness is my only desire, but I pray it lies with me.

Marcus

"You sent for me, my Lord?" Marcus looked up to see Breeson standing at the study's door. Breeson had followed Marcus across Belgium before losing his arm at Waterloo. Upon Marcus's insistence, Richard Breeson had taken a position on the Wellston estate. Marcus's father and Myles had both agreed: As long as the man lived, Breeson would have a home with the Wellston family. Of course, neither he nor his former batman had expected Marcus one day to be the earl. Marcus's family had paid their debt to Breeson's loyalty by showing the man the respect many of Breeson's fellow soldiers knew not.

"Yes. I require your discretion in delivering a private message."

"Of course, Sir."

"At first light, I wish you to ride to Manchester and deliver this letter to a certain lady." Marcus applied the wax to the outside page.

Breeson looked pleased. "I must say, Sir, it is about time."

His former batman often spoke too frankly, even when he had served Marcus on the battlefield, but the man had displayed absolute devotion, and Marcus had blessed the day Richard Breeson had walked into his life. "The lady is an identical twin so be certain you speak to the correct woman."

"A twin?" Breeson mused with delight.

"Keep your observations," Marcus warned with a wry grin.

Breeson reached for the letter. "Is the lady pretty, my Lord?"

Marcus remembered such conversations throughout their relationship. The older man had taken a fatherly attitude towards Marcus. "Very pretty, Richard. You may judge for yourself when you meet her."

"It will be my pleasure, my Lord."

༺༻

Discovering the fact Lord Yardley's lady could often be found alone had surprised Breeson. The lady's sister and uncle regularly rode out, leaving Yardley's love interest to her own devices. Even more unexpectedly, the baron's staff had readily provided the details. Breeson quickly understood His Lordship's concerns and why the earl would risk contacting the woman. The baron had not schooled his staff on handling a questionable situation. Yardley's estate had sustained an attack. Breeson knew Wellston's personality: The earl had felt compelled to protect a woman for whom he cared, and this woman was a twin. It spoke of the earl's nightmare–his not being able to save his own twin.

Breeson waited patiently for the baron and his niece's departure. Within a few minutes, as predicted by one of the grounds keepers, the earl's lady appeared in the upper garden alone. Breeson paused long enough to be certain of her solitary endeavors, and then he approached. "May I speak to you, my Lady?" he asked from some distance–aware he might frighten her.

Surprisingly, the girl rose to confront him. "If this is something to do with the estate, you must wait for my sister's return. I am Miss Cashémere, not Miss Satiné." She sounded as if she had said the words many times.

Breeson offered another bow. "Then I have chosen the correct sister. I have a message for Miss Aldridge from Lord Yardley."

A smile exploded on the girl's face. "Lord Yardley?"

"Yes, Miss. I am Richard Breeson. I served His Lordship on the Continent, and when I sustained an injury at a Frenchie's hands, Lord Yardley provided me a position on his estate."

Her face lit with happiness. "Lord Yardley sent me a message?"

"Yes, Miss." When the girl did not move, Breeson suggested, "Might we step inside a moment? I would prefer others did not see us together."

The girl blushed in embarrassment, but she found her reason and motioned Breeson to the open patio door. When they entered the room, the lady closed and locked the library door. "Tell me," she said as she rushed to the man's side, "that His Lordship is well."

"Lord Yardley is safe, Miss. We had a bit of trouble, but His Lordship can handle himself quite well."

"Trouble?" the girl asked anxiously.

"I am certain my Lord explains everything in his letter," Breeson assured. "The earl is not injured, so rest your worry."

"Do you have a moment so I might read what His Lordship says before you leave? I may have a return reply for him."

Breeson smiled indulgently. "Yes, Miss."

The lady broke the seal and walked away to read in semi-privacy. Breeson watched her carefully. The girl did not resemble any of Wellston's former lady friends, but the batman supposed that opposition was the reason the earl, obviously, favored this one. He could never imagine Yardley risking contacting an unmarried woman without a serious tendance existing between them. The girl sighed heavily and then refolded the letter. Yardley must have said what she most wanted to hear.

"Thank you, Mr. Breeson, for riding all this way and for bringing me His Lordship's message." She impetuously caught the man's hand.

"It was my pleasure, Miss." He laughed nervously.

The girl shot a glance toward the locked door. "I realize you have little time, but would you tell me how you served His Lordship in the war?"

"I was his batman. Do you know the term, Miss?"

"Yes, I am familiar with it."

"He is a fine gentleman, Miss–one of the finest I have ever known."

She giggled self-consciously. "You have no need to convince me, Mr. Breeson." She bit her bottom lip nervously. "Would you take a note to His Lordship?"

"If you make it a short one," he agreed.

The lady nodded and rushed to the small desk in the corner. She removed foolscap, ink, and a pen. Again, Breeson watched her. She was a bold one, a good match for Wellston. His Lordship was always one of the first ones into a battle or a scuffle. Breeson had always thought the young lord had wanted to punish himself for not saving his own sister. And despite the man's compulsion to save others, Wellston had matured

160

into an honorable man. Tweed Hall had suffered from multiple tragedies, which had polluted the family for years, but Breeson had always believed it would be Marcus Wellston who would change the family's luck.

Folding the single sheet of paper, Miss Aldridge rushed to where Breeson waited. "I trust you will refrain from reading my note," she warned.

"Of course, Miss."

She led Breeson toward the patio entrance. "I thank you again, Mr. Breeson. Assure His Lordship I will practice caution."

"Yes, Miss." Breeson presented an awkward bow. "For my part, Miss Aldridge, I would see you at Tweed Hall soon."

Cashé blushed. "Yet, you know nothing of me, Mr. Breeson."

"But I know Lord Yardley, and the earl would not choose a woman without merit. It is not of His Lordship's nature." The man smiled knowingly. "And might I add, Miss Aldridge, Lord Yardley's comment regarding your beauty was perfectly correct."

"Lord Yardley described me as beautiful?" she gushed.

"He did, Miss." Mr. Breeson squeezed her hand with his one good one. "Make the man happy, and you will earn my devotion."

"Tell His Lordship I expect him in London." Cashé laughed with a renewed spirit. "You have no idea how happy you have made me, Mr. Breeson–even with Lord Yardley's warning of danger."

"Farewell, Miss." The man cautiously looked about before exiting.

"Mr. Breeson." She caught his upper arm. "Give His Lordship this." Cashé went on tiptoes and kissed the man's cheek.

"Lord Yardley may strike me, but I will deliver your message, Miss Aldridge." He laughed lightly before slipping into the landscaped hedgerows.

Clinging to the doorway until she could see Mr. Breeson no longer, Cashé watched his departure; then she rushed to her chambers so she might read Marcus's letter again. He had called her his "Dearest" and had said she carried his heart in her hands. Deliriously happy, she locked her chamber door and flopped on the bed. He had broken with convention to warn her because he cared for her, and Marcus had told Mr. Breeson she was beautiful. Cashé could not stop the image of Marcus's desire-filled eyes from forming. The thought budded her breasts' nipples, and she groaned audibly. "London," she whispered. "It cannot come soon enough."

"What is it, Uncle?" Satiné asked, noting the baron's brows furrowing in dismay.

"This letter asks me to come to London." He looked up, taking in both girls' countenances. "It is from the man known as 'Shepherd,' the one currently overseeing the Realm."

"Is something amiss, Sir?" Cashé asked innocently. She had pretended no knowledge of Lord Yardley's attack.

Morton frowned again. "I am not certain; but as it is a matter of the British government, I feel I must concur. Possibly, there is new information on Velvet's abduction."

"Would they not simply send you some sort of report?" Satiné asked in concern.

The baron reasoned, "Maybe it is too sensitive to risk losing the information."

Satiné appeared uncomfortable. "Why would those in charge not ask Viscount Lexford to deliver the message?"

"I am uncertain." The baron folded the letter and placed it in an inside pocket. In his doing so, Cashé suddenly remembered his taking Uncle Samuel's parting letter and executing the same move. She had never finished reading Samuel Aldridge's farewell, but she recalled her uncle's accusations against Charles Morton. Recalled Uncle Samuel's allegations that the baron had planned to ruin him and how she was not to believe anything her mother's only brother had to say about her parents' deaths.

For a few brief seconds, Cashé considered questioning her Uncle Charles about Samuel Aldridge's charges, but she bit back the words. It was not the right time. Instead, she said, "Viscount Lexford is to call on Friday. Shall I send word for him to delay his visit?"

"No." Her Uncle Charles appeared nervous. "I would like to think Lexford was in the house if some renewed danger is the issue. You girls may serve as each other's chaperone. I trust Satiné to oversee Lexford's courtship. I will return by Monday at the latest, especially if I leave on the morrow. Ask the viscount to stay until my return."

Satiné shot a quick glance at Cashé. "Yes, Uncle. You will be careful, Sir?"

"Have no fear, my Dear. I am not some green boy who has not seen the world's evils. Nothing of consequence will occur. I will send Lexford a note explaining my departure and ask his protection be extended to my home."

Distracted by her own thoughts, Cashé kept playing in her mind the scene of Uncle Charles taking her in his arms at Linton Park. Something was different, but she could not remember all the details. While the baron was away, and whileSatiné secured the viscount's affections, she would look for the letter. Her Uncle Samuel had addressed his words to her, and Cashé wanted it: She had a right to it.

Chapter Eleven

"Did you speak to Miss Aldridge?" Not waiting for Mr. Spear to announce the man, Marcus met Breeson in the main foyer.

"Have you ever sent me upon a journey where I did not complete your wishes, my Lord?"

Marcus ignored the smugness playing across his friend's face. He led the man to his study, closing the door and pouring Breeson a much-deserved brandy before seating himself across from the man. "Tell me everything," he said.

Breeson took a long swallow of the brandy. He had known Wellston since taking on the position as his "man" when the young Marcus bought a commission. He had seen the boy become a man. "First, I should tell you I found the baron's staff too willing to share the household secrets with a complete stranger. With a few well phrased questions, I knew the comings and goings of Baron Ashton and both nieces."

That news brought Marcus new qualms. For the past two nights, he had dreamed of Cashé being in danger and his not being able to reach her in time. After this encounter with Breeson, he would send Lexford a carefully worded letter suggesting the viscount do a survey of the baron's ability to protect the Aldridge sisters. Everyone thought he preferred Miss Satiné; hopefully, no one would find anything peculiar with his interest in the baron's household. "I will see what I can do. Thank you, my Friend."

"That being said," Breeson took up the tale, "I waited for the baron and the one known as Miss Satiné to depart for their daily ride, and then approached your Miss Aldridge."

Marcus prayed she was his Miss Aldridge. "No one observed your entrance?" Marcus asked anxiously. Marcus would not have Cashé's reputation ruined.

"No one observed me, my Lord. Each day, while her family rides, Miss Aldridge spends time in the garden. When the lady appeared, I approached and asked to speak to her privately in your name, and the lady led me into the library to be away from prying eyes."

"Did Miss Aldridge welcome my letter?" Marcus pressed.

Breeson winked. "The lady affects you, my Lord. Have no fear in that manner." He took another sip of the brandy, obviously, relishing Yardley's eagerness. "Miss Aldridge's first wish was to know of your well being."

Marcus breathed easier. "Was the lady in health?" he asked deep in thoughts of Cashé.

Breeson grinned knowingly. "The lady is quite well." He paused, elongating what he would share next. "Miss Aldridge is quite as beautiful as you said, my Lord. I observed both young ladies, and although the women appear identical on the surface, Miss Cashémere is the superior choice."

Marcus chuckled. "The world believes I prefer Miss Satiné."

"How could anyone who knows you think as such? I should not disparage Miss Satiné, but even from my brief observation, I recognized the lady is too biddable. You require a challenge. Just the fact Miss Aldridge risked being caught accepting a letter from you tells me she is of the nature that most suits you, my Lord. I found her quite bold."

Marcus confided what he had not voiced to anyone else. "Viscount Lexford staked a claim to Miss Cashémere months prior. How do I deny my interests to advance my friend's happiness?"

Marcus was certain Breeson would observe the feelings Marcus could no longer conceal. "Would it make the viscount happy to know he had brought torment to you and Miss Aldridge? What I know of the man says Lord Lexford would step aside. Besides, the lady prefers you, my Lord. Miss Aldridge asked me to remind you of your required presence in London."

"I want nothing to come between Lexford and me. We pledged a bond to protect each other. The viscount has saved my life on numerous occasions," Marcus reasoned aloud.

Breeson countered, "As you have done for him."

"Yes, I suppose." Marcus looked off, seeing something Breeson did not. "Lord Lexford has known a great loss."

"As have you, my Lord." Breeson paused. "It would seem the thing, which bonded you to your friends, was the common feeling of loss. The empathy created a brotherhood. And although I wish His Lordship his own happiness, I disagree with the idea you do not deserve felicity."

Marcus did not respond for several minutes, lost in his own revelry. "Thank you, Breeson, for taking on this task in my name." He shifted as if to stand.

"Then you do not wish the lady's note?" Breeson teased. "After I risked my good name as your courier?"

"Miss Aldridge sent me something?" Marcus sat forward, extending his hand.

"I thought so." Breeson rose to his feet and pretended to search his pockets for the single sheet of paper. "Now, what did I do with it?"

"Not humorous." Marcus followed Breeson to his feet, gesturing for his man to find Cashé's note.

"Ah, here it is." Breeson made a grand flourish of pulling the paper from an inside pocket of his coat and keeping it out of Marcus's reach.

"Hand it over, Breeson, if you value your position on this estate," Marcus growled.

Breeson barked out a laugh. "You really affect the girl. Well, that is a good thing." He delivered the note. "Because the lady asked me to give you this." Without ceremony, he placed a peck of a kiss on his master's cheek before casually strolling away from a totally flustered Wellston. "Enjoy your day, my Lord," the former batman called over his shoulder.

Marcus blustered as his fingers wiped the unexpected kiss away, but then the reality hit him: Cashé had sent him a kiss, and, instantly, a smile spread across his face. "You deserve a raise, Breeson," he called good-naturedly after the man's retreating form. Then Marcus collapsed in his previously vacated chair, ignoring what his actions did to his clothing. He took a deep breath to slow his rapidly beating heart. Slowly, he unfolded the paper to read Cashé's hastily written response.

My dearest Marcus,
You have brought me the greatest happiness today, and although I grieve for the pain you have experienced and the danger you have endured, my heart embraces the knowledge you have thought to protect me. I wish I had the time to tell you everything, but know my plan of a switch has progressed to a point where, over tea this week, Satiné and I fooled Aunt Charlotte, Uncle Charles, and Lord Lexford. Soon, Satiné will win the viscount's heart, and we may be together without guilt or regret. Believe in me, my Lord, for I believe in you. Yours forever,
Cashémere

"Forever," Marcus murmured. "Dare I think in terms of forever–of knowing contentment–of knowing only her?" He chuckled softly. "The lady will likely drive me insane with her manipulations and demands." Marcus sighed, realizing he held no hope of forgetting the pleasure of being with Cashé. "But what a way to go mad!"

ﾟ

"Lord Lexford," Satiné greeted the viscount, "thank you for coming to Manchester earlier than planned. Uncle Charles will be pleased to know you offered your protection so freely."

Lexford bowed properly. "I am at the baron's command in such a matter. I would not wish you or Miss Aldridge to experience danger."

After entering behind His Lordship, Cashé waited her turn to greet the viscount. "Lord Lexford," she intoned, followed by a curtsy.

"Miss Aldridge." Lexford settled an approving gaze on her.

"Did you speak of danger, my Lord?" Cashé ignored the required civilities and the viscount's admiration.

Lexford grimaced at the reference to menace. "I received a message from Lord Worthing yesterday, several hours prior to your uncle's request. I regret to inform you Murhad Jamot broke into the earl's home less than a week prior."

Satiné gasped, and although Cashé already knew of the events, she rushed forward to grasp her sister's hand. "Tell us, my Lord," Cashé demanded.

"It is Lord Yardley's belief Jamot started a fire at the mill on Yardley's property, and while His Lordship and his men fought the blaze, Jamot entered the manor house and found the easiest access to the structure. Later, the Baloch returned to search Yardley's house for the emerald Mir believes one of us has in our possession."

"An emerald?" Satiné questioned. "What emerald?"

"Did you not realize Jamot held Velvet as ransom?" Cashé declared. She wondered if she had ever been as sheltered as her sister, at least, in essentials.

Satiné appeared insulted, but she said, "I suppose it never occurred to me the man held a motive other than Thornhill's past."

Cashé ignored Satiné's embarrassment. "Might you tell us whether Lord Yardley suffered in any manner? What of his brother Trevor?" Cashé

167

knew neither had been injured, but she thought Lexford might possess additional information.

Lexford accepted the seat to which Cashé gestured. "Yardley cornered Jamot in Trevor's room, and there was a scuffle, but no one in His Lordship's family sustained injury. Jamot made a fast retreat through a preset exit. Unfortunately, two of His Lordship's tenants lost their lives in the mill fire. Lord Yardley takes such losses personally."

In her desire to know every fact of Marcus's life, Cashé had unconsciously taken over Satiné's position as the hostess. "His Lordship has spoken of Trevor on several occasions. I assumed from what Lord Yardley has shared his brother might not handle such an invasion well."

Lexford dutifully explained, "Trevor Wellston never developed properly. His mother was well past her prime when she delivered Trevor, and although he is the oldest son, he is not capable of running the estate. Lord Yardley holds the title as Trevor's regent."

"Then His Lordship and Trevor are from different mothers?" Cashé pressed, although she knew speaking so familiarly of Marcus's family was unacceptable in social circles.

His Lordship smiled indulgently. "Lord Yardley's mother was much younger than the former Earl of Berwick, but she succumbed to a typhoid infection when Yardley was ten. The earl's older brother Myles, who should have inherited, fell from his horse and broke his neck while Wellston and I were in Persia. That event precipitated Lionel Wellston making arrangements for his youngest son to succeed him. Lord Yardley returned home prior to his father's passing so he might learn his duties as the future earl. The old earl passed only recently."

"How awful," Satiné remarked.

Cashé could not stifle her curiosity. "And Maggie? What happened to His Lordship's twin?"

The viscount's brow rose in a question. "I believe Lord Yardley should share those details when he is prepared to do so."

Cashé fought back the frustration before feigning disinterest. "I was just curious because of having a twin myself. I should not have prodded." She looked about expectantly. "Allow me to see to the tea and to Lord Lexford's room."

"You will rejoin us?" Satiné pleaded.

"Of course." Cashé smiled at both of them. "I shan't be long."

"Are you prepared to spend time with Lord Lexford as if you are Cashémere?" Cashé asked as she assisted Satiné into her riding habit. They had spent the previous two days in the viscount's company–sometimes as themselves and sometimes as their twin. Although they found constantly switching clothes to keep His Lordship confused on their personality differences had been exhausting, the viscount appeared none the wiser for their perfidy. During those switches, the twins had laid the basis of their current farce.

Satiné took a deep breath, as if to steady her nerves. "What if today Lord Lexford discovers our ruse?"

Cashé rolled her eyes in exasperation. She had repeated her answer every time they changed places. "He will not," Cashé insisted. "If Uncle Charles did not recognize the differences, His Lordship will not." She straightened Satiné's collar. "Just recall, I am not the horse woman you are. Perhaps you should ask the viscount to assist you in becoming a more proficient rider."

"Then I could pretend to master riding thanks to his attention. You are brilliant, Sister," Satiné declared, giving Cashé a spontaneous hug.

Satiné's ever changing moods irritated Cashé. There were moments when she considered doing her twin bodily harm. "Has His Lordship made any advances or said anything of promise?"

"Lord Lexford told me last eve he thought I might make an excellent mistress of my own home now that I had spent time with Satiné," her twin said ironically. "It is nice to hear myself praised, even as a secondhand compliment. I politely told the viscount 'with her experience in the baron's household, my sister Satiné is superior.'"

Cashé brushed her sister's ego by encouraging, "Permit the viscount to hold your hand or to kiss you."

"I could not!" Satiné protested.

"You can!" Cashé insisted. "Do you not desire the viscount's kiss?" She almost said 'first kiss,' but she would not purposely begin another argument.

Satiné blushed, but she whispered, "Dare I encourage such familiarity?"

"Do you wish this man's attentions? Can you see him as your husband? The father of your children?" Cashé charged.

Again, Satiné blushed. "How can you ask such personal questions?"

"Satiné," Cashé fought the growl rising to her throat. "If you are not serious about Lord Lexford, then why are we performing this switch?

The purpose is for you to capture the man's heart. Yet, if you do not mean fidelity, then do not continue with the farce. The viscount deserves better than a woman who cannot return his regard."

"Listen to you. What would you do about Lord Yardley if I did not wish to earn Lord Lexford's attentions?"

Cashé bit her bottom lip. "I do not wish to bring the viscount additional pain, but my heart dwells elsewhere."

Satiné looked on. "You are serious? You will only settle for the earl?"

"I am quite serious." Cashé walked to the window. "I cannot explain it, but I belong to Yardley even if I never see him again."

Satiné sighed. "Then I should set about truly winning the viscount's devotion."

Thirty minutes later, the trio rode sedately across the manor's greenway. Within a few minutes, Cashé, as Satiné, began to fidget in the saddle.

As expected, the viscount took note. "Is something amiss, Miss Satiné?" Should we return to the estate?"

"This horse is hands shorter than the one I normally ride; therefore, the leather skirt is interfering with my commands to the animal. I should return the seat to the stables." Cashé held little knowledge of sidesaddles, but she knew the disaster of having an ill-fitting saddle.

Lexford did the gallant thing: He stopped their progress. "Then we will all return. I refuse to permit you to know solitary measures when you should be in our company." He gestured to Cashé's twin.

"No, I insist," Cashé told a worried Lexford. "My sister requires a riding lesson. I will rejoin you when Mr. Stewart makes the repair. Mulvanney shall accompany me to the stables."

"Are you absolutely certain, Miss Satiné?" Lexford questioned. "Your sister and I would not wish to be without your company."

"Do not be foolish. I ride daily, but Cashémere is not so fortunate. Uncle Charles just recently arranged a new saddle for her. I would not deprive my sister of your good company."

"As you wish then." The artifice had worked just as Cashé had predicted. Lexford had played the perfect gentleman, but she had outmaneuvered him and then had watched with some satisfaction as he and Satiné rode off. With the groomsman close at hand, Cashé returned to the house to await her sister's triumphant appearance.

"Would you care to rest for a few minutes, Miss Aldridge?" Lexford asked as they approached an outcropping overlooking a waterfall.

"That would be pleasant, Your Lordship." Satiné kept Cashé's dislike of riding ever in her mind. She even stepped gingerly before straightening to walk toward the rocky overhang. Loosening the ribbons of her riding hat and spreading the material of her skirt around her, she took a seat and waited for the viscount to join her.

Lord Lexford tied the horses nearby befoe he sat beside her. Removing his hat, he leaned back on one elbow and stared at the sunless skyline. "We will know winter soon," he said as he tilted his head to take in more of the expanse. "When I was in Persia, the night sky seemed darker and the daylight brighter; it was all quite breathtaking, but I yearned for this." He gestured to the wispy clouds. "I yearned for England with all its miserable weather. Yearned for green grass and not brown vastness."

"Was it horrible, my Lord?" Satiné asked, suddenly very curious about this man.

Lexford frowned, as if he chose his words carefully. She could sense the change in the viscount and wondered what had occurred to upset him. "Occasionally. But mostly it was not England. I had run away from my responsibilities to forget England, but it had haunted me and called to me every day I was away."

She paused, afraid to ask her next question. "What about England did you shun?" What if the thing, which had driven him from his home was another woman? Was she prepared to fight the ghost of a former love?

Instead of answering, Lexford sat up suddenly and took possession of her hand. "I would prefer not to revisit those times. They were too painful then, and although time has lessened the emotions associated with the events, they are still too raw." His Lordship paused, and Satiné wished he had taken her into his confidence. "It is my wish to find someone with whom I can find solace and learn to accept life again. My family has known enough of death."

Curiously, she wondered again what shadows creased this man's life, but she would bide her time in learning more of what drove him. Satiné wished to be as knowledgeable of the viscount's past as her sister was of the earl's. She would not permit Cashé to best her in such matters. "And have you seen such a person?" she asked flirtatiously.

Lexford laughed lightly. "Are we seeking a compliment, my Dear?"

Satiné blustered, "Of course not, my Lord." She blushed thoroughly.

171

"You have nothing to fear: I know none to rival your excellence." Sadly, Satiné wondered if the viscount could not tell her and Cashé apart, which was the excellent one?

She had little time to ponder the situation, however, for the viscount removed one of her riding gloves. He wiggled his eyebrows playfully, and she instinctively smiled at him. One finger at a time, he withdrew each slowly, and then he rotated the palm to face upward before kissing the inside of her wrist.

Satiné gasped, "My Lord!"

Lexford's lips turned up in a smile. "I realize at Linworth I promised to keep my pursuit at a minimum until your Come Out, but I must tell you I am enjoying the changes I have observed in you since your becoming a member of Ashton's household."

Satiné played it coy. "I thought you preferred me as I was, Your Lordship."

"You know I meant not to criticize. You, my Dear, mean to twist my words." He traced a finger down her cheek. "I see a more relaxed Cashémere Aldridge, a woman who has permitted her vulnerability to show, something not found previously."

"It is my sister Satiné's influence," she whispered, wanting him to see her and not Cashé.

"Your sister has many admirable qualities," Lexford began. "I admit I had not noticed Miss Satiné so closely until of late. I see your influence on your twin and hers on you." He pulled her hand closer to his body, forcing Satiné to rest against his shoulder.

As she felt his warmth up and down her body, Satiné remembered Cashé's advice: to make Lexford desire her. "Maybe it is my twin you desire, my Lord. Have you ever considered the possibility?" She lowered her eyes demurely.

"I would never think to act the cad, especially as Lord Yardley has expressed an interest in Miss Satiné." Lexford traced circles across her palm.

Satiné brought her chin up to meet his gaze. "I can assure you, Lord Lexford, the earl has withdrawn his attentions from Satiné."

"I was unawares," he confided. "Is Miss Satiné overset?"

Satiné smiled shyly. "I would say with some degree of certainty Satiné has not considered Lord Yardley as a possible suitor for several weeks, even before our departure from Linworth."

Regina Jeffers

"And the lady has identified a replacement?" he said teasingly.

She brought her chin a bit higher, welcoming his kiss. "Absolutely. Satiné has identified a superior choice."

ⓞⓞ

After sending Satiné off with the viscount, Cashé had returned to the estate. She had held a dual purpose in finding time alone: providing her sister the opportunity to entice Lord Lexford's attentions and discovering her Uncle Samuel's letter. Since recalling how her Uncle Charles had manipulated Samuel Aldridge's speedy exit, the need to know the truth had become a bit of an obsession. She had replayed the scene over and over in her mind, but there were annoying gaps in her memory that were driving her a bit mad. She had imagined how Lord Yardley would find her frustrations amusing, but even thoughts of the compelling earl could not replace her desire to uncover an answer.

Sending her mount to the stable with the groomsman, Cashé had made her way to the house's rear and along the servants' staircase to her uncle's study. By stepping into empty rooms, she had avoided the household staff before sneaking into the baron's sanctuary, closing the door, and quietly locking it.

"Where should I look?" she mumbled as she stepped farther into the room. She had thought of searching the study during the night, but she had assumed someone would see the light under the door. During the day, such detection was not an issue. Light streamed in through the high windows and the patio opening, providing her easy access.

She first searched the desk, shifting quickly through the stacks of correspondence arranged neatly on the surface. Then, Cashé did the same for the stacks on the table behind her. Finding nothing, she sat in her uncle's chair and began to open the drawers. In the third one, she found a folder bound by string and holding letters and receipts, some of which included her parents' names, as well as references to Samuel Aldridge. Impulsively, she slid the bundle under her riding jacket to read later. She would replace it before the baron's return.

Finding nothing more of importance in the desk, Cashé made her way about the room, lightly touching items. She quickly realized she could not look through everything; Uncle Charles collected too many artifacts and books for that possibility. She must use her insights into the baron's personality. From their first encounter in Velvet's rescue, she realized he prided himself on his stratagems. Where would he hide Uncle Samuel's

173

letter? Then it came to her: The baron would hide the letter in plain sight. Turning slowly to take in every item on display, her eyes came to rest on a book on an end table. Obvious, but secretive, at the same time, she realized. Cashé removed the book and laid it upon the cushions of a nearby chaise before opening it. The first page held an elaborate family tree, tracing the Mortons through some five generations. Instinctively, she found her mother, along with the line indicating Chenille Morton's joining with Edward Aldridge and the births of her sisters, as well as her own name. Uncle Charles had continued the lines with Velvet's marriage to Brantley Fowler. A silent sob choked her: Her emotions raw.

Opening the Bible to where the folded paper lay, Cashé chuckled at her uncle's deviousness. She realized, unexpectedly, she was probably more like him that any of her sisters. She would have planned something similar to hide her secrets. In fact, His Lordship's letter rested in a folded scarf on her bureau. In plain sight, but still hidden. "A very nice touch of irony," she whispered. "You hide Uncle Samuel's letter in First Samuel. Which section, Uncle Charles?' She let her eyes scan the page. "Chapter three: the curse on Eli's house. More irony!"

Cashé left the Bible lying open, arranging two loose pillows over it to mask her perfidy from prying eyes. Taking the letter with her, she released the door's lock and latch and then made her exit through a floor to ceiling window, which she left ajar in case she required it to return the items before someone detected her deviousness. Casually, she made her way around the house to the garden, purposely stopping periodically to pull away a dead leaf or to enjoy the last of the blooms. The grounds keepers had seen her do so hundreds of times over the last few weeks. Finally reaching the main entrance, she greeted Mr. Whitcomb, the baron's butler, before hurrying to her room.

◦◦◦

Her boldness had taken Lexford by surprise, but not in a negative manner. He had flirted with Cashé Aldridge on and off for months, but this was different. This time a tingle of excitement coursed through his veins, and pure lust squeezed the air from his lungs. Her gaze mesmerized him, and Lexford found himself slipping into an abyss. She had attracted him from the first time he had laid eyes on her at Linton Park, but now Miss Cashémere held him in a hardy grip of emotions. He had noticed the difference when he had unexpectedly met the baron and called upon the household for tea. Distractedly, the intensity had lessened at the evening of entertainment he had shared with the Morton family, and for a short term, Aidan had wondered if he had been mistaken. Even over the past two days sometimes he had felt an energy when in Miss Aldridge's presence, and other times Lexford experienced the simple comfortableness he had known from the beginning of their relationship. "Miss Aldridge," he breathed her name as she closed her eyes, anticipating his kiss.

✑✑

Cashé had rushed to her room, locking the door behind her. Her heart pounded a defeaning staccato from the moment she had found the letter. Kicking off her shoes and removing her riding jacket, she curled up on the bed, looking for the secrecy the draped four-poster provided.

First, she removed the letter. The morning of Samuel Aldridge's departure, she had read only the initial paragraphs before storming from her room to confront those who had destroyed her known world. Cashé had felt Uncle Samuel's betrayal–felt the caustic manner in which each of the other household members would welcome her defeat–felt the anger of how little she had meant to any of them. How could she not know disappointment? She had been left behind, again. First her parents. Then her sisters. Then her sometimes loving, but often-dreadful grandmother. And just as she had found her place, her Uncle Samuel had joined the exodus. For that reason alone, this time she would read each paragraph carefully, discovering the truth of her repulsiveness. From her Uncle Charles, Cashé had learned how the Mortons and the Fowlers had paid the Aldridges for the twins. At the time, she had thought the Aldridges had chosen her above her sisters, but over the past few weeks, Cashé's identity had suffered as she had learned more of those early years. Apparently, the Fowlers had chosen Velvet because her older sister was closer in age to Eleanor Fowler, providing a ready-made companion for the girl, while Uncle Charles and Aunt Louisa had chosen Satiné because of her youngest sister's propensity for female activities: tea and lace and pretty gowns.

So, where did those revelations leave her? Unwanted? Tolerated? She was the middle sister, the one unnoticed by anyone. Velvet, even before their parents' deaths, had been coddled, held with the highest esteem. Cashé had always thought Satiné a bit self-centered and pampered, but it was she, the one discarded, who had possessed the greatest variety in her traits–in opposition to either of her siblings. Cashé had viewed herself as independent and generous. She had recognized how others thought her emotionally withdrawn and distant, but Cashé considered herself social

175

and knew, despite a quick temper, she could be a strong negotiator. "Then why did no one want me?" she murmured, as her chest constricted from loneliness.

Unfolding the letter, she took a deep breath and read what she had not seen several weeks prior. Although addressed to her, Aldridge's letter was actually an attack on Charles Morton. The viscount had told her he was leaving her in the care of a "pernicious braggart." Lord Averette referred to Thornhill as "the spawn of a black-hearted degenerate." He offered a prayer for her and Velvet's future. Her Scottish uncle had disparaged her English one, as well as Brantley Fowler, and Lord and Lady Worthing. In fact, the letter said very little about or to her. Uncle Samuel did not even apologize for leaving her behind.

The latter part of the letter declared Uncle Charles's accusations of Averette having a part in his brother's accident as "ludicrous"—a refutation that immediately piqued Cashé's curiosity. The viscount asserted a love for his brother. Despite Lord Averette's denials, Cashé now knew enough of Charles Morton to recognize the baron would never level such an affront without grounds. She knew Ashton had once served in a group similar to the one in which Lord Yardley and Viscount Lexford operated. Uncle Charles would not lightly make a charge without evidence. "What kind of evidence" she asked the empty room.

Her Uncle Samuel's adieu was an additional denunciation of something in which he had once taken pride. He disputed his lack of charity within the church. "Well, that is one area in which no one may question Uncle's integrity."

Cashé wished Lord Yardley had remained in Cheshire. She wished to consult with him on what the letter revealed regarding both her uncles. She had recognized the breach existing between the Aldridge and the Morton families long ago, but she had never realized Uncle Charles had thought Uncle Samuel could purposely hurt his own brother. Even as a small child, she was aware of how her grandmother would vehemently turn on her youngest son. How she would say, "You would make an acceptable clergyman, I suppose–never a soldier. You do not have the heart of a man who could murder another. You can never be to me what my Edward was." Had Kentigerna Aldridge prodded Uncle Samuel into doing something he would never have done otherwise?

What bothered Cashé the most was she did not immediately believe Uncle Samuel incapable of such an action. Cashé had known Lord Averette's anger–his unreasonableness–his desire to shame a child before family and friends. Could not a man who taught hate in the name of love devise a plan to seize his brother's title?

"Enough," she chastised herself aloud. "I only have a few minutes. I can dwell on the information I find later." Putting the letter aside, Cashé read through the beribboned bundle. Some were bills of sale; others were notes and letters. Some made sense–others did not.

"I wonder if I should replace these before the viscount and Satiné return?" she remarked after perusing each sheet of paper carefully. She restacked the pages in the same order and closed the heavy parchment over the sheets. Then she retied the ribbon before picking up two heavy tomes from her end table and inserting the bundle between them. She would pretend to visit the library and go through the patio door and in through the window in her uncle's study. Lexford and Satiné had been gone for over two hours. They would return soon for nuncheon.

Slipping from her quarters, Cashé nonchalantly made her way through the near empty hallways, pausing for a maid to see her enter the library, before closing the door.

Behind the closed portal, she hustled through the open patio doors and around the house to the study's window. Clinging to the shadows, Cashé stepped over and through the casement. The door remained closed from earlier in the day, and she rushed about the room to restore the items to where she had found them. Silently, she released the lock to the study's door and turned to admire her pretext. Finally, having it all in place, she exited the same way she had come, through the tall, narrow window, shutting it more firmly this time.

She had just reached the patio when she heard Mr. Whitcomb calling her name. Swiftly the library door swung wide, and a distraught head servant rushed forward. "Miss Aldridge," the man's hands nervously played with a watch chain, "I am grateful I located you. We may have a problem, Miss. His Lordship's horse returned to the stables without the gentleman."

A knot twisted her stomach. Could Jamot have come to Manchester? "Perhaps the viscount and my sister are on one horse. However, we should send someone to seek them out."

"I took the liberty, Miss, of dispatching men to search for His Lordship and Miss Satiné."

"Thank you, Mr. Whitcomb. I am certain it is nothing serious. Lord Lexford is quite capable of handling any situation. I have no fear for my sister's safety." She said the words because they were true, but a deep need to rush into the protective embrace of Marcus Wellston swelled her chest. "You will keep me abreast of the search."

"Certainly, Miss."

꧁꧂

He was going to kiss her. She would receive her first kiss from Viscount Lexford, and Satiné wanted it more than anything else. The fact he had called her by her twin's name bruised the experience, but she was set on replacing the viscount's interest in Cashé with real affection for her. She had thought it a good idea that he would kiss her. Whether Lord Lexford knew it or not, he would be making a comparison between the sisters, and Satiné was determined to win his heart. Instinctively, she allowed her lips to part in invitation, and then his mouth took possession of hers in a powerful need. The viscount's arms came about her, and Satiné slid her arms around his neck.

꧁꧂

He had told her at Linton Park he would wait for her to make the adjustments to her new life, but surely she had welcomed his desire. Her gaze had simmered with heat, and she had closed her eyes in anticipation. "Miss Aldridge," he had breathed her name before lowering his mouth to hers. He had made himself go slower than his body demanded. She was truly an innocent, and although he had blazed to an arousal, Lexford gently caressed her neck's curvature before pulling her closer and tightening his embrace. Even through their many layers of clothing, he could feel her heat rising. Somehow, this kiss was different from the one in Linworth's garden. The first one had been nothing but chaste. Cashé Aldridge had not responded then, but now she pulled herself closer, plastering her breasts to his chest. She clutched his lapels before sliding her arms around his neck.

Lexford slid his tongue along her lips' line, her soft moan lending him encouragement. When she opened further, his tongue invaded her mouth, tasting the soft recesses and sucking gently on her bottom lip. He splayed his fingers across the back of her neck, holding her in place as he reached to remove her hat. Then he caught her about the waist again before escalating the kiss.

"You are magnificent," he gasped as he feathered kisses across her cheek, ear, and neck before returning to her mouth in a fiery, while tender, possession. His mouth plundered hers leisurely, and the lady rewarded him by venturing a lick of her tongue across his lips.

Pulling away, they both panted, fighting for breath–chest rising and falling rhythmically. "My goodness, Darling." He kissed her temple. Unable to resist, he traced the outline of her kiss swollen mouth with his fingertip. Her flushed face increased his need. "Might I kiss you again, Sweetheart?"

She nodded briefly, and Lexford's smile reached his eyes. He did not hesitate–his blatant desire heightened by her enchanting silence. His lips pulled at her ear lobe before he revisited her mouth. The smell of her–lemons, he thought–and that was odd because he would have sworn Miss Cashé always wore jasmine–intoxicated him. As the urge to hold her forever encroached on his sanity, Lexford pressed her backward to lie upon the smooth rock face, his body draped across hers. He did not care any longer about the baron or Jamot or the Realm. Only the lady in his arms mattered; he was lost completely to her.

Thusly engaged, he had not heard the man's approach. Then the blow rattled his brain–sending shades of black where light had existed moments earlier, and although he fought it, the pain and the darkness won out, and he crashed in a wounded heap upon her.

Chapter Twelve

She should have sensed the danger when the shadow spread over them, but the viscount's kiss had taken away all her reason, and Satiné had thought only of how delicious it would be to tell Cashé she too knew the difference between a tender kiss and a demanding one. Then a gush of air and Lexford's mouth being ripped from hers brought a blood-curdling scream as His Lordship's body collapsed heavily upon hers.

The scream continued as she clawed at the viscount's body pressing solidly upon hers; fighting for her reputation, she had shoved at his shoulders to leverage her hands between their bodies. Even when she realized the annoying scream had come from her, Satiné could not stop. Only then did her mind register the fact His Lordship did not move. There was no attempt on the viscount's part to steal her innocence. Finally, large hands replaced hers on Lord Lexford's shoulders, and the viscount rolled easily away from hers. Yet, before Satiné could react, a gruff-looking man, built like a wooden column, jerked her to her feet.

"You be comin' with me!" The stranger manhandled her, shoving Satiné away from where the viscount laid upon the rock face.

"His Lordship?" Satiné gasped when she saw the blood pooling on the outcropping's smooth surface.

Her captor frowned. "Ye be not worryin' on the viscounty's behalf," he ordered as he dragged Satiné toward the waiting horses.

She pulled hard at where his large hands wrapped themselves about hers. "We cannot leave him. He could die!"

The stranger refused to loosen his grip. Instead, he had grabbed her about the waist, lifting her from the ground and carrying her from the scene. Other than a grunt when she had kicked his upper thigh, he had said nothing more. The distance between her and Lexford increased, and Satiné feared she would never see him again.

"Release me!" she yelled close to the man's ear. "Release me at once. My uncle is a baron. He will pay you to return me to my home." Her fists beat a tattoo upon his chest, but nothing Satiné did made a difference. The man had her tightly clamped to him. "Please set me free," she wailed.

"We be goin' home," her captor growled through gritted teeth. "To my home…our home," he clarified.

When they reached the clearing beyond the woods, Satiné saw the small coach waiting along the access road, and her heart froze with fear. "Do not…" she began, but the man caught her in a very uncomfortable grasp and threw Satiné over his massive shoulders. She pounded her fists against his back in a weakened effort. She had had no time to understand the significance of this abduction. All she could consider was the limp and bloody form of Lord Lexford upon the flat overhang. Reaching the small coach, her abductor jerked the door open and unceremoniously tossed her upon the carriage's floor. "Do not do this," Satiné pleaded, trying to scoot away from him. "I will pay you to set me free."

He ignored all her efforts to negotiate her release. Grabbing a rag he had left on the seat, the stranger leaned forward, his face inches from hers. "I be takin' ye home," he sneered. "Ye belong to me, gel. I told Averette I would have ye one way or the other. I will see ye as me wife, Cashémere."

Now, Satiné understood: It was if a gigantic candle had delivered reality. The man thought she was her twin. "I am not…" she uttered, but the stranger had caught her about the neck, his enormous hand covering her mouth with the rag. Satiné struggled to breathe, thinking he meant to kill her, but the darkness crept across her mind, leaving her helpless in his grasp. The last thing she saw was the carriage's roof as it descended toward her.

༼༺༽

He groaned and forced his body to roll to the side, reaching for where the pain radiated through his head. Finding the sticky blood on his fingers did not surprise him, but Lexford frowned just the same, creating a new wave of sharp pains crossing his brow.

Through a deep breath, he opened his eyes and shoved upward to brace himself on his shoulder and forearm. He instantly realized something was amiss, but it had taken him a few moments to recall he had been kissing Cashé Aldridge before someone had struck him. "Cashé," he grunted, looking around for her. Was she hurt? The pain throbbed into his extremities, but Lexford gritted his teeth and rose to a seated position. Turning his head slowly, he searched for any sign of his companion. One glove remained at his feet, and her bonnet sat several inches away, but

181

Miss Aldridge was not in the immediate vicinity. The horses still stood where he had left them. So, she had not gone for assistance. Therefore, whoever struck him must have taken her. Lexford did not know how long he had been unconscious, but he recognized the urgency of his situation.

Shakily, he rose to his feet and staggered toward the tethered horses. Reaching for his mount, he took the reins and with a determined hold on the horn, lifted himself to the saddle. Another deep breath came before he kicked the animal's flanks with his heels. He had gone less than one hundred feet before he found himself reeling in the seat, clutching at the saddle horn to keep his balance, but the blackness had returned; and he could do nothing to resist it. Valí shifted to the side, and the ground rose up to smack him hard. The air rushed from his lungs, and Lexford welcomed the emptiness.

.οΩϙ,

"Mr. Whitcomb, is there any word?" Cashé paced the front foyer. Satiné and Lexford had been gone for five hours, and no one had seen them.

"None, Miss Aldridge." The man looked as distraught as she.

"How many men do we have searching for them?" she demanded.

"Twenty, Miss. Mr. Stewart and I decided to send them in pairs. The men have been given specific areas to search and orders to report back when they are finished. In that manner, we know where everyone is at all times."

"That seems most prudent." Cashé walked to the nearest window to stare out. She wondered where the viscount might have taken Satiné. Cashé did not believe Lexford would hurt her sister; yet, she could not shake the feeling Satiné was in trouble."

"Miss!" a maid rushed forward from the house's rear. "Miss Aldridge!"

Cashé met her immediately. "What is it, Lucy?"

"They found him, Miss." The girl anxiously wrung her hands.

Cashé pressed, "Lord Lexford?"

"Yes, Miss." The servant fought to catch her breath. "I be in the back garden, and Old Davy said Kennett and Mulvanney found His Lordship, but the viscount is hurt bad. The grooms be sendin' for a wagon to bring him in."

"And my sister?" Cashé focused the question.

"Nobody knows, Miss."

Cashé winced. Where was Satiné? Attempting to portray calm amidst the chaos, she said, "Thank you, Lucy. I want you to go upstairs and prepare His Lordship's room. The viscount will require our care."

"Yes, Miss." The maid rushed to meet Cashé's orders.

"Mr. Whitcomb, send someone for a surgeon and notify Mrs. Lacey."

"Immediately, Miss." Finally having something to do energized the household.

As everyone did her bidding, Cashé paused in quiet contemplation. She would have sworn the world had trembled as she looked about for guidance. "Where are you, Satiné?"

Within a half hour, using an old door as a litter, the two groomsmen carried Lexford's lifeless body into the house. Cashé examined his bloody countenance as several footmen lended their support with the makeshift pallet.

She followed them to the viscount's quarters, praying his wounds were not fatal. Cashé swallowed hard. There was no one to assist her in this matter. She desperately wished for her uncle's return–wished for Lexford's recovery–wished for Satiné's appearance–wished for Marcus's comforting embrace. "What can you tell me?" Cashé caught the elderly groomsman by the arm as the household staff moved Lexford from the wooden litter to the bed.

"Found His Lordship by the outcrop overlookin' the falls." Although she knew little of the area, Cashé nodded her encouragement. "Found Miss Satiné's horse still tethered to a tree. There be blood on the smooth rock and on a large tree branch near by. We be findin' the gentleman's hat and ye sister's bonnet and glove on the ground. Mulvanney climbed down the rock face to be assuring everyone Miss Satiné did not go over the edge, but he finds nothing unusual."

Cashé glanced quickly at Lexford's limp form. "Then where is my sister? Lord Lexford would fight to protect her."

The groom followed her eyes. "His Lordship has a nasty bump on his head. Looks like someone be hittin' him with the branch. Plenty of blood there by the rocks. Appears as if he tried to follow whoever attacked him. There be two sets of boot tracks and a set of marks made by a coach on the small road leadin' to the peak. Same boot marks where the carriage be on the road, but no marks for a woman."

Cashé softened her tone. Her uncle's staff had performed admirably. "What do you suggest we do next?"

"First, we should be sendin' for a magistrate, Miss Aldridge," the head groom offered. "Then, seems to me that if'n your sister be gone we should be contacting the baron."

Cashé bit her bottom lip in anxiousness. She had never experienced anything so dire in her short life; yet, the loyalty of her uncle's servants had given her the required confidence. "Thank you for your excellent advice," she told the man and saw relief on his countenance. "Would you send a rider for the magistrate, Mr. Stewart?" The man nodded his agreement. "Meanwhile, I will write a note to Uncle Charles, plus, I will send to Lord Worthing at Linton Park. His Lordship was Viscount Lexford's commanding officer, and Lady Worthing is my cousin. I am certain Lord Worthing can offer his assistance within hours where my uncle may take days."

"That be sensible, Miss." The man gave her a nod of encouragement.

"Then you do what you must to assist the magistrate, Mr. Stewart. We shall permit Mrs. Lacey to tend Viscount Lexford until the surgeon arrives."

"I be getting' a fresh horse and rider, Miss. Soon as them letters be ready, me man will ride to London." He gave Cashé a quick bow and left the bedchamber.

"The physician just rode into the circle, Miss," Lucy informed Cashé and the housekeeper.

"Perfect." Cashé's natural ability to organize had proved useful. In Scotland, she often assumed the role of the manor's mistress, especially in dealing with the estate's house servants. Aunt Alice was not of the nature to speak with authority. "I shall await the doctor's analysis in my uncle's study. I must send a note to the baron to plead for his immediate return."

"I shall bring Doctor Potter to you when he finishes, Miss."

Thirty minutes later, Potter tapped on the door. "Miss Aldridge?"

Cashé rose to greet him. "Thank you for responding so quickly, Sir."

"I have often served Ashton." He accepted the chair to which Cashé gestured. "It is my understanding, Miss, your sister is unaccounted for."

Cashé did not answer. She knew the servants would gossip, but she had wanted to keep Satiné's absence a secret as long as possible. "We are doing all we can to assure Satiné's safety."

"If you require my assistance, I will make myself available until the baron's return."

The doctor tone said he thought her incapable of handling a crisis, and that particular realization riled Cashé's stubbornness. Therefore, she purposely ignored his words. "How is Viscount Lexford?"

The physician relayed his disapproval with a scowling countenance, but he said, "Lord Lexford has a serious head injury. I have cleaned the wound and stitched the area. Of course, my greatest concern is the swelling. If His Lordship's head is swollen on the outside, it is likely swollen on the inside of his skull, as well. We must watch the visocunt carefully. The brain takes its own time in healing, but there is promise. Lord Lexford must have recovered enough to mount his horse because he was found some distance from where his hat was left behind."

Cashé listened carefully to what the surgeon said professionally and what he omitted. The viscount might not recover. If so, it would be her fault. She had manipulated today's rendezvous. Lord Lexford must have been quite distracted if someone had caught him unawares. She wondered if Satiné had enticed the viscount's attentions, allowing His Lordship's assailant to do his worst.

"Then we shall give the viscount the best care possible. You have provided Mrs. Lacey instructions, Sir?"

The surgeon again bit back his displeasure, but Cashé pretended not to notice. "I have." He looked about him, as if he did not know what to do next. "I will call a bit later to see to Lord Lexford's progress."

"Thank you, Sir." Cashé rose to return to her letters. "I shall trust your expertise with His Lordship."

With the surgeon's exit, Cashé took up her pen again, explaining to James Kerrington what had occurred and why she desperately required his guidance. She expressed her fear Jamot had taken Satiné. If people analyzed her actions over the last few hours, they might consider her detached, but Cashé felt it all: the responsibility for Satiné being alone with Lord Lexford and the guilt at having secretly searched her uncle's private papers, as well as the incompetence she had felt at being the one to make life and death decisions. Yet, she would weather whatever God placed before her. It would be what both Uncle Charles and Lord Yardley would expect of her.

"Miss Aldridge."

Cashé looked up to see Mr. Stewart. "Yes."

"The magistrate wishes a word, Miss."

"Send him in, Mr. Stewart."

The elderly gentleman came solicitously to a halt beside the desk. She had met Malcolm Lloyd at her uncle's recent gathering. Surprisingly, his demeanor offered her comfort. He did not judge her as being too young to assume responsibility. "Miss Aldridge, my heart goes out to you. This mystery will resolve itself; I will not rest until your sister is returned safely to the manor."

"Thank you, Mr. Lloyd. Tell me what we may do at Chesterfield Manor to aid in your search." Cashé caught the man's arm and led him to a wing chair. She sat across from him. "My uncle would spare no expense to bring Satiné home, and I feel confident to pledge as such in his name."

"Of course, Ashton would want you to act in his stead," the magistrate assured her.

Cashé wanted him to understand she would willingly accept assistance in this matter. "I have drafted a letter to my cousin James Kerrington, Viscount Worthing. His estate is in Derbyshire, and Lord Worthing and Viscount Lexford served together in the East. He will be here in hours to serve in my stead, but until then I insist on being kept informed. I am not the type to spend my hours crying into a gentleman's handkerchief."

Mr. Lloyd smiled knowingly. "Ashton indicated as much. Your uncle is quite proud of the woman you have become."

Pleased that her Uncle Charles had spoken positively of her, Cashé blushed. "Have you examined the area where our staff found Lord Lexford's body?" She redirected the conversation.

"Mr. Stewart's men performed admirably, keeping the scene clear of outsiders who might destroy the clues. Many of the baron's men have been on search parties for runaways," he disclosed. "Everything was as Mr. Stewart relayed. We followed the coach's tracks to the main road, where they blended with the daily wear of travelers. There are marks where your sister and His Lordship had dismounted and a few leading to the outcropping. It is a popular site, overlooking the falls, but the hard rain earlier in the week washed the area clean. Theirs were the only ones coming from the west, but there are difference boot marks along the tree line to the east. The carriage marks are a quarter mile or so away from the site."

"You were very thorough," Cashé remarked.

"Been doing this for some time, Miss." The magistrate leaned forward to press his point. "Your sister is my chief concern. Is there anything else I should know about this situation?"

Cashé considered telling the man of Jamot and the emerald, but while what the Realm did was not exactly a secret, it was not readily shared with others. "Nothing of which I am aware, Sir," she lied. "Is it possible, Mr. Lloyd, that Satiné ran away when Lord Lexford was attacked? Is it possible she has taken refuge somewhere on the estate or in the area? Perhaps, Satiné is injured, as well. Perhaps the carriage tracks have nothing to do with my twin's disappearance." She remembered how Jamot's kidnapping of Velvet had ruined her eldest sister's reputation. Cashé wished to protect Satiné's name.

"All of what you have asked is possible, Miss Aldridge." The man's voice held a bit of skepticism, but she had planted the seed of doubt. Mr. Lloyd rose to make his exit. "We have a few more hours of daylight to aid our search. Mr. Stewart has recruited every available hand and tenant. We will make a thorough sweep of the area between the manor and the falls."

Cashé stood also. "Mr. Stewart has a rider prepared to deliver the letters to Lord Worthing and my uncle. The letters will be on their way in the next quarter hour," she declared. "Therefore, there is nothing for me to do but to await your success."

.ePe,

Thirty minutes later, Cashé slipped into Lexford's room. "Any change, Mrs. Lacey?" she asked as she pulled a chair close to the bed.

"It is too soon, Miss–not until tomorrow at the earliest." She changed a cool compress on Lexford's head.

Cashé nodded involuntarily. "I will sit with His Lordship for awhile. There is nothing I can do downstairs besides stare out the window and wait."

Mrs. Lacey lightly touched Cashé's shoulder. "It is a great burden, but you have performed well."

"I should not have left them." She reached for Lexford's fingers, bringing the back of his hand to her cheek.

Mrs. Lacey changed out the water in the bowl. "You are not to blame yourself, Miss Aldridge. Another woman would only have added to the confusion."

Yet, Cashé knew better; she should be wherever Satiné was being held.

.ePe,

After sitting with His Lordship for several hours, for the last three, she had watched the hands creeping about the clock's face. Cashé had estimated how long it would take an experienced rider to reach Linton Park and how long it would take Worthing to respond, so when she heard the sound of horse's hooves in the drive, she breathed relief that he had come. Racing from Lexford's room, she was in Worthing's comforting embrace within seconds. She had not allowed herself to cry since the first moment she had heard of Lexford's injury, but now she cried openly in the arms of a man she barely knew.

"Come," he whispered close to her ear, as he led Cashé into an open doorway. Worthing motioned to a maid to bring tea, and then he seated Cashé on a settee. "I am here," he murmured as he caught her in his arms again. "I will allow nothing to happen to you."

Cashé cried her tears of regret and her tears of worry, soaking Lord Worthing's shirt and cravat before sitting herself from him. "I apologize, Your Lordship," she mumbled while patting her eyes dry.

Kerrington smiled with gentleness. "Eleanor placed an extra handkerchief in my pocket before I left Linton Park. She said you would required it."

"Thank you for coming so quickly," she rasped through a stifled sob.

He looked up to see the waiting maid, balancing the tea service. "Permit the maid to serve our tea," he encouraged. "I told the countess recently that when I was in Persia I missed English tea more than anything else from my daily life."

Despite the emotions coursing through her, Cashé nodded, the evenness of his voice bringing her peace. "I shall serve, Lucy," she managed to say.

The maid quickly exited, and His Lordship waited for Cashé to resume her composure before he said, "Now, my Dear, you must tell me everything before I see Lexford."

Ignoring her tea, Cashé related all the specifics of the attack, Lexford's injury, and Satiné's disappearance. "Could Jamot have taken my twin the way he did Velvet?" she asked.

"I have never known the Baloch to repeat his revenge nor would he take Miss Satiné without making a demand for return of the emerald. Jamot planned an elaborate abduction of Eleanor in Hyde Park, but Sir Louis Levering staged his own farce, disrupting Jamot's plans. We are certain Jamot killed Sir Louis to keep the man silent. Then the dual kidnappings of Sonali and Her Grace occurred. Although the Baloch staged an abduction of Velvet, I do not believe he would practice another kidnapping so soon.

The last one produced negative effects. It does not make sense for our old enemy: Jamot considers himself a strategist."

She was thankful the viscount had not asked her how she knew so much of Jamot. "But he broke into the earl's home recently," Cashé insisted.

Worthing's eyebrow rose in question. "I suppose Lexford shared the incident?"

Cashé blushed. "The viscount explained as such when he arrived recently."

He placed his cup and saucer on a side table. "Cashémere, I am going to ask a personal question, and I must insist you respond with the absolute truth." He paused for her gaze to return to his. "Explain to me how if Lexford came to Chesterfield to woo you, that he rode off with your sister, especially after you reportedly had trouble with your saddle. If you were his interest, no matter how much you insisted, the viscount would not desert you for Satiné." He paused before adding, "And also explain the obvious differences in your and Wellston's relationship before he departed for Northumberland from what Ella reported upon your first arrival at Linton Park."

Cashé thought to lie to him, but she required an ally. "You will not tell anyone else?" she pleaded.

"As long as what you say does not put anyone in danger, I will keep your confidence."

She swallowed hard. "Satiné and I came to an understanding of sorts before we departed Linton Park. Despite, Lord Lexford's and Lord Yardley's initial interests, we found ourselves attracted to the other suitor. As few can tell my twin and I apart physically, we devised a switch. We have since traded places several times in the past few weeks, fooling everyone, even Uncle Charles." She noted how Lord Worthing fought back a smile, which gave her confidence. "Today, Satiné pretended to be I. We thought Lord Lexford only found me attractive physically, but Satiné is my equal in that manner. If we could convince him to lose his heart to Satiné in my name, she and the viscount could know contentment." She added for good measure, "Satiné and Lord Lexford share many interests."

"Poor Lexford," Worthing shook his head in disbelief. "Did he not suspect the apparent contrasts?"

Cashé smiled deviously. "I am afraid our ruse worked perfectly, which only proves His Lordship to be besotted in name only."

"Is the earl aware of this plan? Has Wellston given his approval, or do you plan to fool him also?"

Cashé flushed in embarrassment. "I would not say Lord Yardley approves, but His Lordship is aware of our scheme."

"I cannot imagine Wellston willingly would seek to displace Lexford."

"Of course, the earl would not betray his friend," she defended Marcus. "He has expressed a resolve to remove himself from the situation rather than to bring Lord Lexford pain. It is I who will not permit him to do so. Only Lord Yardley engages my heart."

"What an interesting twist of fate," Worthing remarked. "But it explains what I read in Yardley's sudden concern for your well being."

Again, Worthing's words sent a shiver down Cashé's spine. "His Lordship sent Mr. Breeson to warn me of Jamot's household invasion. I knew before anyone else," she confided.

Before Worthing could respond, a knock announced the return of Mr. Lloyd. "Excuse me, Miss Aldridge." The magistrate remained in the open doorway.

"Come in, Mr. Lloyd," Cashé motioned as she came to her feet. "Mr. Lloyd, permit me to present my cousin Viscount Worthing."

"My Lord," Lloyd bowed courteously. "I am pleased to see Miss Aldridge's family has come to her assistance."

His Lordship returned the acknowledgment. "I assume, Sir, you have news of importance to share."

"Yes, my Lord." Lloyd stepped farther into the room. "I found a witness who saw the coach turning from the access road onto the main one."

"A witness?" Worthing gestured the man to a seat.

The magistrate removed his handkerchief to mop the sweat from his brow. "Mr. Tolley, the coachman for the late morning run, recalls the carriage. Said he noticed it because as his coach passed the small road, he had worried whether the man driving the other carriage might turn his coach into Tolley's."

"Did Mr. Tolley recognize the driver?" Worthing questioned.

"Not that he recalled, Sir." The magistrate appeared in his element. "Said the driver was a big man–not only tall, but with big shoulders."

Worthing shot a quick glance at Cashé, and she had understood his silent command to hold her tongue. "Was he British?"

The magistrate appeared confused. "Do you mean did the driver appear to be an Englishman?" His Lordship nodded his affirmation. Cashé was impressed how the viscount knew just what to ask. "Well, I do not likely know for certain, Lord Worthing. I did not think to ask, but I am relatively certain if the man were a foreigner, Tolley would have mentioned it. Besides, I have discovered a name. The man rented the carriage at the inn."

"And the name, Mr. Lloyd?" Kerrington pressed.

"Boyd Livingstone." The man read from a piece of paper he removed from an inside pocket.

"Sounds British," Worthing remarked. Cashé recognized the name immediately, but she managed to stifle her words. However, her emotional response did not go unnoticed. Cashé blanched, turning completely white. "At least, you have a solid lead, Mr. Lloyd," the viscount announced. He placed a reassuring hand over hers and gave her wrist a gentle squeeze. "I assume you have sent riders to trail the coach as far as possible. We should confirm my wife's cousin Miss Satiné was not aboard the coach." Lord Worthing stood to bring the conversation to a close. "Mr. Tolley did not by some chance take note of Miss Aldridge's sister, I presume."

Mr. Lloyd rose also. "No, my Lord. Tolley said the coach appeared empty." He bowed to Kerrington and then to Cashé. "I will see to the riders immediately, Lord Worthing."

Worthing walked the man to the door and motioned for a waiting servant to see the magistrate out. "My cousin and I appreciate all you have done today. I plan to speak to the surgeon regarding Lord Lexford's recovery and then to Ashton's staff. I will call upon you a bit later, if that is acceptable. It is coming upon nightfall."

"Certainly, Lord Worthing." The magistrate made a speedy exit.

Worthing closed the door and turned toward her. Although she attempted to maintain her composure, Cashé swayed in place, a tight grip on her chair's back the only thing preventing her knees from buckling. Worthing caught her about the waist and assisted her to a seat. He knelt beside her. "Tell me," he whispered hoarsely. "Who is Boyd Livingstone?"

"It is the name of Mr. Lachlan Charters' grandfather. Mr. Charters' mother came from the Livingstone clan in central Scotland." Tears formed in the corner of Cashé's eyes. "Mr. Charters once told me the man's parents named him Boyd because he was a tow-headed child. Boyd is a Gaelic word for blond. The man who took Satiné is the one to whom Uncle Samuel once promised me. Mr. Charters thinks Satiné is I." Cashé visibly shook with dread. "He came after me," she whispered.

A Touch of Cashémere

Lord Worthing did not pretend to not understand. It was a testament that the viscount trusted her. "What does Ashton know of Viscount Averette? Why did Lord Averette leave you behind? Help me to assist Satiné."

She slipped her hand into his and held tight. Silent sobs shook her shoulders. "I did not know until today," she murmured. "I returned from the ride to discover for myself why Uncle Charles took Lord Averette's letter. I only recently recalled the incident, and it has haunted my days." Cashé looked deep into Kerrington's eyes. "The baron believes Uncle Samuel had something to do with my parents' death."

His Lordship muffled his curse. "Will you show me what you found?" he encouraged. "Whatever Ashton knows has put your sister in danger. You must realize, Cashémere, I want only to protect Satiné."

Meeting his questioning gaze, Cashé protested, "But Mr. Charters will not hurt Satiné. He will release her when he discovers my sister is not I."

The viscount's eyes narrowed. He spoke earnestly, "Satiné is ruined. Too many people know of her disappearance. Our only hope is to rescue her as quickly as possible, but I cannot do that if I do not know what I am likely to encounter."

Despite her culpability in this matter, Cashé meant to protect her sister. "Satiné will be devastated; she has looked forward to her Come Out for two years." Cashé rose quickly to her feet. "Follow me. The papers are in uncle's study."

As Lord Worthing read the letter and then returned it to its place in the family Bible, Cashé impatiently paced the open space before the desk. Finally, he had read through the bundled file. "Tell me," she demanded.

"You shan't like it," His Lordship warned.

Cashé stopped suddenly. "Nevertheless, I must know."

"This is a statement from a wheelwright. There is evidence that the spokes on your parents' carriage had been cut. Each broke at the same precise angle," he explained.

"Yet, that particular fact does not mean Uncle Samuel was to blame," Cashé challenged.

Worthing continued, "What you say is true, but the baron found other clues leading to a group of men, among them one Lachlan Charters. These men once enthusiastically followed the teachings of Thomas Chalmers, but

192

they have found a means to profit from the parochial system Chalmers advocated to service the poor."

Although Cashé knew quite well Lord Worthing spoke the truth, she vehemently declared, "That is impossible!" Yet, she did not believe her protests. She had read the file herself, and with His Lordship's explanation, it made perfect sense. Cashé stood completely still. In defeat, she asked, "How may we stop them from hurting Satiné? I will do anything to save my sister."

Some time later, Cashé withdrew to Lexford's bedside. She had assisted Lord Worthing with his detailed plans to recover her twin. As part of his scheme, His Lordship had contacted several of the other members of his unit: Baron John Swenton, and the Marquis of Godown, Gabriel Crowden, along with Lexford's man, Lucifer Hill. Although Charters had a substantial head start, His Lordship had assured her they could overtake the carriage before it reached the Scottish border. "The land is rough going in a carriage, especially with a man at the reins who is unaccustomed to driving a coach," he had said before she had retreated to tend Lord Lexford. Worthing expected he and his men could travel north by midnight.

As she watched over the viscount, she caressed Lexford's cheek before pushing away that arrant curl, which forever fell over his forehead. "I wish I could tell you how deeply apologetic I am for placing you and Satiné in danger." She had once told Satiné how annoying she had found the gesture, but Cashé would give anything if the viscount would open his eyes and reach to replace the curl for himself. "I promise to make this right for you and my sister. You will know happiness with Satiné. You must." Her throat cramped with an uncontrollable sob. "I want to see you and Satiné with a houseful of children. I want to hug my nieces and nephews and to see you grow old together." The tears fell upon the hand she held. "Please come back to us," she whispered hoarsely. "For Satiné. For Marcus. For your future, and for mine."

He was floating somewhere between the familiar voice of Cashémere Aldridge and the abyss leading to Heaven. All around him the sun caused his eyes to squint against the glare, and Aidan Kimbolt attempted to delineate the form of the approaching shadow before it overtook him. Warm fingers gently removed the lock of hair, which forever graced his forehead, but a different reality now called to him. The shadow had begun to take shape, and Aidan's mind filled with regret and shame. The apparition did not retreat, nor did the blackness. He had never run from a fight in his life, but he wished to run now. Yet, his feet refused to move. Although he pulled frantically at his legs, he could not loosen the sucking hold of the muck beneath his boots. Angry words. A sharp pain in his side. His arms wrenched behind him. A blow to the side of his head. Tasting his own blood, and then blackness again. There was no way out.

A little after midnight, Worthing and his companions prepared to depart for Scotland. Lord Godown had ridden in from his estate in Staffordshire, Lord Swenton from Yorkshire, and Mr. Hill from Lexford's estate in Cheshire. "I have written to Eleanor," Worthing told Cashé. "She will come tomorrow to stay with you. I suspect it will be another two days before Ashton arrives. I will send word as soon as we know anything."

Feeling very uncomfortable, Cashé murmured, "How may I demonstrate my gratitude, my Lord?" For unexplained reasons, she wished she had not betrayed her uncle by showing Lord Worthing the files on Samuel Aldridge. She had made a mess of everything. When Uncle Charles discovered her deceit, he would send her away; he would never forgive her, and she held no hope of returning to her Scottish home. Cashé had thought of Velvet, but her sister would not welcome her after everything Cashé had said before Velvet's nuptials and everything she had done wrong since that time.

"You will repay me by tending to Lexford. I should wish to see the viscount up and about upon my return." Worthing kissed the tip of her nose. "You are quite remarkable," he whispered close so the others could not hear. "You will be very good for Wellston."

Cashé had returned to her room after looking in on the viscount. Sleep evaded her. In fact, she thought never to sleep again. "How will Uncle Charles react?" She paced the narrow chambers she now considered to be hers. Despite being at Chesterfield Manor for barely a month, she knew she had found a home within these walls. "What will Satiné think of me? If I had not insisted, my sister would be safely in her bed and not on some crazy trek across the northern shires. Satiné will refuse our kinship." Cashé flopped down upon the bed, clutching a pillow to her and curling into a fetal position. "Who will want me now? Even Lord Yardley will likely turn me away." A shiver of regret shook her.

Regina Jeffers

Like a swirling snowflake in the wind, the misery bombarded her. She could easily imagine the countenances of each of those she had hurt with her brashness. "I cannot simply lie here." Cashé sat up suddenly, slamming the pillow against the mattress. She glanced at the ormolu clock on the mantle. "Half past two," she announced to the empty room. "There is still time to set all this right. Lighting an additional candle, she strode to her wardrobe. Within three-quarters of an hour, she had packed a traveling bag with several serviceable gowns before robbing both her sister's and uncle's rooms of stashed away coins and paper money, along with several cheaper chains and costume jewelry she might sell if necessary.

By four she was slipping from the kitchen into the damp morning chill. The northbound mail coach would leave the village inn at five, and Cashé planned to be on it. She had an hour to walk the three miles to the coaching inn. Cutting across the back lawn, she set a steady pace. Cashé understood what she must do to save her sister and to hold onto a chance for a family who would love her.

Chapter Thirteen

Marcus raised his head when Breeson tapped on the door. "Come," he called and then returned to his ledgers to finish his calculations. Breeson waited patiently for Marcus to complete the sums. When he laid his pen to the side, his former batman cleared his throat. "What is it, Breeson?" He spoke more tersely than he intended. Marcus's euphoria at having received a note from Cashé had lessened over the past few days. Her missive had told him Lexford had planned a visit to Chesterfield Manor, and a message from Worthing had informed him Shepherd had extended an "invitation" to Ashton to come to London to answer some questions; therefore, despite her assurance she would redirect the viscount's attentions to Satiné, Marcus had imagined Lexford and Cashé together. He had attempted to control his unreasonableness, but Marcus lacked rationality where Miss Cashé was concerned.

"I was wondering, my Lord, if'n I might have a few days to visit my mother. She is not well, Sir."

Marcus pushed his annoyance aside. "Is Mrs. Breeson suffering?"

"Just age, my Lord, but my sister believes my presence would do our mother well." Breeson rotated his hat through his fingers in an uncharacteristically nervous gesture.

Marcus took no time to consider the matter. Breeson never asked for time away. If the man thought he must return home, Marcus would not question it. "How long will you require?"

"A week, Sir."

"Are you certain that is enough?"

"Yes, Sir. Longer than a couple of days takes its toll on us all. I have been away too long to take orders from anyone but you, Sir."

Marcus chuckled. "Take as long as you require, Breeson." Although he thought he would gladly take orders from his mother if only she were alive to deliver them, he understood perfectly.

"May I be of assistance?" Ashton's butler greeted her.

"I am Lady Worthing." Eleanor Kerrington removed her bonnet and gloves and handed them to the man. "Lord Worthing sent for me so I might assist my cousin. Might I see Miss Aldridge?"

The butler assisted Eleanor with her cloak. "Miss Aldridge has not come down, Lady Worthing."

Eleanor shot a glance at the tall clock. "It is after ten. Please tell me this is not typical of Baron Ashton's household."

Mr. Whitcomb blustered. "No, Ma'am; Miss Aldridge saw Lord Worthing and his companions on their way well after midnight. I would assume the young lady required her rest after a trying day."

Eleanor understood the man's loyalty to Charles Morton's household, but her husband's note said the situation was urgent, and she wished to know more of what had occurred. "Is there word of Miss Satiné?"

"I am Mr. Whitcomb, Lady Worthing. The servants report to me, and I have heard nothing of Miss Satiné's whereabouts."

Eleanor frowned from the lack of information. "And Lord Lexford?"

"His Lordship has yet to awake, Lady Worthing."

Eleanor sighed deeply in exasperation. "I will see Lord Lexford while you send someone to my cousin's room to inform her of my arrival."

"Yes, Your Ladyship." The man reached behind him for a salver. "With instructions to deliver it upon your arrival, Lord Worthing left this message for you, Ma'am." He motioned to a waiting maid. "Lucy will show you to the viscount's room and then seek Miss Aldridge's presence in your name."

Eleanor inclined her head regally. Accepting her husband's message, she followed the maid to the guest chambers. She carried her husband's letter with her to read while she waited for Cashé to dress for the day.

"This is the viscount's room, Ma'am." The maid opened the door and stepped aside. Another maid scurried to her feet upon Eleanor's entrance.

Viewing Aidan Kimbolt lying so helplessly upon the bed, Eleanor gasped. "The viscount appears so pale," she said softly.

"The housekeeper, Mrs. Lacey, say that be expected, Ma'am."

"Would you ask the housekeeper to attend me in Lord Lexford's room?" she addressed the waiting maid. "I wish to hear what the surgeon had to say regarding His Lordship's care."

"Yes, Ma'am."

With the exit of both maids, Eleanor sat on the bed's edge, before capturing Kimbolt's large hand. "I am here, Lord Lexford," she whispered as she bent to kiss his cheek. Eleanor swept away the lock of hair drooping over his forehead. "I shall not permit you to leave us, Aidan," she declared. "Without you, my life would have disintegrated into Sir Louis's evilness." She stroked his cheek. "I never told you how safe I felt in your arms and how bereft I felt when we parted. I thought myself cleansed by your touch, and you restored my hope by sending me to James. So, you must understand I am determined to see you well so you may know the same type of contentment as I."

Before she might say more, the young maid came rushing into the room. "Lady Worthing, oh, Ma'am!" She fanned herself with her open hand. "She be gone! Miss Aldridge be gone!"

Eleanor was on her feet immediately. "What do you mean...gone?" She caught the girl's arm to give the overly excited maid a slight shake. Eleanor had not time for hysterics. She required facts.

"Gone, Ma'am," the maid bit out breathlessly. "There be clothes everywhere, and Miss Aldridge be leavin' these two letters on her bed."

Eleanor snatched the papers from the girl's hand. Scrawled across one was Baron Ashton's name and the other held hers. Eleanor tore at the one addressed to her. Her eyes scanned the hurriedly written words. Her young cousin had made a brazen decision. Devouring the words, her hand shook, but she refused to permit the servant to view her concern. "Lucy," she spoke evenly, "please have Mr. Whitcomb to attend me here."

"Yes, Ma'am."

"And Lucy," she warned, "do not speak of this to another soul."

"Yes, Ma'am."

When the maid disappeared into the corridor, Eleanor permitted herself a moment of dismay. "Oh, Cashé," she whispered. "Impetuous, fiery Cashémere." She glanced at the note again. "If you ever mangage your impulses, you will rule the world." In some ways, Cashé's actions appalled her: The girl had put herself in danger. Yet, Eleanor admired Cashé's resolve to find her sister. Her cousin's decision was one Eleanor might have made when she was the girl's age.

⊙⊙⊙

The Shadow had foisted the darkness upon him, but Aidan Kimbolt had clawed his way toward the light. He had argued with the Shadow. Had pushed aside his fears. Had managed to conceal the pain radiating throughout his body. Eleanor Fowler rested in his arms, and he had kissed her tenderly. It was the first time he had kissed any woman since.... Aidan did not wish to remember the pain. The devastation of his heart. All he wished to remember was those shared moments of intimacy with the woman Kerrington reportedly loved. He had not wanted her as did his captain, but he had been sore to leave the warmth and the tenderness he had found with Fowler's sister. *How can I be whole again without that feeling of familiarity? Without that openhearted welcome I found in her presence?* He had asked himself, and the Shadow ominously responded, "You cannot."

✑✑

"Are you certain?" Jamot asked for the third time.

The timid shopkeeper, Mr. Stanley, whom the Baloch paid for information, shifted his weight from side to side. "That is what I heard. The baron has gone to London on business, but he left the sisters under Viscount Lexford's care. Unfortunately, someone attacked the gentleman, and it is rumored one of the girls has disappeared."

"From whom does this information come?" Jamot formed the words carefully. He hated the English tongue, but he knew it served him well to sound as if he were one of his enemies.

"I heard it myself at the inn. The magistrate questioned the innkeeper."

Jamot, by design, reached into his pocket to hand Stanley another payment. "Keep asking around," he instructed. "I want to know everything. Inform me when the baron returns." The man cautiously accepted the money, and Jamot realized Stanley hated serving a foreigner. The knowledge gave him a certain satisfaction in having the Brit answer to his beck and call. "If anything else of note occurs, you come to me first."

✑✑

As the post coach rolled along the country roads, Cashé stared out the window. She attempted to ignore her fellow travelers. She had worn her most common day dress. Luckily, she had anticipated people's interest in her, and to deflect their estimations, she had purposely slurred her words and had pretended to be an upper servant off to tend an elderly relative. She had spoken as little as possible to the others. It would take a minimum of four days of hard traveling to reach her destination. As the miles led her farther from Chesterfield Manor, Cashé had prayed her sister had not submitted to Charters' rough ways. Satiné had never faced adversity before, and Cashé was not certain how this abduction might affect her twin. If Satiné could continue her pretense of being Cashé, her sister might survive this ordeal. The world would view Cashé as ruined, but there was

199

no other solution. She had set her mind to what must be done. She would see this through: She would set things right.

つつつ

Being rocked forth and back, Satiné woke on the floor of the carriage. The coach's constant swaying had caused her stomach to lurch, and she had fought hard not to lose her breakfast. "Breakfast," she formed the word without the sound. When had that been? she thought. And then the realization had hit her hard enough to knock the breath from her chest. Some man had attacked Viscount Lexford and had carried her off, thinking she was Cashémere.

The recognition sent her insides reeling again. What in the world could she do to make the man release her? Despondently, she acknowledged how this incident would ruin her reputation before she had ever made her appearance in London. However, if she could convince her abductor to free her, she might still salvage some shred of decency; and she could delay her Presentation for yet another year to permit the rumors to die away.

How to escape? She wondered aloud. Uncle Charles. Her uncle would search for her. That was a certainty. "But he was away from home," she whispered. Was anyone seeking her? How long had she been unconscious? How far had the man traveled? With an effort, Satiné pushed herself to a seated position before leaning against the bench seat. The inside of the coach swirled about her, and she gave herself a good shake to clear her mind. She must find a means of escape. "Surely, I can clarify the man's misconception. When he understands I am not Cashémere, he will permit my freedom," she told herself, but as the coach rolled on, she doubted whether anything in her life would ever be the same.

つつつ

Eleanor had read her husband's letter and had completely understood the situation. She was to take control of the household. First, Eleanor met with the servants to demand they refrain from speaking of Lord Lexford's injury, Satiné's disappearance, or Cashé's withdrawal to anyone outside the house, "All inquires are to be referred to me," she had instructed. After speaking to Mrs. Lacey, she had sent a note to Mr. Potter requesting his discretion in handling the viscount's case. Finally, Eleanor had spoken directly to the magistrate. The man's handling of the questioning of witnesses had opened Satiné's reputation to censure. Depending on how quickly Lord Worthing recovered Satiné would determine what story they would spread throughout the neighborhood. Eleanor had had plenty of practice in covering scandals, and with her powerful friends and family, she knew what to do to correct the locals' bungling of the situation.

Although not expecting much success, she had dutifully sent a rider to seek her husband with the news of Cashé's plan to save her sister, but Ella knew the young groomsman would need to be an excellent horseman to outride Lord Worthing and her husband's associates. She held no doubt the Realm members would not stop until they had found Satiné's abductor. As there was nothing else she could do to save Satiné or to recover Cashémere, Eleanor returned to Lord Lexford's beside. She would wait for Ashton's reappearance, more likely some time late tomorrow. Then perhaps, she and the baron could decipher what action to follow.

✿✿✿

"What do you mean no one is talking?" Jamot stormed across the sparsely furnished room.

Despite his evident fears, Stanley brought a report of "no news." In some ways, Jamot admired the man's loyalty, but he certainly would not admit so. "I have asked repeatedly...from everyone, and I keep hearing the same thing: 'I know nothing. If you want to ask questions about the family, ask their cousin. The lady is staying at Chesterfield Manor and is overseeing the house in the baron's absence.'"

Jamot tapped down his anger. "Who is this cousin?"

"Again, I am not certain. It is almost as if someone has warned everyone away from the story. I did confirm the fact Viscount Lexford has not regained consciousness."

Jamot stared out the small window. "And you say the baron is not in residence?"

"No. Ashton has not returned from London...although someone has most certainly sent word of the situation. If so, he will likely arrive in Cheshire some time tomorrow or, at a minimum, the next day."

Jamot nodded his understanding. Deep in thought, he added, "You must discover more before you come again." Without looking at the man, he extended the payment. "I pay for information, not the lack of it, Mr. Stanley. Do you comprehend my meaning?"

"Yes. Yes, I understand perfectly."

✿✿✿

Following the most obvious trail to Scotland, Kerrington led his men through the night. From what Cashé had told him, Charters had never traveled outside of his home land, and Kerrington assumed the man would

201

stay to the main roads; but after finding nothing at the first three inns at which they stopped, he had changed his mind. "No one has seen Charters," he said softly when he rejoined his friends in the inn's common room.

Gabriel Crowden shot a glance to the other customers. It was early, and most of the inn's occupants had broken their fasts and had departed on their journeys. "What do we do next?"

Worthing frowned as he followed Crowden's eyes. "This Charters character planned more fully than I had initially expected. I thought this an impulsive move for the Scot, but he has obviously thought this through. It appears we must split up. Crowden, I suggest you and Swenton continue along the main road. According to Miss Aldridge, Charters resides in Leith, about three miles outside of Edinburgh. I will take Lucifer with me, and we will cut across country. I had hoped to overtake the man before Miss Satiné's reputation lay in shreds, but that possibility may be nul. We will meet up at The Sunset Inn south of Edinburgh."

Crowden picked up his gloves. "I am prepared when you are, Swenton?"

Worthing caught his friend's arm. "Is something amiss, Crowden?"

The always-private marquis paused. "Just family issues. Nothing I cannot address on my own." He removed his arm from Worthing's grasp. "I will be outside checking the horses. Join me when you finish your meal, Swenton."

The coach slowed to a stop beside what appeared to be a deserted barn. Satiné had climbed onto the bench seat and peered out the window. She momentarily wondered if she could jump from the coach and run for assistance before the man caught her again, but there were no other structures in the vicinity. In addition, a heavy fog clung to the trees and hedgerows. As she bit her lower lip in indecision, the coach's door swung open, and the man who had carried her from her uncle's land filled the space. "Come," he ordered, reaching in and grabbing Satiné's arm.

"You do not understand," she protested while fighting his manhandling. However the man ignored her pleas. Instead, he shoved her toward the barn. "Please. Do not do this," she begged as stories of ill abused women flooded her mind.

"There be cover behind those trees." He pointed to a nearby copse.

Satiné stared off in confusion in the direction he had indicated, and then it dawned on her what he had suggested. "You expect me to...to..." She could not form the words.

"Ye be getting' airs while livin' with the baron. Ye kin use the privacy or do without." Her abductor unharnessed the horses. "When I finish, we leave. You have the choice."

Satiné thought to argue, but now he had suggested the need to relieve herself, she could do with the moment of privacy. Dejectedly, she walked toward the tree line. Hidden behind the hedges, she surveyed the area. There was nothing of significance. The moors and the peaks loomed all around with nary anything else in sight.

Without an alternative, she had finished her business and returned to where she might watch the man's methodical movements. Surprisingly, he treated the animals with kindness—a caress along the horse's leg and a brush across the animal's rump. Could such a man hurt her? Fascinated by his actions, it took several elongated seconds before Satiné realized he had attached fresh horses to the coach. "You planned this?" she said in dismay.

The stranger glanced over his shoulder at her. "I keep wot belongs to me," he stated matter-of-factly.

She thought to object, but he walked away from her, leading the two spent animals toward the dilapidated barn. In his absence, her idea of escape returned, but before she could take action, he reappeared.

"Time to go." The stranger caught her arm to lift her to the coach, literally boosting Satiné roughly into the carriage. "There be food and water on the seat." He slammed the door.

"We must talk," she called as the carriage shifted with his weigh. She cursed herself for not speaking to him of his error while she had had the opportunity.

"Nothin' to say," he responded as he flicked the reins, and the horses lurched forward.

Satiné righted herself as the rhythmic sway began again. Looking to the small basket now sitting on the seat, hunger's head appeared. She had not eaten since leaving Chesterfield Manor for her leisurely ride with Lord Lexford. Nearly twenty-four hours earlier. Experiencing the hunger pains, she searched the basket's contents. "An apple," she said aloud just to hear another sound other than the noisy clack of the coach's wheels taking her from her home. Satiné could not think on that particular fact right now. Soon. But not now. She took a large bite of the fruit before finding dark bread and hard cheese. Hungrily, she tore off a huge chunk of both, alternating each item to taste. "Not much worth sampling," she mumbled, "but, at least, the fare will stave off my hunger."

She pulled a flask from the basket's interior and removed the cap. Wondering whether the man packed spirits, Satiné sniffed the contents first, but she smelled nothing unusual. "Smells of water." She braced herself by catching one of the straps as the carriage took a sharp turn to the left. When she righted herself, Satiné took a deep drink of the cool water. It had a metallic taste, but that particular fact was not uncommon in many of the local wells. She took another bite of the bread and cheese and some more of the cool water. Just consuming sustenance had cleared thinking. Once she finished her meager meal, she would set her mind to discovering an escape. Nibbling the last of her apple, Satiné leaned back in the well-worn squabs. The sun streaked across her lap, and she traced the line with her eyes. The day was warmer than expected, and she loosened the buttons of her jacket. Her eyes were heavy, but Saíné forcibly studied the scenery outside the window: It was important for her to learn more of her surroundings so she might flee with the first opportunity. However, her effors were in vain. The early morning light distorted the lines of the cushion's tacking, and she felt her head fall forward as the blackness blurred her senses. "The water," she mumbled before falling across the coach's bench.

❦

With Mr. Stanley's departure, Jamot gathered his belongings. He had stayed long enough. Likely, Stanley would find his conscience before he discovered more information. Therefore, the Baloch moved on to the next place. First, he would ride to Lord Lexford's estate in Cheshire, and if, as reported, he discovered both the viscount and his man absent, Jamot would search the house for the emerald. Several months ago, he had completed a similar search of Lexford's minor properties. The viscount's absence would create a prime opportunity to determine what Lexford kept under lock and key.

❦

Cashé had spent her first night in a small inn outside of Leeds. The roads' conditions had permitted the coach's travelers to make their lay over in a timely fashion. Taking her meal in her quarters and attempting to be unremarkable, she had let an insignificant room. If her Uncle Charles gave chase, she wanted no one to remember her.

Regina Jeffers

"I wish I knew where to seek out Mr. Charters," Cashé told herself as she watched the busy inn yard from her small window. "I pray Mr. Charters escorts Satiné to Leith, or better yet delivers her to Uncle Samuel." By design, she paused to say a prayer for Satiné, another for Lord Lexford, and a few words for herself. Her dreams of a life with Marcus Wellston appeared grim. The earl would likely wish nothing to do with her after this disaster. Leaving Manchester on her own had made her a fallen woman. Compound that offense with Velvet's earlier disappearance and Satiné's kidnapping, and the likelihood of an earl, choosing her had diminished to null. All she could do was to return to Scotland and to intercept Charters before the Scot did something diastrous to her twin. Cashé realized Charters could be volatile when pushed to abstraction, and surely he was exactly that. If her former intended had gone so far as to come to England to retrieve her, then Charters had lost his practical reason, and that fact would not bode well for any of them.

Aidan felt the pressure of the girl's mouth upon his lips and the heat of her body beneath his own, and his heart came alive. Could this woman be the balm to his shattered dreams? Could he finally cast off the mantle he had worn for the past three years? For so long, his failure, his inability to save the woman he had loved, had haunted him. So much so the Shadow kept its tight grip about his chest, and the acrid smell of burning flesh filled his nostrils and his memory with the misery of his own vulnerability. As he searched for the girl's countenance among his scattered memories, her once beautiful expression dissolved into a swirl of sensuous withdrawal. A helpless sigh echoed in his ears as thunder broke in excruciating violence. On the edge of panic, he reached for her, but the Shadow replaced the girl's warmth with the familiar Guilt, which shook Aidan to his bones. Something twisted painfully in his chest before an icy hand plunged him downward into the darkness.

Jamot shimmied the servant door open and slid into the darkness. After thoroughly searching Lexford's manor house for the emerald and finding nothing, he had made the short journey from Cheshire to Manchester. News of the viscount's injury had sent the man's household into an uproar, but the staff had concentrated their frustrations to the servants' quarters, leaving the remainder of the house easy pickings.

Now, two hours after midnight, he invaded Baron Ashton's home—not because he thought the Realm had given the man the emerald for safekeeping, but because Jamot required knowledge of how the baron and his nieces fit into the lives of the Realm members. He would use the information he found against his enemy. Plus, he had wished to see for himself the extent of Lord Lexford's injuries. Stanley provided limited knowledge of the situation.

Carefully traversing the narrow servant stairway, he eased open the door leading to the main hallway and the baron's study. Only one footman remained at his post, and the servant nodded in deep sleep. Taking cover behind potted palms and marble statues, Jamot clung to the wall. He slid into the partially opened door and made his way to the baron's desk. Easing each drawer open, he fanned stacks of papers. The bright moonlight permitted him to read a line or two of each page before searching the next. None of what he found identified a connection to the Realm, but Jamot took several pages with Lord Averette's name on them from a ribbon-bound stack. Aware of how long he had spent in the study, he silently closed the drawers and slipped from the room.

⁂

Freely mumbling words of endearment, as well as expletives, Lexford had threshed about for hours. The viscount's words had not surprised her, but Eleanor had found them a bit embarrassing. Therefore, not wishing to expose the girl to the foul language or to permit others to hear what she supposed to be Realm secrets, she had excused Ashton's maid. Now, she sat beside Lord Lexford's bed, changing out the cold compress. The viscount's color had appeared more normal, but the violence and anger exposed in his dreams had wrenched her heart with pain. He had saved her from Sir Louis Levering and had initiated her return to James Kerrington's care. Now, Eleanor searched Aidan Kimbolt's kind countenance, which was painted with misery and despair, and she wished to ease each frown and furrowed line. "Shush, my Lord," she whispered softly. "I shall find a way to relieve your anguish."

Surprisingly, with her words, His Lordship ceased his worried tales. The renewed silence, however, brought Eleanor's already heightened senses to alert. The nearly silent tread on a loose board under the carpet runner three doors along the hall caused the wood to pop. She knew the sound could signal the maid's return, but something deep within Eleanor's gut said otherwise. Without considering the danger, she caught Lexford's gun in her grasp and stepped behind the hinged folding screen. Yet, before she could settle her nerves, the door opened on a silent rush of air, and a man she knew to be the Realm's enemy stood framed in the darkness. Eleanor bit back the fear that clogged her throat. What was Murhad Jamot doing in Ashton's house, and, more importantly, what did he want with Aidan Kimbolt? Instinctively, she sank further into the room's shadows.

◈◈◈

Jamot quickly glanced about the room. With the draperies of the four poster tied back, he knew by design Lord Lexford's position, but where was the person who attended the viscount? It was not likely the household had left Aidan Kimbolt unattended. There was the possibility the maid had stepped from the room to address personal matters; yet, Jamot would take nothing for granted. He warily peeked through the door's crack to find no one behind it before tentatively stepping into the room. Removing his gun from his waistband, he cross-stepped carefully to his left to view first the darkened dressing room and then behind a small desk set in the room's corner.

◈◈◈

Eleanor swallowed her fear. This was the same man who had shot at her in Hyde Park, who had kidnapped Velvet, and who had slit Louis Levering's throat. She held no doubt the Baloch would kill both her and Lord Lexford without expressing any qualms. It would be her domain to protect the viscount. Unconsciously, she thought of James Kerrington and his absolute faith in her. She would not fail him.

Yet, before she could act, Lexford rasped, "Do not touch her! I beg you." Once more, her husband's friend threshed from side to side. The viscount mind fought hard to free him from his enemies. He growled, "Aarrgghh!" as he struggled with the invisible bindings.

Eleanor's eyes grew in size as Jamot looked to the open door; the Baloch obviously expected someone to return to care for the viscount. Seeing nothing, her husband's enemy edged closer to where Lexford lay.

"Kill me!" The viscount bit out with anger. "But do not hurt her again!" he wailed.

"Always happy to bow to the Realm's wishes," the Baloch vowed as he stepped closer to the viscount's bed. Reaching for a pillow, Jamot placed the cushion over Aidan Kimbolt's face and bore down with all his weight.

In horror, Eleanor watched as Lexford fought the intrusion, and for a moment, she froze. Yet, the viscount's muffled cry brought her to action.

207

Stepping from behind the screen and bracing the gun with both hands, she ordered, "Leave him, or I will shoot."

Jamot's countenance held his surprise. For a second, something like a smirk played across his mouth before he released his grip on the pillow and straightened slowly. "Ah, Lady Worthing," he smiled condescendingly. "I did not realize you were the cousin tending to the viscount and the baron's household. However, I should have suspected as such." Eleanor knew him to be unarmed. The Baloch had placed his gun on the bed when he had retrieved the pillow to smother Lord Lexford.

"You were aware of Her Grace's association with my family," Eleanor countered in a surprisingly calm voice. "It was part of your plan when you kidnapped my brother's wife."

Jamot tilted his head to the side, indicating the truth of her words. "I recognized the former Miss Aldridge's connection to the twin girls who distracted me in Liverpool," he said evenly. "Yet, for some unknown reason, your presence in Viscount Lexford's room has taken me unawares."

"As did yours for me." Eleanor's lips turned upward in wry amusement. "Without further ado, I shall ask you again to step away from Lord Lexford's bedside."

"I will hunt you to the ends of the earth," the viscount snarled as he continued his imagined struggle.

Eleanor fought the urge to glance to Lexford's form. She knew better than to give the Baloch any opportunity to escape. "Raise your hands slowly," she advised Jamot.

The Baloch smiled with confidence. "You are not a person who could shoot another in cold blood."

"Do not tempt me," she warned. "In addition to the attempt on my life, I have reason enough to overcome any deficit you think I might hold."

Jamot eyed her cautiously. "Do you even know how to shoot, Lady Worthing?"

Eleanor returned his contempt. "I suppose we shall both discover that reality together."

Jamot's slight raise of his arms told Eleanor the Baloch, at least, considered the possibility of her shooting him. "You do not need to do this," he whispered in heavily accented English. "Permit me to leave, and we will call it even. I have no desire to kill a woman, especially one with child. Yet, I will not permit you to place me in custody. I will fight you, Lady Worthing."

Regina Jeffers

Eleanor's heart raced: She not only placed her own life in jeopardy, but also the one of her first child. However, she could not permit Jamot to leave. Determined, she motioned with the slight flick of the gun for the man to move. If only a footman or a maid would appear where she might send for assistance, things would be easier. But it was the dead of night, and she was alone with an accomplished killer. "Move to the chair," she nodded to the one behind him.

"As you wish, my Lady." Jamot slid his left foot backward, but, like a caged animal, in the next second he lunged for Eleanor, turning her sideways and wrestling with her–forcing Eleanor to lie awkwardly across the viscount's bed. They grappled for control of the gun, and Eleanor fought with a resolve, which surprised even her. In all her childhood fantasies, she had never imagined herself the warrior princess.

However, despite her best efforts, Jamot wrenched the weapon from her grip. With vengeance in his action, her husband's enemy slapped her hard when Eleanor rose with him to continue the tussle, and for a split second, she knew only the pain. Yet, edging her on, the viscount kicked at her, as Eleanor lay draped across his body. Moving deliberately, Ella fought the ringing in her head, which gave her the impetus to rise. The action brought reality, and Eleanor spotted the Baloch's retreating form. Turning and reaching for the gun lying at Lexford's feet, Ella grabbed it with one hand and caught her skirt tail with the other.

Giving chase, she saw the man scurry down the first flight of steps. Eleanor charged after him; yet, she knew she had no chance of catching him. Skidding to a stop on the landing, she raised her arm–settling the gun in a desperate step to prevent Jamot's escape. "Aim low." Eleanor heard her husband's voice whisper to her. "Your target is below you."

With a steadying breath, she squeezed the trigger. The smoke momentarily blinded her, but Ella saw the Baloch clutch at his shoulder. At the bottom of the stairs, Jamot slugged the advancing footman with a left across the servant's jaw, before turning to the slowly descending Eleanor and giving her an elegant bow of respect. She knew he held Lord Lexford's gun, but she possessed no fear of the man. She had conquered her nightmares: had escaped her father's disastrous reputation and had driven this man not only from the baron's house, but also from her life. The Baloch was no longer her enemy. "Lord Worthing possesses a worthy opponent," Jamot smirked. The sound of others awakening from the noise signaled his retreat. Without incident, the Baloch slipped through the library door and across the balcony to the gardens.

Eleanor watched him go. Her first instinct had been to give pursuit, but her hand instinctively rested on her increasing abdomen, and she protectively refused to risk her child more than she already had done.

"Lady Worthing," the butler was by her side. "Are you injured?"

Eleanor's hand drifted to her bruised cheekbone. "Nothing that will not heal quickly." She glanced at the hand still clutching the gun. Her whole body felt weak now that the crisis was over, and she permitted Mr. Whitcomb to remove the weapon from her grasp. "We must see to Lord Lexford," she heard the words but did not move until the butler and one of the footmen braced her stance. She said weakly, "I suspect the magistrate will not be pleased to hear from us again."

Chapter Fourteen

Very late the following day, Baron Ashton and the messenger sent to retrieve him rode into the circular drive of Chesterfield Manor. Although his bones ached from the pounding ride over the past two days, Ashton was on the ground and running before his horse came to a complete stop. Whitcomb jerked opened the door just as he reached it; yet, he made no notice, instead tossing his hat and gloves towards the man. The tension in his muscles could not be tossed aside so easily. "Satiné!" he yelled. "Cashémere."

"Neither lady is at home, Sir," Whitcomb said softly behind him.

The baron swung around, glaring at the man delivering the message. "What do you mean? Surely someone has found Miss Satiné by now!" His voice rose on each word.

"No, Sir. We have heard nothing since Lord Worthing departed in pursuit."

His earlier hopes dashed, Ashton openly recoiled from the news. "And Miss Cashémere? Where is my niece?"

"Perhaps I might answer your questions, Your Lordship," Lady Worthing spoke from the landing. "Please join me in Viscount Lexford's chambers. I prefer not to leave His Lordship unattended for long." Very royally, Eleanor Kerrington turned and ascended the steps as if she were the house's mistress.

Although a bit surprised at discovering the viscountess in his home, Ashton defeatedly followed Lady Worthing to Lexford's room. Closing the door behind him, he shot a worried glance at Lexford's body. "I assumed His Lordship would have recovered by now," he said softly. "It has been nearly four days since Cashémere sent word of Lexford's injury."

"I have hopes of His Lordship's recovery. Lord Lexford spent four and twenty hours in extreme agitation, but he has been calm for some time. Come." Eleanor gestured to nearby chairs. "Let us confer before the hearth."

A queasy feeling flicked at his stomach, but he allowed the daughter of his late wife's dearest friend to take the lead. "I beg you, Lady Worthing, to tell me everything. Where is Cashémere?"

Eleanor took her seat. "Let me start with Satiné's removal and Lord Lexford's attack." For the next hour, Lady Worthing provided details of her husband's search, of the identity of Satiné's abductor, of Cashé's impetuous actions, and of Jamot's invasion of the baron's manor.

"I should never have departed for London," Ashton murmured.

His companion recognized his regret, but she offered little sympathy. "You have kept secrets, Baron Ashton, which have compounded Satiné's kidnapping. Cashémere has discovered your manipulations and has shared them with my husband. I fear Jamot has also discovered some of your confidential papers for he thoroughly searched your study. While recovering Satiné shall be difficult, I have no doubt of the mission's success for Lord Worthing is the most capable man of my acquaintance; however, I must chastise you for your handling of this matter. My husband and his friends are riding into a situation, which should have been resolved long ago. If you had trusted the Realm and the government to discover the truth, things might have been different. On so many levels, you hold the blame for this debacle. You permitted Cashémere to live with that vile man because you wished to bring down Viscount Averette personally. Now, Cashé returns to set the situation aright." She handed Ashton Cashé's letters. "Cashémere believes she can claim it was she who Charters kidnapped and, therefore, save Satiné's reputation. She shall sacrifice herself to that man to protect your family."

"I will not permit it," Ashton declared. He was on his feet immediately. "I must leave for Averette's manor as soon as possible."

"Darkness has claimed the day, my Lord." Eleanor returned to Lexford's side to change the viscount's compress. "Is that the best choice?" she said over her shoulder.

Ashton glanced toward the window. "I hold no other options," he sighed. "I must be there when Satiné's and Cashémere's lives intersect with Averette's perfidy. Cashé will confront Aldridge. I have no doubt of that particular fact, and I fear for her safety if she does so. Plus, Jamot might recruit Aldridge to bring down the Realm. Averette will want his revenge."

Cashé did not like the suggestive looks the young man had given her as she had registered at the second-class inn between Darlington and

Newcastle. Clutching her cape closer, she pointedly looked away when he had caught her eye. "Anything else, Miss?" The innkeeper obviously disapproved of her presence.

"If you would send a meal to my room," she said flatly, counting out the necessary fee.

"Yes, Miss."

Exhausted, Cashé climbed the stairs. Two more days, she had said the words in her mind, calculating how soon she could arrange Satiné's release. She knew there was a strong possibility that when she reached Scotland, her sister might not be there. Then what will I do? Would Uncle Samuel and Mr. Charters permit her to return to Cheshire? Cashé imagined such a move would likely not meet with their approval. More to the fact, to free Satiné, she would need to stay with Mr. Charters. Cashé did not think the man would permit both her and her twin their freedoms. She leaned heavily against the room's door. "At least, Satiné will be permitted to escape. If nothing else, Uncle Charles can claim they had come to Edinburgh for my wedding."

Saying the words brought her a new pain. She might never see Lord Yardley again. "How will I be able to tolerate Mr. Charters's touch now that I have known Marcus Wellston?"

Worthing and Hill discovered in the most unexpected manner news of the carriage they sought. They had watered their horses and had taken a stretch of the legs along a shallow creek in mid afternoon. However, a rustle behind them brought them to alert.

"Runt, come back!" a child's voice called, and both Worthing and Hill lowered their guns just as a scraggly-looking boy of ten or eleven chased a mongrel dog from the underbrush. "Runt!" The child froze when he saw them.

Worthing smiled as Lucifer caught the dog's nape. "Do not worry, Boy," he said softly. "We will not hurt you."

The child's eyes grew, taking in Lucifer Hill's size. "He be a big one."

Worthing laughed lightly. "He is at that."

The boy edged forward to catch a rope around the dog's neck. "Thank ye for catchin' Runt."

"No thanks necessary." Hill released the animal after giving the animal a pat on its head.

"How big do ye be?" The child asked in awe.

Hill ruffled the dog's fur. "Big enough."

"I thought the other man be big, but ye be bigger."

"What other man?" Worthing asked suspiciously.

The child said importantly, "The one who paid me pa to leave his horses in arn barn."

Worthing sucked in a deep breath. "Could you show me the barn?" He offered the child a coin.

"For that coin I shows ye two barns."

Worthing caught his horse's bridle. "Just the one in which the large man kept his horses."

Breeson's horse had thrown a shoe, and so he sipped weak ale in a stinking inn while he waited for the smith to tend to the animal. He had spent less than two days at his mother's home. As expected, his family had once again treated him as an invalid, and Breeson had hated every moment of it. He knew they meant well, but he required nothing to remind him of his injury. He had lived with it every day since a bullet ripped apart the nerves and the tendons of his arm just above the elbow. He was injured, not incapacitated.

With Lord Yardley's insistence and care, Breeson had taught himself to eat and to shoot and to live without his dominant hand. In fact, Yardley's refusal to accept him as less than a whole man had saved Breeson's life. Every time he missed his mouth with his spoon, the earl had never offered him sympathy. Whenever he nicked his chin with the razor, Wellston had handed him a towel, but had offered no hand of assistance. The earl's seeming neglect had created more than one argument between them during Richard's recovery, but it had been Marcus Wellston who had offered the medicine Richard had required to survive and to set his feet on the straight and narrow. Many of his fellow soldiers had turned to drink and even to drugs to kill the pain of what they had seen in battle and what they had experienced before returning to civilian life. Breeson, on the other hand, owed Wellston his life, and he was anxious to return to the estate he called home, the place where he had carved out a life of his own. Lord Yardley had allowed him to apprentice with the estate's steward, and he hoped one day to assume the position. Plus, he held ideas of claiming Faith Molson as his wife. The girl was the village doctor's only daughter, and Breeson had wanted her the moment he had first laid eyes on the girl.

"I tell you she is alone." Breeson overheard two young bucks at the table behind him. "She will welcome us with open arms."

Breeson shifted his position so he could observe the men in profile. Over the years, he had heard similar posturing among the enlisted men and even a few of the minor officers–young men attempting to prove their manliness.

"How can you be certain?" the tow-headed youth asked, shooting a quick glance about the crowded room. "Should we not just entertain Meddy instead?"

The dark-haired youth turned his nose up in disgust. "I do not want another turn with Meddy. Every man in this place has found himself between Meddy's legs at one time or another. I want to feel clean for a change."

The before-mentioned Meddy appeared at Breeson's table with his evening meal; the barmaid gladly gave him a full view of her ample bosom. He had thought the youths would have to service a woman of such boldness many times before they could bring her to pleasure. "Thank you," he mumbled and diverted his gaze from the tempting globes to observe the youths once more. They meant mischief, and if necessary, he would put himself between the "boys" and the female of whom they spoke. He wondered if he had ever itched to prove himself as these young men wished to do. Not likely. He had known his fair share of women, but no one such as the barmaid had ever caught his attention. He had known from a young age he would find a woman of merit to claim as his own. He wanted no one but the fair-eyed Faith, the type of woman a man never forgets, not even for a moment.

⟨ℓℓℓ⟩

Marcus had spent the evening playing chess with Jeremy, but the game never engaged his mind. He had spent the day thinking on how his house required a female's touch. Despite bits of lace and fringe heavily displayed in several drawing rooms, they seemed too masculine. He and Jeremy and Trevor had existed in a male dominated household, and he had found he despised every minute of it. He ached for Cashé so intensely there were moments he thought he might explode. Marcus had never felt such a void in his life–not even with Maggie's death. How had Cashé taken control of his every thought so easily–he, who had considered himself above love, had found himself wallowing in it? "Cashé," he moaned as he closed the door to his chambers. "I require you more than you will ever know."

215

◦◦◦

She had collapsed across the bed to cry away her fears. The maid had left a simple meal on the table, but Cashé had eaten but a few spoonfuls before giving in to her despair. Now, the night sky filled her window. She had wiped away the traces of her tears and made herself undress for the evening. Her day dress held enough wrinkles from her journey without adding those from her misery. Making her way to the window, she had leaned her head against the cool pane. "Marcus," she had whispered to the stars peppering the darkness. "Where are you, my Love?"

◦◦◦

After the baron had ridden out, Eleanor had nodded off. She could no longer recall when she had slept in a bed for an entire night. With the pregnancy, she could feel the exhaustion setting in quicker than usual, but Ella would not leave Lexford's side. She would not permit the viscount to wake in an unfamiliar bed and with an unfamiliar servant tending him.

When sleep claimed her, she had dreamed of her husband. The man had haunted her every thought since the day she had, literally, stumbled into his welcoming arms. James Kerrington had given her what she had always required: a family who loved and respected her. Tonight's dream included the baby and Daniel; in it, they had sat together on the floor of James's bedchamber watching Daniel blowing soft bubbles on his sibling's stomach. Eleanor had wished she could see the baby's face clearly for she wanted to know whether it was a boy or a girl. Daniel's lips vibrated a moan as the baby cooed a welcome gurgle. Eleanor thought it was a sorrowful moan. Moan? Daniel should not moan. Then she realized it was not Daniel. Eleanor's eyes shot open, and she was on her feet immediately. "Lord Lexford," she placed her hand lightly on his arm. "Aidan, I am here."

The viscount turned his head toward the sound of her voice and slowly opened his eyes.

"Aidan." She lowered her face closer to his. "Do not move too quickly. You have experienced a head injury. Permit me to send someone for the surgeon." His eyes followed her, but Eleanor thought them vacant in their clarity. She rushed to the door and summoned a footman to fetch the surgeon; then Eleanor returned to his side. "Would you like some water?" She leaned over him to maintain his gaze.

"Y...yes," he rasped.

Eleanor lifted a spoon from the bedside table and showed it to him. "The surgeon will not permit me to lift your head from the pillow so I will spoon in the water."

He did not answer, but Eleanor was certain he understood. Slowly and methodically, she fed him six spoonfuls of the clear liquid before he gave a slight shake of his head to indicate he had had enough.

Returning the water to the small nightstand, Eleanor straightened his blanket. "Everyone will be so pleased for your recovery. You have been unconscious for well over four days. We have been so worried for you." She took the wet cloth and wiped his face. "When the surgeon agrees, I will have the cook send up some clear broth."

Lexford's eyes continued to follow her every movement, which shook her composure, but Ella assumed he was adjusting to the room and the situation. She wished it were daylight so he might see better. "Permit me to refresh the water," she said with more enthusiasm than she felt.

However, before she could more away, his hand caught her arm, holding her tightly in his grasp. "Who...who are...who are you?"

ella

When the door to her room burst open, it had taken Cashé a split second to react to the intrusion, and in that short time, the first man through the door had caught her about the waist and had dragged her into his body. One hand cupped her breast as he pressed her into his chest. He reeked of alcohol, and the smell nauseated her, but she fought him–kicking his legs and clawing at his hands.

"Catch her feet," her intruder ordered his partner as he struggled to bring Cashé under control.

Fear meant to hold her in place, but Cashé would not have it. No one would rescue her if she did not do so. Realizing she had only seconds to free herself before these men violated her, Cashé inhaled a deep breath to expand the man's grasp and then expelled it quickly before dropping to a squat. Nearly free, she, instinctively, slammed her head backwards into his groin, momentarily stunning her attacker. A guttural grunt signaled her release, and Cashé was on the run, skirting around the second intruder and exploding into the dimly lit hallway.

She had reached the stairs before the first man, cursing every foul word he knew and cradling his manhood, overtook her. He caught Cashé's plait and jerking her physically backwards by her hair. "Move, Bitch, and

I will slit your throat," he growled. He plastered her body to the wall with his and theatrically threatened her with a long knife.

Cashé's heart pounded with dread, but she defiantly raised her chin and looked the man squarely in the eye. "Then you must kill me," she declared. "Are you man enough to kill an innocent woman in cold blood?"

"You Bloody Bitch!" he growled. The man's moment of hesitation was Cashé's invitation to scream, and scream, she did–loud and long–at the top of her lungs. Somewhere over the roar of her own vocal caterwaul, she heard her attacker's partner say, "Come, Jordan, she is not worth it." Cashé's assailant suddenly released her, but she did not stop her shrieks of alarm. The two intruders ran toward the back of the inn as an onslaught of rescuers scrambled up the stairs toward her. Seeing them, Cashé triumphantly ceased her cries.

"What goes on here?" the innkeeper demanded, assuming a single female without a chaperone brought only trouble.

"Two men broke into my room," Cashé accused, pointing in the direction her assailants had fled.

The innkeeper loomed over her. "Are ye sure you did not invite them in and then change yer mind?" Those who followed the man snickered.

Cashé flushed, but she refused to permit anyone to lord over her. "How dare you?" she charged, but before she could continue, a rustling of bodies on the stairs caught her attention, and Cashé turned to see a familiar face advancing towards her. "Mr. Breeson!" she exclaimed.

∞

Richard purposely bowed low, indicating his deference to her position. "Miss Aldridge." He glanced quickly at those standing about, stepping purposely before Cashé to block others' views of her disheveled appearance. "I know this lady." He eyed the innkeeper disdainfully. "If she claims an attack in this establishment, as a proper businessman, I suggest you contact the authorities."

"Why does she have no attendant if she be a lady?" the innkeeper charged.

"Miss Aldridge was to travel to Berwick to meet her intended's family; I was sent to escort her north, but I did not expect her arrival until tomorrow." Breeson enjoyed the crowd's reaction to the tale he wove. "If the lady is without a companion, it must be for a good reason." Wellston's lady lightly touched his back, silently accepting his protection.

"Who be her affianced?" The innkeeper said snidely.

218

Breeson did not blink from the intended insult. "My master, the Earl of Berwick." A buzz of recognition spread among the onlookers. "And if you know His Lordship, you realize he will not look kindly on your slighting the woman he intends to marry."

The innkeeper cleared his throat. "Anyone know who might be to blame?"

"The two young men sitting behind me in the open room spoke of a girl, but I had no idea they spoke of Baron Ashton's niece." He knew from his long-standing dealings with both the lower classes and the gentry that interjecting names of the peerage into the conversation would draw a reaction. "Ask Meddy. They spoke of her also."

Everyone turned to the bar maid, who was hanging on the arm of a hulking-looking farmer. "It be Jordan and Shayne."

"Those two be as worthless as an Indian damn," one of the locals observed.

The innkeeper herded everyone, except him and Miss Aldridge, toward the common room. "I will send someone for the magistrate."

Breeson expected to observe her approval of his masterful handling of the matter displayed upon her countenance, but the lady appeared disappointed; however, she voiced no objections. "I suspect you wish to dress, Miss Aldridge," Breeson whispered as he led her to her room. "I will stand guard outside so no one disturbs you. When you finish, we should talk before the local authorities arrives."

"Thank you, Mr. Breeson," she said softly before dejectedly entering her room.

ⱺⱺⱺ

It was all she could do not to break into tears. "Well, so much for not permitting anyone to know I am traveling alone to Scotland." Cashé sighed deeply. "I have no choice. I must see it through."

Some twenty minutes later, she and Mr. Breeson sat at the table in her let room–the door propped open for propriety. "I will escort you to Tweed Hall," Breeson stated the obvious.

Biting back her frustration, Cashé rolled her eyes. "I did not wish to involve His Lordship in my family's trouble." She had not disclosed the real reason for her solitary journey. She had simply said Baron Ashton had been called away to London, and she had received word of her immediate presence required in Leith.

"Despite your qualms, Miss Aldridge, the earl would take the skin from my hide if I permitted you to continue this journey alone. This evening was typical of the dangers for a woman traveling unaccompanied."

Cashé sighed a groan. As much as she wished to see the earl again, she knew she could not give herself to Charters if Marcus Wellston assumed control of her mission. And Cashé held no doubt the earl would commit himself to the fight even without their having a relationship. "Could this situation become more convoluted? she murmured in frustration.

With Breeson's suggestion, the local magistrate ordered the two offending youths to serve as stable hands on the earl's estate for three weeks. They would perform their duties under Breeson's direction. Cashé was not convinced the punishment fit the crime, but Breeson privately assured her any retribution more than a verbal reprimand was a victory. Mr. Jordan was the son of Sir William Jordan, who had been knighted for his handling of a smuggling ring, while Mr. Shayne was the son of the local baronet, Sir Gavin. Although neither family possessed peerage titles, they still held local prestige. Breeson had secured the baronet's agreement for his son to be treated with a dose of humility for the baronet was sorely displeased with the youth. Sir William was less enthusiastic, but he acquiesced to the others. Both young men were to report to Tweed Hall in one week's time or face charges for attempted assault.

Breeson let a curricle, the only available vehicle, and placed the lady in it. He was surprised she was less than enthusiastic about the possibility of seeing His Lordship again; he wondered if the girl and the earl had come to a parting of the ways. However, until he knew the truth of why the lady traveled alone, he could not permit Miss Aldridge from his sight.

"I am Eleanor Kerrington, Lady Worthing." Her voice encouraged his memory.

"You...you are married to Worthing? When did that momentous event occur?" Lexford purposely slid his gaze over her obviously pregnant form. "Where is the captain? I would see him now."

The woman's countenance held her dismay. "You remember nothing of what has happened?"

"I recall returning to England from the East with Kerrington and Wellston as my companions." Lexford's anxiousness grew by the moment. "What else should I know?"

Regina Jeffers

She softened her expression. "Permit me to freshen the water so I might tend your wound, and then I will sit with you and answer your questions to the best of my knowledge."

He preferred not for her solution, but he felt too weak to object. Lexford nodded his agreement and released her wrist. His eyes followed the lady about the room. He could not imagine Kerrington would choose this woman. She was too tall–too regal–too blonde for his friend's tastes. Of course, there was the possibility his former captain had seduced the lady and had brought her to child. Such dishonor would have resorted in a speedy marriage in Gretna Green. Yet, that scenario had been improbable for Lexford knew their trio had been in England for less than a month.

When the woman returned to his bedside, she had placed a new compress on his head and then took up his hand in her two. Capturing his gaze, she said, "As I said, I am Eleanor Kerrington, but before I married Viscount Worthing, I was Eleanor Fowler."

"Brantley Fowler's sister?"

She tilted her head to look at him curiously. "I am, and Bran is now the Duke of Thornhill and has married our cousin."

"The infamous Velvet Aldridge?" he asked with a bit of a taunt.

She smiled at him. "The very one."

He wanted to laugh, but even the slightest turn of his head brought shooting pains down his spine. Instead, he said caustically, "I do not know what farce you play, but I am not amused. Admittedly, you are a wonderful actress, but your facts do not match reality. Brantley Fowler has sworn never to claim his dukedom; he and his daughter only recently returned to England from Brittany."

The sound of a small carriage in the drive brought Marcus to his feet and moving toward the door. When it swung open, the night and several lanterns brought two shadowy figures. One he recognized immediately as that of Richard Breeson, but although he could not make out the countenance or even the form of the second, his heart knew her. "Cashé," he spoke her name aloud as if it were some sort of magical incantation. He reached the entrance steps just as Breeson handed her from the curricle. As he skidded to a stop, her head turned in his direction, and everything froze in place. Marcus felt the silly grin spread across his lips, but he did not care. She was with him at last.

221

"I brought you a gift, Lord Yardley," Breeson called from his place beside the carriage.

Marcus chuckled, "You will do anything for another pay raise, Breeson." His eyes devoured her.

"I did not think I could top the last token." Breeson laughed also.

Marcus took the last few steps to where she stood, a look of anticipation upon her countenance. "You have outdone yourself, my Friend." He raised his hand to cup her chin, lifting it to see her eyes reflected in the lantern light. He whispered only for her ears, "I did not think to ever see you at my home." And that was all it took. Cashé launched herself into his embrace. Sobs wracked her body, and Marcus laced his arms about her, pulling Cashé closer. "What is it, Sweetheart?" he coaxed. "Tell me, Cashé, and I will move mountains to set it right."

Biting back another round of tears, she raised her gaze to meet his. "I have ruined everything," she wailed. "Satiné and Lord Lexford and Uncle Charles and you and me. Everything is ruined." Tears exploded in another round of sobs.

Marcus bent and gently scooped her into his arms. "Breeson," he called over his shoulder. "I require an explanation." He walked slowly up the front steps, cuddling Cashé to him. "Mr. Spear, bring tea and brandy and refreshments to my study."

"Yes, Your Lordship."

Cashé laced her arms about his neck, pulling herself closer. "Do not leave me," she rasped. Her words tore at his heart.

"Never, Ma Chère." He nuzzled her neck. "Never in a million years."

Some time later, as Marcus cradled Cashé on his lap, stroking her back and arm, Breeson explained what he knew of Cashé's attack. She had refused the tea and refreshments–simply burying her head into his chest and silently sobbing. She had shared with his former batman how she had outmaneuvered her two young attackers, and Marcus's friend relayed the tale as Cashé wordlessly clung to Marcus for comfort. His heart swelled with pride when he had heard of how she outsmarted the men, and it lurched with anger at knowing what she had been through.

"Thank you, Breeson," Marcus said softly. "I am forever in your debt for seeing to Miss Aldridge's safety. I will trust you to administer an appropriate lesson to Mr. Jordan and Mr. Stayne. I will take some pleasure in our visitors learning how a gentleman should treat a lady."

222

Breeson smiled knowingly. "I thought you might." His friend stood to take his leave. "I will leave you to your reunion, Lord Yardley."

Marcus nodded his farewell and then shifted Cashé in his arms. "Do you feel safe enough to tell me what has happened, Sweetheart? I need to know why you were traveling alone. Where is your sister? What of Lord Lexford?" As he listened to Breeson's tale, Marcus had attempted to reason what circumstances would have driven Cashé to take to the road alone. Had Lexford demanded her hand? Had Satiné changed her mind about the viscount? The last Marcus knew of the situation, Lexford was to call at Chesterfield Manor, and the ladies were to perform a switch to convince the viscount he had chosen the wrong twin.

Cashé swallowed hard and attempted to remove from his embrace, but Marcus refused to relinquish her. "I do not know where to begin." She glanced to the left and then back to his steady gaze. "Uncle Charles was summoned to London. He departed Cheshire on Wednesday, and Lord Lexford came to stay at the manor house." Marcus listened carefully. He had known Shepherd had requested a personal meeting with the baron. "Satiné and I executed our switches, and His Lordship knew nothing of the change. Therefore, we decided to arrange a day for Lexford and Satiné to be alone. That was Friday."

Marcus calculated when she must have departed Cheshire. His embrace softened. "And?"

She bit her bottom lip. "Satiné and Lord Lexford rode out together after I returned to house. His Lordship thought Satiné was I." She paused and took a deep breath. He caressed her shoulder, saying with action rather than words he meant to see her well. Her eyes grew wider, and she heaved a weighty sigh. "When they did not return after several hours, I sent out search parties. Two groomsmen found the viscount knocked unconscious, but Satiné was not recovered." Again, Cashé paused, but this time she caught Marcus's hand in hers. "I held no idea what to do so I sent word to Lord Worthing."

"Kerrington came, did he not?" Marcus traced lines across her wrist with his fingertip.

"Lord Worthing rushed to my side and assumed control of the investigation." Cashé looked away. "When His Lordship asked of our relationship, I confirmed our connection. I pray I have not displeased you."

Marcus kissed her forehead "Worthing held his suspicions when we were at Linton Park. It is of no consequence. The past few days have convinced me I cannot permit you to know another–even if it means the loss of Lexford's friendship."

She confessed, "When I departed Cheshire, His Lordship, still had not recovered."

"If Worthing arrived, why did you feel it necessary to depart for Scotland?" It bothered him that Cashé had not thought to come to him. The knowledge, that if not for Breeson, he might have no idea of the turmoil in which she suffered ate away at Marcus's gut.

"I felt I had to make the effort to save Satiné. I am sorry, my Lord. I held no desire to bring you pain, but Lord Worthing and I discovered the name of the man we suspected of kidnapping Satiné. It was Lachlan Charters. He took Satiné, thinking my sister was I. I must be to Leith to prevent Mr. Charters from hurting Satiné when he discovers the truth."

Marcus's stomach knotted. "You will not give yourself to that man!" Now he understood her impulsive reasoning.

Tears formed. "I may have no choice." Her bottom lip trembled.

"I will assist you in rescuing your sister, but you belong with me, Cashémere." He turned her chin to face him. "My life began again when Shepherd sent me to intercept Jamot. I will no longer live in the void, and neither will you." He knew he did not have the full story, but he would continue to ask questions until she had told him everything. Tomorrow, they would address her crisis. Tonight, he would see Cashé safe in his home. "Permit me to show you a room for this evening. You must be exhausted."

"Would you stay with me?" she asked innocently.

"Are you certain, my Love? I would not have you the subject of more gossip than what has already occurred." His fingers traced her jaw line.

Cashé laughed lightly. "I believe I am beyond the point of salvation in that manner, my Lord. Besides, if I am fair game for the gossip-mongers, then I wish to know the pleasure of what I am accused."

"I will not defile you, but I would cherish holding you in my arms. I have dreamed of such since I discovered your loveliness."

Cashé smiled. "As opposed to my irascible nature?"

"I was blind. Do not remind me of my short sightedness."

"Take me to your bed, Marcus."

He stood, lifting Cashé to him. "We will have tonight."

Her "very large" abductor sat across from Satiné on the coach's bench. She had fought for a lucid thought, but nothing came. Her eyes fluttered open and then closed again.

"We be home by nightfall, gel," he told her; yet, Satiné no longer held a concept of home. "If'n ye be promisin' not to fight me, I will give ye no more of the water." Satiné attempted to make her lips form the words, but all she could do was to lift the fingers on her left hand before drifting again into the darkness.

Chapter Fifteen

Eleanor sat quietly beside Lexford's bed. She had spent an hour speaking of what she knew of the viscount's life, but her knowledge was limited to the present–the past year. Other than a few stories her husband had shared, she knew nothing of the previous two years of Lord Lexford's life. The viscount slept quietly–his brow furrowed in doubt, and Eleanor felt as if she had failed him somehow. She had assured him his memory would return when he had fully recovered, but the viscount had not responded. Instead, he had turned his head to face the other way, closing his eyes and accepting sleep. The viscount had nothing to say, and that particular fact worried Eleanor more than his condition. It was as if he had lost more than his memory: He had lost that spark in his eyes–the one she first recognized in the stranger who had protected her at Gavin Bradley's hunting box. The one which said he was a man worthy of her notice.

As he slept, Eleanor retrieved foolscap and ink from the room's small desk. She penned letters to both her brother and to Sir Carter, explaining Lexford's condition, Satiné's situation, Cashé's disappearance, and her husband's quest. She begged for assistance–begged them to bring a more competent physician to attend their friend.

Cashé had told him of her Uncle Charles's suspicions regarding her parents' death and of Lord Worthing's belief that Viscount Averette had manipulated the church funds for his own benefit. Marcus had known part of what she had confided, but the news of Averette's perfidy was not what bothered him as he held her in his arms. It was when she confessed, "No one has ever wanted me." Now, as she slept spooned in his embrace, all he could think of was how vulnerable she was and how much he loved her.

Streaks of light had summoned the dawn as Marcus gently brushed the hair from her face. The early rays danced through the shadowy blackness of her long locks. She had the most magnificent hair, and he wanted nothing more than to wrap his hands in it–capture fists full of the silken strands to hold her close. He kissed her cheek gently. "Come, Sweetheart," he whispered close to her ear. "We must be on the road soon."

Cashé turned over, burying her face in his chest. "Mmm," she moaned. "I would rather stay here with you." She kissed the indentation of his throat.

Marcus's breath hitched in his chest. He had fought his lust throughout the night, but now it had returned. Every impulse screamed for him to ignore Society's precepts and take what he wanted. After all, they had already ignored many rules of polite culture: the kiss, his touching her intimately, the exchange of letters, and now sleeeoping within each other's arms. One more should be of no consequence. He meant to make her his wife as soon as the law permitted. If nothing else, they could be in Scotland within the hour. "Ah, my Love, I can imagine nothing better." Marcus tightened his embrace. "But we both know neither of us will be happy unless we resolve this dilemma."

Cashé stiffened. "What if at the end I must stay in Scotland?"

Marcus tilted her chin upward where he might observe her countenance. "Cashémere Aldridge, you are going to be my countess. I will tolerate nothing less." He kissed her cheek. "You are compromised by traveling alone, and, more so, by spending the night in my bed." Marcus brought her close again. "And although it has taken, to this point, a Herculean effort to resist your many charms, I will gladly crumble under the temptation in order to secure everyone's cooperation."

Marcus could hear the smile in her voice. "You want us to marry, my Lord?"

He smiled too. "I will have no other."

.ℓℓℓ.

Jamot had ridden throughout the night and part of the day before seeking a surgeon in a small village some ten miles south of the Scottish border. He had cursed Lady Worthing for the physical pain she had caused him, but as he lay on the makeshift examining bed in the surgeon's home, he had thought more positively of the woman. Eleanor Fowler Kerrington had steel in her spine. She had confronted him, wrestled valiantly with him, and had taken a clear shot. Few English women of his acquaintance held such temerity. In his musings, Jamot had thought Ashmita could have learned a great deal from Fowler's sister. The physician pressed roughly against the opening. "A lover's quarrel," he told the doctor when the man asked him how he had earned the wound.

"The bullet when through the fleshy part of your arm. You are lucky the lady did not aim for your heart."

Jamot laughed lightly. "A man must have a heart for that to happen."

◌◌◌

"It would be better if we go overland on horseback," Marcus shared as he and Cashé took a simple breakfast together in his chambers. "Do you think you could tolerate several hours in the saddle?"

His lady appeared a bit alarmed. "I am not much of a horsewoman," she confided.

"I recall," he teased. "I was to teach you–part of my personal list of firsts with the lovely Cashémere Aldridge."

Cashé blushed, but she added, "Might I use a regular saddle?"

Her request should have shocked Marcus, but somehow he thought the idea fit her: unconventional. "I suppose I could find you some breeches and a shirt from one of my grooms."

Cashé smiled broadly. "You never tell me I cannot do something just because I am a woman."

Marcus stood to ring for a servant. "That is because you are my woman, and I am amazed daily by your bravado." He gently kissed her lips. "While we wait for a servant to bring you something appropriate to wear, may we go downstairs. I wish for you to meet Trevor and Jeremy." He extended his hand to her.

Tentatively, she placed her fingers in his palm, and Marcus closed his grip about her hand. Avid curiosity flared in her eyes. "You wish me to know your brother?"

"Soon Trevor will be your brother. It seems only fitting the acquaintance should begin today," he declared. The feeling of how right her hand felt in his surged through him. Marcus wrapped her up in a quick embrace before brushing his lips across hers. Anything more would have him returning Cashé to his bed. "Come along."

She eagerly followed Marcus to the morning room, and he knew the contentment of a dream come true. "Good day," he called as he entered the room. "How are you this morning, Trevor?"

Jeremy Ingram scrambled to his feet, lightly punching Trevor's side as a reminder of Trevor's manners. "Good morning, Your Lordship," Jeremy intoned, while Trevor sported an extra large grin.

"Gentlemen, this is Miss Aldridge. She arrived late yesterday evening under Mr. Breeson's protection. Miss Aldridge, might I present my brother Trevor Wellston and his companion, Jeremy Ingram."

Ingram bowed again without comment, but Trevor said it all, "She is handsome. Just like you said, Marcus."

Cashé blushed, but she lovingly teased, "You told your brother that I was handsome, Your Lordship?" Marcus suspected he sported the same silly grin as his brother.

Marcus tightened his grip on her hand. "My brother has forgotten his manners," he warned good-naturedly. "Your speech is no way to greet a lady, Trevor."

Trevor bowed obediently. "I am pleased for your acquaintance, Miss Aldridge."

"Are you avoiding my question, Lord Yardley?" she taunted.

Marcus spontaneously brought the back of her hand to his lips. "You know what I think of your appearance, my Dear. Cease fishing for a compliment."

Cashé's laughter warmed his heart. "Yet, it was you, my Lord, who taught me to fish."

"Very true." He touched the tip of her nose with a gentle flick, before turning his attention to his brother. "Trevor, Miss Aldridge and I are riding to her Scottish home to settle a situation regarding her sister. I will return late tomorrow or the next day. You are not to worry."

"Yes, Marcus." Trevor shot a quick glance to Cashé. "Will Miss Aldridge be returning with you? You said the lady previously lived in Scotland."

Marcus pulled Cashé closer to him. "Miss Aldridge will return to Tweed Hall. It is my intention to make the lady part of our family. It has been too long since we have had a feminine touch in this house. Do you not agree?"

"Definitely. Miss Aldridge, you must marry Marcus. He has been a true grump of late," Trevor shared.

Cashé smiled broadly at Trevor's description of Marcus. "I would wish for nothing more than to be your new sister, Trevor."

"A sister!" Trevor barked. "I did not consider having a sister."

Marcus interrupted. "We must leave for Edinburgh. Jeremy, you should continue Trevor's lessons, as always. Come along, Cashémere. Our task requires completing before we may become a family."

Charters guided the carriage into the stable overhang behind the small cottage, a quarter mile from his main house. As he had planned, dusk had covered his return. Before he secured the girl, he unharnessed the horses and set out oats. Then he retrieved the woman he would make his wife. "Come, gel," he ordered, grabbing Satiné's arm and pulling her across the seat where he might find a better hold.

Lifting her roughly, he carried her to the cottage. "Ye be stayin' within for a few days until I apply for a license for our joining." He dropped her unceremoniously onto the bed. "There be food and water on the table, a chamber pot in the corner, as well as more water so ye can wash yerself, and clean clothes behind the screen. I will not return until t'morrow." He gently touched her face with his fingertips. "You cannot escape," he told her. Charters draped two blankets over her. "It be colder in Scotland than in Manchester, but ye be knowin' that fact previously, Cashémere." Then, closing and locking the door, he left her inside the little room.

*

Satiné opened her eyes, but the world had spun before her gaze, so she had closed them again. "Tomorrow," she thought, unable to say the word aloud. She accepted sleep's breath. Despite all the craziness, she was alive, and someone would come for her. She had to believe it. For now, she would lie on a clean bed and pray for her speedy recovery.

But sleep would not come. Her mind raced with the sensation of no longer swaying from side to side. "Where am I?" she finally asked the emptiness. She searched her memory for what the man had told her. Permittng the moon to provide the light, Satiné forced her eyes open to focus on her surroundings. She could discern a table and a chair close to the window, but little else. The room's chill brought a shiver down her spine, and she groped for the blankets and wrapped herself tightly in a wool cocoon; yet, she did not close her eyes. The images blurred, but Satiné concentrated on recovering her world. When the light was better, she would venture from the bed. "Maybe there is a way from this disaster on my own. If so, I do not mean to wait for my rescue."

*

Marcus had led her through a rough terrain far from the main road. He assured her this particular route would save them at least twelve miles. Although it had required a slower journey, he had explained, "We will be in Leith by late afternoon, and we can canvass Charters' household before we decide what to do." Now, as Cashé followed him along a narrow path

230

where three hills merged, she could not help but to enjoy the masculine form of his wide shoulders and the narrowness of his waist. "Do you require rest?" he called over his shoulder, noting her distraction. But before she could answer, Marcus brought Khan to a halt and slid from the saddle to catch her horse's bridle. "Easy, Boy," he coaxed the gelding toward a nearby hedgerow. He looped the reins around a low branch and turned to assist her to the ground. "You are doing a magnificent job of handling Triton," he told her with more concern than she wished to hear in his voice. She had thought the man's saddle would be more comfortable than would be the sidesaddle, but it had proved equally uncomfortable. The only good thing was she had no trouble maintaining her balance on the masculine one. "Let us sit under the tree," he coaxed as he caught her arm. Despite her best efforts, Cashé stepped gingerly, and she heard him snigger. However, a deadly glare she had perfected within her Uncle Samuel's household had warned Marcus to keep his own counsel.

"How much farther?" she asked as she lowered herself to the ground.

"Just a bit longer," he said noncommittally. "Here. Drink this," Marcus handed her a flask.

Cashé looked up at him. "What is it?"

"Brandy." He smiled knowingly. "Little sips. It will warm you and numb you." She held her doubts, but Cashé placed the flask's rim to her mouth and tilted the liquid toward her lips. When the brandy crossed her tongue, it burned her throat. Tears formed in her eyes, and she coughed to clear her breathing. However, he had been correct: A warmth spread through her veins. "Stretch out your legs," he had ordered. When she did, the earl massage her calves and thighs.

Cashé took another sip of the drink and closed her eyes. "That feels heavenly," she whispered and was rewarded with an amused chuckle of approval from Lord Yardley.

The combination of his hands on the inside of her legs and the hot liquid seeping down her throat quickly lured Cashé into a moment of desire. "Marcus," she whispered in a shallow rasp.

"Shush, Darling," he murmured. Her equilibrium faltered. He had started at her ankles and had continued until he now caressed the muscles on the inside of her thigh. The soreness had dripped away as he had inched closer to her most private place. When his fingers stroked her softness through the breeches, he whispered her name on a thready sigh.

The lighting shot through her as Marcus circled his fingers across her damp breeches, and the heat from her chest lodged itself between her legs. Cashé opened her eyes to gaze into his desire-filled ones. "I love you," she whispered as Marcus released the buttons of the placket and slid his hand into the tight quarters–his fingers stroking her wetness. When he pushed one finger into her opening, Cashé instinctively opened her legs wider. His finger slid in and out as his thumb circled the nub at her apex. "Marcus," she breathed his name but did not look away.

The earl's chest rose and fell as she bucked, pushing herself into his hand.

"Permit it to happen, Darling," he whispered. "It is ecstasy, and it is time you knew it."

Cashé thrust forward again as he slid in a second finger. "Love me," she begged.

"More than life," he rasped, as he pinched her nipple through the loosely woven shirt. "I want to see you crackle with life; I want to see the desire in your eyes." Then she broke: her body shivering with her first climax. She clawed at his arm as wave after wave coursed through her. Finally, Marcus ceased his manipulations as he gathered her into his arms. "You are so beautiful when you are in the throes of desire. Thank you for trusting me. When you are my wife, we will spend our first week as a couple in my bed."

"Will we sleep, my Lord?" she asked dreamily.

Marcus chuckled. "Occasionally."

"Sounds divine." She snuggled closer. "Can we do that again sometime?"

Marcus found her mouth. "That and so much more."

Having finally achieved the rendezvous point, John Swenton and Gabriel Crowden rode into the Sunset Inn's yard. Hostlers scrambled to take their horses. "I will see if the captain has arrived," Swenton said as he dismounted.

"I will see to the horses." Crowden led his own horse to the stable.

"Swenton." Worthing called, exiting the inn. "You made excellent time."

"Crowden was not in the mood to rest for very long in any one place." Swenton shot a glance over his shoulder where the marquis walked casually toward the barn.

Worthing followed Swenton's gaze. "I wish I knew what goaded him."

"He will tell us when he is ready." Swenton followed the viscount into the inn's private room."

"We have made progress. Charters returned home late yesterday, but he did so on foot and alone. Lucifer is watching the house. I thought to stir things up by making an unexpected call on Averette, while you and Crowden might discover whether Jamot is involved somehow."

"Permit us to let a room and to find something to eat, and then we will be prepared to assist."

.୧୧୧,

Before releasing the knocker, Worthing made note of where every footman waited for Averette's instructions. A proper butler responded immediately. "Viscount Worthing to speak to Lord Averette." He handed the man his card, along with his hat and gloves.

"This way, Sir." The butler showed him into a small drawing room. "I will inquire if His Lordship is receiving."

"Tell Lord Averette this is not a social call," Wothing cautioned.

"As you wish, Sir."

The butler disappeared into the house's depths as he surveyed the room. Very ornate, a bit too ostentatious for his own tastes. He was contemplating the costs of such a display when Averette appeared in the doorway.

"Lord Worthing, to what do I owe the pleasure of your company? You are a long way from Linton Park." Averette gestured toward a cluster of chairs.

Worthing took the suggested seat but remained alert. "I beg your forgiveness for not sending word of my arrival."

"There is no need. You extended your hospitality to my family. It is appropriate I reciprocate." Averette played with his watch chain. "How may I serve you, Sir?"

Worthing cleared his throat. "I fear I bring bad tidings." He paused to judge Averette's reaction. "Miss Satiné has been kidnapped and Lord Lexford attacked."

Averette shifted nervously, but his voice held no guilt. "I do not understand what Charles Morton's problems have to do with me. Satiné is my niece, but I rarely see her. Now, Ashton has assumed the care of Cashémere. I have no contact with either girl."

"Yet, Miss Satiné's abduction appears to have been executed by someone you know." Worthing pried for information and waited for a response.

"I am afraid I still do not comprehend. Who of my associates do you suspect?" Averette's face offered no knowledge of the crime, and Worthing wondered if he had chosen incorrectly.

"Cashémere recognized the name of her former suitor Lachlan Charters among those registered at the Manchester inn. The magistrate traced a let coach to Charters," Worthing prompted. "We assume the man did not realize he had absconded with the wrong twin."

Averette actually flustered with anger. "The idiot! I assure you, Worthing, I knew nothing of this! Charters called upon me nearly a fortnight prior, demanding Cashémere's return, but I never suspected him to attempt something so dastardly."

Worthing sat forward to press his point. "I should tell you, Averette, I have seen evidence, which implies a connection between you and Charters that should be severed immediately. You are my wife's cousin, and I would wish no disdain to fall upon your shoulders."

Averette's voice went up an octave, indicating his anger. "You listen to Charles Morton, Lord Worthing!"

He smiled knowingly. "I am aware of Morton's beliefs, but others have similar thoughts. If there is any truth, it will be found out," he warned. "However, that particular fact is not my concern with this journey. I wish Satiné's return, and I seek your cooperation in saving your niece's reputation."

"Of course," Averette assured Worthing. "Explain what you require of me."

"You will inform me if Charters calls upon you," Worthing explained. "I await my colleagues. Charters attacked a peer. The English courts will not look positively on those who protect him."

"I understand." Averette rose to end the conversation.

Worthing followed Aldridge to his feet. "If you hold no objections, Your Lordship, I will call tomorrow to bring you abreast of the search."

"Absolutely, Lord Worthing. We must secure Satiné as soon as possible."

Satiné had permitted the light to fill the small room before she had departed the bed's security, and then she had explored the space. The room was cramped, but, thankfully, it was clean. "I wonder how long my captor will keep me here," she said aloud just to hear her own voice. She used the chamber pot, before discovering the clean clothes, towel, soap, and water. She said a prayer of gratitude for even that small kindness. "He will not treat me poorly any longer."

Methodically, she stripped away the stained riding habit she had worn for days. "How many days?" she wondered aloud. "At least four." Satiné knew how long it might have taken to reach her Uncle Samuel's house, and she had assumed the man, who had taken her, lived near the Averettes. In fact, she had concluded he was Cashémere's Lachlan Charters. "I wish the water was warm" she commented as she poured some from the ewer into the bowl.

With clean clothes and feeling more human, she explored the basket of food left for her. Taking an apple from the basket, she sank her teeth into it and closed her eyes. She would eat slowly, not certain how long it had been since she had eaten. She remembered the man providing her the water that had kept her drugged. "Probably two days," she reasoned, reaching for a slice of thick bread. "I wonder about the water." She sniffed the pitcher, attempting to smell the metallic odor from before. Smelling nothing unusual, she took a small sip and waited, but no nausea occurred. Therefore, she drank her fill. Finally, replete, she looked out the window, surveying the area. "Only trees and bushes."

Nevertheless, she pulled the chair closer, where she might see the daylight. "What now?" Satiné reached for the small brush she had found on the mantel and began to work the tats from her hair. "What now, indeed?"

♦♦♦

"Lord Averette." Aldridge's former groomsman stepped before the curricle along the road to Leith.

"Get out of my way, March," Aldridge warned. "I have no time for your foolish games. I have told you before you are not welcome on my land."

"That may be, M' Lord, but I have something ye'll want." March tossed a sheet of paper into Averette's lap before disappearing into the underbrush.

Averette looked around suspiciously, wondering if anyone watched him. Slowly, he opened the folded paper to read...

Lord Averette,

I have taken several documents from Baron Ashton's house, which I am certain you will wish in your possession. Meet me at midnight in your stables. Bring a thousand pounds, and they are yours.

Averette swallowed hard. Could it be true? When Worthing had departed from his home earlier in the day, Aldridge had thought the world, as he knew it, had collapsed; but if this note proved true, Ashton might not be in a position to ruin him, after all. If he could break with Charters, he might still survive. He first must make certain this disaster fell on the Scot's head. He would force the man's hand in this sorted business–make the simpleton the guilty party. Setting the horse in action, Averette guided the curricle toward his former associate's home.

⟨◌◌◌⟩

Worthing observed the exchange between Aldridge and the scraggily looking groomsman. As the messenger departed, the viscount abandoned his pursuit of Aldridge. He was well aware of Averette's destination, and he knew Lucifer Hill would oversee what transpired between Lord Averette and Charters. Instead, he followed the stranger.

⟨◌◌◌⟩

Charters had planned to visit Cashémere at the small cottage on his land, but the announcement of Aldridge's appearance had cut those plans short. "Lord Averette," he said coming to his feet, "what brings ye to me house on such an overcast day?"

Averette accepted the seat to which Charters gestured. "We must have a serious talk, Charters. I have entertained a visit from James Kerrington, Viscount Worthing, this morning. The gentleman brings a report of your recent visit to Manchester."

Charters fought to control his initial reaction to Averette's words. He had thought he had covered his tracks well. Rather than to respond, he waited to learn the whole story. "And?" he said quietly into the silence.

"And Lord Worthing makes a good case against you, my friend. His Lordship suggested I remove your name from my list of associates... actually said you might pay dearly in a British courtroom."

Charters ran his finger under his collar. He did not like the sound of Averette's words. "Let us say some of what you repeat be true, I sees no offense in my layin' claim to me betrothed and to puttin' an end to the English viscount's advances toward Cashémere," he declared.

Averette smiled broadly, which made Charters more wary of the viscount. Averette only smiled when he thought he had won the battle. "Then you admit your involvement?"

Creating time to weigh his words, he cleared his throat. "Cashémere be promised to me. Everyone for miles knows it be so. I settled a livin' on

236

her with you, and I be expectin' the courts to not deny me rights." He took a deep breath. "I found Cashémere in Viscount Lexford's arms. The man be takin' liberties that should be mine."

Averette's surprise showed, but Charters wondered if the viscount knew real surprise or artful pretense. "Are you saying you discovered the viscount and Cashémere in a compromising situation?"

"Seen it with me own eyes," Charters assured. "Pulled the Brit off Cashémere."

Averette sat forward, overtly interested in the tale. "You removed the viscount physically and then did what exactly?"

"Carried Miss Cashémere to me carriage." Charters watched Averette's reaction. Years of dealing with the rascally English lord had told him to beware, but Charters could see nothing but concern in the man's countenance. He wondered whether to trust his long-time associate.

"And my niece came without protest?" A raised eyebrow was Samuel Aldridge's only show of disbelief.

Having experienced it before, Charters ignored the viscount's superior attitude. "Of course, Cashémere be upset, but she will understand now she has returned to Scotland."

Averette sat back leisurely into the cushions. "It is to your benefit you have compromised my niece by traveling alone with her from Manchester. That offense was all you did to compromise her, is it not?"

Charters' face flushed with color. "I be gentle with her, even gave her some laudanum so she could rest for the journey be long. I would never hurt the gel. I mean to make her me wife."

"Where have you kept her?" Averette glanced around the room. "Somewhere in the house."

"She be close by." Charters said no more. He would trust no one with the girl's location.

Averette shifted uneasily in the chair. "Then I suppose we must find a means to stymie Worthing's investigation. It is not likely the viscount will walk away from this search. Plus, the man indicated his colleagues were to be expected soon. As a future earl, Worthing has powerful friends in the British government. This will not be easy to sweep away. You cannot keep my niece hidden for long."

Despite his best efforts, Charters' anxiety showed. "What should I do? I will not tolerate their taking the gel from me."

Averette removed his watch to check the time. "Worthing plans to call again in the morning. I would like to tell him his search was in vain, but I am certain the viscount will not agree unless he speaks to my niece."

Charters used a handkerchief to mop his brow. "If'n the gel be compromised, she be mine."

"Yet, she really is not truly compromised," Averette suggested. "Traveling alone could be covered up with enough lies and enough money. Morton also has government friends, and he will spare no expense. In fact, they could say Lexford's actions preceded yours and give Lexford first claim to my niece."

"What are you suggesting, Averette?" Charters demanded. He did not like the implications.

"I am not suggesting anything. I am just stating the facts. If Worthing finds my niece, he and his friends will create a story to explain her days away from her Manchester home, and then the future earl will see you are prosecuted for her kidnapping. I witnessed how he and the Duke of Thornhill manipulated Sir Louis Levering's death. Without a trial, the baronet was sentenced to transportation, and then he was mysteriously killed on the journey to Australia–all this with the blessing of the Prince Regent. It will take little for the man to do away with you. The only alternative is to make my niece your wife today."

Charters fisted his hands. He meant to keep what was his, and he would fight whoever stood in his way. "Ye know that be impossible. There be no time for a license or a proper ceremony. They would be watching the roads if'n I attempt to escort Cashémere to some secluded village to speak our vows over the anvil."

"But there is time for a wedding night," Averette stated matter-of-factly. "If the girl is yours, they must agree for her to remain with you. If it was I, I would mark the girl as my own."

⁂

Palming his pocket pistol, Worthing stepped behind the groomsman. "Do not turn around," he whispered harshly in the man's ear. "You will come with me."

"I have done nothin' wrong," the man protested. Worthing had asked the necessary questions. He knew the man was one of Averette's former grooms, a man named Leyton March. March had lost his position when Lord Averette discovered the groom had whipped one of the viscount's favorite horses.

"Then you have nothing to fear." Keeping his gun prominently in the groomsman's back, Worthing directed the man to the inn's side door. Once outside, he caught the groom by the nape and slammed him against the wall. "I want answers, and it would be to your benefit to respond honestly. Do I make myself clear?"

March swallowed hard, but he managed a nod of agreement.

Worthing kept the man pinned tight against the wall with a foreman across the groom's chest and the gun pointed at March's temple. He meant to frighten the man, but violence was also acceptable. "You delivered a message to Averette this afternoon. I want to know who sent it and what it said."

The groom's eyes grew in size, but his voice remained steady. "Met a man...over a month ago in the inn...bought me ale...had some black powder...thought it somethin' to try once in me life." He darted a glance to the side before continuing. "The man disappeared for several weeks. Came back today and asked for me assistance."

"Describe the man's appearance," Worthing demanded.

"Dark skinned...a foreigner."

Worthing bit back the curse. As he suspected, Jamot was involved. That particular fact would complicate this investigation further. "Did this foreigner give a name?"

"No, M' Lord. He never say, and I never ast."

"What was the note's message?"

March appeared frightened again. "I cannot read, M' Lord, but me friend Joby reads a bit. Joby say the note told Averette to meet the foreigner at midnight in the county's stables."

Worthing quickly released his hold on the groom. "If I see you again before I leave Scotland, you will rue the day."

The groom nodded vigorously, straightened his shirt, and then made a speedy retreat.

"Midnight," Worthing grumbled. "What would Jamot want with Averette at such an ungodly hour?"

ॐ

Averette climbed slowly into the curricle, considering what scenario he had just set in motion. "That bit of deception should put Charters away for life," he spoke his thoughts aloud. "Thinking the girl is Cashémere, Charters will take liberties with Satiné. It will be a suitable revenge on Morton to have his precious Satiné ruined. Her option narrowed to marrying a Scottish bumpkin. Now, who has the upper hand, Morton?" With a smirk and a devilish laugh, Averette set his team in motion.

Chapter Sixteen

Charters silently opened the room's door. He had used a concealed exit to the wine cellar to appear behind several large boulders some one hundred yards east of his home. The tunnels had come with the house when his father had purchased the land some fifty years prior. As a child, Lachlan had spent endless hours playing castle and knights in the darkened passages. Some thought the house, which had been built upon the ruins of a Scottish keep, held ghosts and even a curse, but practical Lachlan had never believed any such tales. Yet, as he had emerged from the hidden entrance, a shiver of foreboding had shot down his spine. "Maybe I should permit the gel her freedom," he told himself as he set out toward the cottage, but he had knew it was too late to forstall his duplicity in the matter. He would execute the plan Averette had suggested.

He had taken the last of the sponges with him. Before he had departed for England, Lachlan had sent to his maternal grandmother, her clan's healer, for an herb or plant to deaden pain. The woman regularly dealt in medicinals not readily found in the bags of country physicians. His grandmother had sent him a mixture of opium, hemlock, and mandragora. Lachlan had seen the woman use sponges soaked in the mixture to ease grown men into a peaceful sleep while she reset their broken bones or removed bullets. It was what he had used on Cashémere to subdue the girl so he might remove her from her English home. He had given her laudanum mixed in water to keep her unconscious through most of the trip. On the road, he could not trust her not to attempt an escape, but now she had returned to Scotland, Lachlan had hoped their joining would not be a repugnant idea for the girl.

"It be good to see you up," he said softly as he closed the door behind him and set the lock. The girl did not turn. She had moved the lone chair in the room to sit before the window, and she appeared entranced by her narrow view of the world. Lachlan placed the small basket he had carried on the table. "I brought ye more food." Still, she did not respond, and he had wondered what bothered her. "I be sorry, Gel, for being so rough with ye, but I had no means of convincing ye to come back to me." He chuckled lightly. "I not be treating you as such once ye be me wife. Ye know I care deeply for ye. I require me a wife to tend the children, but I want a gel with whom I kin show affection."

Without looking at him, she said, "So you will lock me away until we may marry? How long might that be, Sir? Three weeks for the calling of the banns? Oh, I forget. I am in Scotland now. Tell me, Sir, does your village have the same rules of marriage as Gretna Green? Do we require more than an anvil?" Her voice sounded detached. It rang with coldness and pure disdain.

"I would not have ye speak so, Gel." Lachlan moved up behind her. He rested his large hands on her shoulders and felt the shudder of revulsion go through her. "We once shared the same dreams."

"We shared no such dreams, Sir." She stormed from him. "You stole me from my family. You have left my reputation in shreds." She turned vehemently on him. "Who do you think I am, Sir?"

Lachlan knew confusion. "Ye be my Cashémere."

The girl cackled in a most disturbing manner. Had she lost her mind while in England? "Just as I suspected," she accused. "It is so ironic." She sat weakly on the bed's edge. "My sister and I thought ourselves so smart. We fooled Uncle Charles and Aunt Charlotte and our cousin and my uncle's staff. We even convinced Lord Lexford I was my sister, but look how God has chosen to punish me for my falsehood." Her voice grew hysterical.

Lachlan caught her hand to jerk her to her feet. "What mean yer words?" he demanded.

Her face held her contempt, and he instinctively released his grip on her arm. "I am not Cashémere," she whispered hoarsely into the room's silence. "If you once thought my sister your betrothed, should you not know enough of her nature to know my twin when you see her? Tell me you recognize the difference when you look upon me." She thrust her chin upward to give him a good look at her countenance.

Lachlan listened, but his mind refused to acknowledge he had made a mistake. "It cannot be," his voice thundered in the small room. "It be common knowledge the fancy English viscount courted me Cashémere behind me back. Attempted to cuckold me, he did. I seen the county taking liberties. Ye be fortunate, Gel, I be willing to forgive yer wanton ways."

242

His prisoner laughed again, this time more bitterly than before. "My sister no longer affects a mere viscount. Cashémere has set her sights on an earl, the very one who escorted her to Derbyshire two months prior. You have committed a crime for nothing. Your precious Cashémere will become a countess. What makes you believe she might wish to raise another man's children or to accept a glorified farmer over a peer?"

"Ye offer a lie!" Charters' voice boomed off the walls. "Lord Averette called at me house today. He says Viscount Worthing and his friends search for Cashémere. Your Uncle Samuel would not twist the truth."

The woman shook her head as if to clear it. "That reasoning makes little sense. If Lord Worthing is involved, then my Uncle Charles and the household know it is I, not Cashémere, who is missing. Why would Lord Worthing say otherwise?"

"Ye just tryin' to confuse me," Lachlan accused. "But I not be permitting yer return to Manchester. Ye will be me wife today."

"Then you will drag me kicking and screaming to speak vows before a smithy, after all?" She bitterly accused.

Lachlan shook off her words. "I had hoped ye would see I be offering ye an honest proposal, and ye would give yerself freely to me." He spoke earnestly, stressing the truth of his words.

She snarled. "Give myself freely? Even Cashémere would do nothing of the sort, so you cannot expect me to do so; but if you will permit me my freedom, I will intervene with Lord Worthing and my Uncle Charles," she bargained. "I will speak upon your behalf."

In silence, Lachlan watched her for a few moments, and then he walked by design toward the basket he had left on the table. With his back to the girl, he reluctantly removed the dry sponge, opened the water flask and splashed some on the small square. "I be afraid what you suggest be not possible," he said evenly. " As you say, no one be believing a stupid oaf of a farmer." Advancing slowly, he prepared to do what was necessary to save his life. "Especially against an English viscount and his powerful friends."

⁂

Satiné recognized the panic rising in her chest as she skittered away from him. "What do you plan to do?" Her mouth went dry, while her palms were damp.

"Yer Uncle Samuel say I must mark ye as me own." He backed her against the bed. "I mean to take me husbandly rights before the ceremony."

243

She went completely white with fear. "Please do not do this," she begged in a raspy voice. "You will know gaol," she reasoned.

"A man cannot be prosecuted for taking liberties with his wife. The English viscount will excuse me crimes when I accept ye and offer ye the protection of me name," he countered. "It be the only way. Even Lord Averette say so. It be his idea."

Satiné gulped for air. The seriousness of the situation flooded her chest with dread. "Uncle Samuel suggested...that..." She could not say the words.

"Will ye accept me freely?" Lachlan asked quietly. "I will be gentle."

She closed her eyes, as if imagining the possibility of what he suggested. Unaware she did so, she gave a slight shake of her head. Before she formed the words of denial, Charters grabbed her and shoved her on the bed, following her down with his large body. Satiné squirmed and clawed, but it was of little use. Charters held her tightly in place and easily caught her two hands in his one.

"Stop, Cashémere," he ordered as he wrestled her, purposely pressing her body into the mattress's softness. "I do not mean to harm ye, Gel," he growled.

"You just mean to take me against my will!" Satiné huffed as she continued to struggle.

"It be not what I desire," he insisted.

Suddenly she ceased her undulations, and Lachlan followed suit. Very quietly, she acknowledged, "This is beyond the pale, Sir." When he made no move to release her, she spit in his face. "That is what I think of your kindness."

Lachlan released her hands to wipe her mucus from his cheeks. Pure contempt spread through him. He had been lying upon her chest to chest, but now he purposely rose up on his elbows. His slow movements stilled her struggle, and the girl froze: She defiantly faced his granite countenance, and he felt a surge of admiration for her boldness. "Ye should not have done it, Gel," he warned. "It be wrong to show yer husband such dishonor, Cashémere."

"You are not my husband," she declared vehemently.

"Not yet," he growled. "This will make ye more amiable." Swiftly, he covered her mouth and nose with the wet sponge. She clawed at his hand, but he was stronger, and soon she ceased her efforts. Her hands fell loosely to her sides, and Lachlan released his hold. Boistering his shaky composure, he said with false bravado. "Permit me to see what ye bring to me bed." He dutifully unbuttoned the small pearl fastenings down her gown's front. Opening the bodice wide, he reached for the laces of her chemise.

Marcus and Cashémere rode into the curved drive of Charters' small manor house. Marcus quickly slid from the saddle to lift Cashé to the ground. "Permit me to do the talking," he warned as he quickly escorted Cashé up the steps to raise the knocker on the main door.

Within seconds, the door swung wide. "Yes, Sir."

"The Earl of Berwick and Miss Aldridge for Mr. Charters." Marcus noted the shocked look of the butler when he noted Cashé's clothing.

"Permit me to inquire if the master be at home, Sir."

Marcus caught the man's shirtfront. "No inquires," he growled. "Tell me where Charters can be found."

The servant swallowed visibly. "I have not seen Mr. Charters for over an hour."

A footman stepped into the hallway, taking a menacing step in Marcus's direction, but Cashé stepped in his way. "Stop this instant!" she ordered.

From the expression on the man's face, it was obvious he recognized her. "I do not mean to hurt ye, Miss Cashémere," the footman warned.

Suddenly a large form filled the open doorway. "Then I suspect you should not consider interfering."

Marcus shot a quick glance toward the figure. "Nice to see you, Lucifer."

Lexford's man eased into the opening. "I thought you might require my assistance, Lord Yardley." He pointed a gun at the footman, and Cashé moved from the way.

Marcus shook the servant soundly before tightening his hold. "Is Charters at home?" he demanded.

The footman answered instead. "Mr. Charters ordered the cook to make up a food basket, and then he disappeared into the tunnels."

"What tunnels?" Marcus asked insistently.

Cashé stepped beside him and said softly. "There are several tunnels from when this land held a Scottish keep."

"Has Charters a female house guest?" Marcus shot a glance at the footman who had cautiously raised his hands in surrender.

"No one. I swear."

Cashé lightly touched Marcus's shoulder. "She must be here or at Uncle Samuel's," she whispered.

"The gentleman arrived home on foot yesterday afternoon," Lucifer disclosed. "Only Lord Averette has called today."

Marcus nodded his understanding. "Good work, Mr. Hill." Marcus maintained his hold while redirecting his remarks to Cashé. "Assist me in discovering where Charters might have gone. He is on foot and has food, likely for your sister. It cannot be far. Where might Charters be holding Miss Satiné?"

Cashé bit her bottom lip, deep in concentration. "The cottage," she said suddenly.

"What cottage?" Marcus loosened his hold on the servant.

"The one his parents lived in while his father built this house," she said as she turned toward the door. "It cannot be more than a quarter mile." She was leading the way around the side of house and toward the woodlands. Marcus gave each of the servants a silent warning not to follow, and then he chased Cashé along the pathway. Without giving the man orders, he knew Hill would deal with Charters household staff.

◦○○◦

Cashé was running, her men's clothing permitting her the freedom of a longer stride, while he followed closely behind her, neither of them slowing until the cottage came into view. Stopping suddenly, they both bent over, hands on their knees and panting. "What now?" Cashé sucked in a deep breath and straightened.

"We should proceed slowly," Marcus suggested. "We will see what is in the back. Is there more than one way in?" he asked as he caught Cashé's hand and led her on a sweeping arc of the cottage. They avoided being seen from the cottage's windows by ducking behind hedges and trees.

"I do not think so," she shared. "There are really only two rooms. A large room with a kitchen and fireplace and a small bedroom. It was temporary quarters for Charters and his wife." Marcus considered her description. The limited space could play to their advantage.

Reaching the lean to, Marcus motioned to where the let coach. "Charters has been here," he whispered close to Cashé's ear. "Stay hidden," he ordered. "Permit me to discover what is within before we make our entrance." Knowing her nature to be an impatient one, Marcus kissed her forehead and squeezed her hand before he left her hiding behind a hedgerow.

246

Slowly, carefully choosing where he stepped, he approached the cottage. There were no windows along the backside of the structure so he did not worry of someone observing him until he reached the back corner and eased himself about the turn. His gun hand led the way as he squatted below the windowsill. Straightening cautiously and avoiding any tell tale noise, Marcus peered into the filmy window. When his eyes adjusted to the scene, his heart stopped cold. "Damn!" he growled before racing for the front of the small house.

♀♀♀

Cashé had watched each step Yardley had made as he guardedly approached the back of the cottage. She admired the lightness of his step while ogling the very masculine line of his hips and shoulders. Before she had met His Lordship, she had never much thought about a man's body; but those innocent thoughts had disappeared last evening when she had slept in Wellston's arms. He had worn only his breeches, and while he had slept, she had surreptitiously examined his body–every pore, every freckle, every hair–totally entranced by the sight of his chest and his flat stomach.

While her eyes followed his every move, the earl reached the cottage's back corner, and Cashé's mind returned to the danger in which he had placed himself for her sake. It amazed her to have someone care so much for her. As he had edged around the building's edge, Cashé had moved also, literally crawling along the ground to reach a place where she might still observe him. However, when he reached the window, everything changed. Wellston's body stiffened before he was on the run toward the front of the house. Unable to wait, Cashé scrambled to her feet and shimmied between the branches of the bushes, and then she too was running toward whatever awaited them.

♀♀♀

Marcus had not even attempted the front door; instead, he kicked it open before taking three powerful strides, hitting the interior door with a mighty kick. The doorframe snapped, but it did not give completely. As he hit it a second time, he heard Cashé's approach. He did not turn to warn her from danger. There was no time. Instead, he placed a third kick on the door's bolt. This time, the door ripped from its hinges, and Marcus laid his shoulder to it to open it further. As he knew she would be, Cashé was beside him, adding her efforts to force the door to give way.

When it did, Marcus stumbled into the room, but not before Charters could climb from the bed and right his clothing. Marcus launched himself

247

at the man, taking Charters to the floor with him. They were a mix of arms and legs. Punches. Groans. Kicks. He and Charters wrestled, rolling dangerously across the floor. Marcus lost his gun in the melee, but he fought on. The man's actions towards Satiné Aldridge, a woman Marcus had once considered for himself, incensed him, and the thought that the woman on the bed could have been Cashé made him crazy for revenge.

ၥၥၥ

Although Charters outweighed his attacker by some two stones, the Scot did not have the man's training or his impetus. He had known his actions were reprehensible even as he had prepared to take the girl without her consent. He had never hurt a person who did not deserve it, and so he had accepted his assailant's continued pounding. As the man straddled him, Charters instinctively, brought his arms up to protect his face, but he no longer fought the stranger who had come to the girl's rescue.

ၥၥၥ

Cashé had followed Marcus through the door with no idea of what she might find on the other side. The sight of her lovely sister lying partially unclothed on the bed brought Cashé up short, and then she was on the mattress, draping herself over Satiné to hide her twin from the eyes of others. She was aware of the struggle going on not ten feet away, but all of Cashé's energies went into protecting her sister. "Satiné," she rasped as she pulled at her sister's gown, attempting to cover Satiné's exposed breasts and legs. "Oh, Satiné, I am so sorry."

The injustice took hold of Cashé's heart. Her head snapped around to where Marcus pounded Charters' head into the wooden floor. "Get off him," she yelled as she slid from the bed and made her way to the tussling men. "Get off him, Marcus," she urged as she pulled at Yardley's arms. "I want the pleasure of killing him."

Realizing belatedly she was there, Marcus sent Cashé tumbling backwards upon her rear, but she came storming back. "Permit me to kill him," she begged as she crawled on all fours to where Marcus held Charters in place.

Marcus said nothing as she fisted her hands and began to pound Charters' chest and face. "You, Bastard," she hissed as she burst into tears and took her frustrations out on the man. "Give me the gun, Marcus," she demanded. "I wish to shoot his sorry, arse."

248

Surprisingly, Charters accepted her anger, refusing to move as Cashé punched and slapped at him–simply staring upward at the ceiling. When her anger subsided, Marcus caught Cashé's hands in mid strike and pulled her toward him. Taking her tear-stained countenance in his hands, he waited until Cashé's eyes met his. "Assist Satiné," he whispered hoarsely. "I will handle Charters."

A sob of realization caught in her chest, but Cashé gave him a slight nod and then staggered toward the bed.

Meanwhile, Marcus rose to his feet and toed Charters with his boot in the man's side. "Get up," Marcus ordered solemnly. "You have an engagement with a British court."

Cashé's nervous fingers retied Satiné's chemise and worked the buttons of her sister's bodice into place. Throughout, she whispered apologies to the unconscious Satiné. Taking water from a bowl on the table, she wiped the powder residue from her twin's mouth and nose before gently removing Charters' semen from Satiné's inside thigh. "Please, Satiné," she begged as she struggled to pull her twin to a seated position.

⸎

"Leave her," Marcus said softly from behind her. "You take the gun and hold it on Charters. I will carry Miss Satiné."

Cashé looked uncomprehendingly at him, but she did what he said. With a shaky hand, she aimed the gun at the man to whom Averette meant to marry her. Marcus felt the gravity of the situation. The woman he loved more than life could have been the victim of a deviously planned despoilation. "Please provide me a reason to pull this trigger," she said coldly.

"I never meant to hurt her," Charters spoke softly in defeat, "but Lord Averette said it would be the only means to prevent Lord Worthing from prosecuting me."

Before he could shield her from the truth of Charters's words, Cashé flinched in disgust. "Uncle Samuel did what?"

Marcus released his hold on Satiné's limp body. "Worthing called on the viscount?" He realized Worthing must be close because of Hill's appearance in Charters' doorway, but he had not thought his former captain would call on Averette.

"Averette called on me home earlier today," Charters now confessed freely. "He said Lord Worthing knew I took Cashémere."

"I am Cashémere," Cashé insisted.

249

Charters dropped his eyes. "I knows that truth now, but not until today. I swear it. I found the gel in the English viscount's arms."

Marcus confronted Charters. "Worthing knew you had taken Miss Satiné, which means Averette had to know you did not hold Miss Aldridge as your prisoner. Are you telling us Averette never informed you otherwise?"

"I swear it be so." Charters still refused to look at either of them. "The gel attempted to explain who she be, but I refused the truth. She was with the English viscount, and Averette never said anything about her not being me Cashémere. But when I sees no birthmark on the gel's neck, I realized I had been duped."

Cashé's quiet voice told it all. "Uncle Samuel wanted revenge on the baron. What better way than permitting Mr. Charters to ruin Satiné?" The realization shook her, and it was all Marcus could do not to pull her into his embrace to comfort her; but Cashé would require time to absorb this new realization regarding her beloved Uncle Samuel. There would be time enough for tears and comfort once they had seen Satiné securely home. "He killed our parents, and now he has destroyed my sister's reputation."

Marcus caught her hand. "We will see your sister to safety, and then we can address your uncles." Cashé nodded her head in agreement, but Marcus knew she would not readily permit her anger to subside. She would brood over how she could not control all that had happened.

.◌◌◌,

Eleanor possessed no idea how her brother had known she had required his assistance, but when he rode into the circle at Chesterfield Manor, she was out the door and in his arms as soon as he had dismounted. "I cannot believe you have come," she sobbed. "I only sent word yesterday I required your presence in Cheshire."

Her brother studied her countenance, and she instinctively brushed the hair from her cheeks. Eleanor could not recall the last time she had slept soundly. "You are exhausted. Why has Kerrington not ordered you to bed?" Bran asked in concern.

"My husband chases Satiné's kidnapper," she confided.

Bran exclaimed, "Satiné's what?"

Eleanor caught his arm. "We should go inside. Obviously, you have no idea what has happened."

"Shepherd sent word he had questioned Ashton extensively, but he was unable to break the baron's resolve. He asked Worthing and I seek the truth. Because of our family connections to Ashton, Shepherd thought the baron might confide in us. When I arrived at Linton Park, the countess informed me both you and Kerrington were in Cheshire."

"Then you are in for a surprise," Eleanor said. "The world as we have known it has turned itself upside down."

⟨QQ⟩

It had taken Eleanor more than an hour to bring Brantley up to snuff with all the changes of the previous week. Then he had done what her husband could not. He had ordered his sister to bed while he assumed her place in Lexford's room. The viscount had awakened with the changing of his compress, and Bran prepared to meet his long-time friend's confusion.

"Fowler?" Lexford recognized him immediately. "When did you arrive?"

"A couple hours prior. I came to Cheshire seeking for my sister. If I had realized your state, I would have come sooner."

"Although I did not recognize it at first, your sister appears the perfect match for Kerrington."

It bothered Bran to hear the viscount speak with no knowledge of recent occurrences. "Eleanor tells me you wish to converse on events of which she possessed no knowledge. Do you hold questions I may address?"

Lexford closed his eyes, and Bran waited for his friend to compose his thoughts. "Would you tell me about Susan?" Lexford opened his eyes slowly. "I think I know, but I reqire someone to confirm my suspicions. Did I cause Susan's death?"

Thornhill schooled his expression. He knew how Lexford had suffered when he could not save his young wife. He did not want his friend to revisit the pain. "Not directly."

⟨QQ⟩

Marcus carried Satiné's limp body as they exited the cottage. Charters had come next, followed by Cashé, who still carried the gun firmly in her grip. They meant the main house and their waiting horses as their destination, but they had taken no more than a dozen steps when Jamot stepped from the cottage's shadows. He pointed a gun at Cashé's head, effectively bringing their "party" into the jaws of danger. Marcus silently cursed himself for permitting them to fall into the Baloch's hands.

"I will take the gun, pretty one." As Marcus watched, Jamot sardonically took pleasure in his success. He reached around Cashé's shoulder and removed the gun, placing it in his waistband. "Interesting,

Lord Yardley," the Baloch taunted. "Which one is yours? The one in your arms? Or the one who dresses as a man? I suppose such costumes is one means to tell them apart."

Marcus's wrathful focus rested purely on the Realm's enemy. "Permit the ladies their release, Jamot, and I will freely go with you. You want the emerald. I will take you to it, but only if you leave the women alone."

"No!" Cashé reacted to his offer.

Jamot nudged her temple with the gun. "Ah, but you have no idea of the emerald. I know because you are not the type of man to betray your friends, but you are the type to give up your life for someone you love."

"Unlike you," Marcus accused. "You left Ashmita to suffer."

Jamot's gaze lowered. "It is not so easy to be a hero when one follows a man of Mir's temperament."

"You give yourself forgiveness, Jamot; yet, you will find the world less willing to do so. How could a man call himself a man if he permits the woman he loves to be used repeatedly."

Jamot cocked the trigger. "Will you think yourself a hero if I kill this one before your eyes, my Lord?"

Marcus watched Cashé's eyes grow in size, but she did not move. Finally, Marcus said softly, "You hold the upper hand, Jamot. How will this play out?"

Jamot's mouth curled in a satisfying sneer. "Put the lady down, Yardley." Marcus gently placed Satiné Aldridge upon a grassy patch and then stood waiting the Baloch's next order. Jamot tossed a rope to Charters, who stood docilely in defeat. "Tie His Lordship to that tree."

Charters looked anxiously at the earl. "Just do as he asks," Marcus instructed and then placed himself before a nearly bare hawthorn tree. His eyes demanded Cashé hear his unspoken caution. "Save yourself," he told her with a slight tilt of his head, and she answered likewise. Without emotion, Charters obediently laced the rope around and around the tree, lashing Marcus to the trunk.

"Be certain it is tight," Jamot instructed.

Obediently, Charters pulled on the lines to demonstrate he did not risk Jamot's anger by leaving the binding loose enough for Wellston to escape.

Content, Jamot caught Cashé by the arm, keeping the gun pressed tightly to her head and shielding his body with hers. "You may leave," Jamot told Charters.

"What?" The Scot appeared confused. Marcus hoped Charters would do as he was told for if he the man returned to his house alone, Lucifer Hill would send out an alarm for the other Realm members.

Jamot scowled; he countenanced an intimidating glare directed at Charters. "From what I observed, Yardley and his pretty accomplice had taken you their prisoner. I am releasing you. Leave and do not look back."

The Scot stared at Jamot for a long moment, and Marcus knew without being told, Charters had found his honor. "I kin't allow ye to hurt the lasses," he declared. "I have done enough harm."

Jamot barked out a short, bitter laugh. "You wish me to shoot you in cold blood?"

"I dinnae want to die, but I will not desert the lasses," Charters hoarsely confirmed. In some ways, Marcus admired the man. Charters had been a fool to fall for Averette's manipulations, but he held some decency, after all.

"Then bring the other one," Jamot said tersely before shoving Cashé forward.

Marcus looked on with interest as Charters retrieved Satiné's body and fell into step before the gunman. He noted how Cashé had set her shoulders–as if she were a royal princess. She would make him a wonderful countess. Northumberland was a rough land, and it would require a special type of person to survive there. Cashé Aldridge would not only survive; she would thrive.

Jamot turned them toward the rocky shore; yet, before they were out of sight, Cashé defiantly called out, "I love you, Marcus Wellston!"

"Do what you must to stay alive," he called to her retreating form. "I will come for you, Cashémere."

Chapter Seventeen

Cashé was no more from sight before Marcus set to manipulating his bindings. Charters had wrapped the rope across Marcus's chest several times, but Marcus had learned a lesson from the woman he loved. When Cashé related her escape from the two drunken youths, he had marveled at her ingenuity and forethought. Even in a crisis, she had the good sense to find a means from her dilemma. Cashé had told him of swallowing a deep breath to expand her chest and making it appear her attacker had a tighter hold than he did. Marcus had done the same with Charters' attempts to secure him to the tree.

As Charters bound him, Marcus had put Cashé's ingenuity into play and had leaned forward at a slight angle so his bindings appeared tight. Now, with no one in the area, he faced a slackened rope. Maybe an inch–but it would be his discharge. By wiggling against the rough tree bark, Marcus worked the layers down the trunk, as well as his body, gathering them at his waistline. He twisted and scooted up and down, and, the hold gave way little by little. When the lowest strap reached his hand, Marcus laced his wrist through the binding and freed it. Then bending at the knees, he slid down far enough for his fingers to touch the top of his boot, where he kept a small knife hidden in a special pocket.

Slowly and carefully, working it loose from its binding, he caught the handle between his thumb and his index finger. Having the handle in his tentative grasp, he stood again before using the tree's trunk to brace the small knife with his upper thigh. Finally, it was his, and Marcus permitted himself triumph's breath.

Palming the weapon, he brought it to his other hand, using his fingertips of the still bound hand to hold the handle in place while the other released the blade. With his freed hand, Marcus used the small blade to cut the hempen strands. Sawing at the twisted threads, the cord frayed and finally fell in two. Pulling frantically at the ends, Marcus unwound the line–fighting to chase after Cashé. The thought of her being under Jamot's control had nearly sent him into a panic, but Marcus had made himself concentrate on one step at a time. Finally free, he took the knife in hand. "Protect her, God," he whispered. He turned toward the trail Jamot had taken with the others. "Please protect Cashémere."

୦୧୧

Jamot had kept a waiting wagon nearby. When he set out to investigate Lachlan Charters's property, he held no idea he would stumble upon one of his enemies. From a distance, he had observed Lord Yardley and the boy as they had approached the cottage, and he had waited for them to emerge. When they did not do so immediately, he had approached to have a closer look at what had brought one of the Realm to this dissolate location on the Scottish front. For a moment, Jamot had possessed the fleeting hope he had unknowingly stumbled upon the hiding place of the missing emerald. It made sense for the Earl of Berwick to hide the jewel on what might have one time been part of his holdings, and so Jamot had spied on the earl through the filmy window. When he realized there was no emerald, Jamot had known disappointment, but the knowledge Yardley did not travel with a boy had brought another sort of satisfaction. The twins who had foiled his plan with Velvet Aldridge were within the cottage, and he would have his revenge.

Reaching the wagon, he had ushered the one known as "Cashémere" into the back and had instructed the Scot to place the unconscious one beside Lord Yardley's lady. "You drive," he told his willing prisoner, as he climbed in with the women. "If you attempt anything heroic, I will kill His Lordship's favorite."

"Where are you taking us?" the girl had demanded.

Jamot smiled deviously. "Some place interesting."

୦୧୧

Worthing, Crowden, and Swenton rode into the drive before Charters' house. After Worthing had questioned the groomsman, he had gathered his associates so they might learn what Lucifer Hill had discovered. Finding Hill missing from his hiding place and expecting trouble, the Realm members had approached the Scot's home. "Be wary," Worthing warned as they dismounted.

Swenton gestured toward three horses tied nearby. "Is that not Hill's horse?"

"And if I am not mistaken," Crowden added, "that is Khan, Wellston's mount."

255

"What is the earl doing in Scotland?" Worthing remarked as they moved cautiously forward. However, before they could reach the door, it swung open to reveal Lucifer Hill.

"Hill!" Worthing expelled in relief. "Is Yardley within?"

The man looked surprised. "I suspected you might be he. Yardley and Miss Aldridge called upon Mr. Charters earlier."

"What the bloody hell is Miss Cashémere doing in Scotland? I thought I left her in Manchester," Worthing remarked in frustration.

"I cannot say, Sir," Hill confided. "I saw Yardley and what I thought was his tiger ride in. I could not imagine what business the earl had with Charters so I came to see if His Lordship required my assistance. When I arrived, the earl questioned Charters' staff."

Worthing demanded, "Why have you remained behind?"

"Charters is missing...seems the Scot departed the house through a wine cellar's tunnel. Miss Cashémere thought Charters sought a nearby cottage...supposed the cottage was where the man held Miss Satiné. I stayed behind to assure Charters' staff offered their master no assistance."

Crowden asked the obvious. "Where is Miss Cashémere's horse?"

Hill smiled amusedly. "I said Yardley rode in with what I thought was his tiger. Miss Cashémere wears a young man's clothing. She rode astride."

"That girl," Worthing grumbled, shaking his head in disbelief.

Swenton looked behind him. "Which way to the cottage?"

Hill gestured to the left side of the house. "Yardley and the girl went that way."

Worthing was striding toward the horses. "Bring Yardley's mount and the girl's. We should see this cottage."

Fowler sat in silence as Lexford stared at the draped cover over the four-poster. He had answered as many of the viscount's questions as he could. They had discussed their years serving together on the Continent and the years since their return to England. "Basically, I have lost nearly three years of my life," Lexford observed.

"You recall nothing of the things we have discussed? Nothing of even the recent past?"

"I believe everything you have disclosed." Lexford's voice held real defeat. "But without your insights, I would possess no knowledge of the events. The last I recall is returning home to the knowledge of Susan's brush with Bedlam. How do I recapture all I have lost?" Brantley Fowler

256

felt the twinge of guilt. He had not supported his friend through Lord Lexford's unfortunate marriage, at least, not as he should have. Lexford's words spoke of the viscount's recent memories, but they also spoke of Aidan Kimbolt's lost of family and of the man's true love.

∂∂∂

"They have been here," Worthing said as they inspected the small bedroom in the cottage. "There has been a struggle. See the blood stain."

Hill reentered the small cottage. "This rope has been cut." He displayed the remnants of the bindings.

"Let us see if we can discover a trail. We must determine whether Yardley and Miss Cashémere follow Charters and Miss Satiné or whether they are together." Worthing led the way from the cottage.

Swenton examined the tree. "It appears someone was tied here." He pointed to the bent over grass. "Whoever it was exited in that direction." He pointed to where the road turned sharply to the left.

Worthing nodded his understanding. "Another mystery which requires our intervention. We should know haste."

∂∂∂

Marcus growled several expletives when he realized Jamot had made his escape in some sort of wagon or carriage. He and Cashé had foolishly left their horses at Charters' home. A difficult decision rested before him: Should he follow on foot, dropping further behind, or to lose valuable time by returning to the Scot's home to retrieve his horse? Either way, he had permitted Jamot the advantage. Marcus could not shake the image of Cashé's defiance. She would be in danger in the Baloch's grasp. Marcus did not expect Jamot to readily accept Cashémere's impetuous spirit. Turning doggedly to retrace his steps, he experienced the familiar guilt of failing someone he loved; however, a sight he had not thought to see brought Marcus up short.

"Might you be in need of a willing mount, Your Lordship?" Crowden mocked as he led Khan behind him.

Marcus smiled, although he said, "You are a pompous prat, Crowden." He caught the reins the marquis offered.

"What has occurred?" Worthing demanded as he turned his horse in a tight circle.

Marcus sighed in resignation. "Charters attempted to take a drugged Miss Satiné against her will," Marcus reluctantly shared. "Miss Cashé and

257

I stopped the Scot, but before we could return the lady to safety, Jamot appeared. The Baloch has taken the women prisoners, along with Charters."

Worthing questioned, "Then it was you who was bound to the tree."

Marcus smiled deviously. "Did you expect otherwise?" However, he noticed none of his friends asked how he and Cashémere had come to be riding together. No explanation would be necessary. If he had chosen Cashé as his own, his associates would not interfere in what might occur with Lexford. They would not choose one over the other in the matter.

Hill called from where he had been examining the wagon tracks. "Jamot has turned toward Leith."

"How far behind the Baloch are we?" Worthing asked as Hill remounted.

"Somewhere between three-quarters and an hour," Marcus confirmed.

Worthing set his heels to his horse's flanks. "We are wasting time."

Satiné's eyes fluttered opened and closed several times, and Cashé knew renewed hope. "Cashé," Satiné said softly.

"I am here," Cashé soothed. She moved strands of hair from Satiné's cheeks.

From behind her, Jamot ordered lethally, "Do not speak."

Cashé flinched, but she laid her fingers on Satiné's lips to secure her sister's cooperation. Then she gingerly massaged her twin's arms and hands, working the feeling into Satiné's extremities. Throughout, they maintained eye contact, reestablishing their shared relationship. With her touch, Cashé spoke of regret and of an apology while tears pooled in the corners of Satiné's eyes. They rode into unknown danger; yet, Cashé silently announced she meant to protect her twin.

When Jamot shifted to a position of prominence behind Charters, Cashé looked up to see what the Baloch planned for them. "Over there!" he ordered.

"My God!" Cashé gasped, her eyes growing in size as Charters stopped the wagon outside a cone-shaped brick building.

"Out!" Jamot commanded, flashing the gun in Cashé's direction. He, obviously, saw her as the one to manipulate among her trio.

Cashé eased her weight from the wagon before turning to support her sister's decent. Satiné stumbled, but she managed to right herself before accepting Cashé's silent offer. Climbing down from the seat, Charters remained several feet away from the sisters; his head remained lowered

258

in complete defeat. She wished she held some sympathy for her former intended, but benevolence was not in her thoughts where the Scot was concerned. Soothingly, Cashé slid her arm around her sister's waist and eased her steps forward.

Satiné finally raised her eyes to the structure. "What is it?" she breathed the words in Cashé's direction.

"A glass cone," Cashé whispered.

"This way." Jamot gestured to the arched opening.

Walking before Charters and the Baloch, Cashé held the foolish thought of making a run for safety, but she could not conceive of leaving her sister behind; and Satiné was in no condition to sustain more than a short distance on her own. Therefore, Cashé permitted the Baloch to set up the parameters of what she instinctively knew would be a showdown. Without being told, she knew Marcus Wellston would search for her. All she must do was to protect Satiné and wait for the earl's appearance. Therefore, they entered the building unnoticed. Although not complete, the glass cone towered over other buildings in the area. As if it were a lonely lighthouse.

Cashé knew little of the glass industry, but she had seen other examples of the glass cone springing up upon Scottish soil over the last decade. Normally, the circular based building held a large central furnace surrounded by a circular platform on which the workers stood. Fritting floors, constructed of yellow refractory bricks, covered the area. Spaced at regular intervals, single thick brick walls offered protection from the heat and the hot glass.

With a flick of his wrist, Jamot gestured the threesome toward another opening. With uncertainty, she ushered Satiné forward. Entering the tunnels, they first climbed steps and then an incline, edging their way through what would eventually be a flue, one meant to carry the heat and the waste gas of the glass making process to the top of the structure and into the open air.

As they climbed, Cashé noted pieces of clothing and scraps of food strewn about the floor. Evidently, the Baloch had used the structure as his hiding place over the past few days. "What do you plan to do with us?" she demanded.

"Be patient, Miss Aldridge. You will see soon enough."

They continued to climb: Satiné, in the front, obediently leading the way, with Cashé behind. Charters resolutely followed. Finally, they had gone as far as the construction would allow. "Now what?" Cashé faced Jamot. "Do you plan to leave us here?"

"Nothing so mundane." Jamot smiled with satisfaction. "You will to go through there." He pointed to a narrow opening.

"There is nothing through there," Cashé protested. "It is an empty cavity."

Jamot's steely stare told tales of danger. "Open your eyes, Miss Aldridge. There is room for those not faint of heart." He caught Satiné by the arm and shoved her toward the opening. "The men who built this structure have provided a space in case of a fire or some other disaster. It is quite unique. Every three meters they have created a small ledge. See. Instead of mortaring the bricks end to end, they have laid them side-by-side. Although you will not be free to move about, you will have a place to stand against the wall."

"No!" Cashé charged. "I will not do it."

Jamot placed the gun to Satiné's head. "You have an opportunity to live, or you may die now. You must place confidence in Lord Yardley. Do you not trust your lover, Miss Aldridge?"

Cashé swallowed hard. "I will go first."

"As you wish." Surprisingly, approval showed on the Baloch's face.

Cashé stuck her head through the opening to assess the situation. The supposed ledge could be no more than three to four inches wide. Below, some five and twenty meters straight down was the yellow-bricked floor. With her back to the hand-made red brick wall, Cashé edged out onto the jutting tips of the bricks. The curved nature of the structure created a pitched-forward stance. Catching her breath, she extended her hand to her sister. "Follow me, Satiné."

Her twin's face appeared at the jagged opening. "I cannot, Cashémere."

"Satiné, Lord Yardley shall not permit us to die. Do as I do. You have only to stand against the wall and wait for His Lordship to come for us. We can do this together. I will protect you until Marcus arrives." In the back of her mind, Cashé thanked her foresight in not redressing Satiné with the layers of chemises and under skirts. Her sister would require a flattened skirt line on such a narrow perch.

Reminding her sister she possessed no choice, Jamot shoved the gun into Satiné's side, and Cashé flinched when Satiné visibly recoiled. Her sister had suffered so much, and it was all her fault. She would spend a lifetime setting things aright.

Slowly, Satiné followed Cashé onto the narrow ledge. "I am frightened," she said as Cashé reached for her.

"Do not look down," Cashé warned. "Where I should have been all along, I will be beside you." Making room for her sister, she caught Satiné's hand and stepped gingerly to the right.

Finally, Charters' bulky form appeared in the opening. He carefully worked his way through the breach, but his body mass countered the man's efforts in such a small space. The ledge could not support Charters with any security–his large boots finding no hold on the narrow strip. Scooting along the thin ledge, the Scot moved to the left.

"Do not look at him," Cashé hissed. "Look at me or look up at the beautiful sky. No matter what. You are not to look down."

Satiné gave a brief nod, staring intently at her sister.

Jamot amusedly peered at his captives. "I will leave you to your own devices," he boasted. "By and by, you will hear a small blast. But do not fear. I am simply providing His Lordship with a bit more of a challenge. It is all in payment for the small distraction provided me by the lovely Aldridge sisters in Liverpool. Do not panic when you hear it." Then the Baloch laughed, his voice ricocheting off the walls.

Cashé counted in her head. She had no idea how they could escape, but her mind raced to find a solution. In less than a minute, the walls shook. Powder and dust rained down on them. Satiné shrieked, but Cashé was determined to keep her twin safe until Wellston arrived. With every ounce of courage she could muster, Cashé demanded for her sister to remain immovable. She squeezed Satiné's hand. "Look at me!" she emphatically ordered over the noise. "No matter what, you are to look only at me."

With Worthing, Marcus rode at the front. His anxiety grew with each thud of Khan's hooves on the hardened ground. He could lose Cashé in a heartbeat, and the thought shook him to his core. Maggie had died because he was too late and too weak to save her. Would God bring Cashémere to a similar fate?

"Spread out," Worthing ordered as a flat bed wagon appeared beside a circular structure some two hundred meters ahead.

Automatically, the men separated to surround the building, but before they could secure the area, an explosion rocked the ground. As they scrambled to react, Jamot escaped from the arched opening and ran for the wooded hillside backing toward the brick cone. "Crowden, with me," Worthing ordered before he and the marquis gave chase.

.ᴏᴏ,

Cashé felt the walls sway as the explosion settled. Thick dust and powered mortar belched through the small opening as it collapsed. A dust cloud hung briefly in the air before the particles rained down on the fritting floor below. Seeking a better grip, Cashé had dug her nails into the sandy mortar. And although her stomach had done a complete somersault, she held her sister's hand tightly to the wall, refusing to permit Satiné to teeter on the ledge. "Look at me!" she repeated to her sister's distraction. Cashé willed Satiné not to perish. "I love you. I will protect you," she said with confidence.

However, before she could settle her own nerves and secure her sister's safety, a defeated groan announced Charters' despondency. From her vantage point, she watched the man purposely pitched forward and, unceremoniously, followed the dust particles to the ground below. A sickening thud heralded his impact. No other sound followed. Cashé wished to discover whether Charters had survived the fall, but she had her own dilemma as Satiné leaned forward in a swoon.

"Satiné!" she called in a panic. "Stay with me!" Cashé gave her sister's arm a quick jerk backwards, demanding Satiné's attention. "You are not to leave me!" she ordered. "We are twins! I cannot survive without you! Satiné, look at me!" She knew she had said the words before, but it was all Cashé could think to do to settle her sister's stance.

Slowly, Satiné turned her head in Cashé's direction and pressed her back to the wall.

Cashé breathed a bit easier. "I love you, Satiné," she whispered. "Please do not leave me. Everyone else has abandoned me."

"I will stay with you," Satiné responded weakly.

.ᴏᴏ,

The explosion had rocked the very ground upon which they rode, and Marcus's heart plummeted. As Worthing and Crowden chased a retreating Jamot, Marcus raced to the glass cone, a familiar structure found throughout Northumberland. His heart told him Cashé was in trouble. "Please God," he pleaded as he hit the ground at a run. Bursting through the arched opening, he yelled "Cashé! Cashé! Where are you?"

Breathing heavily, his own heartbeat pounded in his ears. At first, he did not hear her. "Marcus!" She sounded so far away.

262

His eyes adjusted to the darkness, and then he saw Charters' body spread out on the brick floor. Blood and grey matter flowed from a cracked skull. Even without checking, Marcus knew the man had breathed his last.

Swenton and Lucifer now stood behind him. Marcus motioned for Lucifer to check the body while he determined from where Cashé's voice came. Looking down at Charters' broken body, Marcus's eyes began to imagine the man's brief flight, and then he saw her. Cashé and Satiné were perched on a narrow ledge some twenty or more meters above him. "My God!" he gasped in a panic.

"Marcus!" Cashé's voice stayed him. "Jamot blocked the only way up." Her words echoed from the walls, repeating her dooming proclamation.

"Damn!" he sent Swenton to look at a gaping hole on the left as Marcus searched frantically for other openings. He knew from past experience with the cones within his own shire that normally a glass cone had several flues, but this building was under construction, and the flues had yet to be installed. The tunnels went nowhere.

Swenton returned to the circle. "Rocks and debris everywhere. We could dig it out, but it would take hours," he whispered to Marcus.

"They cannot wait that long." Marcus's urgency spurred them on. "I must find a means to reach them."

Hill joined them. "Come down from the top," he suggested.

Marcus looked questioningly at Swenton. "It is your call," the baron answered. "Lucifer and I will handle the ropes."

Marcus turned back to the circle. "Cashé, I am coming for you!"

༄

Worthing and Crowden had chased the Baloch along Leith's shoreline and toward Edinburgh. Jamot had hidden a horse in the wooded area, and the Realm now chased a well-trained warrior.

Finally, the Baloch had alighted and had entered the ruins of an old abbey. Worthing and Crowden, only seconds behind, had dismounted cautiously, before following. "Keep your eyes open," the future earl warned. "Dusk approaches, and soon Jamot will have the cover of darkness to his advantage."

"I will take the left," Crowden whispered as they separated and began meticulously to search the remains of a once-magnificent religious house.

"Jamot!" Worthing called, advancing through the narrow space. "Forsake this madness!"

He motioned for Crowden to check behind some tumbled stones before they crept further into the shadows. Cautiously, he wove his way in and out of the still standing alcoves. The painted glass windows cast odd lines across the stone arches and floor. Swirls of red, yellow, and brown streaked the area.

Worthing took several more tentative steps before Jamot appeared on an upper archway. It was a clear shot, but he paused, not wanting to kill any man in cold blood. He had seen enough of death during the war. "Jamot!" he called. "If you move, I will shoot."

It did not surprise him when Jamot laughed sarcastically. "You sound exactly like Lady Worthing right before I took the gun from her. She died with your name on her lips, Your Lordship."

Before he could wrap his mind around the Baloch's wild accusations, Worthing's vision blurred. The image of Eleanor lying dead upon Baron Ashton's floor flooded his mind. "You lie!" he accused through shaky lips.

Jamot looked about, obviously, searching for the marquis. "Do I?" he taunted. "Less than a week prior, I found my way into Ashton's home. Lady Worthing interrupted my dispensing with Lord Lexford. Unfortunately, the lady insisted I leave the house immediately. Foolish woman, I possessed no choice." Jamot snarled. "You have lost a wife and a child, Lord Worthing."

Kerrington could not breathe. A sickening feeling turned his stomach. Could it be? He held no doubt Ella would fight Jamot.

"Do not trust him, Captain," Crowden called from some place behind him. "If Lady Worthing was no more upon this earth, you would know. Your heart would know."

Forcibly, he swallowed his fear. "I plan to kill you, Jamot."

"You plan to try, Worthing."

The bullet whizzed by his head as he dove from its path. Worthing heard Crowden return fire and Jamot running again. "Damn!" He followed the sound of fear.

Reflexively, he chased the Baloch. It seemed their paths would be forever crossed–at least, until one of them died. He could see Jamot ahead, but, as always, the Baloch did the unexpected. He reached in his pocket and dropped some sort of legal papers upon the ground. Then he bolted forward again.

⊙⊙⊙

Morton dismounted in Aldridge's drive. He had slept little over the past three days, and his body ached with exhaustion, as well as with apprehension. Where was Satiné? Where was Cashémere? Were they safe? He handed the reigns to a waiting footman. "Is Lord Averette within?"

"Aye, Sir."

Morton nodded his thanks before mounting the entrance steps. Releasing the knocker, the baron waited impatiently for the door to open. Finally, he was able to say, "Baron Ashton for the viscount."

"If you will wait here, Sir, I will inquire if His Lordship is receiving."

From behind the butler came Aldridge's voice. "Morton, what brings you to Scotland? If you came to claim another niece, I fear I am fresh out of young ladies."

Morton's countenance fell. "Then neither Cashémere nor Satiné are here?"

"I have seen neither since I departed Derbyshire. Now, if you will excuse me, I have business to which to attend." Aldridge turned toward the back of the house.

Morton took several steps forward. In supplication, he said, "Do you not understand, Man. The twins are missing, and they are in trouble."

Aldridge turned slowly, a smile of triumph on his face. "Against my will, you accepted the care of my brother's children. If they now suffer, it is on your head. Blane, show the baron out."

"But wait!" Morton called. "You are telling me you will not assist me in finding Cashémere and Satiné?"

"I am telling you the twins are no longer my concern, Morton." With those words, Aldridge turned and walked away.

"You will pay, Aldridge! If it is the last thing I do, I will see you pay for this insolence!" Morton grabbed his gloves from the butler's hands and stormed from the house.

"Yer horse, M' Lord," the footman bowed.

Morton prepared to mount. "Would you tell me where Lachlan Charters lives?"

"Take the main road, M' Lord. When it forks, bear left. Another mile. There be a big tree in the middle of the road. The entrance to Mr. Charters' house be on the right."

Morton tossed the man a coin. "Thank you." He reined the horse in a tight circle before continuing his search.

Marcus, Swenton, and Hill climbed the narrow outside steps circling the brick cone. Marcus ignored the danger, but his companions took it more carefully. Reaching the top, he looked down into the cavity. Cashé and Satiné clung precariously to the "smooth" wall of the cone's interior. "There is no place to tie off the rope," he announced.

"I can hold it," Lucifer spoke seriously. "I will be your anchor, Your Lordship."

"We should lace the rope through the small opening between the bricks," Swenton suggested.

Marcus peered over the edge again. "Is the rope long enough?" He quickly counted the rows of bricks. "Three to four meters."

Swenton removed a looped rope from over his head and chest. "I found this one in the tunnel. The space appeared to be Jamot's hiding place."

"And I have this one from the tree."

Marcus nodded. He had striped off his coat and waistcoat before their climb. "Then we should begin. Lucifer, wrap this end around your body and then sit on it to hold it in place. Swenton, you will guide the rope so it does not tangle on the ledge above where the ladies are standing. You will be supporting the women's weight and mine."

"We will not fail you, Yardley."

Marcus moved precariously on the narrow stairs, making a looped harness before perching on the ledge. "Cashé," he called to her. "Do not look up. I am coming after you."

Slowly, Marcus lowered himself over the lip of the cone, testing the rope with his weight. "Release a bit more of the rope," he ordered.

He could see the women some two meters below him. Cashé kept a cooing tone going as she spoke to Satiné. He could not make out every word, but she spoke to her sister about "love" and "fear" and "trust," and Marcus had thought her the most remarkable of women. They would survive this because of her determination.

Finally, he reached their level, the toes of his boots touching the ledge. "Do not move too quickly," he warned. He shot a glance at Cashé, and her eyes met his. "We will do this slowly and carefully. Are you both well? Any injuries?"

Cashé gave him a slight shake of her head. "Take Satiné first," she ordered. "I will wait for your return."

Marcus's heart lurched. He wanted Cashé safe. "Are you certain?" he asked softly.

"As certain as I will be your countess by this time next week." Cashé gave him a delicate smile. "You see, my Lord, in my conceit, I hold no doubt you will save us both and no doubt in our love."

"You are incredible," Marcus whispered.

Thus decided, he worked his way closer to Satiné. When he was within reach, he placed his arm across Satiné's waist to keep her balanced. "I want you to place your arms about my neck. When we push off, you must hold on with all your might. I will catch you to me, but I must have one hand on the rope. Therefore, you must hold tight even if we are jostled. Do you understand?"

Tears streamed down the lady's face. "I am frightened," she sobbed.

"So am I," Marcus said evenly. "But soon you will be my sister, and I will not permit you to fall. Come now, the men above cannot hold me forever." He nudged her into action.

Satiné hesitated, but Cashé purposely broke their physical contact by pointedly releasing her twin's hand. "Satiné, our lives are yours to lose or save. Move now."

Thankfully, Miss Satiné wrapped her arms about his neck, and Marcus pushed off from the cone's side with his legs. "Lay out across me, and wrap your legs about my waist," Marcus ordered. He leaned at a forty-five degree angle and, literally, walked up the wall. Looping the rope through the notches on his waistband, Marcus pulled their combined weights toward the sky.

Satiné continued to sob, but Marcus coaxed, "We are almost there. Another meter. See the light."

When they were close to the top, Swenton reached over and caught Satiné by the shoulders and lifted her from Marcus's body. "Release your hold, Satiné," Marcus encouraged as she refused to loosen her grip. "The baron has you."

With a gargantuan tug, Swenton pulled Satiné free, sending them both staggering backwards on the narrow stairs. Marcus climbed over the lip to follow Miss Satiné to safety. He watched with curiosity, as the baron caressed the girl's cheek. "I have you," Swenton told her as he righted himself and steadied his stance. Catching her to him, he embraced her before turning Satiné toward the steps. "Can you sit here safely?"

She nodded her head and sank down where he indicated, and Swenton scrambled to Marcus's side. "Are you all right?" The baron asked as Marcus caught his breath.

"I will be when we retrieve Cashé from that damnable perch," he grumbled. "Can you do this again, Lucifer?" Marcus looked carefully at the man. His friend's face was blood red from the strain.

"Allow me a moment to relax my arms." As he said the words, Hill adjusted the ropes about him. He flexed his shoulders and shook out his arms. "I be ready, Lord Yardley."

Marcus nodded briefly before beginning the descent once again. His blessings were many, among them the loyalty of these men.

"Be careful, Marcus," Cashé warned as he swung out over the three inch ledge above her.

Finally, he rested a meter or so from her. His toes touched the ledge, and the ropes supported him in place. "Come, Sweetheart." He extended his hand to her. "Come to me." Cashé nodded her understanding. The ropes would not permit him to reach her on his own: She must shift to the left to catch his outstretched hand. She bit her bottom lip and concentrated on each of her movements, and Marcus had never been prouder of anyone. This woman he had chosen was remarkable. Gingerly, Cashé slid her foot along the rough brick and then brought the right to meet her left one. "That is it, Sweetheart. Nice and steady," Marcus coaxed when she repeated the movement. "Come on, Love. Almost there."

Cashé's eyes met Marcus's; she did not look to the ledge. Instead, she permitted her foot to feel its way along the bricks. "Tell me you love me," she whispered roughly.

"I adore you; you are my life," Marcus rasped as he examined her every move. "A few more inches, Cashé," he cautioned.

He watched with guarded interest as Cashé steadied her nerves with a deep breath before moving again. Their fingertips touched as she slid her foot another six inches; but when she shifted her weight from her left to the right, the shelf crumbled under her left foot, and Cashé pitched forward. Her left hand reached for Marcus, but all he could see was open air under her feet. Her scream echoed from the walls.

Like a whip, Marcus's hand snapped downward to catch Cashé's arm, but her weight swung them away from the wall as they dropped another meter before Swenton and Lucifer caught the slack and stayed their fall. Together, they slammed into the interior wall with a mighty thud, and Marcus heard her grunt in pain.

He could not see her, just feel her weight pulling at his shoulder socket. "Cashé!" he pleaded

With a gush of air, she answered, "I...I am here."

Marcus steadied his breathing. "Do you have it, John?" he yelled before he moved. A growled affirmation said they strained, but they would not fail him. "Cashé, catch my arm with both hands," he ordered. Never displaying doubt, the girl, thankfully, reached for him with her free hand, clasping Marcus's arm with all her might.

Gritting his teeth, he began to flex his arm and lift her to him. "Use your legs, Cashé, as I did earlier. Walk up the wall."

He marveled at how his courageous Cashémere followed his every order. She was the most spectacular woman he had ever known. When she was beside him, Marcus pulled her arm across his body, literally wrapping her grasp about him. "Catch my other arm, Love," he instructed. "One hand at a time."

Cashé was close enough now for him to see the sweat forming on her forehead, but he also saw the determination in her eyes. How had he ever lived without her? When both her hands clasped his arm holding the rope, he caught Cashé about the waist and lifted her to his body.

"I have her!" He told Swenton as he adjusted Cashé in his embrace. "We are coming up." He kissed the top of Cashé's head. "Do like your sister, Sweetheart. Wrap yourself about me."

Cashé wrapped one arm around his neck and the other under Marcus's arm and across his shoulder. Her legs snaked about his waist. "I love you," she whispered as she buried her face in his neck.

Marcus caught the rope with his left hand and pulled them upward. Then he did the same with his right. Left. Right. Left. Right. His arms felt as if they were being pulled from their joints, but he swallowed the pain. Left. Right. "Nearly there, Love," he rasped as he reached with his left again. "Say it for me, Darling. Count off the steps." He rested for a split second, adjusting his feet against the wall. "One," he grunted as he pulled again.

"Two," Cashé said softly into his ear. "Three." Pause. "Four." Pause.

"Two more," he growled.

"Five." Pause. "Six." She said with triumph.

"Take her," Marcus groaned in obvious pain.

Swenton allowed Lucifer to hold the slack alone as he snatched Cashé to sit on the wall. Immediately, she scrambled to the other side and grabbed a hold on the line. "Get him over," she cried as she leaned back to brace herself against the wall.

Marcus's fingers clawed at the opening's ledge as Swenton caught his shoulder and pulled him inch by inch over the wall's lip. When Marcus finally supported his own weight, the other three collapsed on the narrow stairs.

Heaving for breath, they each appeared beyond moving, but as Marcus looked on, Cashé, on hands and knees, crawled to where Lucifer Hill sat with his eyes closed. "If you require anything," she breathed, "I am forever in your debt." Impulsively, she kissed the man's cheek. Then she moved on to an exhausted Swenton. "You were phenomenal," she said as she kissed his lips. Finally, she reached Marcus. Lying across the steps, he simply raised his arm, and Cashé draped herself across his body. "We made it," she moaned.

Sending his hand up and down her back, Marcus leaned back with his eyes closed. It was the most exquisite moment he had ever known. He had not failed her. Unlike with Maggie, he had not permitted Cashé to perish: Cashé's survival would heal him.

Chapter Eighteen

Worthing and Crowden had given pursuit. They had scooped up the papers the Baloch had left behind, Jamot's plan to convert the documents into ready cash thwarted. "Jamot heads into the southern mountains," Crowden noted as they turned toward a hidden valley. "Will we continue the search?"

Worthing pulled up on his horse's reins. "God!" he expelled, as his eyes scanned the area. "I know we should continue the pursuit, but, in reality, all I want to do is race home to assure myself that Ella is well. I am exhausted by this life. Is it beyond reason to simply want to live out my days as Eleanor Kerrington's husband?"

Crowden had paused beside him. "I believe you should return to Cheshire, Captain. You have a family to protect. Chasing the kidnapper of your wife's cousin is an honorable quest. A family obligation should always take precedence in a man's life. Chasing a crazy Baloch across Scotland is someone else's mission. Have we not given enough years and faced enough dangers?"

"You sound introspective, Crowden?" Worthing took an account of the marquis's countenance. "Is there something you wish to say?"

Staring at the trail they should be following, Crowden remained silent for a several minutes. "I want what you have. What Fowler has found. What Wellston has, obviously, discovered. If I possessed it, I would be on the road to my estate so quickly people would question whether I had ever been here."

The viscount turned his horse in a tight circle. "You have the right of it, Crowden. Someone will find Jamot, or the Baloch will return to his homeland. Either way, I am to Manchester. I will deliver Ashton's papers, and the baron can choose whether to prosecute Aldridge. At the moment, all I wish is to sleep with my wife held tightly in my embrace."

Crowden nodded seriously. "I will assure myself Yardley and Swenton have recovered the ladies, and then I will be to Staffordshire. I am of the persuasion I can assist England more by being a voice of reason in Parliament than I can by tracking Jamot."

"We will report we lost the trail," Worthing confirmed.

"Farewell. Be safe, Captain." Crowden extended his hand in parting.

Worthing accepted it and then turned his mount toward England, his wife, and home.

∞

Grace lurked in the shadows as the house's mistress sought her husband. Having been the governess to the Averette family for some five years, Grace Nelson had seen the manipulative ways of the man, but, of late, the viscount's temperament had taken a darker turn, and Grace feared Lord Averette would harm his wife if someone were not present to witness his cruelty. "What is the matter, Samuel?" Alice Aldridge wrung her hands anxiously. Packing away papers and ledgers, her husband rushed about the room.

For a few minutes, Lord Averette ignored his wife, but when she did not withdraw, he turned on her. "Remove yourself, Woman!" He shoved past her, sending Alice stumbling backwards into a bookshelf.

She righted herself before Grace could step in to save the woman. "Please tell me," Lady Averette begged. "I have a right to know what has occurred."

"You have a right!" His Lordship charged at her, and Alice Aldridge recoiled. "Since when do you have a right? You are my wife, and you will do what I say."

He raised his hand to strike her, but Grace Nelson burst through the open doorway. "Your Lordship!" she spoke with authority.

Aldridge turned his contempt in Grace's direction. "No one asked for your presence in this matter," he declared viciously. "Take yourself from my sight."

Grace glared defiantly. "Gladly, Viscount Averette, but first I shall see Lady Averette to her room." She placed her arm around the woman's shoulders. "Come, Viscountess. Gwendolyn requires your attention."

"I want you gone from my house," Averette ordered to Grace's retreating form. "Before the day is out."

Grace ignored the man's posturing. Instead, she said, "I have ordered your maid to pack several items for you and for Gwendolyn, Ma'am. I suggest you spend time with your parents."

Regina Jeffers

Alice Aldridge glanced uncomprehendingly over her shoulder to where her husband ranted about the lack of assistance from his servants. "Viscount Averette will object," she said tentatively.

Grace continued to guide Lady Averette's steps to the main staircase. "His Lordship plans a journey of his own. He has arranged for his coach," Grace said encouragingly. "The servants have their orders. Something evil is happening at the Ridge, and you and Gwen must not be a part of it."

"But what of you?" Always of a subservient nature, Lady Averette permitted Grace to lead the way.

"I have long wished to return to Lancashire," she lied. "I have family there." Grace directed the viscountess toward the mistress's chambers. "If you could provide me a letter of reference, I will find another position. Perhaps, something closer to my home..."

"What of Gwendolyn? My daughter shall miss you. My husband is simply out of sorts. Something concerning the estate or his nieces. I am certain Lord Averette shall forgive your interruption. You shall see. Everything shall return to normal."

Grace gently touched the lady's arm. "On more than one occasion, His Lordship has voiced his displeasure for my part in the Duke of Thornhill's revenge on Sir Louis Levering. Although I was an unknowing participant, Viscount Averette has permitted his ire be known. I am certain my most recent interference has sealed my fate. And as to Gwendolyn, she shall have your parents to dote upon her and her cousins with whom to play. She shall adjust quickly. I have spoken to her of my departure, and Gwen understands my reasons for leaving. I have explained how I miss my brother and younger sister and England."

"I shall think of you kindly, Grace Nelson. You have been a Godsend. When you are prepared to take your leave, your letter shall be waiting." Wiping the tears from her eyes, the viscountess entered her quarters.

Grace sighed heavily. "I shall be happy to be free of this place."

With dusk looming, they forced themselves into action. Stretching and straining, Marcus and Cashé rose as one to stand at the cone's highest point. "Here rides the marquis." Marcus pointed to an approaching figure on horseback.

Swenton followed the line of Marcus's arm. "Where is the Captain?"

Marcus mumbled, "I do not know, but we should find out. Swenton, would you see to Miss Satiné?"

"Certainly, Yardley." The baron edged closer to Satiné Aldridge. "Permit me to assist you, Miss." He caught the crumpled Satiné by the shoulders and lifted her to a standing position. "I will guide you. Stay close, and you will be safe." It bothered Marcus that Satiné said nothing, but she followed Swenton down the narrow circular steps, and he supposed he should be thankful for small miracles.

Lucifer Hill, his hands raw with rope burns, descended before the pair. Then Marcus took Cashé's hand, bringing it to his lips. "Did you mean what you said, Darling?"

Cashé moved easily into his one-armed embrace. "What was that, my Lord?" She kissed Marcus's cheek.

"That you would be my countess by this time next week," he said huskily.

"We are in Scotland, Lord Yardley. It could be sooner," she teased. Then glancing toward where Crowden rode, she said, "After we address yet another crisis."

Marcus accepted her evaluation. "Crowden does not ride with urgency," he noted. "It may be nothing."

"I certainly hope so." She permitted Marcus to brace her stance.

As they reached the structure's bottom steps, the marquis overtook them. "Where is Kerrington?" Swenton asked when Crowden came to a halt.

"We lost Jamot's trail after a confrontation in a deserted abbey near Edinburgh. Yet, in the midst of the fight, the Baloch claimed he had harmed Lexford, as well as Lady Worthing and the captain's unborn child. Although His Lordship did not believe Jamot, I thought it best that Worthing leave for Cheshire. We have recovered Ashton's papers regarding Lord Averette. Worthing will return them to the baron. The viscount would be of no use to us here."

Marcus understood what Crowden had not said. Inside a glass cone, Marcus had left his ghosts behind. He had spent six years of his life attempting to deaden the feeling of inadequacy he had carried with him from the day he had not saved his twin sister. He had rescued countless souls in more countries than he cared to remember, but none of them had healed the void he toted across the Continent. Now, all he wanted to do was to return Cashémere Aldridge to Northumberland and raise a dozen children of his own. He held no desire to chase the dream any longer. He had found it. "We must do something about Charters's body."

274

Regina Jeffers

"There is a blanket in the tunnel. I noticed it earlier," Swenton noted. "We should contact the authorities."

"I suppose we should find a magistrate," Marcus suggested.

Hill volunteered to fetch the man, but a group approached from the village. Instinctively, Marcus draped his coat about Cashé to cover her unusual attire.

"Wot be gonnae on?" The group's spokesman demanded.

Marcus stepped forward. "I am the Earl of Berwick." Despite his title being an English one, his ancestral land had once been a part of Scotland. These men would recognize the title, even if they knew nothing of him. "This is the Marquis of Godown and Baron Swenton. From Manchester, we have followed a man who kidnapped one of the young ladies. Along the way, we discovered another assailant, who has been hiding in this structure."

The man gestured to the other villagers behind him. "How come ye not ast fer hep? This be Scotland."

"There was not time. The ladies were in danger."

The leader of the group touched his hat. "Didnae ye find the man, M' Lord?"

"One man is dead inside. He fell to his death."

"Wot now?" he asked suspiciously, and Marcus noted how the others edged forward as if expecting trouble.

Marcus recognized the general dislike of the British found in the southern area of Scotland. The countries had fought many a battle over the land. "We will speak to the magistrate."

Cashé stepped beside Marcus. "Is that you, Hamish?" she said to the dark-haired man on the left. "Hamish, it is I, Cashémere Aldridge, Lord Averette's niece. You deliver grain to my uncle's lands."

"I knows her," Hamish quietly told the leader. "I sees her at the Ridge manor before."

Marcus lightly touched Cashé's hand. With her knowledge of the area, she likely had just defused a difficult situation. "Miss Aldridge and her sister were the victims," he explained.

The man had one more question. "Wot be ye in Manchester, gel?"

"My maternal uncle resides there," she said simply. "Now, how about someone locating the magistrate as Lord Yardley has asked?" Predictably, Cashé had taken control, and Marcus was not a bit annoyed. He would give her her lead when it proved to an advantage. "It is nearly nightfall, and I wish to see my sister to safety."

"Yes, Miss." Hamish hustled away to do her biding.

Marcus looked carefully at the group's makeup. They were honest men protecting their property. "I will stay behind to answer the magistrate's questions, but the ladies have suffered greatly. I insist my friends escort them to the nearest acceptable inn. They should not be out in the cold night air with no coats or shawls to keep them warm."

The villagers eyed the group. "Ye be stayin'?"

"I will stay," Marcus said evenly.

The villagers agreed, and Marcus organized the departure. "Crowden, take Miss Aldridge up with you. Swenton, you assume the care for Miss Satiné. See if you can locate some clean clothing for the ladies." He lifted Satiné into Swenton's waiting arms. "It will be over soon," he whispered to the girl. Since her recovery, she had withdrawn into herself, a fact he knew would play poorly on Cashé's composure. He handed Cashémere up to Crowden. "You are to stay with your sister tonight: Satiné requires your sensibility and your loving heart."

"You shall require both also, my Lord," she answered softly, and Marcus's eyes locked with hers. "I shall wait for your return." Louder, for the benefit of the waiting villagers, she said, "We shall be at the Sly Fox. It is two miles along the Harbor Road toward Edinburgh."

Unable to say anything else before the others, Marcus nodded his agreement. Feeling foolishly bereft of her presence, he reluctantly stepped away. His friends were barely from sight when the magistrate appeared.

"Yer Lordship." The man offered an appropriate bow. "Hamish, here, says ye have had some difficulties. I am Alastair Dougal, the closest thing to the law in this area. How might we be serving you?"

Marcus gave Dougal an abbreviated bow. "This is a complicated story. Could we find some place to share it privately?"

"Me house be jist o'er the way, if'n you possess no objections to sittin' with a Scotsman." Dougal gave a toothy grin, which held a bit of a taunt.

Marcus rose to the test. "As my land previously sat in Scotland, I believe I have the right to call myself part Scot."

"Can you hold yer brew?" Dougal challenged.

"I suppose we will discover the truth together." Marcus gestured for the man to lead on, as he caught Khan's reins to follow.

Two hours and three stiff mugs of homemade brew later, Marcus had explained in some detail how they had come together in Dougal's "back land." Marcus had omitted the attempted rape of Satiné and the fact Cashé had traveled with him. He led Dougal to believe she had returned to her former home under the marquis's protection. He told Dougal, as Cashé's intended, she had sent word of Satiné's mistaken abduction, and he had traveled to Scotland to assist her with Charters.

"So, thinkin' to change the lady's mind, Lachlan took the wrong gel?"

"That is how this started," Marcus confessed. "Mr. Charters would not accept the fact Baron Ashton had chosen my suit over his. Miss Aldridge will be my countess."

Dougal smiled knowingly. "Scottish lasses are not like those in London," he teased. "I noted the affection of which you speak of the lady. Ye have found yer match."

"I hold Miss Aldridge in true regard." Marcus stood. "We will be at the Sly Fox if you have other questions."

"After I takes a look at it, I be havin' Hamish to escort Charters' body home." Dougal followed Marcus to his feet. "The man never was smart, but I be surprised he goes so far."

"It was an impulsive act, which cost Mr. Charters his life," Marcus shared.

Marcus noted how Dougal worked in questions in the midst of his side remarks. "And ye be sayin' this other man set off the explosion, which captured the gels on the ledge?"

Needing to end the interview, Marcus worked his way toward the door. "I believe he is a drifter, supposedly a very dark-skinned man. I imagine he thought he had found a means to make some fast money. Lord Crowden followed the stranger to an abandoned abbey, but he lost the man's trail. You may ask His Lordship for a better description if you care."

"I be doin' jist that, Yer Lordship. I be callin' on your associates in the morning."

"I will advise them to expect you, Dougal. Now, if you will excuse me, I wish to see to the safety of my future family." With that, Marcus exited the man's house. He prayed the Scotsman believed his story. Marcus did not want to involve Shepherd in this. The Realm's leader would be most annoyed for how little control they had exercised over the chaos.

When he had called at Charters' small manor, the servants had turned him away, but Morton had recognized the stress among the man's staff, and instead of leaving, the baron had found himself a place where he could watch the house. Turning up his coat's collar against the cold, he prepared to wait it out. "Someone in that house knows something," he said aloud. "And I mean to discover the truth of it."

He waited impatiently, but his efforts finally proved productive. Some three hours after nightfall, a flat bed wagon rolled into the drive, and Morton came alive. Before the worker had stopped the team, the baron set his feet in action. He would require a closer look. When the footman stumbled from the door to meet the driver, he was hiding in the shadows.

"Wot have you there, Hamish?" the footman called.

"Yer master." The one known as Hamish pulled back the blanket to give the footman a look.

The servant backed away from what was obviously a gruesome sight. "Wot happened?"

The wagon driver appeared to relish the role of town crier. He puffed out his chest with importance. "Some English lord be makin' a loud noise 'bout Charters takin' some English gel, thinkin' it be Miss Cashémere. Seems the lord plans to marry Lord Averette's niece."

Hearing Aldridge's title mentioned along with Cashémere's name, Morton stepped from his hiding place. "What lord?" He pointed his pistol at the men.

The wagon driver froze, his gossip stifled. "We be wantin' no trouble."

"I just want to know what lord and where I might find him. Then I will leave you alone," Morton assured them.

"Name's Yardley. He and Miss Cashémere and some others are at the Sly Fox on the Harbor Road, goin' back toward Edinburgh."

Finally, he thought. Finally, a piece of information he could follow. Morton touched his hat and with a nod, he hurried to find his family.

Marcus sat with his friends and Cashé in a private room in the inn. They had had a quiet meal as he had shared his interview with Dougal. "The man will call on us in the morning."

"I hope the magistrate is early. I wish to be on the road to Staffordshire."

Marcus shot Swenton a questioning look regarding Crowden's sullenness, but the baron gave a slight shake of his head as a warning. Instead, Marquis inquired of Cashé, "How is your sister?"

Regina Jeffers

"I do not know. Satiné will barely answer me." Cashé slid her hand under the table and into Marcus's. "I possess no knowledge of how to make Satiné whole again?" Marcus knew her pain would drive Cashé crazy.

However, before he could respond, a ruckus in the main room caught his attention. "I mean to see Yardley," Charles Morton argued with the innkeeper.

Cashé was on her feet immediately. "Uncle Charles," she squealed as she ran to the man's waiting embrace. For infinitely long seconds, they simply enjoyed the renewal of family while Marcus looked on with satisfaction. He was pleased the baron had not chastised Cashé for her impetuousness.

"You are here," Morton caressed her cheek before pulling her hard to him again. "I was so worried for you, Child." He hugged her tightly. "Please tell me you have discovered your sister."

With the reminder of Satiné's ruination and her part in the debacle, Cashé eased from his embrace. "Satiné is upstairs, but I am worried for her."

Morton looked up to see Marcus standing in the doorway. "So, you are here also, Yardley?"

Marcus bowed. "Come, join us, Your Lordship," he said to Morton before turning to the waiting innkeeper. "Please send some food and drink for the baron."

"Yes, Lord Yardley." The innkeeper started away.

"Mr. Wallace."

"Yes, Sir."

"Baron Ashton will require a room also."

"Right away, Sir."

Marcus's friends made polite conversation, but they quickly withdrew, leaving Marcus and Cashé to explain to Ashton what had occurred. "So, do you wish to tell me how you two came together in this matter?" the baron demanded. "The last I heard from Lady Worthing, you had traveled alone, Cashémere."

Cashé started to respond, but Marcus cleared his throat. "It is not as you insinuate, Your Lordship. My former batman found Miss Aldridge in a dangerous situation at an inn outside of Darlington. Mr. Breeson thought it best to bring Cashémere to me for my protection."

"Cashémere?" Morton's eyebrow rose in question.

279

Marcus smiled with satisfaction. "Cashémere," he said confidently. "It is my intention, Ashton, to make Miss Aldridge my wife."

"Are you telling me, Yardley, you have compromised my niece?"

Marcus did not approve of the baron's tone or of the degrading way of which he spoke of Cashé. Again, Marcus halted Cashé's response. "Miss Aldridge's traveling alone has put her reputation in jeopardy. Yet, Your Lordship, it has been my intention to seek Miss Aldridge's hand since our days at Linton Park." Marcus watched with satisfying interest as the baron covered his surprise. "And although I have not compromised your niece in the strictest sense of the word, Cashémere's exploits, her staying unchaperoned in my home, and our traveling together speaks of a speedy marriage. But you should know, Sir, I love Cashémere."

Ashton did not answer immediately. "And you feel the same, Child?"

"Yes, Uncle. It is my wish."

Marcus noted how Ashton did not agree, nor did the man object. "And what of Satiné? Your sister had aspirations."

Cashé turned pleadingly to Morton. "You do not understand, Uncle. Satiné and I decided Lord Lexford was more to her preference. I explained our switch in my letter to you."

"I read the letter, Cashémere, but I will not see Satiné slighted."

Marcus cleared his throat. "May I speak of a delicate matter, Sir?"

Ashton looked carefully at his niece. "Before Cashémere?"

Marcus thought it a bit hypocritical for Morton to speak of Cashé's ruination to her face and then to want her removed when speaking of the same possibility for Satiné. "Miss Aldridge observed the situation of which I will speak, but if you wish her absence, I will understand."

"Is it that horrid?" The baron paled with the possibilities.

"Yes, Uncle." Cashé took his hand to offer her comfort.

Marcus continued. "Charters kept Miss Satiné drugged with laudanum throughout most of the journey from Manchester. When they arrived at his home, the braggadocio placed your niece under lock and key in a small cottage near to his main house. When Miss Aldridge and I discovered the cottage, Miss Satiné was unconscious, and Charters was taking the most intimate of liberties with her."

The baron sucked in a deep stilling breath.

"After Marcus subdued him," Cashé added, "Charters confessed Uncle Samuel had convinced him defiling Satiné was the only means to avoid prosecution. Mr. Charters still thought it was I. Lord Worthing had previously told Uncle Samuel Charters had taken Satiné by mistake. Uncle Samuel purposely set the wheels in action for Charters to claim Satiné's innocence."

Morton visibly recoiled. His actions told Marcus the baron understood the implication–the unspoken assumption. "And did Charters succeed?"

"We have no means of knowing, Your Lordship." Marcus spoke softly; he had no desire to hurt the baron further, but the man needed to know the truth of what had happened. "Miss Satiné did not recover consciousness until an hour or more after we had found her. She would hold no memory of the act, and Charters died before the girls' rescue. We cannot question the man. He was apologetic for his action, saying he did not know the difference until he noted the lack of a birthmark on Miss Satiné's neck. Your niece, Sir, was unclad when we broke into the locked room. Charters was in a position to complete the act." He paused to allow the baron to absorb the information. "The whole situation has left Miss Satiné quite despondent."

Morton, sounding totally defeated, said, "Might you tell me what happened after you rescued Satiné from the cottage?"

Marcus quickly explained about Jamot's surprise maneuver, his chasing the Baloch and Cashé, Jamot's crazy punishment, Marcus's rope rescue, and what he had told the magistrate to cover some of the gossip.

Afterwards, Morton sat dazed for several minutes. "I suspect I should see Satiné," he said softly.

"Do you wish me to go with you, Sir?"

Morton squeezed Cashé's hand. "It might be easier on your sister if I speak to her alone."

An hour later, her uncle found Cashé asleep, her head resting in Marcus's lap. They had remained alone in the same small private room. Marcus watched the dying embers of a fire while stroking Cashé's hair. Morton silently slid into a nearby chair. "I am not certain, Lord Yardley, that I approve of your newfound familiarity with my niece."

"Then force me to take Cashémere to a border village to make her my wife," Marcus answered confidently. "I hold no qualms with saying vows over an anvil."

Morton shrugged away his vexations. "Satiné refuses to return to Manchester." He rubbed his face with both hands to fight off the exhaustion. "She fears too many people know of her ruination."

"I assumed as much," Marcus considered the baron's words. "I have been thinking, Sir, what might be best after a situation with such devastating ramifications. If I were you, Baron, I would escort Miss Satiné on an extended holiday, say to Italy, for example. You must keep your niece away from prying eyes until you are certain Miss Satiné is not with child."

Morton swallowed hard. "And what if Satiné is truly ruined? Even without her being with child, no gentleman would accept her with all the gossip. All Satiné ever wanted was her Society debut."

Marcus turned his eyes from the baron's obvious anguish. He knew he would sound cold, but he looked upon Cashé's strength against all odds, and thought her twin could use a bit of resilience of her own. He understood the lady's despondency, but he was always one to believe God aided those who saved themselves. He judiciously offered hope. "I believe you are in error, Morton. Miss Satiné has many fine qualities. Despite the gossip, a gentleman would welcome her as his wife, but if you cannot convince your niece as such, there are many Italian ducas and French comtes, and Spanish marquises, who would gladly align their titles with an established English family. The Continent has changed with the war's end. Miss Satiné's beauty will turn many heads, and traveling will provide her with the confidence to face the worst of British society with a raised chin."

"A lesson Cashémere learned in the worst of conditions," the baron's tone expressed additional regrets. "Once we have met with the magistrate, I wish to call on Averette. I would have you accompany me, Lord Yardley. I cannot guarantee my sanity otherwise."

"Of course, Sir." Marcus recognized the unspoken acceptance of his relationship with Cashé. He would be part of the baron's family. "I thought we might retrieve the coach Charters brought from Manchester, and then you and your nieces will be my guests at Tweed Hall. You can develop your plans from Northumberland."

"Thank you, Lord Yardley."

"Permit me to carry Cashémere to her sister's quarters." Marcus gently lifted Cashé's head from his lap and deposited it on the settee's soft cushion. "You would have been so proud of her, Sir." Marcus looked lovingly on Cashé's sleeping form. "Cashémere expertly fought off her attackers at the inn; she was singular in finding her sister, and it is thanks to her that Satiné lives. If I had removed Cashé first from that narrow ledge, Satiné would have plummeted to her death before I could return for her. And how Cashé

282

fought to survive when the ledge collapsed was unbelievable. I thought her lost to me, but she clawed her way back–persevered over it all."

Morton said softly, "Cashémere is the best of her sisters. She has triumphed over the worst of conditions and has come out stellar."

Marcus knew he thumbed his nose at propriety, but he gently lifted Cashé to him. It was well after midnight, and no one but the baron would be the wiser. She stirred in his arms, and Marcus permitted her to curl closer to him. The baron followed silently behind him, so Marcus swallowed his words of endearment. Pushing the door wider to the room she shared with Satiné, he carried Cashé to the bed and left her beside Satiné.

"Uncle?" Satiné mumbled as she woke.

Morton assured, "Nothing is amiss, Child. His Lordship and I brought Cashémere to bed. Be certain your sister does not sleep in her dress."

"Yes, Sir."

Marcus led the way to the door. "I will see you in the morning, Sir."

In complete exhaustion, the baron rubbed his face with his dry hands. "I will be happy to leave Scotland behind."

Marcus could not agree. Scotland had given him the woman he loved, and even with all they had encountered, he could not help but feel a softness in his heart for the country.

✑

Cashé had insisted on accompanying her uncle and Marcus to confront Samuel Aldridge. Dougal had taken statements from Crowden, Swenton, and Hill. The Scot previously had visited the cottage and observed the destruction as being consistent with Marcus's tale. Dougal made his sincere apologies to Ashton for the pain the baron's family had suffered. Upon the man's departure, Crowden had made his excuses and had set a course for Staffordshire. Swenton had agreed to accompany the baron's family to Tweed Hall. Although his hands were still raw, Lucifer offered to drive the coach.

With everything settled for their return to England, the chaos surrounding Averette's household upon their arrival had taken them unawares. Marcus permitted Cashé to lead the way through the open door. Servants scrambled from room to room, gathering what appeared to be anything of value. Raising her voice about the din, she demanded, "What goes on here?"

The servants froze in place, each looking a bit guilty at being caught. A man Marcus recognized as Aldridge's butler stepped from behind the stacked items in the front foyer. "Miss Cashémere," he said evenly. "We did not anticipate your return." Marcus was surprised anyone would speak to her; he had never seen Cashé's anger so evident, even when she had attacked him in this very house.

Cashé huffed. "Obviously." She gave each man and woman in the room a look of pure disappointment, and Marcus pitied them for crossing her good nature. His servants would know her disdain if they did not perform to her standards. He quite liked the idea; it was unusual to discover a young woman so prepared to lead a household.

"Would you care to explain, Blane, why the household staff seems intent on ransacking my uncle's personal belongings?"

"Lord Averette has departed the country, Miss." Marcus stayed Morton with a touch of his hand on the man's shoulder. "Her Ladyship and Miss Gwendolyn have retreated to the mistress's family home in the north." He gestured to the piled goods in the open area. "The staff has not been paid for last year's wages, Miss Cashémere, and this year be nearly gone," he offered as an excuse for the servants' actions.

Cashé's hands fisted at her waist. "So you thought it acceptable to steal from my aunt? A woman who has treated each of you with kindness?" He noted how she did not mention her reprehensible uncle. It appeared Samuel Aldridge meant to evade the authorities. "Did you allow the viscountess the opportunity to make good on my uncle's debts?"

The servants all dropped their heads in shame. "No, Miss," confessed a maid Marcus recognized as the one who had accompanied Cashémere during their rescue of the duchess.

"When did Lord Averette depart?" Marcus protectively stepped beside Cashé.

Placing down a silver goblet, the maid, Edana, responded, "Yesterday evening, Sir."

Not so easily pacified, Cashé continued to eye each of her uncle's employees. "And my aunt?"

Edana kept the floor. "Miss Nelson asked us to pack Lady Averette and the child's belongings. The master be in a snit, of late."

Morton finally joined the conversation. "How do we know Aldridge departed Scotland?"

The butler answered, "Callum saw His Lordship to the docks and placed the viscount's belongings on board ship."

Morton cursed under his breath and turned toward the door in frustration.

Cashé pleaded softly. "We cannot permit this to happen to Aunt Alice and Gwendolyn." She motioned toward what the servants had accumulated. "Is there nothing we can do?"

Marcus eyed Morton cautiously. He knew the baron required a means of revenge on Averette, and Marcus would lead him in the best means currently possible. "What say you, Baron, to our using a bit of our governmental influence to revoke Lord Averette's bank privileges for his personal use and to revert them for his wife's."

"Can you do that?" Cashé looked in awe at Marcus.

"For you, my Dear, I will certainly give it the noble attempt."

Cashé gave the servants a warning glare. "You will cease this madness until our return. Is that understood?"

"Yes, Miss Cashémere."

ه‍

Before appearing at her uncle's bank, Marcus had recruited his original government contact–the one Shepherd had told him to use if he had found difficulty with Jamot in Edinburgh. "Well, this is certainly what could be termed 'difficulty,'" the man had reasoned aloud. Gordon Keating maintained a presence as a respected local businessman, and his word at the bank proved invaluable.

Aldridge had withdrawn two thousand pounds from his personal account sometime yesterday afternoon, but nearly five thousand remained. Marcus and the baron used their status as part of the British aristocracy to lock the funds for Alice Aldridge's use only. Mr. Keating guaranteed the servants' pay with his signature. At Ashton's suggestion, Lady Averette would seek Keating's advice before making major withdrawals from the funds, and Keating would issue her a regular allowance from the investments and other sources of income.

"That is an excellent idea," Cashé confided to the baron. "Aunt Alice is not adept at managing her own expenses. Uncle Samuel never permitted her the responsibility."

"The lady will learn. Keating appears a fair man."

"Might we also remove Uncle Samuel from the church account? He, Mr. Charters, and Mr. Stowbridge have equal access to the funds for the school and the other programs for the poor in the parish. I want no one else to suffer because of my uncle's deceit."

Marcus turned to the agent. "Keating, will you make certain Stowbridge is a fit match in handling these church funds?"

"I will start my evaluation this afternoon, Lord Yardley."

With everything in place to curtail Averette's future funds, they departed the bank offices. As Cashé expressed her gratitude to Mr. Keating, Marcus caught the baron's arm to speak privately. "I know this is not the outcome you sought, but it is the best we can do for the moment. Remember, if Averette departed for Europe, we will soon learn of the viscount's whereabouts. Between your former and my current connections, you might locate the viscount easily. Mayhap even as you and Miss Satiné take in the sights. And do not forget, a duel to defend your family's honor would not be against the law in many European countries."

"I like the way you think, Yardley," Morton whispered.

"Allow us to return to The Sly Fox. I am anxious to be on English soil."

.೦೦೦,

Along with Keating, they called upon Averette's household to announce their success. Cashé released the services of everyone except Blane and Edana. "My aunt may choose to secure your services again upon her return. I will write her this evening to explain what I have done to protect her home." When the servants retreated, she turned to Marcus. "May I stay and pack some of my personal items while you retrieve my sister? I will require them in Northumberland, and I have some mementos from my parents I wish to keep for our own children," she whispered. "I wish to hold my parents' memory dear. To place my items beside the lace from Maggie and those keepsakes of your brother and parents. To truly blend our families as one."

Marcus smiled at her. "You know too well how I cannot resist you. We will return in a little over an hour. Is that enough time?"

"More than enough. I am prepared to start my new life in my new home," she teased with a pouty mouth.

"Please do not tempt me." Marcus said as he pulled Cashé behind a door to steal a kiss. Like a man who had never known peace until this moment, he drank of her lips.

It pleased him how Cashé clung tightly to him as she returned his passion. "It is too long before I am truly yours," she groaned.

Although he still kept Cashé in his embrace, Marcus withdrew. "I will secure a special license when we return to England," he whispered.

Cashé kissed his chin line. "Then let us be about our life. I have seen enough of Scotland."

◦◦◦

Late in the evening, the loaded inn coach came to a halt before Marcus's home. His footmen scrambled to assist the guests to debark and to dispatch Cashé's trunks to the chambers Marcus had ordered for her before they had departed for Scotland two days prior.

"We are pleased you are home safely, Your Lordship. Lord Trevor will be beside himself with joy with the additional company," Mr. Spear declared as he accepted everyone's wraps.

"Miss Aldridge's sister, the Barons Ashton and Swenton, and Mr. Hill will also require rooms, Spear," Marcus ordered. "Ashton and Miss Satiné will remain for an extended stay."

"Yes, Your Lordship."

"Might Mrs. Marling see to a quick meal for everyone. I am certain we are all famished. Whatever she might provide will be appreciated."

Spear bowed to Marcus's guests. "I will speak to Cook immediately, Sir. The blue drawing room has a full fire, Your Lordship. I will see to tea for the ladies and brandy for the gentlemen."

"Thank you, Spear. And tell Mr. Ingram to ask Trevor join us."

◦◦◦

Despite the chaos of the previous fortnight, everyone enjoyed an evening of friendship and family. Even Satiné accepted quiet time with Swenton as Trevor entertained the others with innocent stories of a young Marcus's many escapades. "How is it you remember exactly what I said to you when I was ten, but you cannot recall your history lessons?" Marcus sat easily beside his older brother.

Trevor smiled that adorable lopsided smile he presented to everyone. "That is easy. I do not love my history lessons."

"Your brother knows how best to silence your objections, my Lord." Cashé smiled largely at him before turning her attentions to his brother. "Lord Trevor, might I persuade you to escort me to my chambers?"

Trevor scrambled to his feet. "I have never been asked to be a lady's escort before," he confided over a blush.

"Then it I who shall claim the honor and to say I shan't make it the last time you are asked," she assured him. "Good night, Gentlemen," she said to the room before giving Marcus a lingering gaze.

287

When everyone retired, the baron remained. "I have considered what you suggested, Yardley, and I believe your plan to escort Satiné abroad is a sound one. I will send word to Chesterfield Manor to prepare our trunks for an extended journey."

Marcus sipped his brandy. "I am sorry it has come to this. Needless to say, you are welcome at Tweed Hall as long as you require sanctuary, Sir."

The baron sighed deeply. "I realize you are most anxious to marry Cashémere, but I worry for how Satiné will react," the baron confided. "Satiné is on fragile ground."

Marcus nodded his understanding. "I came to the same conclusion as I observed your niece today, and I do not expect Miss Satiné will recover quickly." He realized how what he once had thought of as Miss Satin's biddable personality to be one of weak resolve. The lady would never survive in Northumberland's harsh environment. "However, I offer a caution: It would be unfair to permit your preference for the child you have raised as your own to overshadow Cashé's need for a family. Cashémere has known nothing of what family means. I do not wish to criticize you, Sir, but I have sworn to protect Cashémere, and I will do even if it makes you uncomfortable."

Marcus paused for several elongated seconds. He knew the baron would take the responsibility for both sisters equally once he had time to weigh the facts. Satiné appeared to be very vulnerable, but Cashé hid fraility. She was equally as susceptible to Society's censure. Marcus continued, "It would also not be proper for Cashémere to reside in my household for a prolonged stay. We can twist the rumors to our benefit at this point, but not for months on in. How say you to Cashé and I asking Lord Worthing for permission to marry from Linton Park's chapel. If you recall, the earl made such an offer at Thornhill's joining. The Kerringtons would welcome our marrying in Derbyshire. Lord Worthing or His Grace could act in your stead for presenting the bride. You could remain at Tweed Hall solidifying your plans, while Cashémere and I holiday."

"Again, it appears you have an answer for everything, Yardley," the baron observed without enthusiasm.

"It is not my purpose to assume control of your life, Ashton. I want only to protect Cashémere, as well as her sister. I would not see Miss Satiné suffer, but neither will I permit Cashémere to do so." Marcus sat his glass on a side table. "Think about my suggestion overnight. I am at your disposal when you are prepared to take action." Marcus made his way to the door.

The baron said a bit sarcastically, "I suppose you also know where I might find a knowledgeable steward. I will require someone other than Mr. Thorne, who has grown too old to do the job competently, to oversee my land and holdings while I am away."

Marcus smiled deviously and turned to face the baron again. "Actually I do. Mr. Breeson, my former batman, has been apprenticing on my estate since his return from the war. Yet, it is not likely Breeson will assume the position any time soon. Might I send him to speak to you about the estate? Breeson would be delighted. For some time now, he has had his mind set to ask Faith Molson to be his wife, but he required a position of his own before he did so."

Ashton accepted Marcus's manipulations reluctantly. "Why not? Send the man to see me in the morning. What else do I have to occupy my time?"

Marcus bowed from the room, but he took great satisfaction in seeing his dreams coming together.

Chapter Nineteen

"How is Lexford?" Sir Carter Lowery asked as he accepted a seat in one of the drawing rooms. The baronet had arrived at Chesterfield Manor with a renowned physician in tow.

Fowler had met them in the front foyer, gladdened by the physician's appearance. The duke shook his head in disbelief. "The viscount's wound is nothing more than a dark bruise behind his ear, but he still possesses no true memory of the time after Susan's death. I certainly do not relish Lexford's grieving for his wife again."

Lowery nodded in agreement. "I thought we might lose Lexford on more than one occasion. As if he punished himself for his wife's weaknesses, he took on the most dangerous assignments."

The physician stood. "Perhaps I should make my own evaluation. Could someone show me to the viscount's room?"

Thornhill rose to reach for the bell cord. "My sister's maid Hannah sets with His Lordship at the moment. We will await your diagnosis."

"I will return late tomorrow or early the next day depending on the road conditions," Marcus told Cashé as he prepared Khan's saddle straps to his liking. "The archbishop visits Durham, and I am prepared to pay heavily for a special license, but such a 'outlay' would be worth the expense rather than a ride to London. I hope a journey to Doctors' Common will not be required. However, if that proves necessary, I will send word of a change in my plans."

Cashé bit her bottom lip, a sign of her agitation. "I feel guilty for being so happy."

"Cashé, I do not wish for Miss Satiné to suffer, but your sister has a long recovery; and despite her own despair, I cannot believe Satiné would deny your happiness. I regret to say Miss Satiné will not welcome our joining, but, deep down, she knows it is right." Marcus lifted Cashé's chin with his fingertips so he might look into her countenance. "Besides," he said as his breathing became shorter, "now that I may claim you as my own, I will not tolerate our wasting one second of our time together."

"It amazes me how much you care for me. I have never known such affection." Tears crept from her eyes' corners and down her cheeks.

Marcus used his thumbs to wipe them away. "No more tears, Love. You have healed me, and for that, I will forever be at your side."

∂∂

"Satiné, may we speak?" Cashé found her sister in her chambers. As much as she had dreaded this conversation, Cashé knew there were things to be said between them.

Without changing her expression, Satiné said, "I suppose."

Cashé came to sit beside her sister before the hearth. "I am worried about you."

Satiné shuddered. "I cannot feel warmth. Do you not think it bizarre that even with a roaring fire, I still can feel the coldness seeping into my bones?"

Composing her expression, Cashé looked away for a second. "I wish I could change what has happened," she whispered.

Satiné picked at invisible lint on her gown. Cashé had shared several of her day dresses with her sister; she had ordered Marcus's staff to burn the dress Charters had provided her twin at the cottage. Satiné required no reminders of her trials. "I am healing," Satiné said weakly.

Cashé paused with dread over sharing her news. "Lord Yardley has asked me to be his wife."

Satiné's eyes misted with tears. "It is as you planned then."

"Please do not say it in that manner. You know I never meant for you or Lord Lexford to suffer."

Satiné bit back a sob. "But we both have suffered. You possess no idea how it feels to imagine yourself dirty–to imagine a stranger's hands on upon your person."

Cashé felt guilty about her twin's ordeal, but she was also a fighter. If the situation were reversed, Cashé would certainly not have bemoaned her fate. She would never accept Charters' attack as her defining point. "Are you dirtier than Velvet? Jamot touched her innocence as revenge against Thornhill. And what of Eleanor? Abused by her father, as well as Sir Louis Levering. And what do you think happened to me while I was rushing to reach your side? Two men broke into my room to take advantage of me." Cashé swallowed hard to steady her pulse. "Satiné, what happened to you is tragic, but do not make the situation a tragedy. You do not know if Charters violated you, but even if he did, you are still the same person you were when you departed for that fateful ride. Charters only wins if you permit him to do so."

"Do you not understand?" Satiné snapped. "No gentleman will ever consider me fit material to be his wife!"

"You would allow a man to label you? Uncle Samuel attempted to break me, but I was above him. Jamot thought to best us; yet, we survived. Luckily, Mr. Breeson assisted in my escape from those two men, but only after I had taken my vengeance on one youth's manhood. I will never be subordinate to anyone. Lord Worthing adores Eleanor because our cousin refused defeat. The duke holds a new respect for Velvet because our sister took her rescue into her own hands. A true gentleman does not judge a woman on her innocence."

"You know nothing of a man's regard. Of love," Satiné charged.

Cashé folded her arms across her chest. "If what you describe is love, then I want none of it. Lord Yardley knows my faults, but he still desires me. I am thankful Mr. Jordan and Mr. Stayne's violent attempt to know me was thwarted; yet, I do not believe Lord Yardley would have turned from me even if those two ruffians had been successful. Marcus Wellston understands life is not kind to women. Nor is it kind to men. People must make the best of what few times of happiness they possess." Cashé caught Satiné's hand in hers. "I love you. If I could have taken your place, I would gladly have done so. Without regrets. However, God has given this to you to bear. Our Lord wishes to know if you will thrive. What will you answer Him?"

"Marry your earl, Cashémere. You do not require my blessing," Satiné said sarcastically.

Cashé squeeze the hand she held. "You are correct. I do not require your permission to marry Lord Yardley, but I desire your good wishes."

"I will attempt to know peace, Cashémere. That concession is the most I can promise."

Late on the third day of his journey, James Kerrington reached Chesterfield Manor's drive. He slid from the saddle and ran for the steps. Mr. Whitcomb opened the door as the viscount reached it, and Worthing skidded to a stop in the entryway. "Eleanor! Eleanor!" he bellowed as he

292

searched the nearby rooms. He ignored the butler's attempt to take his hat and gloves. "Eleanor!"

Fowler appeared from the back of the house. "Have you gone mad, Worthing?" the duke taunted.

Kerrington's knees nearly buckled in relief at seeing his wife's brother. "She is well?" he pleaded, nevertheless.

"I am here."

His eyes fell on the woman he loved, and this time his legs did give out. He sank to his knees before covering his face with his hands. Then his wife was kneeling before him. He caught her violently to him and began slowly to rock her in a rhythmic sway of thanksgiving. "Jamot claimed to have done you harm," he whispered to her hair. "I thought to have lost you."

They had spent over a week apart. "I am here," she repeated.

"Will you two continue to make a spectacle of yourselves, or would you care to join me in the drawing room?" Fowler looked on in amusement.

Worthing growled, "I have never appreciated your humor, Fowler."

The duke laughed lightly. "Unfortunately for you, the woman you claim as your own is my sister. You must tolerate me as family."

Worthing cupped his wife's chin before kissing her softly. Then he stood, bringing Eleanor with him. "Come, Sweetheart. I do not plan to permit you from my reach for a long time."

Fowler continued to do the talking. "So, Worthing, you rushed home to learn how our Eleanor thwarted Jamot's plans to do away with Lexford by shooting the Baloch in the shoulder?"

Worthing stopped suddenly, catching his wife's arm in a tight grip. "You did that?"

Eleanor shook her head in the affirmative before asking, "Did you find Satiné and Cashémere?"

He simply smiled at his wife. She always put others before herself. That particular characteristic was one of the reasons he loved her. "Let us order a meal. I am suddenly famished. We have hours to figure out what is what."

※

Over the next week, everything progressed. Mr. Breeson arrived at Chesterfield Manor with letters from the baron naming him as the new steward. Wellston's former batman was to be given a small cottage near the manor house for his personal use, and he told Worthing he had proposed to Faith Molson before departing Northumberland. The man also delivered letters from Wellston to Worthing and from Miss Aldridge to Lady Worthing.

"Cashémere and Lord Yardley plan to marry at the end of next week." Eleanor read from her cousin's letter.

Her husband added from his own, "And they seek permission to use Linton Park's chapel for the ceremony."

Eleanor perked up. "With that news, do you not think, my Lord, it is time we returned to our home and our family. I cannot have the countess overseeing everything for the wedding."

Worthing continued to read. "Wellston says it will be a very small affair. Only he and Trevor and Mr. Ingram from his family. Mr. Breeson, of course. The baron plans to escort Satiné abroad for an extended stay. It appears Satiné suffers greatly from the ordeal."

Bran remarked, "Satiné was the lesser sister, after all. With all her beauty, she does not have the mettle found in Velvet or our Eleanor."

Worthing noted his wife's raised eyebrow, but he kept his thoughts of the duchess to himself. "Or Cashémere," he confided. "Mr. Breeson related some of the goings on since we have last seen her. He found her fighting off two thugs in an inn outside of Darlington, and Wellston has related how he saved her from the glass cone while she dangled at the end of a rope."

"It is a shame," Fowler added. "I had hoped when Lexford recovered his memory he would also discover a fondness for my wife's youngest sister. But I would not want him to do so, if the lady had not the wherewithal to encounter her dilemma with resolve. Shepherd was correct in that respect. He once told me those who served the Realm require a different type of woman to be satisfied with our civilian lives. You found that in my sister. I did so in Velvet, and the earl will have Cashémere."

Eleanor interrupted his thoughts. "None of us can say Satiné will not blossom into a fit companion for His Lordship? She is young still." Worthing recognized his wife's desire to create a perfect happily ever after, but he knew much of what her brother said to be true.

"She is but two years your junior, Eleanor," her brother reminded her. "One year less than Velvet and the same age as Cashémere. Ashton sheltered Satiné too long. She has never known hardship."

"We once said the same about Velvet," Eleanor countered.

"But Velvet learned to be a fighter from her books," Bran smiled. "She was Scheherazade, staying alive in Jamot's crazy scheme. I did not think it possible, but she proved me wrong, and I am proud of her for it. The same as I am with you, Ella. You faced Jamot and protected Lexford." He smiled at his friend. "We are lucky men, Worthing. Very lucky men."

"And I hope Velvet reminds you of that particular fact daily," Eleanor laughed.

Bran smiled knowingly. "As often as you remind Lord Worthing."

Already organizing Cashémere's wedding, she paused as if deep in thought. "I should make a list of who to expect. Bran, shall you send for Velvet?" Eleanor asked, but did not wait for a response before adding, "What do we do about Lord Lexford?"

"The viscount should remain here until after the wedding," Fowler stated. "Although Lexford has no memory of his initial interest in Miss Aldridge, there is no reason to make everyone uncomfortable on such a momentous day. As soon as the physician agrees the viscount can travel safely, I have made arrangements for Lexford to spend time in Kent with Velvet and me. I was in Brittany the last time Lexford went through his guilt and his grief. I will see him through it this time."

Eleanor rose from her seat. "I shall set Hannah to the packing. If we leave by noon, we may be home by supper, James. I have missed Daniel terribly."

"As have I, Sweetling." He kissed her fingers. "Your brother and I will make final arrangements and confer with Mr. Breeson."

"Hannah is quite efficient; she shall have my belongings packed within the hour. However, when you finish your preparations, I would prefer we visit with Lexford together."

"Of course."

✍

"You have mumbled and grumbled your way across three shires," Cashé had teased.

"And you know perfectly well why," he growled. Each time he had reached for her, Marcus had quickly withdrawn his hand. Cashé found it all quite amusing to know he enjoyed touching her and only propriety kept him from doing so. Of course, she had purposely tormented the earl with lingering gazes and suggestive glances. It was wonderful to practice a bit of flirtation.

On Tuesday, Marcus's large coach appeared before the Linton Park circular fountain. She, Marcus, and Trevor rode in luxury, while Jeremy Ingram, Marcus's valet, and a maid for Cashé had followed in the smaller

295

coach. It had taken three and a half days to reach Derbyshire. Where Marcus had seen it as pure torture, Trevor had seen it as a great adventure. Because Marcus's brother rather traveled, he had asked hundreds of questions. It reminded Cashé of herself and her sisters when they were small, and she wondered of her own children. Would they be curious? Would they drive the earl crazy with insistent questions? She found the possibility quite amusing.

.ℓℓℓ.

His head resting on the coach's window, watching for the estate, Trevor remarked, "It is a large house."

"Yes, very large, and quite beautiful." Cashé patted Trevor's hand. Marcus adored how she always made time for his brother. He had predicted she would be a very patient mother with their children. The only difficulty with such a mundane thought was it led Marcus into considering creating those babies, and he would be hard again and grumbling again.

"Two more days," she whispered as she prepared to dismount.

Marcus caught her hand and pulled her to him. "If you keep taunting me," he growled, "it will be tonight."

Cashé smiled prettily. "You want me, my Lord?"

"More than you know," he groaned.

A footman jerked the door open, and Worthing and his mother, the Countess of Linworth, greeted them. "Welcome," Lady Linworth said as they stepped from the coach.

Cashé curtsied before walking into Worthing's waiting embrace. "How do I apologize, my Lord?" she whispered.

"Make Wellston happy, and we will forget any irregularities," he teased lightly. "Come into the house. It is turning colder." He placed Cashé on his arm. "Mother, did you meet Lord Yardley's brother Trevor?"

.ℓℓℓ.

"I apologize for such short notice, Lady Linworth," Marcus said over his second cup of tea. "We had thought to use Tweed Hall, but Baron Ashton and Miss Satiné remain in residence. As the lady is still recovering from her ordeal, it did not appear appropriate to celebrate mine and Cashémere's new beginning with Miss Satiné so distraught."

"Think nothing of it," she assured him. "We shall have a close intimate celebration." She sipped her tea. "Linworth was quite delighted with your and Miss Aldridge's following in the tradition set by our James and Eleanor.

Regina Jeffers

We have made arrangements for ten on Thursday morning, and we have engaged Doctor Perry for the ceremony. I hope that choice is acceptable."

Cashé said earnestly, "It sounds heavenly, Lady Linworth. With all the chaos surrounding my twin's abduction, we wish to keep our joining simple. A few friends. Our families. That will be perfect."

∞

"I plan to ride to Manchester," Marcus whispered as they sat together in the Linworth drawing room after supper.

Cashé understood immediately. "You plan to call upon Lord Lexford?"

"I know it may sound odd, but I must address Lexford in person." He lifted their laced fingers to his lips. "He is my friend."

"Shall I accompany you?" she offered.

"And give Lady Worthing apoplexy? The viscountess has but one day to fit your gown."

Cashé squeezed his hand harder. "Give His Lordship my regards."

∞

Having been received, Marcus made his way to Lexford's room. After knocking, he entered to find Lexford sitting up in bed, reading a book. "Ah, Wellston," Lexford said upon seeing Marcus at the door. "You have saved me from a fate worse than death: a book of poetry."

"You were always more a man of science, Kimbolt. What fool brought you poetry?" Marcus moved the stack of books perched on the edge of the chair before taking the seat.

"Fowler means to vex my good humor," Lexford confessed. "The duke has appointed himself my caretaker."

Marcus watched Lexford play at being in a good mood. He knew it was how his friend dealt with pain. "I was under the belief you held no memory of current times; yet, you speak of Fowler as a duke."

"Fowler enjoys being a duke. It provides him an opportunity to outrank Crowden." Lexford adjusted his position in the bed. "However, I do not believe you called upon me to speak of poetry or dukes."

Marcus frowned. "No, not poetry or dukes." He paused awkwardly. "I plan to marry Miss Aldridge tomorrow morning in the Linton Park chapel."

"And what do you wish of me, Wellston? My blessings?" Lexford refused to meet Marcus's gaze. He suspected Lexford searched for a memory upon which to base his remarks. "When Susan started the fire, which killed her, it was you above all the others who understood how I

297

felt in not knowing success to reach her–not saving my wife. Although our time together was plagued by past circumstances, Susan did not deserve to die such a horrible death."

"It was never your fault," Marcus swallowed. "You devoted your heart to the late viscountess. Few men would have accepted the life your father thrust upon you." He sighed with defeat. "What you wish to know is have I betrayed you also." Marcus swallowed hard, searching for the right words to explain how things came to pass. "I never meant to fall in love with Cashémere. I told myself you were my friend, and I would never come between you if your attentions to Miss Cashé were sincere."

Sarcastically, Lexford observed, "But I proved myself otherwise by kissing Miss Satiné. Is that it, Wellston? It was a ruse, perpetrated by the young ladies."

"It is not of how you speak, and you recognize the truth, although you would prefer to deny it. You viewed Miss Cashémere as a safe choice–someone you enjoyed–someone who could dull the memories of what happened with Susan, but I never observed in you what I saw in Kerrington's and Fowler's countenances when they looked upon the women they love. I suspect if true love existed for you, if you felt that soul-cleansing love for Cashémere, you would never forget it–no matter what Charters did to you. Do you recall such a love, Lexford? If you say you love Cashémere in that manner, I will cancel the wedding; I will withdraw. I will allow you the opportunity to make Cashémere return your love."

Lexford remained silent for several minutes. "No, I do not remember such a love. Surprisingly, I remember kissing Lady Eleanor during the farce involving Louis Levering. And I remember feeling clean afterwards. I also remember passionately kissing someone whom I suppose was Miss Satiné, but I hold no memories of love. Miss Cashémere was never part of my memories."

"And, yet, I cannot breath unless Cashémere is near," Marcus whispered into the muted room.

Another long silence ensued. "Then I suppose you should marry the lady," Lexford remarked. "I would not wish to be the cause of your demise." He reached out his hand to Marcus. "We are brothers, Wellston, and brothers never stand in the way of the other's happiness. You have my sanction."

Marcus gladly took his friend's extended hand. "Thank you, Lexford." He breathed relief's sigh. "Now, tell me how much you will pay me not to

Regina Jeffers

tell Worthing you kissed Lady Eleanor." Marcus taunted good-naturedly, attempting to restore normalcy between them.

"I will withdraw my blessing," Lexford countered.

Marcus smiled joyously. They would get through this. "My lips are sealed."

⟡⟡⟡

"Dearly beloved," Doctor Perry began. Marcus heard little else. He supposed he had spoken his vows at the correct times because within a quarter hour, the man had pronounced Marcus and Cashémere husband and wife. Her dancing eyes said she found his confusion quite amusing, but Marcus did not care. His heart had healed.

"Are you happy, my Love?" he whispered in Cashé's ear. They signed the church's registry.

Cashé went on her tiptoes to kiss his lips. "Does my open affection not answer your question, my Lord?"

"Must we attend the wedding breakfast?" he said as he pulled Cashé closer.

"Oh, my poor darling," she teased. "You must be patient a bit longer."

"One hour," he growled.

"Two," she contradicted.

He laughed lightly as he nibbled on her ear. "One and a half." He removed his pocket watch to check the hour. "You are being timed, Countess."

"Lord Yardley, I object," she slapped at his chest with her gloved hand.

Marcus placed her on his arm to meet those who waited for them outside the chapel. "One and a half," he repeated.

⟡⟡⟡

Marcus did not believe it possible to experience so many erections in so short a time. If Cashé had not been an innocent he would have taken her in his coach, but he had schooled his patience. They had ridden for nearly three hours to the inn where he had reserved rooms for the evening, and during that time, every gesture Cashé made created havoc with his body. She placed a loose curl behind her ear, and Marcus had imagined removing the pins from her curls and allowing her coal black locks to drape across his bare chest. Instant erection.

She ran the tip of her tongue along her lips to wet them, and Marcus went hard again.

299

Cashé stretched out her legs, and Marcus remembered massaging her legs that day they had raced to Satiné's rescue, and again he found himself in full arousal.

"I am Yardley, and this is my countess," he aristocratically told the innkeeper. "You have received my instructions."

"Aye, Sir. Everything is as you required." The innkeeper preened. "It is good of you to honor us with your patronage, Sir."

Marcus paused impatiently. "Then might we see our rooms?"

"Immediately, Sir."

Within minutes, they were alone. "Would you care for champagne?" He gestured to a waiting bottle.

Cashé, suddenly shy, shook her head in the negative before shooting a wide-eyed glance at the largest piece of furniture in the room: the bed.

Marcus smiled, her innocence a comforting reality. He stepped forward slowly. "Do not tell me, my bold warrior princess, that you have unexpectedly developed a case of the nerves."

Cashé swallowed twice before answering. "Not exactly. It is just...what if I cannot please you, my Lord?"

Marcus breathed easier. "I do not expect that particular fact will be a problem. I simply look at you, and my world opens to new possibilities."

"That is what I mean," Cashé held back tears. "You tell me such things, and I cannot help but fail. How can I give you what you require? I am far from perfect...very flawed, in fact. I am impulsive. Do not always think before I speak. Am sometimes insensitive. Singular in my views, and, obviously, manipulative. Look what I did to Satiné." Her voice rose on each word.

Marcus slowly wrapped his arms about her. "Aye, Love, you are all those things, but you have the type of heart that will protect our children with a vengeance–never thinking of yourself; the type of heart that loves with an undying allegiance; the kind of heart that accepts the failures of others because you have known defeat yourself." A faint smile grazed his mouth. Marcus's fingers splayed through the lose tendrils of her hair. He threaded the coal-colored strands in and around his fingers. Slowly, he tilted her head back.

He kissed her then, slowly and purposefully, igniting fires in them both. Kissing her was like kissing no other woman of his acquaintance. She tasted of home. Her mouth warm and inviting. Her hair tumbled down over his fists, and Marcus caught it in a tight ball of silk. As Cashé

300

wound her arms about his neck, Marcus lifted her to him. He caressed her buttocks, holding her where he could grind his erection against her sweetness. "Cashé, I desire you...now," he growled close to her ear. The powerful lust he had experienced in the coach drove him to possess her completely. Her kiss, tentative at first, increased in its answering need. A red-hot jolt of passion shot through Marcus's veins.

As he backed her toward the bed, their gazes caught. Cashé toyed with a wisp of his hair. "I hope our sons resemble you," she murmured. Her innocent remark warmed his heart. He prayed their daughters were as beautiful as she.

Her fingers worked at the knot of his cravat, and if he were not busy with his own assault on the buttons running down the front of her dress, Marcus might have assisted her. As each button gave way, he recognized his own personal heaven. Embers caught in her eyes as his mouth trailed fire down her neck and across Cashé's shoulders. He hissed a groan. "Allow me to look upon you, Darling."

He watched as Cashé swallowed, drawing a tightened breath. Her tentativeness added to his desire. He would be the only one to know this woman. "Teach me of love," she rasped. With a soft sigh, she leaned into him.

The buttons undone, Marcus released the dress and permitted it to slide down her body as a silky feather. The swell of her breasts pushing against the corset stayed him. "I have dreamed of this for months," he whispered hoarsely. "I should be ashamed to admit how often this moment has played through my sleep time mind," he said with a smile.

His fingers touched the laces of her corset, and Cashé shivered. "You are exquisite," he whispered as he returned to her mouth. Marcus's hands weighed her breasts as his thumbs stroked her nipples through the material.

"I should be embarrassed by my wantonness, but I wish to see you also," she said with false bravado.

Marcus reached for the bed linens, jerking the counterpane back. "I will step behind the screen and undress. I will not shock your sensibilities by doing so before you." He kissed the tip of her upturned nose. "I will meet you beneath the sheets in a few minutes."

"What if I wish to see you now?" Hesitation softened the defiantly raised tone.

Marcus laughed lightly. "You will have years to look upon me." He tapped the bed as if directing where he wanted her and then walked leisurely toward the screen. "And who said anything about dousing the candles." He winked at Cashé.

"Yes, my Lord." Cashé smiled broadly and spun about in happy circles.

Within a few minutes, they were once again in each other's arms. Marcus could not keep his hands still. They roamed at will across her breasts, her arms, her legs. He kissed her in earnest. She tasted of sunshine and the air after a spring rain and the beauty of a Scottish moor covered in heather. She tasted of happiness. "Not so many minutes prior, you called yourself flawed, but you are pure perfection in this manner." He sat upon his knees to look his fill.

He caressed her breasts gently, stroking her nipples. His mouth followed his thumbs across her breasts, sucking gently at first, but then more demanding. Soon excitement had constricted Marcus's breathing, but when Cashé arched toward him, he knew she was ready for him. His fingers stroked along Cashé's cleft, spreading the wetness. Marcus touched her very much as he had done that day in the Scottish midlands. He meant her to know the familiarity of their intimacy before sharing more. When she climaxed, he set himself between her legs. "Are you prepared to know my body, my Love?"

Cashé opened her desire-filled eyes. "I want to be yours forever, Marcus." Their gazes locked, and he positioned himself to enter her. Slowly, he slipped into her wetness.

"You are so hot...so wet," he groaned. All conscious thought evaded him. Cashé arched again, welcoming his strength, and Marcus gritted his teeth not to come undone. He lifted her hips and pushed deeper. Experiencing her barrier, he leaned forward to kiss her again, and then with a hard thrust made her his. Cashé stiffened for a few elongated seconds, squirming in a manner that left him fighting not to explode too quickly. He paused too, waiting for her to become accustomed to their joining. Then he set up a comfortable pace, she joined him in a rhythmic coupling. Hard strokes buried him to the hilt, and Marcus pounded his body against hers. "Let it happen again," he growled. He made a sound of need, one buried in his very core. Finally, Cashé's body tightened around him—muscles contracting, and Marcus snarled his release—an exclamation of need and a shuddering pulsation, as he filled her with his seed. He collapsed upon her, fighting to recover his breathing and his reason. While still buried within her, he had found the hope for a future. The disorder of his soul abandoned.

302

Taking her with him, Marcus rolled to his side. He did not wish to leave her body. Cashé rested her head upon his chest and drew circles across the line of hair down his body. "Is it often like this? Like flying without wings?" she asked innocently.

"I cannot speak for others, but never in my experience until now," he rasped, his heart, pounding in his ears. "Perfection again," he whispered hoarsely.

They lay together, arms and legs entangled in a passion-filled embrace. "Did I hurt you?" he asked as he brushed a sweaty curl from her cheek. Mindlessly, Marcus removed the pins from her disheveled hair.

"Only for a brief moment." She appeared a bit embarrassed. "I did not disappoint you? I could not bear it if you disapproved of me as your wife."

"How could you disappoint? Did I not just tell you that you are perfection?" Marcus suspected it would be some time before he could convince Cashé he required nothing but her love. Unfortunately, Aldridge had left his mark on her confidence. "May I tell you how I know you will never dishearten me?"

Although she buried her face into Marcus's chest, Cashé agreed with a mumbled, "Yes."

"When I was a twelve, my twin sister Margaret...Maggie and I holidayed with my father and older brothers. Trevor, as you know him, has learned some civilities, but in those days, Father permitted Trevor to do as he wtshed...with few restrictions. On this particular day, we were in the Peak District. Father had thought to take Myles into the earth, so to speak, to teach his heir about the land, but also about courage, as Myles was terribly afraid of small enclosures. Father and Myles were to descend the steps into one of the caverns in the area." Marcus mindlessly stroked her back, and Cashé snuggled closer.

"Although I was quite keen on the idea of an adventure, there was no way for the entire family to make the trek. Being the youngest son, I always wished to prove myself to the Earl, and I was sore to understand how Trevor would have created havoc for everyone. So, Maggie and I were left to fend for ourselves under the less than watchful eye of my sister's maid. As Myles fought his demons below the surface, I foolish fought with Maggie above. It was over something completely childish. I had teasingly told Maggie the color of her dress had made her skin appear yellow. It did not, but young boys always tease their sisters. In anger, Maggie had stormed away with Trevor in tow."

When Cashé moved to where she could look upon his countenance more clearly, he breathed easier. She understood this was an important part of his life and meant to know more of him. Their eyes cleaved.

He swallowed hard before continuing. "What actually happened, no one knows. Trevor had witnessed my sister's peril, but he could not tell us, nor did he set up an alarm. After ten minutes or so, Trevor returned, without Maggie, to where I played with a hard ball against a stone wall. When the maid and I asked where Maggie was, he simply said, 'In a hole.' It likely took us another ten long, excoriating minutes to find her at the bottom of a walled-up well. She treaded water, but was exhausted. I attempted to reach her. Really I did. Used the abandoned boards to make a flimsy platform from which to dangle. Surprisingly, somehow our fingers touched, and I pitched forward to catch Maggie's hand.

"My sister's eyes spoke of her fear, but I kept telling her I would save her. That I loved her. That I was sorry for being an idiot and for teasing her. Told her she was my other half." He paused to permit the emotions to settle. "I pulled, Cashé, with all my might. I swear I did! Attempted to lift her from the water. Maggie's wet fingers clawed at my hands, but I was not strong enough to hold her. The maid, and even Trevor, held my legs to steady me, but the wood cracked, and then everything happened so fast. Maggie fell back into the water, her head hitting the brick wall, and, just like that, she was gone. I mean they found her...Father and some other men, but she was gone. I had failed her. It was my fault. I should have gone in after her. Should have died saving her."

Cashé eyes remained glued to his countenance. "Oh, Marcus, it was not your fault. Do you not recognize that fact?"

He turned his head towards hers. "I do now. I learned to master heights, you see, and I have saved many others. My time with the Realm gave me those intangibles. Yet, none of them mattered until I saved you. You are a person I love dearly, and I was able to save you. Part of it was because you fought so hard to survive, but mainly, I was now strong enough mentally and physically to save a person who meant the world to me. I know it sounds ridiculous, but it changed everything."

"I would go through it again if it made a difference in your life," Cashé claimed. "Every hair-raising second if it gave you peace." She clung tightly to him.

Marcus kissed her softly and then more passionately. "I plan to know you again, Ma Chère. Let us create beautiful children together. A dozen of them."

"A dozen?" Cashé smiled amusedly.

"We will begin with a little girl who we will name Margaret...Maggie," he whispered into Cashé's hair as he pulled her closer.

"Twins," she corrected. "We shall have twins...a boy and a girl."

Finis

Life is a culmination of the past, an awareness of the present, an indication of a future beyond knowledge, the quality that gives a touch of divinity to matter.

- Charles Lindbergh

About the Author

Regina Jeffers, a public classroom teacher for thirty-nine years, considers herself a Jane Austen enthusiast. She is the author of several Austen-inspired novels, including Darcy's Passions, Darcy's Temptation, Vampire Darcy's Desire, Captain Wentworth's Persuasion, The Phantom of Pemberley, Christmas at Pemberley, The Disappearance of Georgiana Darcy, Honor and Hope, and The Mysterious Death of Mr. Darcy. She also writes Regency romances: The Scandal of Lady Eleanor, A Touch of Velvet, A Touch of Cashémere, A Touch of Grace, and The First Wives' Club. A Smithsonian presenter, a Time Warner Star Teacher and Martha Holden Jennings Scholar, Jeffers often serves as a consultant in language arts and media literacy. Currently living outside Charlotte, North Carolina, she spends her time with her writing, gardening, and her adorable grandson.

Website www.rjeffers.com
Blogs http://reginajeffers.wordpress.com
http://austenauthors.net
http://englishhistoryauthors.blogspot.com/

Twitter – @reginajeffers
Facebook – Regina Jeffers
(Books available from Amazon, Barnes & Noble, Books-a-Million, Kobo, Joseph Beth, White Soup Press, and Ulysses Press.)